THE 45th

BOWEN ISLAND LIBRARY
3 0947 0005 5914 2

THE 45th

D.W. BUFFA

Cover and jacket design by 2Faced Design
Interior designed and formatted by E.M. Tippetts Book Designs

ISBN 978-1-947993-53-2
eISBN 978-1-947993-74-7
Library of Congress Control Number: 2019935861

First hardcover publication May 2019 by Polis Books, LLC
221 River St., 9th Fl., #9070
Hoboken, NJ 07030
www.PolisBooks.com
Interior formatted by:

emtippettsbookdesigns.com

ALSO BY D.W. BUFFA

The Defense
The Prosecution
The Judgment
The Legacy
Star Witness
Breach of Trust
Trial By Fire
Evangeline
The Swindlers
The Dark Backward
The Last Man
Helen
Hillary
Necessity
Rubicon (as Lawrence Alexander)

CHAPTER ONE

Louis Matson tapped his thick fingers on his desk, regretting before it even started the meeting he did not want to have. For forty years the majority leader had been a member of the House or a member of the Senate, forty years in which he had known what he thought every kind of charlatan and fool, but of all the various categories of shameless, small-minded, ruthless and vindictive men of ambition, there were few he disliked more than the ones who had become party chairmen. He had known every chairman of the national Republican party for the last half-century, and though it might just be an embellished memory, nostalgia for a past that had never existed, none of them had seemed quite such an embarrassment as the one who was now about to steal an hour of his life. Matson picked up the telephone.

"Send the son-of-a-bitch in."

The majority leader's office was a long rectangle in which the door for visitors was at the other end of the room from the senator's desk. There were two tall narrow windows at the end, with a gray leather sofa below. An oil painting of the White House on fire during the British attack on Washington in the War of 1812 hung above a marble fireplace that had not been used in at least half a century. Matson liked to watch the reaction of first time visitors, the way they walked, the way they held themselves, as they came down the length of the room. He rather liked it if they seemed slightly nervous, a little unsure of themselves. It meant, in most cases at least, that they had a regard for the traditions of the place. Reece Davis came in brimming with confidence, eager to impress. He stopped at the painting and with an evil little laugh, remarked, "Might be a good idea to do it again."

Davis dropped into one of the two blue wingback chairs in front of Matson's desk, reached inside a black briefcase and removed a large manila envelope.

"This is the speech we would like you to give at the convention."

With his elbow on the arm of the chair, Louis Matson placed his thumb and two fingers against the side of his face and said nothing. Davis had a dozen different responses ready, but he had not prepared himself for perfect silence and the absence of all expression.

"I know it isn't much notice, but....You are planning to be there, aren't you? Part of the Michigan delegation?"

A brief, understated smile cut across Louis Matson's aging, jagged mouth.

"Chairing the Michigan delegation," he corrected.

"Chairing. Yes, of course; I knew that, of course," said Davis, with a quick, nervous grin.

"In any event, you now want me to give a speech. And this suddenly occurred to you two weeks before the convention is scheduled to open? The answer is no."

"No?" cried Davis, startled.

"I'm chairing the Michigan delegation. Don't you think that will give me enough to do? I mean, Jesus Christ!" laughed Matson, "I've never seen such a mess: the convention in two weeks and no one knows who the candidate is going to be!"

Louis Matson was over six feet tall and more than a little overweight. He had a full head of graying chestnut hair, a large, hawk-like nose, and deep-set hazel eyes that usually seemed full of suspicion. Even standing still or, as now, sitting at his desk, he seemed to be in motion. It was a reflection of the politician's need, a need grown out of habit, always to be busy with more than one thing. His speech was often abbreviated, sometimes fragmentary, even at times incoherent, and yet, at the same time, seldom disconnected with the subject under discussion. Occupied with something he had to read, or a brief conversation on the side, he would seem to be paying no attention at all, and then, suddenly, as if he had not missed a word, make a remark that settled everything.

"The party has been taken over by people who think the only government we need is a well-armed militia. They want to go back to what they think the country used to be. Well, consider this a first step: a convention that may not be able to agree on a candidate in less than a hundred ballots. We are back in the 1920's. Who could complain about that?"

"That is the reason we need you, Senator," said Davis with a thin, practiced smile

"You think I can solve your problem with a speech? I'll be interested to see what it says, because if it isn't as good as the Gettysburg Address you don't have a chance."

Davis nodded a little too eagerly.

"That good! - You must have a speechwriter I've never heard about."

"Not the speech," said Davis, irritated that he had not yet been understood. "It's a good speech; a very good speech, in my opinion. But – if you'll just look at it, you'll understand."

"If I just…?"

He opened the envelope, removed an eight-page double-spaced speech, read the first line and looked at Davis as if he thought him out of his mind.

"You want me…? You expect me…?"

"To chair the convention. No one else can do it; no one else can do this without seeming to favor one side or the other. The candidates know you can be impartial."

As he had just reminded the chairman, Matson knew that there had been convention fights before, and that it had taken sometimes dozens of roll call votes before the party's candidate had been chosen. It had not happened for more than half a century, however; and, for those Americans who thought history started and ended with themselves, that meant there was no precedent for what had happened in the last few months. Everyone on television said so, and everyone who was asked about it agreed.

"You're in a lot of trouble, aren't you?" asked Matson, suddenly.

It caught Davis off guard. "Trouble? What do you mean?"

Matson studied him through narrowed eyes. He did not like anything about him; he never had. It started with his looks: the slick, black, wavy hair; the eyes that seemed to dart all around; the eager, too eager, smile that followed each well-rehearsed word. Trying hard to underscore his sincerity, he only proved his inherent duplicity. He reminded Matson of a young Dick Nixon, the only difference that Nixon, whatever else you thought about him, had intelligence.

"You were elected chairman because the right-wing – the Tea Party types and the Libertarians – drove out most of the old-line conservatives. You were going to become the hero, the chairman who led the party in a successful rebellion against all those, like me, who don't believe you can just shut down the government every time you don't get your way. But now, with a fight – a knockdown, drag out, bloody, take no prisoners fight - a fight that could go on for days, or even weeks, in a convention the whole country will be watching, you are going to be blamed, which is to say hated, by damn near everyone. Whoever wins will blame you for not doing more; whoever loses will blame you for doing too much. The first thing the winner will do is name someone else as chairman." He paused to let this sink in, and then added, "Unless you have already made a deal with one side or the other – or made a deal with each side separately."

With a look of injured innocence, Davis sat straight up. Then he leaned forward.

"My job is to make sure the convention can make its own decision. It isn't my place to help one candidate more than the other. Every one will be given the same opportunity to make their case to the delegates."

"They will all be given the same...," repeated Matson, with a jaundiced look. "The same opportunity to kill each other! What do you think is going to happen? You heard what they said about each other in the primaries. They think this is the most important election in the history of the republic. What else could it be when they're the candidate? They hate each other so much, the only wonder if that one of them hasn't had the other one murdered. Don't try to look shocked. Do you know why they don't?" A caustic smile twisted across his mouth. "Because part of them knows that the only way they will ever win is if the nomination goes to someone else."

Reece Davis could recite from memory the number of delegates each state had, he knew by heart every detail of the sometimes arcane procedures by which each delegate was selected, but he had nothing of the insight of the seasoned politician into the weaknesses of ambitious men and women. Matson tried to explain.

"Because beneath all that shiny self-confidence, the belief that they are, each of them, destined for greatness, they know if they get the nomination they'll lose."

Davis started to object, to insist that Madelaine Shaw had too many negatives, that there were too many rumors, too many scandals. Matson ignored him.

"Whoever wins, loses; which means whoever loses, wins. It's easy," he said, with a shrug. "Whoever loses can claim the nomination was stolen, that the convention was not fair, that the other side, the winning side, had advantages – had made a deal with the chairman," he added with ruthless amusement. "Which was the reason the rules were applied the way they were. And then, the most effective argument of all: they stole the nomination and because of that we lost our only chance at the White House. Because of that, thanks to them, we have Madelaine Shaw in the White House. And what follows from that, if not that the only way to make things right, the only way to take back the country, is to nominate the one who was cheated out of the nomination the last time. Who could resist that argument? – Not any of these self-righteous moralists you and your friends have brought into the party."

"Self-righteous!" sputtered Davis, struggling to contain himself. Matson was one of those who with any luck at all would lose in the next election to someone who understood what the country was all about. He would have given anything to tell him that, but Matson was one of the few Republicans left that even Democrats seemed to like. He had to become the face of the Republican convention. It was the only way to make what the party stood for seem measured and reasonable.

"Self-righteous?" he repeated, sitting back as if taking it under advisement. "I suppose that must be the way it appears to people who don't follow things too closely. It is what sometimes happens when you have candidates who feel so strongly about what they believe in."

"Or are too goddamn sanctimonious to know their own stupidity. But never mind all that. Just tell me this: which one of them, Rivers or Lochner, does better against Madelaine Shaw?"

Davis shifted uneasily in his chair. He began to fidget with his smooth, manicured hands, started to say something, and then looked away and shook his head. Folding his arms over his chest, he crossed his legs and began to swing his foot.

"It's too early; the polling means nothing," he explained, forced to confess an inconvenient fact. The words seemed to stick in his throat. "Shaw is ahead, but…."

"Far ahead?" It was not really a question; it was the assertion of someone who already knew how badly the Republican candidates would be defeated.

"Rivers runs slightly better."

Matson lifted an eyebrow as if astonished at the chairman's attempt to put a good face on disaster.

"By slightly better you mean what, exactly?"

"Rivers runs eight points behind her; Lochner twelve," admitted Davis, without expression.

Matson bent forward as if to share a confidence.

"Do you think the difference is because Edward Rivers looks like Lyndon Johnson's illegitimate son?" Matson burst out laughing; Davis did not know what to do. "I've seen the polls," said Matson, suddenly serious. "Shaw is way ahead, but she isn't yet at fifty percent; she isn't even close. There is still a chance, or there would be if we had a candidate anyone could support."

"And we will," insisted Davis with the mechanical enthusiasm that had become second nature, "once you explain to everyone why whoever wins the nomination is a far better choice to lead the country. No one can do it but you. That's why the speech is so important; why we want you not just to chair the convention, but to give the speech, the keynote speech."

Even had he made up his mind, Matson would not have given him the satisfaction of an answer.

"The convention is in less than two weeks," Davis reminded him.

"And you just asked me today," said Matson, rising from his chair. "I'll let you know."

Davis started to leave, but stopped before he had taken three steps.

"It's the chance of a lifetime. The major address, a speech televised to millions of people. Why would you hesitate, why would you need time to think about it?"

Matson went toward him, put his hand on his shoulder and looked him straight in the eye.

"Maybe because I haven't heard more than two or three speeches in the last forty years I would not have been embarrassed to give."

"Well, I think you'll find that…." He could not finish. The look in Matson's eyes, the knowing laughter that seemed to dare a contradiction, would not allow it. "I hope you'll agree to do this, Senator," he said instead. "We can come out of this convention more united that we have ever been. I'm sure of it."

Matson shook his hand, and in response to the sense of urgency in the chairman's eyes, promised to let him know the next day.

"But I can tell you right now I won't agree if you expect me to give the speech you brought me."

"You haven't read it yet," replied Davis, confused by this sudden, strange demand. "I think when you do, you'll -"

"I won't agree to give a speech I haven't written myself."

"But no one writes their own speeches – Do you?"

Matson looked at Davis as if he were seeing for the first time the inexperience, the limited knowledge, the inevitable dependence on the assumptions of his age.

"You ever read any of Lincoln's speeches; ever read any of Churchill's? It's a funny thing. Neither of them was too busy to write his own speeches. Of course, all they had to deal with was a civil war, which the North almost lost, and a world war that without Churchill Germany would have won – nothing like the things a beleaguered member of Congress has to worry about. But, still, it makes you wonder why what they said remains a permanent part of the language, while the things that these speechwriters of ours write today are less memorable than the graffiti on a bathroom wall! But you asked if I write my own. No, I don't. And you know the reason? – I'm not good enough; I never had the gift. But I know when something is well-written and when it is not; and I know how to make changes, how to edit, if you will, so that I don't make a complete fool of myself when I speak to the Senate. I'm not going to write a speech for the convention, but if you want me to give one, I'll decide – not you, not anyone else – what I want to say and who I want to write it."

"I understand," said Davis, though he really did not. "But if you'll just look over what I brought," he went on, nodding with a quick, superficial smile, toward the speech he had left on Matson's desk, "I think you'll find all the basic ideas that have to be expressed. That is the important point. How you want to say it, who you want to write the final draft – that of course is up to you."

If Matson had not given an immediate answer to the chairman's request it was only to make his eventual agreement seem more difficult to obtain and his conditions, for that reason, easier to accept. The question was not whether he was going to do it; the question was why. He was too old to think about the presidency himself, too old to think of this as the best possible chance to have everyone start thinking of him as someone who ought to run the next time, after the election had come and gone with a Republican defeat. There was nothing in it for him, and yet there was everything in it for him: the chance to set an example, to be the kind of man, the kind of senator, he had always tried to be. It was strange how archaic that now seemed, after so many things had changed.

Standing in the middle of the room, his eyes, following his thought, came to rest on the framed photographs that lined the wall opposite the fireplace. There were not that many of them, nothing like the endless pictured chronicles of the public careers of senators and congressmen that covered the walls, and even the hallways, in offices all over Capitol Hill; no photographs of those happy families that, sooner or later, every disgraced, scandal plagued politician left office supposedly to spend more time with; just a half dozen old photographs of people now only vaguely remembered, if remembered at all. The two in the center brought a smile of nostalgia. One was a picture taken the day he was sworn when he was first elected to the House of Representative. It was January, 1977, and he was standing next to Bob Griffin, the Republican senator from Michigan, without whom he never would have been elected to anything. The other, taken four or five years earlier, when he was a young assistant on Griffin's staff, was in its way symbolic of how much Washington had changed. In the annual springtime softball game between Griffin's staff and the staff of Michigan's then senior senator, Phil Hart, known as both a liberal's liberal and the conscience of the Senate, Hart and Griffin, both in shirtsleeves, were grasping a baseball bat, after going hand over hand to decide which team would bat first. Griffin had reached the highest position on the handle, and should have won, but Hart, smiling at how he had broken the rules, had put his hand over the top. Griffin was laughing as hard as it was possible for anyone to laugh. They had never voted the same way on any issue of significance, and they were great good friends.

Matson felt a sense of regret, a sense of something lost, something that he had wanted, and even expected, and had never had. He had never known the friendship of a political adversary; he had never known the friendship of a friend. It was not just that he lived his life in Washington, that place where Harry Truman had said that if you wanted a friend you should get a dog, but because for all the thousands of people he had come to know, he had not really liked very many of them, and those he had were either people he had looked up to at the beginning, men like Griffin and Hart, much older than himself, or those, much younger, who had come to Washington after he was a senior member of the Senate and, some of them at least, had looked up to him.

Turning away from the photographs and his own remembered past, he want back to his desk and started reading the speech Davis wanted him to give. Halfway down the second page, he pushed it aside, grunted an obscenity, and then, the corners of his mouth bent down in disgust, pulled it back in front of him. By the fourth page he was bobbing his head and, in a sing-song voice, mocking what he read. Stretching back, he lifted his legs onto the corner of his desk and crossed his ankles. Holding each page as if it carried a communicable disease, he glanced over the typewritten lines, until, turning the page, he let the one just finished drop, unmourned, onto the carpet below.

When the last page finally fell, he muttered one last obscenity, gathered them up, stacked them together in a single pile and put the speech back in the envelope. He pushed a button on the console

"Can you come in for a minute?"

Ismael Cooper had been administrative assistant to the majority leader for nearly six years. Unlike most of those who worked on the Hill, Cooper had once been a member of Congress himself. A moderate Republican running for a third term in the House, he lost the primary to a political unknown when he refused to sign a pledge never to raise taxes. The small minority who voted in the primary thought Cooper's explanation that only a fool would agree never to do something that might be necessary in a national crisis was all the proof they needed that the congressman was not one of them. The day after the election Matson offered him the job as his administrative assistant.

"How old are you?" asked Matson, as Cooper lowered himself into the same chair Reece Davis had used. Unlike Davis, who had sat with rigid formality, Cooper dangled his right leg over the arm.

"Forty-three – forty-four next month," he replied. The question, he knew from long experience and from the way Matson's large head was bouncing to some strange rhythm of its own, had almost certainly nothing to do with his age.

"And how old am I now?" Matson's eyes were making a slow circuit of the ceiling.

"Too old to ask the question; too young not to run for another six-year term."

Matson scratched his ear. His mouth trembled with more than amusement - anticipation, at what would come next.

"You are without doubt the most dishonest man I've ever known. And despite that, you still managed to lose your last election."

"That's the problem with being dishonest: I lied so often I thought I was telling the truth."

There was, somewhere below the surface, wisdom in that, but Matson did not have time to pursue it. He shoved across the desk the speech he had just finished reading.

"Here, give me your lying, dishonest opinion of this. It's the speech that idiot Davis wants me to give, the keynote speech, at the convention he also wants me to chair."

Cooper blinked twice, pulled his leg down and shot forward.

"Davis wants you to…? You said yes, didn't you? You had to say yes."

"I told him I'd think about it; I said I'd give him an answer tomorrow."

"But you're going to do it. It's…. What are you going to say? You haven't decided who you are going to support."

The sunlight through the windows at the far end had come halfway forward across the room. Matson could keep time by it, the line made by the summer sun on a late afternoon in July.

"I wanted to see if you thought the same thing I did: that this is one of the worst…." He caught himself. There was another way to look at it, the way most people would look at it. He remembered the way Davis reacted when he asked if he had read Lincoln or Churchill. "I suppose it isn't actually that bad. That is what everyone will say, if I give it. They'll even prove it - these television geniuses we all listen to – some of them former speechwriters – telling us how someone said the right thing, or the wrong thing, and then – a dozen people, turning a dial one way or the other in approval or disapproval - and then the chart that shows whether the speaker struck a chord."

Matson threw up his hands, and then brought one of them down hard on his desk and shook his head in frustration. He studied Cooper as if he thought Cooper might understand the problem better than he did himself.

"We don't give speeches anymore; we chant tested words and phrases at an audience of empty-headed fools. There is no argument, no attempt at persuasion; no sense of the importance of explaining the condition of things, of the problems we face; no sense of urgency about what is needed, the kind of sacrifices required; nothing to create an understanding of the need to take the longer view of what is in the best interest of the country. All we talk about is what the polls tell us people want, when we should be talking about what people need to do."

Dressed impeccably in a dark well-pressed tailored suit, striped shirt and handmade bow tie, Ismael Cooper ran his hand over his reddish short cropped hair and then tugged at his small clean-shaven chin. With his round face and penetrating blue eyes, he looked more like an English teacher in some private New England school than a brilliant lawyer who had graduated at the top of his class at Michigan. He was nothing if not analytical.

"In other words, senator, the speech is shit."

"That is a nice way of putting it."

"You want me to find someone who can write a better one."

"Sure, if you could; but there isn't anyone. We have people here who write speeches, and they're as good as anyone, but they all sound the same, as dull and lifeless as a lawyer's brief. All the points are made and no one really gives a damn what happens next. I want to give a speech that matters, that changes the way people think, that gives them some reason to believe – or at least hope – that the country still has a future, a future better than the past."

Ismael Cooper scratched his chin. Staring into the distance, he smiled to himself.

"There is someone who could do it, write a speech like that- If you knew where to find him."

"Know where to find him?" asked Matson, with a blank expression.

"Julian Drake. He could have…."

Cooper stopped in mid-sentence, astonished by the sudden look of anguish in Louis Matson's eyes. With a deep breath, Matson stared down at his hands, trying, as it seemed, to clear his mind, to remember what had happened all those years ago and what it had cost. He looked up at Cooper, a sharp glance that seemed to demand an answer to a question, or, rather, two questions at once, the first of which, a shield to the second, was how much he knew. He did not wait for an answer.

"I haven't thought of Julian in long time," he remarked in a low, almost inaudible voice.

"You've never heard from him?"

"No, never; but I did not expect I would. Once he decided he had to leave….You knew him; you served with him in Congress. His last term was your first, if I remember."

"That is not quite right," replied Cooper. He was careful to make it seem a matter of no importance. "We never actually served together. I took his place; I ran for the seat when he ran for the Senate. Or when he started to run. But I knew him; I worked in his first campaign. I never did understand what happened, why just a week before the primary election he suddenly withdrew. He would have won – not just the primary; he would have been elected to the Senate. There isn't any question. I never heard anyone do what he could do with an audience – any audience. It was extraordinary, uncanny. You got so caught up in what he was saying, carried away by the force and power of that astonishing voice that seemed to come at you from every direction at once. And then, suddenly, with no warning – and no explanation – he just quits. And the day after he does it, disappears, vanishes without a trace. No one ever knew why. There was a rumor that it had something to do with a woman, but no one knows for sure."

"A woman? Yes, that was true," said Louis Matson, with a grim smile. "I'm the one who had to make the announcement that Julian was withdrawing, that he would not be a candidate for the Senate, that he was quitting public life. Julian asked me to do it, and because I knew why he was doing it - why he had to do it - I agreed."

"You knew? He told you?" asked Cooper, intrigued that Matson had kept the secret this many years. "Did he quit, have to quit, because of a woman?"

"Oh, yes – it was about a woman; it was all about a woman," replied the senator. Far from regret, the look in his eyes seemed almost triumphant.

"It was because of a woman, but he was not caught in some scandal that would have destroyed him politically?" asked Cooper, just to be sure.

For some reason the words, the suggestion of some commonplace wrongdoing, the daily litany of political sin and temptation, made Matson start to laugh, and then, an instant later, he was as serious as Cooper had ever seen him.

"He did what he had to for a woman, and it was the least disgraceful thing I ever heard of. I wish I could tell you what it was. I can't. I promised I would take his secret to the grave." Matson glanced pointedly at the speech that still lay on his desk. "You're right: Julian could do it, he could write a speech worth giving, a speech worth listening to. Although," he added, as a smile slipped over his mouth, "he never wrote his own."

"Someone else did?"

"No, not someone else - No one wrote them. Julian did not need a written speech. Hell, he never needed notes. He could speak for an hour - never repeat a line - and all of it, the whole damn thing, every sentence, every phrase, the instant creation of his own remarkable mind. He tried to tell me once that it was the way people used to speak, in whole paragraphs, before the days of radio and television. I did not believe him. I thought he was looking for a way to disguise the fact that he was simply smarter than the rest of us."

"But it was a woman that brought it all to an end?" asked Cooper, hoping Matson would tell him more.

"Yes, it was a woman, an extraordinary woman from what little I know."

But that was all he would say.

CHAPTER TWO

Louis Matson did not bother to give the chairman his answer directly. He read in the morning paper, under the byline of a columnist who quoted unnamed, but unimpeachable, sources that the Senate Majority Leader had been asked to chair the convention and give the keynote address. The story could only have come from Davis, and if Davis did not want to keep their conversation private, Matson saw no reason not to follow suit. He called a press conference and made the announcement himself.

"Yes, it's true," he replied to the first question. He was standing in the hallway, just outside his office, under the glare of the television lights. "Chairman Davis asked me if I would, and I am happy to be able to accept."

Matson was used to the give and take with reporters. He frequently knew before they did themselves the questions they were going to ask.

"But if you chair the convention, can you still chair the Michigan delegation?" asked Cedric Turner, who had covered the Congress almost as long as Matson had been a member.

Matson threw back his head and laughed.

"You're the last of the polite reporters, Cedric. Chair the delegation? Don't you mean, control the delegation? Isn't that what you really want to know?"

It was almost impossible, at least if you were a reporter, not to like Louis Matson. He knew what you wanted to know, and he did not make you ask four or five different questions to get there.

"The Michigan delegation is the only delegation that is going to the convention uncommitted and -"

"Not uncommitted, Cedric – committed to me. But I'll let you in on a secret: I'm not running," he said, with a huge smile. "And I'll try not to feel too hurt by how many of you just now laughed. Look, you all know what happened. We had one of the last primaries. None of the candidates had won enough delegates; no one was going to have a majority in the convention. The Michigan secretary of state decided at the last minute to put my name on the ballot. The result is that -"

"That you control the delegation, and maybe the convention," shouted someone from the back.

"I don't control anything. The delegation is pledged to me on the first ballot. After that, every delegate is free to vote for whomever he or she wishes."

Rachel Good of the New York Times, who never shouted out a question, stood on her tiptoes and raised her hand.

"If you take the Michigan delegation out of it, the rest of the delegates are divided almost equally between Lochner and Rivers. Your delegation can decide which of them becomes the nominee. Which do you think would make the better candidate, and, more importantly, the better president?"

It was almost irresistible, the temptation to tell the truth, that the election of either one of them would be a disaster for the country and the beginning of the end for the Republican party. Almost irresistible.

"My party – the Republican party – is not going to nominate anyone who isn't qualified to lead the nation."

"Which one?" Rachael Good was looking at him with a thin, teasing smile. "Which of these two qualified candidates is the best qualified, in your judgment?"

There were dozens of reporters crowded together, but Rachael Good had the manner - the presence, if you will – that, when she asked a question, drew you toward her as if she were the only one there.

"That is what makes it so interesting, Ms. Good," replied Matson, as if they were having a private conversation. "It's been a long time since we've had a convention that was not tantamount to a coronation, a four-day television event that decides nothing of real importance. You've been to as many of them as I have. Have you ever covered anything with less drama? Conventions have become infomercials. Not this one; no one knows who the nominee is going to be. No one has a majority of the delegates, and," he added with a smile that seemed to signal some deeper meaning, some deeper design, "those delegates are only pledged to a candidate on the first ballot. After that they become free agents. After the first ballot, the convention can choose anyone it wants. Isn't that the kind of convention you always wanted to cover? It could go on for weeks."

A young reporter for an internet service was certain Matson was wrong.

"That can't happen," he insisted. "Not today."

"Is that a question?"

"Not unless you want to make it one."

Reporters who had been jotting down notes suddenly looked up. Heads turned.

"I mean, it's obvious, isn't it? The nomination has to go to either Rivers or Lochner. They ran in the primaries; they were in it at the end – they're still in it. Several of the others dropped out. What would it say to everyone who voted if the convention nominated someone else? – Voting doesn't matter?"

Matson wondered why people, and reporters especially, now seemed to know less and less, or, rather, more and more about things that did not matter.

"It would say just the opposite: that the way you win an election is to get a majority of the votes. A primary election allows members of the party to choose delegates who will support the candidate they prefer. No one won the majority of the delegates chosen. The election – the choice of a candidate – now goes to the convention."

The young reporter was unimpressed.

"The polls – whether polls of the voters, the Republican voters you talked about, or polls of the delegates themselves, the ones chosen in all those primaries – show a majority for Rivers. Doesn't that mean the race is over? Doesn't that mean that this won't be any different than any other convention, that we know the result before the convention even begins?"

Matson exchanged a glance with Rachael Good, a quick, almost furtive glance, enough to remind them, what they both understood, that the best proof that things would not go as predicted was that everyone was so certain that they would. He looked back to the reporter.

"You may be right, but I doubt it."

Other reporters tried to get him to say something that could be taken as a hint that he preferred one candidate to the other. When they could get nothing that suggested anything but a strict neutrality, they asked what he thought about other candidates, dark horses that might suddenly capture the imagination of a convention cut loose from its first ballot obligations.

"A sudden stampede to a third candidate? I doubt the convention would turn to someone who was not able to win in the primaries. That isn't to say that they were not all fine candidates, but the fact is they lost, and -"

"Lincoln lost his Senate race, two years before he became president!" someone yelled, to the great enjoyment of the crowd.

"Yes, and if he were still around I'm sure the convention would nominate him again!"

"Are your sure?" asked Rachael Good. "Are you really sure of that?"

The press conference was over, but Rachael Good lingered behind while the other reporters began to move away, down the long dimly lit marble corridor. The network technicians went about their business, dismantling the television lights. Louis Matson leaned against the doorway at the front entrance of his office, talking quietly with Ismael Cooper.

"You promised me a private interview," Rachael Good reminded him.

"I did, didn't I?" replied Matson. A brief, slightly embarrassed grin told her he had forgotten all about it.

"Actually, you promised me dinner," she said, with a look of mischief.

"I never promised that. I asked – first time I saw you, thirty some years ago. Promised? How could I promise what you refused?"

Her green, limpid eyes danced with the antic memory of time, of youth not so much misspent as misunderstood, the past reinterpreted through the veil of thirty years. What had once been her unknown future had become her history.

"I would have said yes, if you had asked again; and – remember? – you promised that you would."

He was seeing the same thing she was, what had happened when they were both much younger, but from a different perspective, a different side, as it were, of the same picture. He did not know what he looked like then – he had never been all that conscious of himself – but he remembered how she looked, how the first time he had seen her she had taken his breath away.

"I never promised you that; I promised myself – someday, if I ever thought I might have a chance." Then, somehow, he knew, and his aging, tired eyes brightened with the certain knowledge that, like other beautiful women, she had never doubted who she was and the effect she had. "You always assumed – didn't you? – that anytime you said no to someone the only question – the only real question – was how long before they asked again."

"If you had asked a second time, I would have said yes," she told him again.

"If I had asked a second time, that would have just given you another reason to say no."

"Another reason?" she asked, tossing her head in the schoolgirl way that instead of something remembered had once been second nature.

"Insufficient pride."

"Bury your pride. You owe me an interview. You may have forgotten, but you absolutely promised that."

"Yes, I did; but I can't do it right now. There are some other things I have to take care of first. So why don't we meet somewhere in Georgetown around eight?"

"For dinner?" she asked, raising her eyebrows with the kind of eager anticipation she might have shown had he ever asked again, the time that had never happened because she had been too beautiful and he had had too much pride, and too much fear of another refusal.

There was only one thing Louis Matson had to do, and despite the impression he had left Rachel Good with, it had nothing to do with the Senate, and nothing to do with presidential politics. He had an appointment with his physician.

A little after six, he left the Russell Senate Office Building and caught a cab for the short ride to a building on L Street, just a few blocks from the White House, where his doctor, Estelle Steinberg, had her office. She always scheduled his appointment for the end of the day after everyone had gone. This had never been discussed. Dr. Steinberg understood the need for discretion. Matson let himself in through the doctor's private entrance.

"How are you feeling?" she asked, as she pressed a stethoscope to his chest.

He sat on the end of the examining table, his shirt unbuttoned, taking, at her direction, one deep breath after another.

"About the same. A little dizzy at times, mainly when I first get up in the morning. Sometimes if I get up from a chair a little too quickly."

She put the stethoscope away and gave him a long, serious look. With her steel gray hair pulled straight back and her pale blue eyes, she had a way of making him feel that, though ten years younger, she was somehow older and more experienced.

"You should be home, resting; you can't keep on the way you do. You remain in the Senate and…." She said this with a stern expression that just below the surface was as warm and sympathetic as anything he had known.

"It's the damndest thing. You talk to me like you're my mother, and you're almost young enough to be my daughter."

"What's the difference? Mother, daughter – anyone who cares about you would tell you you were crazy."

"It's usually the people who don't care about me who say that."

Dr. Steinberg raised an eyebrow, taking his point. She sat down on the only chair in the narrow examining room.

"You're seventy-four years old," she said in a slow, methodical voice. "You have cancer. We can keep you comfortable and alive for -"

"Two, maybe three, years. Yes, I know," he said, immediately sorry for the sudden rush of anger that had come unbidden into his voice. With a quick glance of apology, he added, "I know I'm dying. If I go home and lay down and don't waste any energy, if I take all the medication I'm supposed to take, I can live – if you can call it that – a few more years. If I don't do that, if I keep living the same way I have been doing, the time I have left will probably be cut in half. But that really is no choice at all, is it?" He searched her sympathetic eyes with the certainty of an agreed upon fact. "You wouldn't give up medicine – go home, lay in bed, waiting for the end to come. Suppose you had a chance to find a cure for something, but you were told that if you didn't stop, if you didn't give it up, you would be dead in a year instead of two or three. The question answers itself, doesn't it?"

Dr. Steinberg nodded slowly in apparent agreement. The lines in her high white forehead deepened.

"And is that what you have a chance to do? In the next year, find a cure for something?" Her voice had a sad, distant quality, the gentle weariness that comes with the knowledge that there is nothing that will make any real difference. Louis Matson was going to die, and medicine had no answer for that.

"A cure? I doubt it. But I may have a chance to do something so that things don't get any worse." He glanced out the window where, in the distance, part of the White House was visible. "When I was a kid in college and Kennedy was running for president – it was right at the end of the campaign – he came to Ann Arbor and gave a speech outside the student union. It was close to midnight when he got there and it was cold, freezing. There were thousands of us waiting. We had been there for hours and no one had left. I had not decided yet whether I was a Republican or a Democrat. It did not matter. When he spoke I never felt better in my life. And I never felt that way again. When he died – and I am of the generation that no matter what happened to us later never forgot exactly where we were, exactly what we were doing, the moment we first heard that Kennedy had been shot – when he died it was as if something had gone missing in our lives, something nothing, that no one, could ever replace. And we were right - nothing ever has. If I could do anything to bring back that sense of hope, the belief we had that we were a great country, that we could do anything if we put our minds to it....What if I could do that, if I could help do that – I probably can't; it's probably too late, but still, what choice do I have? Why bother to live at all, even a year, except to try? There are worse things than failure."

Estelle Steinberg gave him a prescription for something to help with the pain, something stronger than what she had given him before.

"My father died when he was almost ninety. He should have died six months sooner. He did not want to live anymore. They had him all doped up on morphine. What is the point of it? I'll use what you give me, but only if it doesn't cloud my brain. You have to promise me that, promise that you won't give me anything that won't let me function the way I should."

"No, I promise I won't. But the pain will only get worse, and then…."

"And then I'll do something about it." He began to button his shirt. He noticed his mottled, wrinkled skin and the way it fell loose around his ample waist. "I'm seventy-four and I never think of myself as old. Is that common? Do all of us think that getting old only happens to other people? I know I'm dying, I know there is nothing you or anyone can do, and the truth of it is I still think I'm the same kid who stood out in the cold night air in Ann Arbor listening to JFK. Some mornings I wake up and worry I might be late for class."

Estelle Steinberg scratched the side of her face and smiled.

"I had a patient some years ago who got up every morning and made breakfast for his wife. She had been dead for almost five years. They had been married for almost fifty years before she died. Why wouldn't he think of her as if nothing had changed? She was all he had ever had, all he had ever wanted. You wanted something else, and from what you told me you still do. Consider yourself fortunate. You want something serious, something worth leaving behind."

CHAPTER THREE

Louis Matson liked riding through the city at night. The massive tan stone buildings that lined the broad avenues had an even more majestic look, especially in the sultry heat of summer, illuminated in the shadows, than they did in the harsh light of day. There was a sense of purpose, a sense of power that made it somehow different from what he experienced in cities in which soulless steel skyscrapers crowded life into narrow streets and vacant glass-walled spaces. Paris, London, and Rome were the only other cities of importance that had kept intact a sense of great accomplishment, of a history worth remembering, instead of this modern obsession with mere technical achievement. Four cities, four capitals, and, at different times, four empires, each of which had for a while dominated the world. And all of them, Matson reminded himself, empires that had fallen victim to their own arrogance and ambition, and, more than that, the belief that after all they had done, all the sacrifices they had made to acquire what they had, nothing like the same effort was required to keep what they had gained. If there were only some way he could make everyone see that, see it before it was too late, then his life might be worth something after all.

The taxi pulled up outside the Georgetown restaurant where he was to meet Rachael Good. The well-lit street was full of people, young couples, some with small children, going nowhere in particular, a summer evening stroll after what for many of them had been a long day working in an executive office or on Capitol Hill. Matson recognized a few of them, and nearly everyone recognized him. He was used it, the sudden looks, the quick whispered conversations in which someone told someone else that he was there. It was not vanity, and it certainly was not because he especially liked to draw attention to himself, but the constant notice, the fact that everywhere he went in Washington he was always recognized made him feel, not so much important, as useful. The look in their eyes meant that he still had a connection with the unknown future, that any attempt to anticipate what would happen next in the world of politics had to take him into account. Estelle Steinberg had been right: He did want to do something serious, something worth leaving behind; it was just that he had no very clear idea what it should be or how to accomplish it if he had.

The restaurant was full of chatter, full of noise. White jacketed waiters moved like acrobats between the tables, balancing trays of food and drink above diners too absorbed in their own eager analysis of the latest rumors and the latest scandals to notice what was passing just above their heads. Rachel waved to him from a booth in the back corner, and, apologizing each time he bumped into someone's chair or the back of their shoulder, Matson made his way through the softly lighted room.

He ordered a Manhattan and, when the waiter brought it, greeted it like a long lost friend.

"The best part of the day," he remarked, as he took a drink.

"Was the day that bad?" asked Rachael.

"The day was good. Better than most," he added with the show of confidence he could summon on even the worst of days.

Rachael Good reached across the table and gently touched his hand.

"We've known each other a long time. How are you – really? You seem a little distracted lately. Are you sure you're okay?"

"You mean my health - because I had that surgery last year? I'm fine. As a matter of fact, I just saw my doctor – that was one of the things I had to do this afternoon."

It was a minor deceit, a slightly larcenous evasion, a way of keeping things as they had always been. No one looked at you the same way when they knew that death was waiting just around the corner. You might get sympathy from your family, if you had one, or your friends, if you had any, but the only meaning that death and illness had in Washington was that suddenly there was a new opening, a new opportunity, for someone else.

A look of wistful malice suddenly came into Rachael eyes. She leaned forward on her arms.

"Do you ever think about – her?"

Matson did not understand, and then, a moment later, he knew whom she meant.

"Linda? No, not really; not for a very long time. It was years ago and.... Why?"

"And you never thought about re-marriage?"

"No, but why are you...?"

"Because she's here, and she's coming over."

Matson had been married once. He fell in love, or thought he had, because given how easily he had gotten over the divorce he wondered if it had ever been anything more than a temporary infatuation, a passing obsession for a gorgeous young woman. Linda Lattimore was still attractive, but she was no longer young and when men looked at her it was to admire in the faded remnant the beauty that had once been hers.

"Hello, Louis. How are you?" she asked with a glittering, made up smile. Matson wondered if he would have recognized her had they passed each other in the street.

"Fine, just fine. And you?"

She had always managed to make it seem that the moment, whatever the moment was, belonged to her. In a reviewing line at the White House, she had stood in front of the president as if he had passed through the line waiting to see her. The world belonged to Linda Lattimore, she seemed to say with every breath she took, but she had her mind on other things.

"I haven't seen you since that embassy party two - or was it three? - years ago. Well, good to see you," she said, and then, without another word, turned and walked away.

"She remembers you at least," remarked Rachael Good with a wry, impish grin. "We were roommates for almost a year, when we both first arrived in Washington. She had just graduated from someplace in Texas and had a job in the office of a Texas congressman. I had just come down from New York.... But of course you remember that. You met her through me."

"You told me you thought I would like her better. That was your way of saying no when I asked you out."

"And I was right. You married her."

Matson took another drink, a long one this time. He arched his eyebrows and laughed.

"I would have thought it proved you wrong. Her father owned half of Texas. How do you think she got that job in the congressman's office? She was not looking for money; she had all anyone could want of that. She wanted what she did not have; she wanted power. She was young and so damn good looking it hurt to look at her. I was just starting my second term. I had a future. Listen," he said, as he slowly stirred his drink, "there was a great story Gore Vidal wrote somewhere about a Hollywood actress, so dumb she thought the way to get ahead, the way to get a role in a movie, was to fuck the writer. Linda thought the way to get ahead in Washington was to marry a congressman. What could be dumber than that? But she wasn't dumb – not like that, anyway. She had a kind of genius, if you take my meaning: an instinct for the main chance. We had not been married a year before she realized that no one threw Georgetown parties for a second term congressman, but everyone fell all over themselves for a senator or a member of the cabinet. Married two years, and six months after the divorce she's married to Clyde Wilkerson, then a senator from North Carolina – remember him? But Wilkerson was never going to be president so...."

"Another divorce, another marriage. Yes, I know. And look who she is with tonight."

Rachel nodded toward a table on the other side of the room. Matson followed her gaze, but did not recognize the man his former wife was with.

"You could look at it this way," continued Rachael. "She had a career like most of the men she married. One term, that is to say one marriage, in the House; then the Senate – several terms, as in several marriages; a failed candidacy for the presidency, and now, finally, like nearly everyone who ever held elective office in Washington, a lobbyist. She isn't married to this one, however. Rumor has it that he prefers someone younger. Now, let's order dinner and then you can tell me the real story, the truth; not that nonsense you told the press conference. Nothing on the record; I'm not looking for a quote - background only. What do I need to know?"

"The truth?" asked Matson, after they ordered. He finished his drink and felt better for the warmth of it. "You think I know what I'm doing? But someone has to do something, stir things up a little; remind everyone that this isn't just a question whether Rivers or Lochner can win over enough delegates pledged to the other one to get the majority they need. Remind everyone," he added with sudden emphasis, "that there is no rule that says the nomination has to go to someone just because they finished first or second in the primaries."

The waiter brought their order. Matson asked for a second drink. Rachael Good furrowed her brow, trying to make up her mind about something.

"What?" asked Matson, as he began to pick at his salad. "What is going on in that devious, suspicious mind of yours? You think I had something else up my sleeve?"

"Yes, absolutely! You could have insisted that it is precisely what everyone thinks it is: that one of the two has to be chosen, but you decided to insist, that because they did not win the primaries they should not become the party's nominee. What I want to know is why you decided to do that?"

Matson's second drink arrived. The noise in the restaurant now seemed like a wall, isolating them from the crowd. Matson stared into the amber colored liquid, remembering suddenly, as it were, several different things at once: the duplicity he had seen in the mean eyes of the chairman, Reece Davis; the solid good sense on the face of his physician, the only one who knew his secret; and, for just an instant, the buoyant eagerness glowing in the eyes of the girl he was about to marry, a look that in his young and innocent heart he had not doubted was true.

"You're smiling at something, Louis. Is it your own ingenuity, the way you have figured out how to make sure no one gets the nomination unless you want them to have it?"

"Lincoln," he said, suddenly looking up from the glass.

"Lincoln?"

"The question you asked at the end – Did I really believe that Lincoln could get the nomination. Think about that." Matson was quite serious. "And then think about the question you did not ask. If you took that as a standard – if you used Lincoln as the measure – where would you find anyone who was even close?"

"But Lincoln – that was another time. Everything was different then."

"I used to think so," replied Matson, as he took another drink.

"That isn't the reason - Lincoln, I mean," said Rachael, dismissing the suggestion out of hand. "It isn't some new nostalgia for the past. You're trying to do something. You don't want either one of them….You want someone else. Who is it, who do you want to be the nominee?"

Louis Matson shrugged, and looked down at his glass and tried to remind himself that he had to be careful not to drink too much. The thought made him laugh. What difference could it make what he did? So what if he told Rachael Good more than he should? He took another drink.

"Someone else? No, there isn't anyone. I wish there were. And, who knows, maybe there will be if the convention goes beyond the first ballot. All right," he said, pushing first his glass, then his plate, aside. "You want the truth, off the record, background only. I want to do whatever I can think of to pull the party back from the brink and make it see reason. I have two ways to do that. The candidates think that because I control the Michigan delegation, I hold the balance. They will come to see me – each of them – and will promise anything they think I want to hear, promises they will forget the moment they have the nomination. The other thing I have is the speech, the keynote speech. I intend to put the party on notice. I am going to remind them, and the country, what the Republican party stands for – what it used to stand for – what conservative really means. I am going to remind everyone that it does not mean the 19th century liberalism – what they used to call 'the night watchman' theory of the state – they disguise under the name libertarian; and that it does not mean this mindless opposition to government that all these Tea Party patriots seem to think was what the American Revolution was all about. I'm going to give our party a history lesson. At least, that is what I would do if I could find someone who could write a speech like that. Do you remember Julian Drake?"

The name was thrown out so quickly for a moment Rachael Good was not sure she had heard it right. An instant later her eyes lit up.

"Remember Julian Drake? Who could forget him? He was extraordinary, unlike anyone I had ever seen. But why do you ask? Has Julian Drake suddenly come back to life?"

"Back to life? He didn't die."

"He might as well have, the way he disappeared, vanished as if he had never existed. All I ever heard was that he had gone out west somewhere, but no one really knew, and after a while....But you knew, didn't you?"

"I knew why he disappeared, but I didn't know where he went, and I don't know where he is now."

Rachael Good had barely touched her food. She did not care about that. She was much more interested in what Matson had just told her.

"You knew why he quit, why he disappeared?"

"I've never told anyone; I promised that I wouldn't. When it happened, when he knew he had to leave, to give up everything he had achieved, everything he might still accomplish – he would have won that Senate race in a walk – he asked for my help. Someone had to handle things, to take care of the people who had been working for him. If I tell you now, it's because I'm going to try to find him, and if I do, then...."

"The speech! You want him to write it; you want him...." Her mind raced back twelve years to the last time she had heard Julian Drake speak to a crowd. "Can you imagine the kind of speech he could give at the convention?" she said without thinking. She looked at Matson, ready to apologize, but Matson understood. He smiled and shook his head.

"That's the problem. Even if I could get him to write the speech for me, I'd never be able to give it the way he could. But it would still be better than any speech I have ever given. That is the point, you see. This has to be the speech of my life."

He had not meant to say anything about Julian Drake's disappearance, he certainly had not meant to tell her that he would tell her why it had happened, but he realized suddenly that it was exactly what he wanted to do. He had carried the secret with him for twelve years. He had kept the promise he had made late one summer night in the privacy of his study when Julian Drake had told him what he had to do. He knew Rachael would understand, and he trusted her to keep a secret that in a strange way had become a private possession too valuable not to be passed on, and perhaps become an example others might one day want to follow.

"It was because of a woman," he began, remembering the rumor that earlier in the day Ismael Cooper had repeated. "Not some woman he was involved with. It was nothing like that at all. It was his sister. She and her husband were killed. They had two small children, a girl and a boy. There was no one else, no other relatives, no one who could take on the responsibility of raising them. Julian had to do it."

Rachael Good stared at him in open-mouthed astonishment.

"That makes no sense at all. Why would he have to give up his career, why quit a Senate race he was about to win? There are all sorts of people – single parents – who raise children while they work."

"That was exactly the argument I tried to use. Hire someone, get whatever help you need. I could not understand it, but then, as I quickly learned that night, I had never really understood him, who he really was. I don't think anyone ever did. He said something that makes more sense to me now than it did then: 'You can only do one thing well.' That was it – one thing. He had to make a choice: continue what he was doing, only now with small children to raise - which would mean he could not spend all his time in politics and government - or devote all his time and attention to the two small children of his sister, a sister he adored. For him it was no choice at all. His sister had helped raise him after their parents died; he was not about to do anything less than all he could for her two orphaned children. That was the reason, not just why he quit the Senate race and put an end to his political career, but why he disappeared. He did not want those children exposed to the kind of public attention they would have attracted. He wanted them to have as easy a transition as it was possible for them to have."

"And did they – the children, I mean - have a normal life with Julian Drake as their surrogate parent?"

"I don't know. I never heard from him again. That isn't quite true. I got a long letter from him a few months later, thanking me for what I had done, and telling me that he was even more certain than he had been before that he had done the right thing. And then, after that, after that letter, nothing, nothing at all."

"You said his sister and her husband had been killed. What was it – a car accident?"

"No; they were murdered. That is what he told me. Somewhere out in California, where they lived. I did not ask him anything about it. I was too shocked by what he was going to do. I don't even know what his sister's married name was. I don't know why they were murdered or if the murderer was caught. All I know is that Julian Drake, who would have been elected to the Senate, and who might have become president, was willing to give it all up because he loved his sister. I've been in this town a long time and I can't think of anyone else I've ever known who would have done that. Can you?"

CHAPTER FOUR

There were more than three hundred passengers on the flight from Washington to San Francisco but Ismael Cooper, so far as he could tell, was the only one wearing a coat and tie. He had come straight from his office, but even if he had had time to change he would not have bothered. No one dressed for anything anymore, except for weddings and funerals, and sometimes not even then. It was everywhere now, the breakdown of propriety and decorum, the common obligation to conduct oneself in a certain way. Scarcely anyone even spoke in sentences anymore, just the fragmentary, abbreviated incoherence with which three words become the equivalent of a whole paragraph, and words themselves replaced by single letters that symbolized things best left unexpressed. Everywhere he looked, passengers who were not eating or asleep were watching on thin well-lit screens movies without even the pretense at dialogue. And here he was, flying across country to convince someone he had not seen in years to write a speech that no one would forget. It made Don Quixote seem the most reasonable man who ever lived.

The plane landed on schedule, a few minutes after two o'clock in the afternoon. With only a single overnight bag, Cooper did not have to wait for the baggage to be unloaded. The rental car was waiting and ten minutes later he was heading south on Highway 101 toward Monterey and, beyond that, to the wilds of Big Sur. The traffic was not too bad, and he was glad he had not taken a later flight when he might have had to deal with the nightmare of the daily commute in and out of Silicon Valley. An hour after he left the airport, Cooper passed through the outskirts of Salinas where a sign on the highway said something about John Steinbeck. Cooper wondered at the irony of posting a reference to the author of East of Eden in a place that was now full of gas stations and cheap roadside motels. Heavy trucks thundered by him as he slowed down, careful not to miss the turn he had been told to take to the Monterey Peninsula. The road ended, twelve miles later, at a highway running along the Pacific shore and he headed south on Highway 1. He passed Monterey, and then, just beyond it, Carmel, the village where artists used to live in the 30s and 40s, when rents were cheap and there was no one else around. Then the tourists started to come to see what the artists did, and those with money thought it might be a good place to have a summer home, and then, soon after that, the first resort was built with a golf course by the sea, and then the writers and the artists, the real ones, the ones who had come here to try to do something serious, found somewhere else to go.

Ismael Cooper remembered that. He had been here several times before, and on one of those visits had picked up a copy of something Henry Miller had written about living in Big Sur in the 1940s. Cooper remembered a conversation he had with Julian Drake about it. He thought it strange that he would think about that now, just as he left Carmel behind him and started into Big Sur on a two lane road of twisting hairpin turns through the coastal mountains that fell straight down to the Pacific; strange the way that one thing could suddenly bring back a conversation, a brief exchange of words, he had had with someone fifteen or sixteen years ago. They had been standing outside a committee room in the Capitol. Drake had told him that he had just come back from Big Sur, that he had spent a week out there visiting. And then – and Cooper remembered this as if it had just happened – he got a look in his eyes, the look of someone who has just discovered the one thing he wanted, the place where he could spend his whole life, a place he would never leave.

Cooper hoped it was true, hoped that Julian Drake had come back here, to Big Sur, for that very reason, and that it was everything he had thought it would be. He had never quite understood Julian Drake, never understood the nature of his ambition. There was no question but that he had been ambitious. He had run for Congress and he had run for the Senate, until he quit. You did not do that unless you were ambitious. But there was something different about it, something Cooper wished he had: a kind of indifference to his own success, as if it did not really matter to him if he won or lost.

He studied the road, careful to slow down each time he saw a signpost or a numbered address at the top of a long driveway that led from the narrow two-lane highway down toward a lonely looking house perched on one of the rocky promontories high above the swirling water below. He must have gone fifteen miles before he finally found it, a dirt and gravel road that cut through a small grove of windswept cypress trees for about a quarter mile and then dead ended at a large single-story house that, as he knew immediately, had to belong to Julian Drake. That day, years ago, when he had seen the look in Julian's eyes during that brief conversation about his first visit to Big Sur – he understood now what that look meant. Cooper felt it in himself, the sense of perfect peace, complete contentment, a place that from the moment you first arrived you never wanted to leave, because you knew, in a way you had never known anything before, that there was no other place that would ever give you this same feeling again.

"Shangri-la," muttered Cooper, as he got out of the car and stretched his arms.

The house, all glass and weathered gray siding, was cantilevered out above the sloping ground, which made it seem almost as windswept as the trees that towered high above it on the landward side. The living room, a long rectangle with three glass walls, had a massive fireplace built of light colored flat stones in the tapered shape of a pyramid. The distant murmur of the ocean underscored a silence so profound that the cry of an eagle circling somewhere high overhead seemed as if it were coming from just a few feet away.

"Did you come to tell me that I was elected to the Senate after all and they have only now noticed my absence?"

Too caught up in his own impressions, too entranced by what he saw,

Cooper had not been aware of anything until he felt a hand on his shoulder and heard the voice that in an instant took him back twelve years in time.

"Most of them don't know where they are. Why would they notice someone missing?" He turned and found himself face to face with someone who seemed not to have changed at all.

"I heard you come," explained Julian Drake. "I heard the car turn off the road."

"You heard…? It must be a quarter of a mile; it must…."

"Live here long enough, you know when something is different. But never mind that," he said, as he gave him a searching glance. "How did you find me? How did you know where I was… and why?" Suddenly, he seemed embarrassed. "That isn't what I meant to say. Don't misunderstand. It's good to see you. I never thought….But, come along, let's go inside."

They started toward the house, but before they had taken three steps Julian stopped and shook his head.

"No, there is something wrong. You didn't just decide to drop by to say hello. What is it? What's happened? Is it something about Louis – Louis Matson?"

Julian Drake was in his late forties but could have passed for thirty-five. There was not so much as a touch of gray in his light brown hair and the only lines visible on his face were the ones that appeared on his forehead when he furrowed his brow. The gray-green eyes were as full of light and quiet laughter as they had been when Ismael Cooper first met him, nearly twenty years before, though lit now with what seemed a deeper intelligence. It was uncanny, inexplicable, but Julian Drake seemed almost to have become both older and younger at the same time.

"I'm sorry," said Julian, apologizing again. "I don't get many visitors. Many visitors!" he laughed. "I think you must be the first." He shook his head, amused at how awkward he had suddenly become. "I mean, people I'm not expecting. No one from the life I used to lead."

It was Cooper's turn to apologize, and to explain.

"I would have called first, but…."

"But I don't have a telephone. I have one," he added, cryptically, as he started again for the front door, just a few steps ahead. "It isn't listed. You could have written – but that…."

"No one could find an email address."

"An email…? No, I meant regular mail. Never mind, it doesn't matter. You're here, and I can't tell you how good it is to see you."

They went inside and for a second time Ismael felt he had entered into a different world. The house, designed almost certainly by an architect who had studied under Frank Lloyd Wright, had an immediate hold on him. Everywhere he looked, from the wooden floors that glowed like fire to the vaulted ceilings that seemed to climb straight up; from the clear glass windows that made the difference between inside and outside all but disappear, to the bookcases that lined the walls with cloth and leather volumes of every shade of color, everything about it was a magician's secret: a house, a thing of wood and glass and stone, somehow given life. Ismael thought he could hear it breathe.

"You'll stay here tonight," said Julian, as they sat down on two facing cream-colored sofas in front of the stone fireplace that towered to the timbered ceiling twenty feet above. "If you like, I mean. And not just tonight – as long as you can stay." With a sudden, embarrassed laugh, Julian jumped to his feet. "What can I get you? Something to drink? I have a couple of bottles of wine somewhere; I might even have some beer. I'm afraid I don't have anything else…."

"No, nothing; I'm fine. Well, actually – would you have some coffee? After the flight out, then the drive, I could use something to clear my head."

While Julian was in the kitchen, Ismael walked around the living room, studying more closely the meticulous manner in which several thousand books had been arranged on the floor-to-ceiling shelves. There was nothing random, nothing to suggest the ordinary household practice of volumes whose only function was to fill up empty space. There was an order that, so far as he could see, allowed for no exceptions. Each section, which might be as little as a single shelf or have as many as a dozen, held only books that fell within a single category: history, divided in turn among American, European and ancient; philosophy, economics, and then, among the various sciences, physics, chemistry, botany, and at least half a dozen others. There must have been thirty or forty separate subjects, and each of them organized alphabetically by author. Ismael's eyes came to rest on the shelves reserved for literature, which included among its other divisions American, English, French and Russian. Next to War and Peace and Anna Karenina, Tolstoy, he found Turgenev.

"That was Jennifer's doing," explained Julian, handing Ismael a cup of coffee. "My niece. She is nothing if not meticulous. It used to drive her crazy if I put a book in the wrong place. I tried to remember, but sometimes I forgot. Her brother, on the other hand, did it on purpose. He made a game of it. She knew where everything was – where it was supposed to be – and so he would take something from the very top shelf where, as you can see, it's hard to make out the title on the spine from this far down, and put it on one of the bottom shelves where you practically have to be on your hands and knees to see what it is."

"Your niece – and your nephew…?" asked Ismael with a puzzled expression.

Julian bent his head to the side. He looked at Ismael as if he were trying to remember something. It had been twelve years.

"Louis never told you…? No, of course not. I asked him not to tell anyone. But, still," he went on, smiling to himself, "after all this time, it would have been understandable if….Did he send you? Is that why you have come?"

Ismael sat down on the sofa and drank some coffee and held the warm cup in his hands. He had wondered how he would begin, how he would tell Julian Drake why he had come without sounding like a perfect fool. Julian had been out of politics for twelve years, and not just that, out of Washington for so long that no one remembered him or what he had been capable of doing. But now that he was here, now that he had seen him, seen the place he lived and the kind of life it implied, it all seemed to make perfect sense.

"He's giving the keynote speech at the convention, and he wants you to write it."

Julian started to laugh. His eyes, just for a moment, sparkled with cheerful malice.

"I can do that," he said, with a quick, decisive grin. He reached inside the tan sports jacket he was wearing, pulled out a black fountain pen, jotted a few words on a small notepad he carried in the right outside pocket, tore out the page and handed it to Ismael.

"'I herewith resign from the Republican party,'" Ismael read out loud.

"It isn't just the words, of course; it all depends on how you read it," explained Julian with a droll expression. "But if you want to say something that no one will ever forget, that is as good as I could do. And besides, unless Louis has changed, become someone completely different from the man I once knew, that single sentence is probably exactly what deep down he would most like to do. Or do you think I'm wrong?"

Ismael leaned back, more certain now than ever that what he had remembered about Julian Drake was true, that he could get to the heart of things as quick, or quicker, than anyone he had ever known.

"He would love to say that, just walk off, leave all those mindless rightwing fanatics to their own devices; let them fight among themselves over the best way to destroy the country. But he can't – or he won't. He thinks he has to somehow save them from themselves. He wants -"

"To give a speech that starts from the beginning, that reminds everyone what the Republican party believed in at the beginning, what it has stood for over the years. A speech, in other words, about the real principles that should inform its conduct, what has to be done to recapture the original intent; a speech that shows – that teaches – why everything the people who now claim to represent it is wrong."

"Yes, exactly; I haven't heard him say it quite like that, but…. You must have followed politics pretty closely all this time. You must have -"

"Hardly at all. Almost never. I read the Sunday Times – every month or so. I don't have a television. I had the children, and I didn't want them to be…." Julian noticed the look of confusion on Ismael's face. "You wouldn't have come all this way, you wouldn't have gone to all the trouble to find me, if this wasn't something Louis thought important. He's never asked me for anything, not once, all this time."

Stroking his forehead, Julian looked past his guest, looked back through the years, the lifetime, that had passed since that awful night he had gone to Louis Matson and asked for his help.

"I was running for the Senate. Maybe you remember. There seemed to be a reasonable chance I might win."

“The only question was how large the margin was going to be.”

“Perhaps, but I would not have been a candidate – I would not have won my first election to the House six years before – if it had not been for Louis Matson. He did almost the same thing for you. I remember. And if you had not lost in that primary, he would have helped you run for the Senate, later, when he thought the chances were good. And, unless I miss my guess, when he decides he’s had enough, when he decides not to run again, he’ll work things so that you become his successor. No,” he insisted, when Ismael started to protest; “he did not ask you to head his staff just because you lost that primary. He knew that if he could keep you in the center of things; keep you in the public eye, you would be in position when the time comes. That’s the reason he has you go back to Michigan every couple weeks to give speeches on what the majority leader is doing, to meet with the editorial boards, to do all those interviews on television.”

Ismael was astonished. “But how could you know that? How did you know – if you don’t have a television, if you only read a paper every month or so?”

“Because I know Louis, and I know you. Nothing else would have made sense. Louis has too high a regard for his responsibilities to let his seat in the Senate go to someone he does not think the best person to fill it.”

“That is certainly what he thought of you.”

Julian got up and walked over to the window. He stood there, silent, watching the blood red sun slowly sink onto the ocean’s edge.

“The election was just weeks away. I was in Ann Arbor giving a speech. I had just finished and someone passed me a note telling me something had happened and that I had to call California. It’s odd, but I think I knew that suddenly everything was going to change.”

Turning away from the window, Julian looked back across the room to his unexpected guest. He was struck by how little Ismael Cooper had changed. There was still the same serious scholarly look, so unlike most members of Congress, so unlike most people generally. He had known he could trust him the first time he had seen him, known that anything he told him would always be treated as if it had been said in the strictest confidence.

“My sister and her husband had been killed. They had two small children:

a boy just turned six, and a girl who was almost ten. There was no one else to take care of them, no one else to raise them. I knew that I was named guardian in their parents' will and trustee of the estate, which, fortunately, was quite large. My brother-in-law was one of those computer geniuses who built a company that made money from everywhere." Julian made a sweeping gesture with his hand. "This was their weekend getaway, a place they could come to be alone. It became our home – the three of us – and our school."

"Your school? You mean, where you taught them what they didn't learn in school?"

"They did not go to school. I made sure of that. It was my responsibility to give them the best education possible. But, never mind that. This is about what Louis did. And he never told you anything?"

"About what happened that night, the night you quit? No, never. I asked him. The rumor was that it was something about a woman. He said it was true, that a woman was involved, but not the way everyone seemed to think."

"My sister," remarked Julian, nodding twice to emphasize the distance between the rumor and the fact. "She was a woman all right, the best woman – the best person – I've ever known. That's why, you see – why I had to do what I did, quit the Senate race, get out of Washington. I could not let someone else raise her children while I was working eighteen hours a day on legislation and then going off for long weekends campaigning around the country. I had to do this; I had to give them a home; I had to make them feel safe. And I had to give them an education, not the kind they give in schools these days, teaching everyone what they have to learn to make a living, to be able, in that awful phrase everyone now uses, to 'compete in the global economy,' but the kind that teaches what it means to live. I didn't want them to learn how to make money - my sister wouldn't have wanted them to learn how to do that - I wanted them to learn what it means to be a human being, our place in the order of the world. I tried to teach them what it means to have a mind. But before I could teach them anything I had to learn – or try to learn it – first myself. That is why I brought them here, why we never had a television, why we never had a computer. It is why we lived here part of every year and the rest of the time in Europe."

It had been a long time since Julian Drake had talked with anyone he had known from the years he had been in Congress, years before he had become, if not exactly a recluse, an essentially private person. He felt a sudden urgency to explain what had changed, why everything was different now, how what had once seemed so important to him had lost all meaning. He wanted to tell Ismael Cooper everything; to take him step by step through what had happened, how in the course of educating two children he had educated himself. But Ismael had other questions, one in particular, that he was not quite sure how to ask.

"Why did Louis…? Why did he, instead of you…?"

"Make the announcement; explain to everyone – especially the press – that I was quitting the race? If I had done it, I would have had to give the reason; I would have had to answer questions. It was better to let everyone draw their own conclusions; better if they believed whatever rumor they heard. The one thing I could not do was let anyone know the truth. I had to protect my sister's children. They could never know the truth – until they were both old enough to handle it. My sister and her husband did not die in an accident; my sister was murdered by her husband who then killed himself."

CHAPTER FIVE

Louis Matson sat at his desk, listening with growing fascination as Ismael Cooper described his trip to California and what he had learned from Julian Drake.

"Has he changed?" Matson bent his head slightly to the side. "Is he the same as you remembered?"

"Imagine someone with his intelligence, smarter than anyone you had ever met, who then spends twelve years studying every important book ever written so that he can learn how to teach. Is he the same? - Yes, and no. He's the same, only more so; quicker, more agile, in the way he thinks. I don't know if he can give a speech the way he used to – I don't know if he would still have the passion – but…."

Matson nodded, scratched the back of his head, and then rubbed his chin. His eyes darted in one direction and then in another.

"But will he write one for me? What did he say when you asked him?"

Cooper had come straight from the airport. He opened his briefcase and removed a sealed manila envelope.

"Here it is: the speech you wanted him to write."

Matson looked at him in astonishment, and then, smiling, shook his head.

"Probably did it at one sitting; probably wrote it straight through and never changed a word. Have you read it?"

"I didn't even know he was going to write it. I told him what you wanted, that you hoped he would help. Before I could say anything else, he told me what he knew you would want to say. Just a couple of sentences, but – at least it seemed to me – a perfect summary of everything you have been talking about, all those -"

"All those weird ramblings, those vague thoughts, I could never quite put together. Yes, I know; he could always do that."

"As I say, he tossed off those few sentences, and then we started talking about other things, including what you did for him, what happened the night he found out that his sister had been killed, the night he found out she had been murdered by her husband and her husband had -"

"He told you that?" Folding his hands in his lap, Matson narrowed his eyes, trying to penetrate the thickening mists of time. "I'd never seen anyone look the way he did that night. I don't mean just his sister's death – that would have been hard enough – and though this may sound strange, not even the fact she had been murdered. It was that she had been murdered by her husband, the father of her children, and there was no reason, no reason at all. It was not jealousy; she wasn't involved with someone else. It wasn't because her husband was a violent man; he did not even own a gun. He bought one that afternoon, went home, sent the kids down the street to stay with a neighbor, and then murdered his wife and shot himself. And no reason, no reason at all. That is what Julian could not deal with, what he could not accept. It meant that there was no reason for anything; that there was nothing you could trust, nothing you could believe in. But he had enough sense to believe in himself, to know that there was something he had to do, something only he could do – raise those two children, to think only of them. I never had any doubt he would do it, and do it well."

"He certainly did it in a way different from what anyone else would have done," said Ismael with a glance of puzzled admiration.

"That he kept them out of school, taught them himself?"

"Not that, exactly; the way he did it, as if it was not terribly important what they learned, or if they learned anything at all. He made a strange remark, which, when I thought about it later, was not really strange at all: He asked me if I knew anyone who could not read; and then he asked me why, if everyone learns how, it should be thought important that someone learned it faster than someone else. All of us eventually learn well enough. He was not interested in having his two charges – he called them that, his nephew and his niece – compete with others. He asked them what they wanted to do. He told them stories out of Homer, stories about Helen of Troy and the Trojan War, stories about Socrates and ancient Greece. And then he asked them if they would like to see what it was like in ancient times, and, like any children, they were thrilled with the thought of adventure, and so they went to Athens and lived there two years. And then, because he taught them history by in a way living through it, they lived two years in Rome. They picked up languages the way other kids pick up games. They knew Greek and Latin before they were teenagers, and then, after a year or so back in America, they were off to France, Great Britain, Germany and Spain. And everywhere they lived he found in the things they saw something by which to lead them to want to learn something they had not known before. They looked at things, wondered how they worked or how they came into being – and he told me this was the most important thing - they learned how to ask questions."

"The boy would be what now – eighteen or nineteen; the girl twenty-two or twenty-three. He's not still teaching them?"

"No, they're both now in school," replied Ismael, tugging on his ear as he tried to suppress a grin. "The boy is in his second year at Harvard, majoring in physics. The girl has just finished her first year in medical school at Yale. She is going to be a neurosurgeon."

Matson roared with delight. "Finally, a member of Congress who knew what he was doing! Now, tell me, about the speech…."

"We talked until – I don't know – it must have been midnight before I got to bed, three in the morning east coast time. I was exhausted; I slept until almost nine in the morning, and when I got up he had it done. He said he worked on it for a few hours, went to bed around three, got up at seven and finished it then. He didn't say anything about it, but I had the feeling that this was not unusual, that he doesn't sleep more than a few hours. He studies all the time. He said that when he started teaching the children, he suddenly realized that everything he had always thought he knew was wrong, that he had never really understood what it meant to question our assumptions because – and this really struck me – we have no idea what our assumptions really are. Anyway, he gave me the speech and said he hoped you would forgive him, that it might not be anything like what you had in mind, that he had not given a speech in years, and that he was glad he did not have copies of the speeches he used to give. He thought they would be too embarrassing."

"Have you read it?" asked Matson. Smiling to himself, he tapped with two fingers the sealed envelope.

"It was sealed when he gave it to me."

"What about the other thing? Did he say he'd come?"

"He laughed when I asked him; but when he realized I was serious, that it was important, that you wanted to have him close by to work on any changes that might have to be made, he was not happy about it. He has no interest in politics anymore, but it is more than that. I think he's afraid of the memories it might bring back." With a grim look in his eyes, Ismael shook his head. "What would it be like to wander around the floor of a convention where, but for an inexplicable occurrence, a death without reason, everyone would have known you; wander around the floor of a convention where now no one recognizes you or even remembers your name?"

"But he'll come?" asked Matson, whose only interest was in whether Julian Drake would be there to help.

"Yes. He owes you that."

"He said that – that he owes me that?"

"Yes. No, actually he said that he owes you a lot more than that."

"Good. I had a feeling I could count on him."

"He did say one other thing," remarked Ismael, as he rose from his chair and gestured toward the sealed manila envelope on Matson's desk. "That after you read it you might decide that you don't need him there after all because you won't need his help to burn it. I think he was serious."

With his broad forehead, his sometimes sullen mouth, and the thick tangled hair that fell over the back of his shirt collar, Louis Matson had the slightly disheveled look of a failed musician, a composer whose mind, while not exactly absent, was working on something other than the passing noise of conversation. With an odd, off-center smile, he nodded in agreement with what Ismael had just said. He had understood immediately what Julian Drake had meant and it was not anything like what Ismael had assumed. He remembered enough about Julian to suspect that he had written a speech that almost no one would want to give, not because it was not good enough, but because there would not be a line in it that was written for applause; not a word, not a phrase, written for the crowd. He could not wait to read it.

He was not the only one. Ismael asked whether, after he was finished, he might have a chance to read it as well.

"Of course," replied Matson, as Ismael started for the door. "Unless I burn it first."

Matson resisted the temptation to open the sealed envelope and glance through the first few pages. He wanted to wait until he could give it his undivided attention, later that night, after a dinner at the Mayflower Hotel at which he was forced to sit at the head table and applaud the kind of mindless remarks that only an American politician seemed able to make without embarrassment.

"What is it you're clutching in your hands like a secret briefing from the CIA?" asked Rachael Good, as the dinner finally broke up.

"A little light reading for later, something to clear my mind after all the deep profundities we heard tonight."

He had known Rachel for so many years, she seemed not to have aged at all. There was something youthful in her eyes, a teasing sparkle that told you she knew all your secrets and could not wait to hear more.

"It's the speech I plan to give next week."

Rachael Good stepped closer. There were people everywhere, men who all looked alike in their tuxedos, women who did not always succeed in looking all that different in dresses that cost more than one of the waiters clearing their places made in a year.

"Are you going to let me read it in advance of that much anticipated event?"

"You never know – I might."

"You might?" she inquired cautiously, surprised that he would even consider the possibility.

Matson laughed at her reporter's reaction.

"You're like a cat who sits there purring, as content as anyone could look, and all the time watching for the first sign when to pounce. Yes, I might let you see it; then, again…."

"You rat!" she whispered. She looked at him with straight-faced larceny, and asked in a much louder voice, "But it will have to be awfully good to rival what we heard tonight, don't you think?"

The reporter and the majority leader were suddenly the center of attention of everyone who in the sudden silence was near enough to hear.

"The speeches tonight were among the best I have heard the candidates give during the campaign." Matson paused long enough to let everyone see the sudden laughter in his eyes. "And after all the speeches they have given, it's a wonder they still have the strength to give another. Fortunately, I only have to give the one next week."

"But you didn't answer my question, Senator," said Rachael Good, playing the innocent. "You didn't say if you thought your speech would have to be remarkably good to rival the ones given here tonight."

"Good? No, it would have to be a lot better than that."

"So you thought the ones given tonight were…?"

"I thought they each said what they wanted to say."

"And what is it you want to say, Senator? What is it you want to tell your party and the country?"

He started to give her the usual predictable response - he could hear the words echoing in his mind – that the party had to give the country a new direction; instead, he said something he had not thought he would ever hear from anyone.

"That the only thing worse than losing an election is winning one you deserve to lose, and that a political party that does not believe in the American government – the only government ever created by the free choice of its citizens – doesn't deserve to exist." Matson smiled broadly. "Or something like that," he added, as he turned and walked away.

Rachael Good caught up with him in the lobby of the hotel. She could hardly contain herself.

"Are you really going to do that – what you said back there? Is that what that speech says?" she asked, nodding toward the envelope he held tucked under his arm. "Come on; let's go someplace. I'll buy you a drink."

"Thanks, but not tonight," he said, as he headed for the doors to the street. "I still have things to do."

"The speech, the one you're going to let me see before you give it?" she shouted after him as he waved goodbye.

Matson walked past a long line of limousines parked in front of the hotel. A door suddenly opened and a familiar voice called his name. Edward Rivers invited him to get in.

"Let me give you a lift. It'll give us a chance to talk."

Matson could barely tolerate being in the same room with him, and that, in a strange way, made it almost irresistible, a chance to discover just what it was that made Rivers so despicable. It was a little like taking a tutorial in abnormal psychology. No one liked Ed Rivers; Rivers knew it, dismissed it as a tribute to the stupidity of others, and thought to turn what anyone else would think a distinct disadvantage into the best reason why he was certain to be president.

"I'm going to win this thing," he announced, almost before Matson had settled into the seat opposite. The Texas twang seemed artificial, contrived, something that, after Harvard Law School, he had taught himself. "I'm going to win – I just need a little help; a little help I know you would like to give me because you know I'm the only one who can win in November."

Stifling a yawn, Matson looked down at his shoes. He wondered why he had not remembered to have them polished. Rivers thought Matson was smiling at what he had just said.

"Look at the polls. They all show I do better than..., better than anyone else."

Matson had been careful in what he had said in front of a crowd of politicians and rich contributors, but there was no reason, none that he could think of, not to tell this brazen upstart what he really thought of him and his chances.

"You're going to win, but you need a little help! That means you aren't going to win without it. And you're sure I'll give you the help you need, because you're going to win?"

He wondered if Rivers would recognize the flaw, the basic inconsistency, in his argument. Rivers just sat there, waiting for the majority leader to finish what he had started to say.

"You're right, Senator: the polls show that you run better than any of the others; but – and this would seem to be important – they only show that you lose by a smaller margin. They don't show you have any real chance of winning."

With the kind of enveloping sincerity learned from long practice, Rivers leaned forward and tried to convince the majority leader that things now had a new meaning.

"That's because half the country still doesn't know who I am. All that changes with the convention when I get the nomination, when I give my acceptance speech. Then I become the only one anyone is talking about. It isn't a problem running behind Shaw in the polls; it is a huge advantage. Because, don't you see, it means that I come out of the convention with an enormous surge of new interest. That's just it, don't you see – I'll be the new face, the center of attention, the one everyone wants to interview. What can anyone say about Madelaine Shaw that hasn't been said before? Everyone knows who she is; everyone knows all about her and her husband. They're old news. What is the one thing everyone in this country is always looking for, the one thing everyone is afraid they might miss? – The next new thing. Remember what happened in 08? No one seems to understand what it meant. No one had ever heard of Sarah Palin, but the moment McCain announced she was going to be his running mate you could have murdered someone on live television and no one would have noticed. All anyone wanted was to hear more about this political unknown who was suddenly going to be a heartbeat away from the presidency."

"And we know how that turned out, don't we?" remarked Matson, as he looked out the window at the lights of Washington sliding by in the darkened shadows. A light rain had begun to fall, and he watched with a nostalgia he had only recently begun to feel a young couple, laughing as they ducked under an umbrella, cross the street half way up the block.

"You're right – what you said about Palin, that everyone is looking for something new," he said, turning back to Rivers. "Have you ever wondered why that is?"

"Have I ever wondered…?"

"Yes, wondered. What accounts for this constant dissatisfaction, this itching eagerness to abandon everything we have done and do something completely different? You, for example. What makes you think the country would be better off if we did the things you and your Tea Party friends say you want? As near as I can tell, you seem to think the best thing we could do is shut down the government and give everyone a gun."

Rivers clenched his teeth and raised his chin, a gesture of defiance with which he invariably met a challenge to whatever he wanted everyone to think he believed. Matson almost laughed at the patent dishonesty of it.

"I don't mean to suggest that you want to do either of those things. But the people who support you, the ones who came from all over to volunteer in your campaign in the primaries – the ones who a few years ago thought Sarah Palin would actually be good for the country – isn't that what they say they want?"

Rivers lowered his chin; his eyes softened into a look of mutual understanding. It was the assumption of an agreement among men who spoke the same language, the common mathematics of political calculation.

"There is enormous frustration out there. People feel a loss of control. Everything seems to be changing. The old traditions, the moral discipline, everything that made this country great, thrown aside, the only thing thought important whatever anyone happens to want. Sodomy, which was always a sin and everywhere a crime, now not just protected but given special status. Minorities, especially if they are here illegally, given rights and benefits, government subsidies, that everyone else has to pay for. Everything is falling apart, and the government not only does nothing about it, but does everything it can to help it along. That is the reason so many people got excited about Sarah Palin. She may have been an uneducated fool, a woman who never read a serious book in her life, and would not understand it if she had, but that only meant she was like nearly everyone else who spends half their lives in front of a television set or a computer screen. She captured the imagination of a lot of people, and the resentments of a hell of a lot more. And if she could do that, think what I can do. I know a lot of people in Washington don't like me, but my worst enemy never called me stupid. There is a movement in this country, Louis, and every movement has to have a leader."

"I'm afraid it's a movement I don't want to be a part of. But even if I did, I could not give you the help you want. I'm neutral in all this. I'm chairing the convention; I'm giving the keynote -"

"Yes, I know," interjected Rivers, unable to restrain himself. "You control the Michigan delegation. All I'm asking is that you let your delegates vote the way they want on the first ballot. A majority of them will vote for me; and that's enough to put me over the top. You're not a candidate, and even if you were...." He stopped himself, but it was too late. Matson understood.

"I was elected as a favorite son. I wouldn't have been able to win anywhere else. No, don't try to explain, don't try to convince me that you didn't mean it. Lie to yourself about your own chances; don't lie to me about something I never wanted anyway. And besides, Senator, I've never found you the least bit persuasive. Now, let's stop this nonsense. You don't like me, and I don't like you. You want my help – what price are you willing to pay for it? If I release my delegates, let them vote as they wish on the first ballot – what do I get in return?"

Rivers had never really believed that Louis Matson would agree to help him, but he was shrewd enough to understand that asking for his help was a way to make the majority leader feel respected. If it did nothing else, it might make his next request, whatever it might be, a little more difficult to refuse.

"I see you haven't thought of that," said Matson. "Perhaps you thought I would give you the help you need without anything in return."

"No, not at all. I just need you to tell me what I can offer."

"Let me be very clear about this. If I release my delegates, I will not release them to you – or to anyone else. They would be released to vote for anyone they choose to support. That is as far as I would go. I will not endorse anyone. I will not even suggest they consider anyone. I would simply stand aside. Do you understand this?"

"Yes, absolutely," replied Rivers, eagerly. "I understand you have to appear neutral. But what is it that you would then expect from me?"

Matson studied him closely, as if he were trying to decide how far to go. He wanted Rivers to think that this was nothing more than a deal, a trade, the kind of backroom bargain politicians make all the time. He wanted him to think that he was no different from anyone else to whom Rivers had made promises he did not keep.

"The deal is this: I release my delegates and if you don't win on the first ballot you withdraw and second the nomination of whomever I then decide to support."

"But that would mean that if I don't win on the first ballot, even if I have more votes than anyone else, I would have to pull out."

"Take it or leave it, Senator. I don't want a divided party, and that means I am not going to let this convention go much beyond a first ballot, if it goes even that far."

They had reached the corner where Matson lived.

"Think about it, if you want. But this is the only way the Michigan delegation gets released." Matson opened the door and started to get out. "One other thing. It would have to be in writing."

"In writing? My word isn't…?"

Matson smiled. "If it isn't written down I might forget I was supposed to release my delegates."

The rain had become a drizzle and Matson stood watching as the limousine pulled away. He took out his phone and called Ismael Cooper.

"If I released our delegates, who would they vote for? Rivers thinks a majority would vote for him. Make a few calls, find out what you can. I think he's wrong, but I want to be sure."

Matson went inside, loosened his black tie and unfastened the top button of his starched white shirt. He made himself a stiff drink and sat down in the comfortable cushioned chair he had owned for years, turned on the lamp and opened the sealed envelope Ismael had brought back from California.

He read the first paragraph, reached for the glass of scotch on the table next to him, but then, his eyes still on the page, he pulled back his hand. Halfway down the second page, he was on his feet, walking slowly back and forth, reading so intently that, quite without knowing it, he began moving his lips as if he were speaking out loud, giving the speech he was reading. He did not stop until he had finished the ten double-spaced typewritten pages, close to three thousand words. He stood still, staring straight ahead, the speech dangling from his hand, imagining the effect it could have, not just how an audience, the convention, might react, but what all those millions watching on television would think about a speech the likes of which no one had given in years. He went back to his chair and took a long drink. Then he took another.

First impressions were sometimes misleading. What seems at first astonishing can turn out on a sober second thought to have been nothing more than empty noise, the euphoria of great plans and promises made during all-night revelries turn to ashes in the cold light of dawn. Slowly, methodically, like a critic searching for a writer's fatal flaw, he read through it again. Stopping at the end of each sentence, pausing even longer at the end of every paragraph, he tried to consider what, if anything, should be changed; what, if anything, might be said a different way, what should not be said at all. When he was done, he put the pages back in the envelope and called Ismael Cooper a second time.

"You said you had a way to reach Julian? Tell him I need him at the convention, but I want him here first – now, tomorrow… whenever he can get here. Tell him it's important, and that I wouldn't ask if it wasn't."

CHAPTER SIX

Ismael Cooper was right. Julian Drake looked exactly as he had twelve years ago, only more so. It was almost uncanny. Everything Louis Matson had remembered about him seemed more vivid, every characteristic deeper and more pronounced.

"Julian!" he cried, as he jumped up from his chair and hurried across the long, rectangular room to greet him.

An inch or so shorter than Matson, and much slighter of build, Julian shook hands with surprising strength, and for just an instant Matson felt himself go cold. Julian Drake was a young man in vigorous good health, he was old man with little time left.

"The years...," he started to say, but stopped himself with a laugh. "I should have followed your example and taken early retirement. But, what am I thinking! Come and tell me everything that's happened."

Matson sat on the far end of the leather sofa under the two windows that looked onto the street; Julian sat in an easy chair just next to it. Stretching his legs across the corner of the coffee table, Matson clasped his hands behind his head, and remarked, "If someone walked in here now, you in that gray pinstripe suit, white shirt and perfect striped tie, me in my tattered shoes and wrinkled shirt, they'd think you were the senator and I was some tired old press secretary listening to what you wanted me to put in some speech you wanted to give. Christ, Julian, you looked more like a senator your first day in the House than most of those clowns with their off-the-rack suits who had been here thirty years."

Julian gazed at the carpets and the crystal chandelier, the ornate furnishings of the office that every majority leader for a hundred years had occupied. He got up and went over to the painting of the White House on fire in the War of 1812.

"We've been lucky," he said, in a voice that to Matson's ear had not changed at all, "lucky that it happened only once, foreign troops on our soil just that one time; lucky that, after that, the only battles fought here were those of our own Civil War."

Matson sat up. "Lucky? The Civil War?"

Julian Drake kept his eyes on the painting

"Not in all the lives lost, but in what happened. Without the Civil War we would have still had slavery; without the Civil War," he continued, turning to Matson, "we would not have had Lincoln. And without Lincoln, without that example, I'm not sure we would have had anything."

"Wouldn't have had anything…? I'm not sure I understand."

"That remarkable intelligence, the deep understanding - the nobility of his soul, to use an older expression – that made Lincoln the embodiment of the best of what freedom can mean. Lincoln gives everyone someone to look up to; he proves the possibility of greatness. He becomes the standard by which to judge everyone who claims the ability, much less the right, to lead." A smile drifted across the fine, straight line of Julian's mouth. "Without Lincoln, we might not know what fools we are."

Sinking back into the soft folds of the sofa, Matson bent his head to side as if to study him from a different perspective.

"And bigger fools every year. This place has become an echo chamber for all the insanity in the world." Matson reached for the speech he had left on the table. "Which brings me to this."

Julian shoved his hands into his pockets and grinned proudly.

"Is that what I've done? – Put all the insanity in the world into ten pages! I had not known I could be so concise."

"You know damn well it's a great speech. The question isn't what you have written; the question is what will happen if I give it, whether anyone will understand it. The question," he added with a raised eyebrow, "is whether I won't be thought crazier than all the rest of them."

Julian nodded slowly, and Matson had the impression that Julian had wondered the same thing himself.

"You could give this speech," said Matson, holding it up in the air. "At least you could have, twelve years ago, when you were still in Congress. No one else could do what you did; no one else would have even known how to try. It's a great speech, but I'm not a great speaker."

Matson set the speech down on the table and hunched forward, resting his elbows on his knees.

"A few years ago, I saw something on television. Winston Churchill's grandson had edited a volume of Churchill's most important speeches. He was doing a reading in New York. I thought about you – it was the reason I watched: what you used to tell me about Churchill, how he learned to speak, how he had to memorize everything, thousands of words, before he spoke in Parliament. His grandson read from several speeches. The words were all majestic, words that once you heard them you could never forget, Winston Churchill's words, but it was not Winston Churchill's voice." With a self-conscious laugh, he jabbed his finger at the speech that lay just beyond his reach. "I know I can't give this speech, but it's such a great speech - it says everything I want to say, everything that needs to be said - that I'll be damned if I won't do it anyway. 'What fools we are.' We are that, all right, and I may be the biggest one of all, but it doesn't matter anymore. At least I know I'm not Lincoln."

"No one is, but you're closer than any of the others. But, tell me," said Julian, coming back to the chair. "Ismael explained your dilemma. No one has a majority going into the convention. You must have seen that coming, and so you arranged things so that you would have the Michigan delegation and with that the balance of power. What is it you want to do? You wouldn't be doing what you are doing unless you wanted the nomination to go to someone other than one of the major candidates."

"That question would be easy, if you had spent the last twelve years in the Senate."

"After twelve years," replied Julian with a quick, self-deprecating laugh, "there wouldn't be anyone left I had not offended."

"Maybe," said Matson, with a long, pensive gaze; "but there also wouldn't be anyone who did not have more respect for you than for anyone else in this place. I told you – do you remember? – that if you ran for the Senate, it would not be the last office you would ever run for."

"I have no regrets."

"It's true, what Ismael told me – the girl is in medical school, the boy is at Harvard? Your sister would have been proud of what you've done – and grateful, too. You asked what I was trying to do. I haven't yet quite figured that out," he said, with a sly grin. "I knew I couldn't just do nothing: I couldn't just let the nomination go to someone who has no right to be president. It isn't a question of whether one of them could win. That is a lie. That is precisely the question, but not the way everyone else seems to think I mean it. If I didn't think there was a chance one of them might win, I wouldn't be so damn worried," he remarked, with a gruff laugh. "Madelaine Shaw could lose. She's old, and she's been around forever. And there is this other thing – I don't mean her husband, his character, the life he leads, that whole business. No, something else. I could not quite put my finger on it before, but when I read that speech of yours -"

"Your speech," insisted Julian, with a sparkle in his eye.

"The speech you wrote. She could never give it. It isn't – what is the word I'm looking for? Careful, or, better yet, cautious. You're dealing in fundamentals; she's never done anything but talk about the small details, changes at the edges of things. This speech – it's like FDR talking about the New Deal! Give a speech like this – she'd win in a landslide. But she won't; she can't. She won't say anything that might offend anyone who has not decided how they are going to vote. What she doesn't understand is that the country is looking for something totally different from all these feeble half-step policies and politicians they have been forced to deal with the last twenty, thirty years. And that means that unless I can do something, someone may get the nomination who might get elected precisely because, not knowing any better, he convinces everyone that what the country really needs is a government whose only claim to govern is the promise that it will never try to govern anything.

"Which isn't anything like what you would have me say in this speech of yours. Hell, I may get shot before I am halfway through it," he said with a huge grin, as he got to his feet. He walked over to his desk and from one of the drawers pulled out a bottle of scotch. "Join me?" he asked, as he started looking for a glass. "No? I forget, you don't drink at all, do you? Still? Probably would have been better if I never had either," he muttered, as he found the glass he was looking for and filled it halfway to the top. He came back, glass in hand, but instead of sitting down, pointed to the speech stacked neatly on the dark lacquered coffee table. "Best goddamn speech I ever read. Wish I could have written it – written something even half as good. What a goddamn waste," he remarked, shaking his head, a baffled expression rising in his tired eyes. "I don't mean what you did – I'd never question that; but that you had to, that you could not stay, that you couldn't do what – I swear to God – I never knew anyone more perfect for."

His gaze still on Julian, he took a long, slow drink.

"You really think I should do this? It will cause holy hell – which would be a good enough reason by itself." He stared at Julian through narrowed eyes, pondering the thought that had not left him since the first time he had read what Julian had written. "I know from what Ismael told me that you don't watch television, that the only news you get is the Sunday Times every month or so, but you had to have known that some of what is in that speech isn't anything I've ever been known to support."

" I did not think you sent Ismael all the way out to Big Sur to find me just to write something anyone in Washington could do as well or better. It's the keynote speech at the Republican Convention, a national audience. I did not know what you wanted to say about specific things; what policies, if any, you wanted to emphasize or support. All I could do was write the speech that, if I were in your position, I would want to give."

"I wish to hell you were giving it. The damn thing is diabolical!" exclaimed Matson, with a sharp, deep-throated laugh. "Diabolical. I'm reading the damn thing, hearing your voice, the way I remembered it from the speeches you used to give, and I suddenly realized – too late, in a sense you'll understand – that I'd been so swept up in what you're saying – in what that speech is saying – that I did not even notice that half of what it says about what the country needs to do are things I never would have voted for. Now how do you explain that? – And you really think I ought to give it?"

It was Julian's turn to laugh.

"No, unless you think that if we don't do something, something like what I tried to suggest, things will just keep getting worse. I knew that, whatever you might think about it, you would take it seriously; I knew you never believed that America is the exception to all the rules of history and experience, that what worked two hundred years ago will still work today because nothing has changed. Nothing has changed, but not the way everyone seems to think," he added, eager to make a distinction Matson was not sure he quite grasped. "But it's your speech. It's just a draft. You can do whatever you like with it."

"Damn it, Julian; I wanted to give a great speech, and you've written one. The question," he said with an almost fierce intensity, "is whether a great speech can be given by someone who is not great himself."

Julian gave him a very odd look, disturbing in its implications.

"When you read it, you said you were carried along by it. That only happens if, in a sense, you take the speech inside yourself and make it your own."

"But everyone who hears a great speech does that."

"Yes, precisely; so the only question is whether, when you give it, when instead of listening you speak the words yourself, the words come from deep inside."

"Some might say that is a conjurer's trick, an actor speaking a writer's lines."

"Yes, but there aren't many great actors," remarked Julian. His eyes danced with a paradox that had just occurred to him. Staring down at the floor, a slight smile on his mouth, he thought through the various possibilities. "I read somewhere that the speaker does not give the speech, the speech gives him. I think what that means is that, as he speaks, the words begin to define who he is. You can read history to the end of time, read all about what famous figures did, the battles they fought, the victories they won, but we don't really feel we know them until we read what they said. Whatever you say in this speech of yours, it is what people will think you are."

Julian looked at Matson as if to study his reaction, whether he was now convinced that he could give the speech Julian had written. Matson moved his head from side to side, like a fighter's bob and weave, or a politician's indecision. Another analogy leaped to Julian's mind, and though it might have been thought arrogance in someone else, Louis Matson would not think it of him.

"She's the best looking girl you've ever seen, but you're afraid she'll only laugh at you if you ask her out?"

Matson's shoulders heaved up and his chest began to rumble. He broke into a harsh, caustic laugh, a laugh that was directed less at Julian than at himself.

"That's close, all right; you're right about the fear, the fear of making myself look a fool. But, I have to tell you, it's not a fear that ever stopped me before. I wish it had. It was just the way you described it: the best looking girl I had ever seen. I was sure she'd never say yes, and maybe that was why I did it, thought it better to be a fool than a coward. So I asked her out, and to my astonishment she said yes, and then, before I knew it, I was married, and learned what real misery could be." His exuberance dwindled into a jaundiced grin. "I'm the majority leader. Making a fool of myself goes with the job. If I don't give that goddamn speech it won't be because I'm afraid of what anyone else might say or think; it will be because…because it's like what you just said: the best looking girl anyone has ever seen. Look at me: I'm a wreck. Would you want to take a picture of a beautiful woman with someone like me standing next to her? But, never mind, I may do it anyway; but maybe with a few changes. We can talk about that later. Besides helping me with the speech, there is something else you can do – if you don't mind, I mean. Someone is coming over."

He checked his watch, nodded to himself, tossed down what was left of the scotch in his glass, and went back to his desk.

"I had a conversation the other evening. Wish you had been there to hear it. I knew it was going to happen at some point." His tangled reddish-gray eyebrows shot up, a signal that something of more than ordinary interest was going on, and that what had happened earlier was in some way connected with what was about to happen now. He pressed a button on the console. "Is he here…? The hell you say. The son-of-a-bitch is late?" A wily look marched through Matson's eyes. He looked across at Julian as he finished. "Let me know when he gets here."

Matson sat down on the heavily creased leather chair behind his desk, but he could barely keep still. His eyes darted one way, than another; he looked up at the ceiling, he looked again at Julian. He looked as if he wanted to laugh.

"He asks to see me. He heard – everyone hears everything in this town – that I had a private meeting after the big dinner the other night, a private meeting where certain matters were discussed and, I'm sure he believes, decided. He wants me to know he knows; then he wants me to explain, to give him assurances, and then, once he has them, he wants me to do something that will give him the same kind of advantage he considers it unfair for the other guy to have. He asks to see me, but to make sure I don't think he's worried, or concerned, or angry, or ready to kill, he makes sure to come late; not too late – he doesn't want me to think he's rude or disrespectful – just a little late to show there is nothing urgent about it." Suddenly, Matson smiled. "I can't tell you how glad I am you're here. If you didn't think we were in trouble before, wait till you see this!"

Five minutes later, Matson's secretary called on the private line. A moment later, the door opened and Ronald Lochner walked into the majority leader's office, but Matson, instead of greeting him, was too wrapped up in conversation to notice that he had even entered the room. Lochner was used to attention; he was not used to waiting. He was not sure what to do. He cleared his throat and regretted immediately what he had done. Irritated as much with himself as with Matson, he turned and started to leave.

"Ronald! Come in, come in," said Matson at his jovial best, as he shot to his feet and came to greet him. "You'll have to forgive me," he said, as he put his arm around his shoulder and escorted him the few short steps to the sofa. "This is Julian Drake. He has been helping me on the speech I have to give at the convention."

Julian stood up and offered his hand. Lochner took it, but barely, and without exchanging a word. He sat down at the far end of the sofa and began to tell Matson why he was there, but then he remembered, as if he had not noticed before, that they were not alone.

"But perhaps we could discuss this….."

The smile on Matson's rugged face grew brighter, larger, really quite immense. This was even better than he had imagined.

"Julian doesn't work for me; he isn't on my – isn't on anyone's staff. Julian was once my colleague. He was in the House for a number of years," he said, deliberately exaggerating the length of time Julian had served. "He would have been elected to the Senate if…if he had decided to run."

Lochner looked at Julian as if he were seeing him, as in a sense he was, for the first time.

"I'm afraid I don't remember….But you were in Congress, and you're here to help the majority leader with the speech he is going to give?" He turned back to Matson for the answer.

"Louis asked if I would write the speech, a first draft, if you will. It's been a long time, but I -"

"Yes, that's very interesting," said Lochner, as he began to fidget with his small, thick-fingered hands. His eyes were still fixed on the majority leader. "I certainly don't want to interrupt, but I thought we really had to talk, and I wonder if we might…?"

"Say what you came to say. It's always good to have a witness, don't you think, in case there is any misunderstanding later about anything that was said."

Dressed in a blue suit, white shirt, and red tie, Lochner looked like a rumpled American flag. He sat with his legs spread apart and his elbows on his knees. His face was too bloated to allow any obvious changes of expression. He had a blank look on his face and a wintry, slightly suspicious look in his pale blue eyes. With his squirrel's nest of bleached blonde hair and his round, rather weak chin, he seemed a carnival barker, a small town hustler drawn from the pages of Sinclair Lewis. There was something missing, the capacity to doubt, the ability - the intelligence, if you will - to understand that money and fame might not be the measure of a life worth living.

"I understand you had a meeting the other night with Rivers, which I thought -"

"I didn't have a meeting, I was offered a ride home after the dinner. We had a brief conversation in the car."

"It comes to the same thing; you had -"

"It does not come to the same thing," insisted Matson, who took an obvious pleasure in the correction. "When you say we had a meeting, it suggests something arranged in advance, something done because both parties have something to discuss. You and I are having a meeting; Rivers and I had an accident – we met by chance."

Lochner blinked twice. He did not see the significance, and he did not like the waste of time. Julian, watching, tried not to smile. Lochner, who thought business the only important profession, cared even less than he knew about the subtleties of politics and power, something that was the lifeblood of a master of the craft like Louis Matson.

"He was just leaving," Matson continued, adding, quite on purpose, one meaningless detail after another, a method meant to be irritating. "He saw me walking on the sidewalk and he gave me a ride. He asked me if I would consider releasing my delegation at the convention and let them vote as they wished. I said I did not think that would be a problem."

Julian had moved his chair a little farther to the side, so that he could see Matson more clearly. A casual observer, he leaned against the side of the overstuffed chair and as he studied the expression on the majority leader's face noticed that no matter how much he had aged, he looked exactly the way he remembered when he was playing with other men's ambitions, building them up, breaking them down, evaluating their strengths, explaining their weaknesses, whatever he thought necessary in that shrewd and sometimes unscrupulous mind of his, to get what he wanted, or needed, to have. It was what kept him going, the game itself, because whatever the outcome, the game never ended. There was always something more to do.

"You didn't think it would be a problem?" asked Lochner, refusing to believe what he had heard. His face started to turn red. "If you do that….Do you realize what will happen?"

Matson shrugged with indifference. "Rivers thinks a majority of the delegation will go for him. I really wouldn't know."

"We both know – everyone knows – he's a lying hypocrite."

"Aren't all hypocrites liars?" asked Matson.

Lochner scratched the side of his face, trying, as it seemed, to stop himself screaming.

"Look, you have to make a choice. The convention is split almost evenly. No one has a majority, the Michigan delegation – your delegation – has the votes to give the nomination to whichever one of us you want."

"And what is the reason he would want one of you instead of the other?" asked Julian, as if the question were not only of interest, but one he had every right to ask. Lochner did nothing to hide his surprise, or his irritation. "Seriously," persisted Julian, "when you get right down to it, what really is the difference." He was looking straight at Lochner, but he could sense Matson's approval. "Rivers may be what you say he is: he may be someone you could never trust, but both of you seem to be saying the same thing. He may be more willing than you are to talk about shutting down the government, but neither one of you seems to be in favor of using the government to do anything important."

It was only with a show of reluctance that Lochner had looked at Julian. He immediately looked back at Matson.

"I came here to talk to you about the nomination. I didn't come here -"

"To tell anyone why you should have it?" remarked Julian, with a mocking laugh that made Lochner grind his teeth.

"Does he speak for you?" he demanded of Matson.

"I don't speak for anyone – not even for myself," added Julian, with a strange, inward smile. "I have no standing here; I hold no office. But you're playing for rather high stakes, and I thought I ought to ask you the question that my old friend here may be too polite to ask."

Matson could barely keep from laughing. He was not sure what Julian was up to, but he was perfectly content to sit back and watch what happened.

"It's one thing, Mr. Lochner, to go around telling everyone what the Democrats have done wrong; it's something else to explain the real source of the problems we face. Unless of course you really do believe that all we have to do is have government get out of the way and everything will take care of itself."

"Government is the problem, Mr…, it's not the solution."

"You have reversed the line, but the thought is still Ronald Reagan's. You believe the government should provide protection for life and property – defense and the police – and that with their safety guaranteed everyone should be free to do whatever they choose. Or have I misstated your position?"

Now the silent observer, Matson remembered what he had earlier tried to explain: that the voice, how the words sounded, made all the difference in the world. Julian's voice drew you toward him, make you feel that even if you disagreed with everything he said, you wanted to hear more. The anger, the impatience, the intense dislike that marched through Lochner's eyes had all but vanished.

"You haven't misstated my position. That would be a fair summary of what I think the principle involved. But you asked the difference between Rivers and myself. He insists – and he's either a fool or a liar when he does – that you can change everything overnight. I know better than that. You can't just dismantle Social Security or Medicare. You have to do it gradually, introduce free market reform, give people a choice to stay in a program the government provides or take the money – their money – money they have earned, and invest it in the kind of securities that will let them pay for what they need."

Julian nodded three times in quick succession, tapped his fingers on the arm of the chair and appeared to agree.

"The difference, then, is that Rivers can't do what he says he will, because it can only be done the way you say it can - with time?"

"Yes, exactly."

"Which means, does it not, that there is no real difference at all?"

"What -?"

"He can't do it – except the way you say you'll do it, so both of you would end up doing the same thing the same way."

CHAPTER SEVEN

There were a thousand different rumors, and a thousand different interpretations of what those rumors meant, as the delegates poured into Cleveland from all across the country. The most interesting rumor, and one that needed no interpretation at all, was that some of them, though pledged to one or the other of the candidates, might decide to vote for someone else instead. No one had a clear majority. There was nothing to stop a delegate from changing his mind, nothing to keep anyone from looking to their own advantage, the chance to own the gratitude of a candidate who could not win without them; nothing, that is to say, except their own sense of honor, and no one thought it safe to count on that. Julian Drake thought the whole thing fascinating, comical and completely insane.

"Two minutes after it's all over, two minutes after someone gets the nomination, everyone will insist they knew it all along, that it all makes sense." He nodded toward the crowded tables in the hotel coffee shop where he and Ismael Cooper had come to talk alone. "Every restaurant, every bar, every place you can find a place to sit and something to drink, the same conversation: What is going to happen, who is going to win? Ask any of them who they think it is going to be – they won't even guess, afraid they might be wrong. All they want to know is what everyone else has heard. But after it is over, after it has been decided...."

Ismael Cooper leaned forward on his elbows, holding a cup of black coffee in both hands. He blew gently on the dark, impenetrable surface though it was already getting cold. It gave him something to do as he tried to clear his mind. Julian's remark made him smile.

"And you? Who do you think will get it?"

It was a fair question, fair to ask if his own criticism did not also apply to him, but instead of being put on the defensive, Julian's eyes were suddenly full of mischief.

"I have no idea, and, worse yet, when someone finally has the nomination, I still won't believe it."

"You still won't...?"

Julian sank into the corner of the booth and, laughing quietly, casually crossed his arms.

"Believe what defies all reason. Because whoever it is, it isn't going to be anyone who should be president."

Ismael put his cup down on the table and with the tip of his finger began to trace random circles on the liquid surface.

"That's the whole reason Louis has gone to so much trouble with the Michigan delegation – to stop anyone winning on the first ballot, because, after that, anything is possible."

Julian shoved his own half-empty cup to the side. It was nearly nine-thirty on the night before the convention was scheduled to open, but dressed in a suit and tie he looked as if he were just starting the day instead of near the end of it. Ismael remembered that Louis had once told him that Julian would sometimes work straight through the night and not sleep at all until the night after that.

"Yes, well," he said, starting to pick up where he had left off. "There is more to it than that. You were there when he had that meeting with Lochner – You made quite an impression, by the way. Louis said Lochner turned red when you were finished – After you left, he told him the same thing he told Rivers, that he would allow the delegation to vote however each of them wished."

Ismael trembled with suppressed laughter as he shook his head at the eager willingness with which vain and ambitious men heard only what they wanted to hear. He looked at Julian, certain that Julian understood.

"The moment they heard that, they thought they had the nomination. In a way, you can't blame them. Spend two years doing everything you can think of to get it, be that close, just a handful of votes away, know that the difference is in the hands of one state's delegation, start believing that the only reason you might lose is because the majority leader – an old man who never liked you; an old-style politician who has spent so many years in Washington he doesn't know what is going on in the country, the new forces that are reshaping politics in the party – and then, suddenly, he agrees to give you the chance of convincing his delegation that you're the only one who can win in November! The nomination is all but yours!" Ismael's laughing eyes narrowed into the shrewd certainty of someone who knows the secret of the game. "What they don't understand is that, once released to vote as they wish, almost all the delegates are still going to vote for Louis, the favorite son. When the roll call is taken, they'll both think, not that they were stupid, but that they were betrayed."

Julian bent his head to the side, trying to understand something that did not seem to make sense.

"But whatever the Michigan delegation does, one of them is going to win."

"Not if Louis has anything to do with it."

Julian threw up in his hands, a friendly gesture that confessed his own confusion.

"He can stop the convention choosing anyone on the first ballot, but the convention has to choose someone, and it can't be someone who lost in the primaries, it can't be someone who tried to run and had to quit. Who is left? Who does Louis want? Does Louis even know?"

Ismael glanced around the crowded room, as if to make sure no one was close enough to hear.

"He won't say, but whether that means he knows and won't tell, or he doesn't at this point have any idea – whether he wants to come up with a name on his own or just let the convention decide, start with a clean slate as if the primaries had never happened – I don't know."

"He has to know," insisted Julian. "He has to have some idea. He can't leave it up to the convention, he can't simply throw it open; he can't make sure no one wins on the first ballot and then go to a second ballot, when everyone is free to vote as they wish, if he wants a third candidate to have a chance. Without another candidate that suddenly everyone is talking about, the margin is too narrow for it not to become a bidding war. Whichever one of them – Rivers orLochner – can get to a few dozen delegates that came in pledged to the other side.... Rivers, Lochner, they're different versions of the same thing: No one who changes sides is going to think themselves traitors to a cause."

Julian had become eager, intense, his eyes flashing with growing certainty as he followed out his argument. Suddenly realizing what he had done, he laughed in apology.

"You'd think I was still in Congress, arguing about what was going to happen in the next election."

"That is pretty much what we used to do, wasn't it?" remarked Ismael, with a look of nostalgia for his own remembered past. "We treat politics like sports: a game in which the only thing that matters is whether you win or lose. Then, the game is over, but there is always next season - the next election - and you have to get ready for that. It all runs together now, the permanent campaign; it never ends. It's worse than that. For some of them, maybe for most of them now, the campaign is the only thing they know, the only thing they like. They give all the reasons they should be elected, but the only reason they want the office is so they can run again. They don't want to govern – they don't know how. All they want is to have everyone know who they are, and think of them as somehow unbeatable."

"You're talking about the Clintons."

"They're the best example, but all of them – Who would have thought twenty, thirty years ago, that you could be nominated for the presidency without having done anything except get famous? Not famous for anything worthwhile, just famous because you figured out a way to be on television."

"But if it weren't for television we never would have had Sarah Palin," said Julian, with a droll expression. And then, immediately, he became serious. "Television has only speeded things up; Americans have always been in love with whatever is new, because whatever is new is supposed to be better. It is how we've all been trained, isn't it; what we all believe – this year's model is better than last year's; the new invention that will change everything, the new drug that will save more lives. A hundred years ago – no, farther back than that, after the Civil War – the country changed. Science, industry – everything became provisional; change became the rule, and the rate of change began to accelerate. Everything was now about the future; the past, instead of the standard, something to be preserved, was forgotten, dismissed as of no importance."

Ismael Cooper stared down at the coffee left in his cup. The lines in his forehead deepened. His mouth tightened at the corners. He looked up, a question in his eyes, a question he started to ask, and then, suddenly, was not sure he should. Julian asked it for him.

"Is this what I have been doing, these last twelve years – reading history, trying to understand how we got to where we are? Yes, but other things as well. It isn't that difficult to understand. The more I learned, the less I knew." There was an almost boyish enthusiasm, an embarrassed pride, in the way he tossed off this seeming paradox, this epigram of studied ambiguity. "And the less I knew, the more I had to learn."

Julian's eyes, full of laughter at his own inability to explain any more clearly what he had done, and why he had done it, held Ismael's gaze just long enough to let him know that even this was more than he would have told anyone else. But then, as Ismael immediately grasped, who else could he have told, having lived an almost perfect recluse all these years? Even when Julian was spending all his time in politics surrounded by other people he had been something of an enigma: always in the center of attention, and always, in the most serious sense, alone.

"So, who would you choose, if you were Louis, what third candidate?" asked Ismael. "After Louis gives that speech of yours – a speech he has not let me see – after no one wins on the first ballot, what happens then? I think you're wrong, by the way."

"Wrong? Probably, but about what?"

"That left to its own devices the convention would end up picking one of those two. It's because what you said is right: that they are both different versions of the same thing. It is the reason both of them would lose in the general election. Everyone knows what the polls are saying. There are two competing emotions in this convention: the desire to have the candidate you support win the nomination, and the desire to win the election. Once the first ballot is over, once it becomes doubtful that your candidate can win the nomination, you are free of the burden of worrying about anything except who has the best chance to win in November. It is strange, but true. I'm certain of it. They want to win; they know, or at least they are afraid, that their candidate can't, but they are committed, they're loyal. But now, suddenly, they don't have to think about anything except finding someone who can lead them to victory. Watch it happen; watch their faces, the tremendous sense of relief, the catharsis, the sudden knowledge, the hope, that everything is going to be so much better than they had feared. I can feel it; it's real. It isn't going to be Lochner or Rivers or anyone like them; it will be someone, a conservative, who in comparison will seem almost a moderate."

Julian signaled for the waitress and asked for another cup of coffee. She was young and pretty and even when she was pouring a new cup for Ismael kept her eyes on Julian. But Julian was too interested in what Ismael was saying to notice.

"A moderate conservative; that makes sense, the way you describe the situation. Someone who can win. You asked me who I would choose. I still don't know. There aren't that many moderate conservatives left, and -."

"The governor of Ohio. He's a conservative who knows how to work with the other side. He served a long time in Congress. He knows how to get things done. But – the look on your face – you don't like him, you don't think…?"

"I knew him when I was in Congress. He's all right. There's nothing wrong with him. He has ability, he's hard working, but we're talking about the presidency. There should be something more, at least a hint of greatness. But, you're right: he would be better, much better, than the others."

Ismael was too intrigued by what Julian had just said to let it go.

"Better, but without a 'hint of greatness'?"

A smile full of skepticism and doubt slipped across Julian's lips.

"How could there be? We've not only forgotten what it means, we've changed out of all recognition the meaning of the word. We're embarrassed by what greatness used to mean. Look at it this way: if Lincoln was great, what are we?" The look in Julian's eyes deepened and became profound. "But if you went so far as to compare any of the presidents, anyone who ran for president, in the last half century with Lincoln, what would be the response? That it isn't possible to make the comparison because we live in different times, and that – astonishing, if you think about it – we have made more progress, are more developed, more sophisticated, if you will, and because of that no one now would use the kind of language Lincoln did. Though it isn't entirely clear where the progress is in that."

Ismael finally had the answer he was looking for.

"That's what you did – with this speech of yours – write something only Lincoln could give. That explains why Louis is so worried he can't give it. He keeps telling me that it's a great speech, the best he's ever read, and how he wishes he was twenty years younger, just starting out, because if this was the first speech anyone had ever heard him give, everyone would sit up and take notice, would line up and follow wherever he wanted to take them. Now he's too old, too well-known, the speech is too much for him, too big a departure from what he has done before. But there is a look in his eyes that tells me something altogether different, that he thinks this speech is going to change everything. So, no, despite all his grumbling, all his late-night misgivings, he's going to give the speech. That's the reason he insisted you be here, to help with whatever last-minute changes that might have to be made. Though," he added confidentially, "that isn't the only reason. He seldom talks about it, and, as far as I know, only to me, but he's never forgotten what happened twelve years ago. You want to know something? I think he would have given up his own seat in the Senate if that had been the only way to get you there."

Julian's reaction was a kind of distant nod, the polite acknowledgment of a known fact, as if he had never doubted that Louis Matson would have made that kind of sacrifice for him. It was stunning, really, how easily he accepted it, as if there was nothing the least bit unusual about it. Was it because he had always felt such gratitude to Matson and knew, perhaps better than anyone, how generous he could be; or was it, Ismael began to wonder, that he thought Matson's high opinion deserved? Julian seemed to dismiss it.

"But think how much better it is that nothing like that ever happened.

Louis would not now be in a position to do what scarcely anyone has ever done before: decide, or at least help decide, who the next president is going to be. And unless I miss my guess, he's enjoying every minute of it, despite all his false complaints about the speech he has to give."

Ismael checked his watch, gulped down what was left of his coffee, and got to his feet.

"There is a meeting. Louis said to bring you with me, if you wouldn't mind. You should come. It will probably prove you right."

"Right? About what?"

"That Louis is enjoying every minute of this."

It was the last thing Julian wanted to do. He had to remind himself that he had an obligation, if only to himself, to learn what he could, even if it were only to learn what he had learned years ago and tried to forget. He was here, and he had to stay here, but only until the end of the week. And so, without any outward sign of resentment, with in fact a show of gratitude for the chance to witness something few others would ever see, he followed Ismael Cooper through the swarming hotel lobby to the elevators, up to the top floor and the penthouse suite where the chairman of the party was trying to maintain a modicum of civility among a dozen men and women who looked like they wanted nothing so much as to start a war.

They were sitting around a long, rectangular table in front of a glass wall with a view of the city and, in the distance, the river that years earlier had been so polluted it had actually once caught on fire. Everyone was shouting at once, all of them looking toward the end of the table where the majority leader, undaunted by their complaints, sat alone. At the far end opposite, the chairman, trying to run the meeting, was virtually ignored.

"Come in, come in, Ismael," shouted Matson over the noise. "You brought Julian – even better!" he added in a loud, boisterous voice that silenced the room. Everyone turned to see who had just come in. "Most of you know my chief of staff, Ismael Cooper. Some of you may remember, as all of you should, Julian Drake, once a brilliant member of Congress and now a private citizen who has been kind enough to help me with that speech I am going to give."

If anyone remembered Julian they did not show it. All eyes were back on Matson.

"The goddamn speech we've been talking about!" cried a heavyset middle aged man with sloping shoulders and a double chin. His eyes, buried under thick folded lids, moved back and forth like a teller counting money. "The goddamn speech no one has even seen. We didn't come to Cleveland to be taken by surprise. Goddamn it, Louis, we have a right to know what you're going to say!"

"A right to know?" exclaimed Conrad Wilson, gray haired and distinguished, with a voice that promised perdition to anyone who even thought to disagree. "We have a right to a lot more than that; we have a right to decide what is going to be said." He looked at Matson to make sure he understood. "Do you have any idea, senator, how much money we contribute to this party of yours? Tens of millions for conservative causes and candidates."

"I probably know it to the penny," replied Matson, unimpressed. Sitting sideways to the table, his left arm resting on it, he looked like a gambler who holds all the cards. "You've told me often enough; every time you've come to see me, if I recall. Your money can buy you a lot of things, Conrad but it doesn't buy you anything when it comes to this speech." Wilson started to interrupt. Matson stopped him with a look. "No, don't bother. I don't want to hear it. All you need to know is that it's the best speech I've ever seen." He bent closer, as if to draw Wilson, and everyone else in the room, into his confidence. "Now, do you really think you're a better judge of that than I am? Do you really think you can write a better speech, give a better speech, than I can? If you do, go run for office somewhere. But if you do, be glad you have all that money of yours, because I can't think of anyone else who might want to contribute to your campaign!"

Wilson was halfway out of his chair.

"I don't have to listen to this, I don't have to -!"

"Yes, you do, if you want to be part of what happens here this week. You'll listen to everything I have to say. Now, sit down. I asked for this meeting; you didn't. There was a reason. You're right, Conrad – you, and most of the others here as well, have contributed most of the money that has funded conservative candidates and causes for the last twenty years, and most of the time you have failed. The two candidates you backed this year have managed to divide between them most of the delegates. Neither one of them got a majority and if either one of them gets the nomination it is almost certain we're going to lose the election No, don't bother – you can criticize me later," shouted Matson when the representatives of the two campaigns who had been invited to attend began to protest. "I may be wrong. Maybe the polls are all wrong; maybe the country is tending more to the right than I think it is. None of that matters. What I want is an agreement. It's very simple. Whoever wins the nomination, whether they win it on the first ballot or only later, whether the candidate is Ronald Lochner or Ed Rivers, whether it is some third candidate – whoever it is – everyone agrees that he, or she, will have everyone's full support. And to make this as clear as I can, if anyone – and by this I mean in particular anyone associated with either of the campaigns represented here – does not agree, does not take a blood oath to do this, I will do everything in my power to convince everyone, including my own delegation, to vote for someone else!"

"Does that mean that you agree to stay neutral, that you won't support, directly or indirectly, either Lochner or Rivers?" asked someone.

"Or anyone else?" added a voice from the other side of the table.

"The only vote I control, the only vote I will try to control, is my own."

There was nothing in Matson's expression to suggest the slightest reservation, nothing to suggest he was not completely sincere. He meant what he said. They all thought so. Except Julian, who understood the difference between the literal meaning of words and the usual way in which words are used. Whatever else he was promising, Matson was not saying that he would not try to convince others, whose votes he did not control, how to cast them. Julian watched with growing fascination as Matson, who was not finished, asked for more.

"If this goes to a second ballot – and it could go much longer than that – it becomes all that much more important to show that beneath our apparent division there is a solid, united foundation. Everyone has an obligation – and I know this is what the chairman wants," he said, casting a glance down the table; "it is what he told me when he asked me to chair the convention – to repeat as often as possible that whoever wins the nomination not only has our full support, not only is far more qualified to be president than the other party's nominee, but is the best person we could possibly have chosen."

The chairman, who could not remember having ever said this, nodded at the wisdom of his own unimpeachable advice.

"I should also tell you," continued Matson, "in case any of you are at all reluctant, that I have spoken privately to both Lochner and Senator Rivers, and both have agreed to throw their full support to whomever the nominee may be." Pausing, he smiled and then added, "Of course they both assume that this is an obligation that only others will have to meet. But they are honorable men, and honorable men keep their promises."

"Even promises they can't remember they made," whispered Ismael to Julian who was sitting next to him.

Julian stared into the middle distance, a slight smile on his mouth. He had forgotten how good Matson was at this, the way he could make everything he wanted sound like the most reasonable thing in the world. The wonder was that, even after all these years, no one seemed to realize that what Louis Matson claimed to want was seldom what he was really after. What was he asking now but a simple pledge of unity, an agreement that everyone would support the eventual nominee. He could have done that without letting everyone know that if either of the two leading candidates, or anyone like them, were to win the nomination the result would be almost certain defeat in November. He was setting them up for a shift away from what most of them had spent their lives trying to get: a right wing candidate and a presidency that would mark the triumph of economics – what they liked to call free-market economics – over politics, a presidency that would govern by refusing to govern very much at all.

Glancing around the table, Julian was struck by the single-minded determination he saw on the faces of what were some of the wealthiest people in the country. He did not doubt that this had been one of the reasons for their success, this ability to concentrate on what they wanted; he was even more certain that it was the reason why, when it came to politics, serious politics, they were nothing more than spoiled children. Money may or may not be the source of all evil;, but it is certainly, as Julian reminded himself, the source of a great deal of stupidity.

The meeting was not quite over.

"If it goes past the first ballot, if some other candidate ends up with the nomination, what guarantees do we have that he will be someone we can trust?"

Matson looked down the table to Rufus Chambers, sitting just to the right of the chairman. He had raised more money than anyone for the Tea Party and done nothing to disguise his desire to replace the majority leader with someone more sympathetic.

"Trust is a two-way street," said Matson, with a thin, lethal smile. "How much you can trust someone may depend on how much they think they can trust you. No one is going to be nominated without a majority of the delegates, and those delegates are almost evenly divided between two of the most conservative candidates we have had in years. Do you really think the convention is going to nominate a liberal?"

Matson said this with a grin, but that grin meant more than what Rufus Chambers and the others thought it did. It meant, as Julian understood, Matson's satisfaction with the way he had managed once again to use the language with effect. The seeming opposition, the difference, between liberal and conservative, disguised the real alternative between a right-wing fanatic of the kind they thought should run the country and the traditional, time-tested conservatism that thinks nothing more important than the preservation of the best of what has been accomplished by the generations that have come before.

The meeting broke up. Louis Matson had what he wanted, an agreement that, as Julian noted, meant something different from what everyone thought it did. But why Matson wanted it, and what he meant to do with it, were questions Julian was not certain even Louis Matson could yet answer. If he had a candidate, someone he wanted to win the nomination, someone whose only chance was a convention that on its own could not decide, he was not telling anyone.

CHAPTER EIGHT

It was the governor of Ohio. Immediately after Louis Matson met with the group of major financial contributors, the meeting that both Ismael Cooper and Julian Drake had attended, he met privately with the governor. By the next morning everyone had heard the rumor that there might be a third candidate, the proverbial dark horse who, without a single pledged delegate, might win the nomination. The governor denied the rumor, which convinced everyone that the rumor must be true.

"I thought that might work," said Matson to Ismael Cooper. They were sitting alone in the majority leader's suite.

"It's all anyone is talking about this morning," remarked Ismael, as he buttered a piece of toast, all he wanted from the room service breakfast Matson had ordered. "The governor's people put out a statement. It denies everything and nothing at the same time. The guy would kill his mother for the chance."

He bit into the toast and meticulously brushed the crumbs from the cloth napkin in his lap. He glanced across the table. Matson's face was ash white, the skin mottled and sagging around his jaw. His eyes were clouded, his speech slow and halting.

"Are you going to be all right?" he asked, careful to make the question sound routine, as if he were asking nothing more important than whether he had gotten enough sleep.

There was a flash of anger, and then, just as suddenly, a look of gratitude, a silent acknowledgement that of all the people he knew, Ismael was, if not the only one, one of the very few who really cared what happened to him.

"I'll be fine; I'm just not as young as I used to be," he said in a distant, barely audible voice. "When I first started coming to these things, I wouldn't sleep at all; there were too many things to do, too many people to meet, too many people you wanted to stay in touch with. Surprising, when you think about it," he added with a weary smile, "but after two or three conventions you get to know people, and they get to know you. You send them cards at Christmas; they become part of the list you keep: names, but names with faces, names with lives, families, ambitions, of their own. Sometimes you can do something that helps them in some way, do a favor, put in a good word. That is what most people miss when they wonder why someone like me stays with it as long as I have: you can be useful, help others, and, best of all, once in a while help someone who might be able to do something good for the country."

"But not for the governor of Ohio?" asked Ismael, who found a few more crumbs to brush away.

Matson was still wearing his pajamas and a white terry cloth robe with the hotel's insignia on the chest high pocket. It was a few minutes after ten. He had gone to bed sometime around two in the morning, but his mind was too full of what he had done, and what still had to be done, to sleep, and he had only finally dozed off just before dawn. If it had not been for Ismael's knock on the door he might have slept all morning. The question about the governor quickened his senses. The color began to come back to his face; his eyes became clear. He remembered the meeting with the governor, and, because what we remember about conversations has all the benefit of careful and detailed analysis, because the memory invests words with their true proportion and significance, he recalled what had happened with an eagerness that he had not felt at the time.

"Only if you assume that he isn't smart enough to know that not every effect has a cause."

Matson said this with a look with which Ismael had become familiar. When someone wants something as much as the governor wanted the presidency, anything other than an emphatic and openly offensive refusal was taken as an implied promise of support.

"He did not ask to meet with me. He could have - and in some ways it would have been not just normal, but even expected. He's the governor of the state hosting the convention; I'm chairing the convention. But he didn't ask; he was waiting."

"Waiting?"

"To see what happens, to see how things fall out, with a convention this divided, with enough people suggesting that this might be the first convention in the modern era that doesn't end on the first ballot. That would open the way for a third candidate. That's why he didn't call me, and that's why he thinks the fact I called him so significant."

"What did you tell him about why you wanted to see him?"

"I just said I thought it would be good to have a talk before the convention opened, because after that we might not have the chance. So he came here…at midnight, and we spent about an hour together."

"And you decided…?"

"Nothing; nothing was decided. He asked a lot of questions: Did I really think it might actually go beyond the first ballot? Didn't I think there was a chance a deal might get made? What was the Michigan delegation going to do? All good questions," said Matson, scratching his ear; "and no good answers - or, rather, answers that did not answer anything. Yes, I thought it could go to a second ballot, or even beyond. Yes, there could be a deal, but I couldn't imagine what it might be. No, I didn't know what our delegation would do: they were free, each of the delegates, to vote for whomever they wished." Matson leaned back in his chair, trying to suppress a grin. "I told him they could even vote for him, the governor of Ohio, on the first ballot, if they decided they wanted to do that."

He could still see it, that moment of hope and indecision in the governor's eyes, the instant hesitation about what to say, how to reply; the quick, fumbling calculation, as he wondered whether, more than a meaningless remark, this was a test to discover the degree of interest, an invitation to ask for the opportunity to address the delegation so he could by the power of his personality and the force of his rhetoric convince them to withhold their support from anyone until, with a second ballot, everyone would be free to look for a third, a new, alternative – him.

"I mentioned to Julian that the governor might end up being everyone's second choice; that once it goes to a second ballot everyone will start looking for someone who can win," remarked Ismael, nodding in agreement with what, though Matson had not said it out loud, they both understood.

"And Julian was not all that enthused, was he? Let me guess: too ordinary, too much like everyone else; a competent governor, but that's all." Matson shoved himself back from the table, folded his arms across his chest and looked at Ismael from beneath a lowered brow, his gaze thoughtful, serious, and nostalgic. "We all grow up with heroes and dream of one day becoming what, when we were young, we thought they were. I don't think Julian ever did. I think he knew from the beginning that there was not much difference between those who made it to high office and those who were never elected to anything. I think he knew that most of what happens happens by chance. Most – not all; because he knew he was different, better, than everyone else. Yes, I know," he said, waving his hand to ward off the obvious objection. "Half of Washington thinks they're better than anyone else; but that's because they see all too clearly the weaknesses, the failures, of others and forget their own deficiencies. Julian never compared himself with anyone. If he had been a Roman – don't forget," he added with a quick self-deprecating smile, "I was a history major – he would have been a Stoic, convinced that all the things we prize – money, power, fame – are nothing so much as the mark of our own vanity and stupidity, the failure to understand that the only life worth living is the one dedicated to learning all we can and making the lives of others a little better than they are. So, no, that Julian would find the choice of the governor shall we say, uninspiring, does not surprise me. That is what Julian would think about almost anyone the convention might choose. It's one of the things that makes him so damn interesting." With a rueful laugh, Louis Matson shook his head. "You want to know the truth? – I think the same way he does. There isn't anyone I look up to. The strange thing is that if I could start all over again, if I could be like anyone, it would be someone just like him."

Matson glanced over to the desk and the speech he was scheduled to give that evening.

"The first time I read it, that was the thought I had: that I wished I could have done something half as good as that," he said with a look of the utmost seriousness. "And he did it in – what – a couple of hours the night you were there, out in California?"

Suddenly, Matson remembered what time it was and what he had to do. He got to his feet and started to the other room to dress. He stopped at the door.

"I didn't tell you. When the governor was trying to figure out whether he ought to ask for the chance to say something to the delegation – I invited him. He'll be there at one o'clock. I told him that because he was the governor of the host state, and because he's almost as well known across the border in Michigan as he is in Ohio, the delegation would love to have him say a few words of welcome. And then I told him that it might be useful if he stayed while we listened to Lochner and Rivers each make their case, why they ought to have the nomination."

"And did you remember to tell him that the meeting of the delegation is going to be open to the press, that the debate will be on television, that anyone who speaks will have a national audience?" asked Ismael, drily.

"I may have said something about that. In any event, he'll be there, and he has never been shy about injecting himself into an argument. It may get interesting. Make sure Julian is there. As soon as it is over, I need to go over the speech. He promised he would help."

Ismael looked across to where the typewritten speech lay stacked in ten pages on a fake French desk in the style of Louis XIV that sat below a copy of a painting done by a French Impressionist more than two hundred years later.

"It's better if you haven't read it; that way you won't have any preconceptions when you hear it tonight like everyone else."

Ismael had the feeling that Matson had not spent any time with it himself. It was still there, in the same position that it had been the day before. And if Matson had not been studying it, learning the way each line should be phrased, where to pause, where to take a breath, neither had he made any arrangements to have it put on a teleprompter so he could read what he was supposed to say without the constant need to look down at a written text. When he had asked if Matson wanted him to do it, he had put him off with the vague suggestion that there was nothing to worry about, that everything would take care of itself.

"Later, after this is over," said Matson, when Ismael asked again, just before the door shut and the Michigan delegation was called into session.

They met in a hotel ballroom with pink painted walls and two crystal chandeliers. The delegates sat on cushioned metal chairs. When the state party chairman introduced, "Our senator, Louis Matson," two hundred men and women rose as one and in what was more a gesture of respect rather than any new sense of excitement greeted him with a long round of sustained and dignified applause. Matson, genuinely moved, raised both hands in acknowledgement, which instead of bringing to a stop only increased the intensity with which they signaled how they felt. They did not know he was dying – that was still his secret – but they knew that he might not run again and that, such is the term of our existence, it would probably be the last time that, gathered all together, they could tell him what he had meant and how much, whenever that time might come, they were going to miss him.

With the cheerful cynicism of the seasoned politician, a part he had learned to play and, like everything played well, had come to love, Matson changed the mood to laughter by the announcement that he had not realized just how grateful they would be, released from their commitment, not to have to waste their vote on him.

When the room went quiet, Matson got right to business; or started to, because, as everyone soon discovered, he had a surprise for them.

"We are delighted to have with us today the two leading candidates for the nomination. They are each going to speak about why we should give them our support, why they would be the best candidate we could choose, why – and this is the ultimate question – they would be the best president the country could have."

The two candidates were sitting in the first row on opposite sides of the room. They tried to appear calm and dignified, happy to be there and eager to make their case. They each exchanged a friendly nod with Matson when he mentioned their names.

"Before we start, however, our friend, the governor of Ohio, has a few remarks -" A sly grin stole across Matson's jagged mouth. "Now that you are free to vote for whomever you want, perhaps the governor wants to share with you who he has decided to support. But before we get to that, before we start the discussion on as serious a matter as we will ever have to decide, there is someone else that I know you will want to hear from, someone that many of you know and all of you will remember, someone who once honored us with his service – Julian Drake."

Julian had come in just a moment after the majority leader. Most of those in the room had their eyes on Matson, but some had noticed the younger, well-dressed man a few steps behind him. They thought he looked familiar, but could not quite place him. The mention of his name, however, ran like a current through the crowd; they had, almost all of them, been active members of the party for years and they remembered, even after a dozen years, Julian Drake and what he had once seemed to promise. The applause was scattered, doubtful; no one knew quite what to make of the fact that Julian Drake was back. A moment after he began to speak it was as if he had never left.

He spoke to them as if they were the most intelligent people he knew. There was none of the "how great you are, how glad I am," the routine remarks with which too many speakers advertise in advance that they have nothing important to say. He said nothing at all about himself. He had always known what an audience needed to hear; not what they wanted to hear, not what would make them feel satisfied with what they had done, but what would help them see what had yet to be achieved.

"You are here to decide who the next president of the United States will be. After almost two years of endless campaigning, after dozens of primaries and dozens of debates, no one has won a majority, and for the first time in more than half a century, the convention, and the convention alone, will decide who will be the nominee. The Michigan delegation – your delegation – can now decide if the nomination should go to Senator Rivers or Mr. Lochner who, between them, have divided up most of the vote; or whether you should withhold your support and in that way open up these proceedings to someone else, a third, or even a fourth, candidate. It is not for me, an outsider, someone who does not even have a vote, to advise you what to do, but no one who calls himself a conservative will fail to recognize that the first rule in making any decision is to take whatever time is necessary to get it right. Listen to what those who speak to you today have to say; listen, and then ask yourself whether this is someone you trust, not just to win an election, but to lead the country. And remember, finally, that the real task of a conservative is not to tear down what has been built up over the years, but to rescue from the oblivion of time what is worth keeping from the past."

Louis Matson stood off to the side watching the reaction. No one cheered, no one applauded; they did something he could not remember having seen outside a formal ceremony in a church: they stood up, every one of them, and waited until Julian Drake walked to the back of the room and took a chair. Resuming their places, no one spoke, no one said a word; the only sound an abbreviated cough or the scraping movement of a chair. Matson stepped back to the front.

"And that is just one of the reasons why those of us who knew him when he was a member of Congress wish he had never left," he said, as he looked to the far end of the ballroom where Julian sat quietly. "But now, let's begin our work. We will hear first from the governor."

Rachel Good could only shake her head in wonder. She had started scribbling her first impressions in her reporter's notebook almost before Julian had finished speaking. Quite without knowing what she was doing she had risen to her feet with the rest, stood there in the silence of that mute applause, witness to something extraordinary. But when she tried to find the words to describe it, she failed to discover a comparison, something by which to show the reader what the reader had not seen. A minute later, when the governor began to speak, and when, after him, the two candidates each tried to plead their case, she realized just how far Julian Drake's brief performance was beyond the common measure: no one – not the governor, not the candidates - even tried to rival what they had heard; they changed nothing in the way they spoke. The governor lavished praise on his own achievements, all the things he had done to make Ohio a model for the nation, which, by implication, could best be done by someone who had done it once already. The two candidates repeated the same arguments, the same time worn phrases, about the urgent need for "bold, new leadership" they had used so often before that now, with the race almost over, they exaggerated all their gestures, intensified their mannerisms, from the perhaps unconscious fear that they might otherwise appear bored with what they were saying. The truth of course was that their own voices were the only ones they heard, those self-same speeches the catechism of what had for them become the received wisdom of the only belief that mattered: what they wanted, what they had by now convinced themselves anyone with any decency and intelligence would want as well. They were like soldiers who had marched so long in the same direction the only thing they had to follow were their shoes.

If Julian Drake had not spoken, Rachel Good might have missed it. The contrast between what he had done and what the others did taught her a difference that, if she had known it before, she had known only vaguely. It was one thing to understand that nearly everyone in politics said the same kind of things and had, almost all of them, the same kind of ambition; it was something else again to see how predictable, how fundamentally uninteresting, they really were, the phony enthusiasm, the empty rhetoric, the thoughtless conviction with which they tried to convince everyone that they could better than anyone else lead them where they wanted to go.

"I remember you from your years in the House," said Rachel Good.

Julian looked up; a modest, almost bashful, smile slipped slowly across his lips.

"I don't remember doing anything memorable."

"Who in the House ever did?" she replied.

Her cynicism could not quite conceal the deeper meaning of the glance with which she studied, or tried to study, the look in his eyes, a look that seemed to mark something that was far more confident than that modest smile suggested. She waited for an answer, some comment that almost anyone who had been in Washington would make, an agreement that on their best days members of the House were insignificant, incapable of doing anything, much less something worth remembering. But Julian said nothing. The silence was not awkward; it was just different. She started over.

"Louis told me you were helping with his speech. Were you surprised - when he asked you to do that?"

The meeting had broken up; the governor and the two candidates were trying to shake as many hands, pose for as many photographs as they could. Everyone was milling around, waiting to exchange a few words with someone they thought important or wanted to meet. There were hundreds of people in the room, but only a few of them came over to say a word to Julian Drake, and most of them older delegates who had known him when he was a rising star. Much later, when Rachel Good looked back on things, she would remember this and decide it had been one of the first clear examples - that and the way his brief remarks had been received - of the hold he had on people; the respect, bordering on reverence, for the way he spoke to them, as if they were every bit as serious and intelligent as he.

"Surprised?" He motioned for her to take the vacant chair next to him. "If you had asked me if Louis Matson - or anyone else - would ask me to write the first draft of a speech, I probably would have laughed. But surprised? No, I can't say that."

Rachel was confused. "But if you didn't expect it; if, as you say, you would have laughed if anyone had suggested…? Well, never mind. That isn't what I really wanted to ask you. What I really want to know is - Who do you support? Who does Julian Drake think should be the Republican nominee?" she asked, narrowing her eyes as she leaned forward, as curious as she had ever been. "I remember what people were saying about you, twelve years ago, when you were in that Senate race."

"That it was only the next step; that after a few years in the Senate I'd be running for president," he replied, shaking his head at what now seemed the absurdity of it. "Does it surprise you - that I remember, or that I'm willing to tell you that I had that thought myself? That isn't the same thing as saying that it would have happened; there are all sorts of reasons why it might not. But I must have had some ambition, running for the House, then the Senate; so it would not have been out of character to think about what might happen next. All I can tell you for certain is that I'm glad that it didn't."

"Glad that it…? You mean you're glad that you're here only to help Louis Matson with his speech, and not as a candidate for the nomination?"

A smile started onto his mouth, at first distant and remote, and then, suddenly, close and almost intimate.

"Can you keep a secret? I'd rather not be here at all."

Rachel thought she understood. "But you thought you owed Louis a favor. I've known Louis a very long time," she explained when Julian gave her a puzzled look. "He has told me a few things…about what happened, twelve years ago."

With a look of sympathy and disapproval, Julian let her know that what had passed between him and Louis Matson was, and would always be, a private matter, and that he had no wish to hear whatever Louis may have told her.

"But you were asking me whom I favored for the nomination." Pausing, as if the question were more complicated than it seemed, he folded his arms over his chest, crossed his legs and began to study the movement of his foot as he swung it back and forth to some short rhythm in his mind. After a few moments, he gave it up and looked at Rachel Good with a teasing grin, the only answer he was willing to give. She understood immediately what he meant.

"It isn't that you don't want to say, that there is someone you support but want to keep it private," she said, just to be sure. "The truth is that you don't think either of them - or anyone else who has been mentioned, all those dozens of would-be third candidates - ought to be the nominee."

Julian fixed her with a sidelong glance. A faint smile played on his mouth, again the only answer he would give. He seemed to be enjoying this. Perhaps, she thought, because he had not talked to a reporter for so long that it had at least the interest, if not the charm, of nostalgia.

"I don't remember you being so reticent," she said, smiling back. "As I recall, you were one of the few people in politics who never refused to answer a question, however stupid or beside the point it might have been."

The smile on his mouth grew broader, the look in his eyes more eager, and more alive.

"And never, as I remember, quite honestly," he replied, daring her, as it seemed, to challenge what he said.

"More honestly than most. The problem with most of them," she added, confidentially, "is that they don't even know when they're lying. They only repeat what they have been told everyone wants to hear and never bother to ask themselves if what they're saying makes sense. How else would you describe what you just heard in there, what the governor - who thinks he has an inside track to the nomination - and what those two - Rivers and Lochner, who think the nomination is already theirs - said to the delegation? They have been saying the same thing, over and over again, for years, like wind up dolls you just set in motion." She stopped, suddenly, and gave Julian a searching glance. "You wouldn't vote for any of them, would you? Then what kind of speech have you written that makes Louis so excited? It can't be anything anyone who has a chance at the nomination wants to hear. What in the world is Louis going to do? What is it that after twelve years away from all this - twelve years in exile, if I can put it like that - you thought you could write that would be so much different from what all these people now seem to believe? Is that the reason no one has been given a copy of it, why no one has been allowed to see it - because of the reaction, because if anyone knew what Louis is going to do, what he is going to say this evening, they would not let him do it?" she asked, becoming more intrigued, more excited, with every word.

Excited is not too strong a word. Rachel Good had covered Washington and national politics almost as long as Louis Matson had held office. She had become not just disenchanted, but seriously depressed, by the changes she had witnessed: the almost violent hatreds with which political opponents viewed each other, the shameless disregard for what others thought important, the absence of intelligence, the almost total lack of learning, the growing admiration for those who showed their disdain for any serious studies or any serious works of art or history. We had become barbarians and thought ourselves the most civilized people who had ever lived. And now Julian Drake, whom she remembered as one of the few with the sensibilities of an earlier age, a time when members of Congress had respect for, and even friendship with , members on the other side, had written a speech that Louis Matson could not wait to give. She had to know what was in it.

Julian would not tell her.

"I can't; it isn't my speech, remember. I'm just a poor scribbler, an unpaid one time assistant, a senate staffer who, like every staffer should, understands that my main purpose in life is to remain anonymous," he said, as he stood up. Ismael Cooper had just signaled that Louis Matson was waiting for him. "I have to go. If I don't see you again - I'm leaving, going home, as soon as the speech is over. It was good to see you after all this time. If you ever come out to California, come by. I'll show you what the tourists never see in Big Sur. It's worth doing," he added with an insistence she found almost moving. "It puts things in perspective, lets you see the difference between what is worth knowing and all this…, this noise," he said with a quick, dismissive glance at the ballroom still crowded with eager, ambitious men and women whom, it is safe to say, would not at the moment have been much interested in nature's solitude or things that never change.

Rachel Good watched him go, watched the way he walked, the apparent indifference to what was going on around him, the easy way he talked with Ismael Cooper, like two old friends that no matter how much time has passed could always pick up a conversation as if, instead of years, it had only been a few hours since they had last talked. She did not know why, she could not have given a reason, but she was almost certain that something was going to happen, something no one had anticipated, something no one could have foreseen, something that, once it happened, would change everything. She could not wait to hear what Louis Matson was going to say.

CHAPTER NINE

Everyone knew something was about to happen; no one knew what it was. After all the primaries, after all the debates, all the money raised, all the money spent, it had come down to the question what Louis Matson was going to do. Thousands of people had gathered together in the massive arena, the office holders who were concerned less for who might win the nomination than how it might affect their own careers, the true believers drawn to politics and a candidate because of what they thought a principle worth the sacrifice of time and money, the reporters ready to make a story out of any unsubstantiated rumor that came their way, all of them waiting, breathless, for the convention to open.

Julian Drake sat on a folding chair at the very back of the platform. Louis Matson sat next to him, going through the speech Julian had written, pronouncing each word in a slow, whispered voice, trying to get the cadence, the rhythm, just right. He held it in both hands, his head bent over it, stopping to look up whenever he wanted to make sure he was doing it the way Julian thought he should. Too late to make any changes, it was a last rehearsal. Julian nodded his encouragement and told him he would do fine.

Watching the crowd, the delegates sitting in their respective delegations, each delegation separate and apart from the others like the units in a military parade, all the cameras, all the noise, Julian had a strange sense of something missed, the chance he might once have had to be here on his own, a candidate himself. He could have done it, run for the presidency, if only out of a kind of curiosity to see what would happen. That was what he could ever explain to anyone: that it was curiosity, more than ambition, the desire to know what would happen if he let himself be involved. People who run for office may believe in nothing else, but they believe in themselves. Julian Drake believed in fate. He thought himself an actor playing a part in a play in which he, and all the other actors, were given the pages only one at a time, a play in which neither the actors nor the audience knew how it would end.

An anonymous voice on the public address system announced the opening of the convention. The Senate Majority Leader was introduced. Louis Matson looked at Julian for a brief moment, a look that conveyed a kind of fatality, the knowledge that there was now no turning back, that what he was about to do, whatever the consequences, would be the last thing of importance he would ever do. He rose from his chair, lifted his arm in acknowledgement of the applause, respectful, expectant, and uncertain, and with the speech in his left hand, started toward the podium. He placed the ten page speech on the lectern, reached inside his jacket pocket for his glasses and smiled as he put them on.

"Even without glasses," he laughed, "I daresay I'm more clear sighted than some of my Democratic friends who think that…."

The laughter died on his lips, the words seemed to echo lifeless in the air. Gripping the lectern, he stared straight ahead, and then, suddenly, his legs gave way and he started to fall

"Julian!" he gasped.

Julian was there in an instant, holding him up, helping him to the nearest chair. Everyone was on their feet, waiting to see what would happen, wondering whether Matson was in danger, seriously ill, whether he would be able to go on. In politics, as in war, casualties become the basis for a new set of calculations. If Matson was disabled, if he could not give his speech, if he could not dictate what the Michigan delegation would do, what would happen to the chances of the candidates, and not just the two leading contenders, but all of them? That was the question, unspoken and unspeakable, that dominated the minds of nearly everyone there, the thousands of delegates and spectators who stood watching as Louis Matson was half carried to a chair.

"You give the speech," whispered Matson as Julian lowered him into the chair. "No one else can do it."

Julian looked at him with a question in his eyes.

"Don't worry about me; I'll be fine. Give the speech; everything else will follow from that."

"Everything else…?"

"Go!" insisted Matson, patting the hand with which Julian still gripped his shoulder. "Give the speech, give it as if you were the candidate, the one everyone has come to hear."

A half dozen others had rushed over to see what they could do to help. As Julian turned and started toward the front of the stage, Matson gave them a searching glance that froze them in place and focused their attention on what he wanted them to do. He brought his hands together, slowly and, as it were, with an effort, the way an invalid, someone suddenly stricken, might make the attempt, and began to clap. Without quite knowing why, they began to clap as well. Turning away from them, Matson followed Julian with his eyes, and their eyes followed as well. With the instinct of the crowd, all the delegates were on their feet, clapping their hands, a show of sympathy for Louis Matson and encouragement for the unannounced speaker who had suddenly been thrust into the spotlight, forced on the instant to give a speech for which he had not been given so much as a moment to prepare. What no one realized, what only Louis Matson understood, was that Julian Drake had been preparing all his life.

Julian stood at the glass lectern, waiting as the applause died away. And then he waited some more. The arena, that enormous auditorium, was now still as a church, and Julian just stood there, ten seconds, twenty seconds, and did not speak. He placed his left hand on the edge of the lectern and stepped back an arm's length away. His head bent, staring down at the floor, he gripped the right lapel of his dark blue suit coat. His lips began to move, but no sound came out of his mouth. He seemed lost in a trance, and then, suddenly, his head came up and his eyes were ablaze and he swept his right arm out to the side.

"We have spent months, years, talking about everything that is wrong with the present administration!" he cried in a voice that by its richness and strength seemed to come from everywhere at once. "It is time we started talking about what is wrong with us." He paused, giving his audience, the twenty-thousand in the hall and the millions more watching on television time to make certain that they had heard him right. "We have, some of us, done nothing but criticize everything the president has tried to do; we have not yet put together three consecutive sentences explaining how, if we are elected, we would govern better. We have lost our way and, worse than that, do not even know it. Think what we have done. When anyone suggests that the rich should pay more in taxes, we call it class warfare, which more than implies, insists, that those who suggest it are somehow unAmerican. And what do we offer as the best way to provide the money we need to pay for the kind of schools we want and the military we need? - To have the rich pay even less, because with more money to spend on themselves, more people will be employed and more revenue will result. We have put ourselves in the strange position, without precedent in history, of saying that we can meet our responsibilities at home and our obligations abroad, that we can be - as we all say we want to be - the greatest nation on earth, by doing nothing more than encouraging the self-indulgence of the rich!

"We talk about the Constitution, but we have forgotten what it means to be a citizen and think only of the right to do whatever we wish. We call ourselves conservatives and without realizing we are doing it act like the most radical liberal, eager to get rid of everything we have built through two centuries of effort and sacrifice, two centuries of war and triumph, two centuries in which our parents and grandparents, and their parents and grandparents, gave their treasure and their lives so that their children and their children's children could live in freedom. We call ourselves conservatives and demand that we throw everything aside and start all over, as if it were for this generation alone to know what is best for the country."

High up in the gallery, in a section reserved for the press, Rachel Good watched the reaction of the vast audience to everything Julian Drake was saying. She could also look down and watch the way everything he did, every gesture, seemed to fit flawlessly with what he said. Or so she had thought when he first started to speak, because three sentences into it, she found herself so swept up in what he was saying that she had to force herself to pull away, to remember that she was there to report on what she saw. It was mesmerizing, that was all she could think, this strange power that let him teach these people, most of them as fanatical in their beliefs as any political convention in recent memory, that everything they believed, everything they thought they believed, was wrong. A power, but what kind and where did it come from and what did it mean? It was more than the speech, more than the words, words which if spoken by anyone else she could think of would have been treated with angry derision and righteous contempt. It was not because the speaker, Julian Drake, had a call on their loyalty; there were not more than a dozen people there who remembered who he was. It was not what he was saying, and it was not who was saying it; it was how he was saying it that allowed him to do what he did. He spoke with a force built out of speed, the words coming with the kind of velocity that it seemed nothing could stop, coming, as it were, out of some necessity that nothing, no reasoned argument, no settled opinion, could resist. And more than that, there was his voice, a voice that seemed to come from everywhere at once, wrapping you up in it, enveloping you as if, instead of coming from somewhere outside, it was your own voice, the one that came from deep inside yourself. It was a voice that, though you have never known it, you had wanted all your life to hear, a voice of such confidence and self-assurance, that just listening to it you knew that, finally, there was someone who understood what you had always wanted to say. It was hypnotic. Everywhere Rachel Good looked, the same thing, every face filled with astonishment and wonder as they listened to Julian Drake take apart the basic principles by which the leading contenders for the nomination had sought to establish their conservative credentials.

"If there is any conservative principle to which we should all be committed, whether we are Republicans or not, it is that we should not tax unless there is a need, and that when we tax we should so far as possible raise the revenue we need without taking money from those who need every dollar they have to feed and house themselves and their children. If there is any conservative principle worth fighting for it is that the country always comes first, and we would do well to remember - those of us who talk about taxing everyone, rich and poor alike, at the same rate - that there has never been in the history of the world a country that for long survived divided against itself. We have a choice to make: either to go back to what made us a great country, the light, the hope, of the world; or to keep pretending that because we are Americans we don't have to do anything because things will somehow always turn out for the best. American exceptionalism means nothing unless it means that what set us apart from every other country is our willingness to sacrifice for others, our determination to place the public interest above what we think our own private advantage. What kind of people are we? What kind of people do we want to be? - Eager, all of us, to spend our lives trying to make more money than we need, or the kind of people who never hesitate to give their lives in the cause of freedom? What kind of children do we want to raise? What kind of citizens do we want to have? - The kind who dream of all the things they can acquire, or the kind who dream of one day deserving the honor that comes with service to their country? What do we want to show by our example? - That we honor athletes by paying millions, tens of millions, to grown ups who play the games of children - or those who risk their lives on the battlefield and then, when they come back with missing limbs and broken bodies, are not given the kind of medical help they deserve and too many of us seem to think this country cannot afford?"

Julian Drake raised his chin a defiant half-inch as if he were about to challenge that vast, silent audience to think again about what they really believed.

"No one should be nominated for the presidency, not by a party that claims it wants to restore the greatness of the country, who is not willing to change all this. No one should be elected to the presidency who is not prepared to promise that those who risk their lives to defend us are guaranteed the best medical care this country can provide. Let us be clear about this. No one should leave this convention with the nomination who doesn't swear an oath to provide state of the art hospitals for the men and women on active duty, and free, quality health care for veterans and their families. There is more. When a member of the armed forces is killed in the line of duty, it should be considered an obligation of the government - it should be an obligation of all of us - to provide for the care of his or her children until they have completed their education and can take care of themselves. If it it be objected that this will cost money, it costs more than that: it costs lives. If anyone think it unfair that some of us will have to pay more in taxes, you may wish to remember that without men and women willing to sacrifice their lives, you would not have to worry about taxes because you would not have a country left to defend. The question, the only question, is what price freedom? What are we willing to do? Are we to be the first generation unwilling to sacrifice, to do what is necessary, for the next? Are we so devoted to our own ease and comfort, so convinced that what happens to us as individuals is more important than what happens to us as a country, more interested in the speed of communication, the latest technology, than in the study, the serious study of our responsibilities to one another, more concerned with what is on television than in learning about the world and how to live a decent life? Or is there some part of us that still remembers what it was like to be an American when we looked on each other as fellow citizens instead of competitors for the tarnished glow of the proverbial brass ring?"

Rachel Good had never seen anything quite like it. Every eye was on Julian Drake, everyone seemingly mesmerized by what he said. Whichever candidate for the nomination they had come to support, they were, all of them, convinced that government was at best a necessary evil and that taxes, if they could not be eliminated altogether, could always be reduced. And yet, here they were, not just listening with tolerance, but, to judge by the intensity of their expression, eager to do what Julian Drake was asking them to do. Suddenly, her gaze moved from the crowd to the back of the stage. Louis Matson was sitting straight up on the edge of his chair with no sign of illness, nothing to suggest a recent collapse, watching Julian Drake, smiling to himself at the way that this speech Julian had written and that, as he had confessed to her, he knew he could not give, had made everyone forget everything except what they were hearing. Then she noticed the other reason Louis was smiling. Julian Drake was not reading the speech. He had shoved the text to the side, pushed it away. He was speaking from memory, the speech so much a part of him that he did not need the written word to remind him what he wanted to say or how to say it.

"We call ourselves conservatives, and those who more than anyone ought to be conservative, those entrusted with the sacred obligation to preserve the Constitution of the United States, those with the main responsibility for pulling us back when we start to go off in a different direction from where the founders of the nation, the framers of our Constitution, the Constitution that for more than two hundred years has kept us on the steady path of freedom and greatness, those who sit on the Supreme Court pledged to conserve the institutions that are the very foundation of everything the generations have built, those who, as I say, more than anyone else ought to be conservative, have forgotten what it means."

Rachel Good scribbled in her reporter's notebook a brief note about Louis Matson, a question whether he had feigned his collapse; whether he had known from the beginning that somehow Julian Drake would give this speech. But why, what was his motive, what was he after? The question, however important, vanished from her mind as Julian Drake began what seemed an attack on the court.

"It is a loss of all standards, a failure of the understanding and a contempt for all the wisdom of the past, an arrogance born of ignorance. There is no other way to describe a decision that for the first time in our history has turned what has always and everywhere been thought a private vice into a public virtue. By deciding that members of the same sex may marry in the same way as members of the opposite sex, the court has shown an utter failure to understand what marriage laws are all about. The laws about marriage have, until now, always been considered the most important laws there are. Marriage has only one serious purpose: to ensure that there will always be a new generation to take the place of the old, to ensure that the next generation will be raised, and educated, in a way that they will carry on the work that has been started, to ensure that our way of life, the way of life that for generations has been fought for, will be continued. Why else did Lincoln insist that the Declaration of Independence be our civic religion, that the principles of freedom and equality be the first thing taught to our children? But now, we are told, everyone has the right to live with whomever they choose. Let them! But that scarcely requires that what some do in private should be seen as no different, as something to be equally honored, as those whose marriage produces the generation that make up the life of the country.

"All of us desire immortality; it is our nature as human beings. Some seek to live forever in the memory of men, famous for something they have done; many believe in the immortality of the soul, and believe that after death another, eternal, life awaits us. Most of us, whatever else we believe, hope to live forever in our children and our children's children. And what do we as conservatives believe if not that what binds us together, what makes us one people, is the great chain of being that connects one generation with the next, that by honoring what our parents and our grandparents achieved, by honoring the past - the past we inherit in ourselves - we gain guidance for the future. That is why marriage has always been considered sacred: the responsibility it bears for what will happen in our future. And that is why…."

But he had to stop, the noise in the hall, which had begun to rise as he spoke, had reached a crescendo, deafening, unstoppable, coming now in waves, sweeping everything before it. Julian Drake stood still, he did not move, his gaze piercing, intense, ready the moment the crowd, which was now on its feet, let him go on.

"…And that is why, despite what the court has done, we must, all of us, do everything we can to bring back, to restore, to its rightful place, marriage and what it really means. It is one thing to obey the law - we can and should always do that - but that does not require that we stop doing everything we can to give whatever help they need to the men and women who are trying to raise children in a way most in keeping with our most honored traditions."

There was a long pause. Julian Drake stepped back and looked from one side of the vast arena to the other. A slight smile creased the corners of his mouth. His eyes sparkled as if at some sudden thought. He stood at an angle to the lectern, raised his head in the way of someone about to give a friendly warning, held up his index finger and slowly waved it back and forth. The arena fell silent.

"We all say we are in favor of the second amendment, but we have forgotten what it means. We claim it is the right to bear arms and, some of us, insist there can be no restriction, that the right is absolute. We say, some of us, that the right can never be infringed because we have, all of us, the right to defend ourselves. The Declaration of Independence, the Declaration Lincoln thought our civic religion, tells us that we have, all of us, the right to 'life, liberty, and the pursuit of happiness.' And so, some of us seem to think that there is nothing wrong when some teenager, deeply disturbed, or some want to be gangster, takes possession of an AK-15 and murders as many people as he can find to shoot.

"Every right has a limit, because every right has sometimes to give way to another right. We have, all of us, the right to defend ourselves. That is what the second amendment guarantees. Not just the right, the obligation. That is what no one seems to understand, that the second amendment was drawn up to make sure that we would, as a people, have the ability to defend ourselves, not just against each other, but together, against invasion and attack. Thomas Jefferson - and you would hope our Democratic friends would understand this - insisted when he was governor of Virginia that every citizen between the age of sixteen and sixty be required to be a member of the state militia and that they be required to have a rifle, and, if they could not afford one, they be furnished with one at public expense. A militia was necessary, an armed citizenry was necessary, to defend against Indian attack because in those days it might be weeks before the regular army could get there.

"We have a right to bear arms, and, as citizens, an obligation to do so, when it is required by reason of national defense. That obligation is, if you will allow me to put it this way, also a right - the right to participate fully as a citizen, the right to help defend the freedom we enjoy. It is - or it should be - the right of every citizen to do this. No one should be given this party's nomination who is not willing to support this. No one should be given the nomination who is not willing to propose to the Congress legislation under which citizens between the age of eighteen and twenty-five can, as he or she chooses, join the armed forces of the United States; legislation that in exchange for four years of service will provide at public expense four years of college. This is nothing more than the obligation of one generation to provide the education and training for the next generation of Americans, the education and training that will restore what we have come dangerously close to losing: a sense of honor, a willingness to sacrifice, a love of country, scorn for the mindless pleasures which have always accompanied the downfall of nations."

He was speaking rapidly now, faster with every breath, hammering home the conviction that everything he said was right. It was powerful, irresistible, carrying everyone with him. They would, as some of them would later recall, have agreed with anything he said, the only thought they had the words they heard.

"Again some will say it will cost too much if too many wish to join. Is your country worth so little that your only worry is about your money? Some will say that the sons and daughters of the wealthy won't have the same incentive to join as the sons and daughters of the poor. Is this the prize of wealth in America, that your children think patriotism only for fools and honor something you can buy and sell? The price of freedom is paid with blood and sweat, it is paid with effort and hard work, it is paid, it can only be paid, by those for whom honor, duty, country are things they would rather die than live without. Remember what made this country great. Remember those who gave their lives in this nation's wars. Remember what the dream, the great American dream, was all about, not how rich we could become, not how many houses, how many cars, we could acquire, but what kind of people we could be, free to live our lives in the pursuit of human excellence, free to do everything we can to make the lives of those around us better, free to answer of our own volition our country's call. Remember what made us great, remember that we, and we alone, have the chance to make us great again. Remember those 'mystic chords of memory' that, as Lincoln taught us, bind together all the generations; remember, while there is still time, that greatness can only come to those who remember what it means; remember, while there is still time, the dangers that we face; remember, while there is still time, that without discipline and sacrifice no danger was ever overcome. Remember that it was the American example, not American power, that once made us the inspiration of the world. Remember, if you remember nothing else, that it is not too late, we can still light the way and show the world, and ourselves, that freedom is not freedom from our obligations, but freedom to meet them in the way we should, with strength and courage, generosity and goodwill, with a sense of honor and high purpose. Remember, in other words, that if we have been made by our history, we can make some history of our own, that we can pass on to the next generation an even better country than the one we inherited. That is our challenge, that is the great adventure on which, if you are willing, we start on tonight, the great endeavor that will determine whether we were worth all the effort, all the sacrifice made by all those who came before us. On your decision rests the fate, not just of this party, but of the country. Choose wisely, choose well, choose someone who holds within himself a promise of the greatness we as a country so desperately need, someone who can make us once again the envy of the world."

The crowd was on its feet, cheering, before he had even finished, the last words barely audible, buried under an avalanche of deafening, heart-stopping noise. And it kept coming, as if the crowd were competing with itself to see how loud it could be. People clapped until their hands began to ache and shouted until their throats grew hoarse. A reporter standing next to Rachel Good started to say something, realized that nothing he said could be heard, and laughed at the futility of the attempt. Julian Drake stood there, taking it all in, but, it seemed to Rachel Good as she watched him, somehow almost detached, as if what he were witnessing, a crowd of twenty-thousand giving him all the approval anyone could ever ask for, had little, if anything, to do with him. She had seen the same thing on the face of an actor, one of the great ones, acknowledging the plaudits of an audience after a performance; she had never seen it on the face of a man or woman in public life, certain, as all of them seemed to be, that far from playing a role what they did was real. Julian stood there a moment longer, and then, with one last wave of his hand, a gesture of gratitude for the kindness of their response, he turned and walked back across the stage and took his seat next to where, twenty minutes earlier, he had left Louis Matson in a state of near collapse. Louis Matson was not there.

Rising with the crowd as Julian came to the climax of his speech, Matson had moved to the far side of the stage where he waited until Julian turned to go back. Then, as the applause finally died down, he seized the microphone and in a few brief sentences changed history.

"What you just heard was the speech I wish I could have given, and knew I never could. Only Julian Drake could give that speech; only Julian Drake could have written it. He served in the House; he would have been elected to the Senate had not a personal tragedy stopped him from doing so. And if he had been in the Senate, the nomination for the presidency would have been his for the asking. We face too many challenges, we have too many problems, we have wasted too much time with second-rate politicians and their third-rate minds. We have a chance to do something that we can proud of for the rest of our lives. Ladies and gentlemen, I nominate as our candidate for the office of President of the United States Julian Drake. As chairman of the convention I am suspending the rules and ask that you make the nomination unanimous!"

CHAPTER TEN

Julian Drake stared out the window, listening to the voices on television jubilant in their confusion about what had just transpired. Louis Matson sat in an easy chair, a scotch and soda in his hand, enjoying the moment. Ismael Cooper occupied the end of the sofa, shaking his head at his failure to see what he should have seen from the very beginning.

"Listen to that," remarked Matson, slapping his knee, as one of the most conservative commentators on television launched a vicious attack on what had just been done.

"He had no business, no right," insisted Ian Flannery, in a strident voice. "Nothing like this has ever happened. Someone should do something about it; someone should demand that the convention reconvene and start all over. Let the other candidates have their chance. All the primaries, all the debates - Louis Matson thinks that counts for nothing, that they don't even get to have their names placed in nomination! Why they let this guy chair the convention, why they thought they had to have him - I mean, he isn't what anyone would call a real conservative - give the keynote speech…!"

With a jaundiced grin, Matson leaned toward Ismael Cooper.

"He's right; he's an idiot, but he's right - I'm not anything close to what he thinks is a conservative. And he is right - I had no right to do what I did." The look on his face changed into one of the utmost seriousness. "I had a duty." He glanced at Julian who was still looking out the window, silent, withdrawn, pondering some thought of his own. "Sometimes you have to break the rules to save what is essential. I meant what I said, Julian: you're the only hope we have."

His hands shoved deep in his pockets, Julian turned around and looked at Matson with something Ismael Cooper thought close to anger.

"When?" he asked. "When did you decide to do this?"

There was no point pretending that had it not been for a temporary loss of balance, a brief collapse, it would not have happened at all. Louis Matson only lied to people who lied to him.

"The first time I read the speech." A distant smile worked its way along the sagging corners of his mouth. For a brief moment his tired eyes drew back on themselves. "No, probably a long time before that. When you were still in Congress, when you were running for the Senate. " He shook his head, and drew back from the past. "When did I decide to do what I did tonight, when did I know it was what I had to do? When you spoke to the delegation, when I saw the effect it had. And if I ever had any doubt about what I did, I don't anymore. All these plastic politicians, all they can think about is the presidency - and you don't want it! Well, goddamn it, Julian, if you had wanted it like all the others, I wouldn't have bothered!"

Ismael switched channels, going back and forth to get the best cross-section of opinion he could. The networks were coming in with the early polling. The results surprised even Louis Matson.

"Almost eighty percent approval. That's unheard of. Eighty percent think you're the best candidate we could have nominated." He glanced at Cooper. "What do you think he's saying now?" he asked, referring to the outraged Ian Flannery who, a few minutes earlier, had been insisting that the convention should disavow what in a moment of false enthusiasm the delegates had been tricked into doing. "No one is going to question what happened. Watch! They'll be lining up to tell everyone it was the best thing that could have happened. They'll all be writing - all those reporters who have to be the first to tell everyone what things really mean - that 'Julian Drake took the Republican convention by storm. After the speech he gave, there was never any question who was going to be the nominee!'"

Julian was not interested in what anyone was going to write.

"Is that the reason you didn't say anything to me about this?" he asked, wanting to be sure of something. "Because you thought I would say no?"

"Yes, exactly; you would have."

A strange look of disbelief, a look of shrewd skepticism, entered Julian's eyes.

"There is more to it than that, though, isn't there? Because if you had asked me, and I had agreed, you would have made me a co-conspirator in a lie, part of a set piece fiction, in which you pretend to be ill and I act the part of the innocent bystander forced to do something he had never wanted to do," he said, daring him to disagree. "There is a third alternative, but never mind that now...."

A third alternative? Ismael Cooper wondered what it could be, and then, suddenly, he thought he knew. The speech. Julian had known when he wrote it that Louis Matson could never give it. Was it possible, was it conceivable, that without actually planning it, Julian Drake had foreseen the possibility, had taken the first step, written a speech only he could give, the first step in a sequence that would then have to follow?

There was a sudden, loud knock on the door. Matson and Ismael looked at each other.

"I told them to hold all calls," said Ismael, as he got to his feet and turned to Julian. "It must be a madhouse down there, everyone waiting to hear from you. This will be the chairman, wringing his hands, wondering what he should do."

Julian shrugged. "Tell him I left town and no one knows where I have gone," he said, laughing. And then, to spare Ismael the trouble, answered the door himself. It was the chairman.

"What can I do for you?" asked Julian, with a friendly grin as he shook his hand and invited him inside.

"I didn't think..., I thought that...."

"That Louis or Ismael...? They're right here. We were just discussing whether I ought to go downstairs and hold a press conference or have a few selected reporters come up. What do you think I should do," he asked, giving the impression that he would gladly do whatever the chairman thought best.

"Well, I don't..., the place is just a zoo. I mean, as you can imagine, no one was prepared for anything like this; no one ever thought that....It was a great speech," he added, remembering that Julian was after all the nominee. "And I think that - what the convention did, the unanimous support, without precedent in my experience - well, I think that...."

"I'll come down," said Julian, before the chairman choked himself to death. "Shall we say ten minutes? Will that give you enough time?"

The lobby was packed with reporters eager to get their first chance to see close up this new phenomenon who in a half hour's time had gone from anonymity to the only person in America anyone could talk about. There was a frenzy of expectation, a kind of mystery about what it all meant, a sense that something more than a bizarre ending to a year long fight for the nomination had taken place, something that threatened the known assumptions, the way that politics was understood. The place was buzzing with anticipation, and then Julian Drake walked in, alone and unannounced, and the silence itself became electric.

It was curious, the way everyone seemed to take a step back to let him pass; curious, the puzzled expressions, as if they were trying to discover in the way he looked the secret of what two hours earlier they had watched him do with an audience who had not known who he was. Slight of build like a long distance runner, with dark brown hair and gray-green eyes, he moved toward the microphones set up in front without any noticeable hesitation or doubt as to why he was there. If he felt in any way self-conscious, awkward or uncomfortable, worried about this, his first experience, with the national media, he did not show it. Just before he reached the microphones, he bumped into a reporter who, too late, tried to get out of the way. Julian grabbed his shoulder to steady him, smiled and apologized for not being more careful. Astonished, the reporter smiled back.

Julian Drake was still smiling when he took his place behind the battery of microphones and looked out at the sea of faces looking at him. He waited a long moment, and then, the smile broader, he tossed his head to the side and announced, “Well, if no one has a question, I’ll....” Everyone was on their feet, shouting, asking, demanding, to go first. Julian pointed to someone in the back.

“Doesn’t it feel a little strange, suddenly to find yourself, someone no one knew, the Republican nominee for the presidency?”

“It isn’t true that no one knows me,” replied Julian with a sparkle in his eye. “And it isn’t strange - it’s an honor - to be the nominee.”

“No, what I meant - “

“I know. It’s a fair question. A few hours ago I could have walked through the lobby of this hotel, or anywhere else, and no one would have noticed, and now I can’t go anywhere without being recognized. But that is how we live now. Fame comes in an instant. The only real question is what you become famous for, and, once you have it, that fame so many people seem to want, what you do with it.”

“There is a rumor that Louis Matson staged the whole thing,” shouted someone closer to the front; “that he did not want the nomination to go to Rivers or Lochner or any of the others, that he wanted you; that he wasn’t ill at all, that he faked that collapse so you could take his place and give his speech and in that way -”

“That sounds pretty unlikely, don’t you think? Who could have known, who could have predicted, what happened tonight? I certainly did not know I would be giving that speech. If I had known what was going to happen,” he added with a modest, eager grin, “I would have stayed in California.”

“You mean - you really expect us to believe - that you wouldn’t have wanted the nomination if you had known you were going to get it?” asked a reporter from the Washington Post.

“If I had known...?” Julian threw up his hands. “I did not know anything. I left politics twelve years ago and never imagined I would be coming back. I wrote that speech because Louis Matson asked me to write it. It was the first time he had ever asked me for anything. It was a chance for me, not to pay back - nothing could ever pay him back for what he once did for me - but to at least show the gratitude I have always felt, and the respect I have always had.”

“What did Louis Matson do for you? What was the reason you thought you had to write that speech?” a reporter with one of the cable shows, a young woman with long dark lashes and bright painted nails, cried above all the others clamoring for attention.

Julian quickly shook his head, as if the questions were somehow impermissible, an intrusion into what was private and personal. He took a deep breath, sighed, and shook his head again, but this time with an air of resignation.

"Twelve years ago, I was a candidate for the United States Senate. I had to quit the race. Louis Matson understood the reason and gave me the help I needed."

Watching from the side, Rachel Good could hear in her head the inevitable next question and did not doubt for a minute that Julian Drake could hear it too.

"What was the reason, the reason you had to quit, what was it that Louis Matson understood?"

The look on Julian's face seemed to say that his comment about staying in California had he known what was going to happen was not as light-hearted, as bright-witted, as it had seemed; that it had covered something tragic.

"My sister and her husband were killed. They had two young children. There was no one else to take care of them, no one else to raise and educate them. There really was no choice. They had lost both their parents; I could not let them be raised by someone who could never be there because I was always out campaigning."

Someone started to ask another question, another question about the same thing. Julian stopped him with a glance.

"There is one thing, the only thing, I will not take questions about. The children are grown up now; they have their own lives. That is all anyone needs to know."

A heavy-set reporter with heavy-lidded eyes and a pockmarked face stood with notebook in hand on which he had written out the question he wanted to ask. Some thought it was a trick, a way to make his questions seem thoughtful and important; others, less charitable, insisted it was because if he did not read the question he would not remember what he wanted to ask.

"Nearly everything you said in your speech is a direct attack on what the Republican party has stood for since at least Ronald Reagan."

Dropping his right shoulder, Julian bent his head to the same side and raised his eyebrows.

"And your question is…?"

"Are you really going to turn your back on what the party stands for?"

Julian stroked his chin with his thumb and two fingers.

"I did not get the nomination and then give that speech," he said, a shrewd glint in his eye. "I gave that speech and then got the nomination. It seems to follow that instead of turning my back on what the party stands for, the party agrees with me."

Pausing, he shook his head, dissatisfied with what he had said. He looked at the reporter who had asked the question and, to everyone's astonishment, apologized.

"I'm sorry; that was not a fair answer. It was not an answer at all. Most of what happens in politics, most of what we talk about, is a response to what seems to be the immediate situation in which we find ourselves. The Reagan Revolution, as it was called at the time, was a reaction to what was commonly seen as an unprecedented growth of governmental power and control. The New Deal under F.D.R., the Great Society under Lyndon Johnson, government was involved in more and more of our lives, regulating, or trying to regulate, everything we did, and taxing everyone to do it. Reagan promised lower taxes and better times, a new beginning, 'Morning in America.' Taxes would be lowered, and because government was the problem, not the solution, as he liked to say, government would do less than it had, but do what it still had to do, especially on the question of defense, much better than it had before. There is nothing wrong with trying to make government, government at every level, more efficient and less expensive; nothing wrong in trying to relieve people of the burden of undue taxation. The problem was the assumption that, left to their own devices, free of governmental control, everyone would be able to take care of themselves, that it did not matter, that it was in a sense all to the good, if the workings of the free market made some incredibly rich and a great many others struggling to survive. Economics became more important than politics, making money more important than what we could do together as a people. That is what I was trying to speak about tonight, that money is a means, not an end; that the only thing worth pursuing, the only thing that will make a nation great and worth remembering, is human excellence."

Another reporter, a middle-aged woman with deep wrinkles around her eyes and a scratchy, no-nonsense voice that made every question seem an accusation, jabbed a crooked finger in the air.

"You just said that you did not get the nomination and then give that speech," she quoted from memory. "You did not make that speech as a candidate seeking the nomination, you wrote it for Louis Matson. He wasn't running, either. It was supposed to a keynote speech, a statement of why the Republicans should win, a statement -"

"'Of sound and fury signifying nothing,'" interjected Julian. "Sorry. What is your question?"

"Would you have given the same speech if you had been speaking as a candidate?"

"No," he replied with a blank expression.

"No?" asked the reporter, stunned by his response.

"No, it would have been much shorter. A speech of withdrawal usually is."

"A speech of…?"

"How many primaries do you think I would have won, suggesting the kind of things I did tonight?" he replied, as the room erupted in laughter. "I'm serious," he insisted. "This is a national convention, a national audience. When you talk to the whole country, you can - you should - talk about things on a large scale, what the country needs to do. Look," he said, his tone now intimate and casual, "it's one thing to speak in a crowded hall; it is another thing altogether to speak in someone's living room to a dozen people come to decide whether you might be the candidate they want to support. What happened tonight - what kind of headline will there be? - 'The impossible has happened: Republicans nominate someone no one has heard of!' What I spoke about, the things I tried to say, could not have happened anywhere else."

"What everyone wants to know, though," insisted a reporter who had written books about the last several presidencies, "is whether you meant what you said. Is it what you really intend to try to do if you are elected in November?"

The words were civil enough, but there was a skepticism, a doubt, that now that Julian Drake was a candidate he would act or think the same way he had before. It was the cynic's certain knowledge that speeches should never be taken seriously, except for the effect they might have on an audience. Julian was not amused.

"Did you think I was lying, that I wasn't serious about what I said; that I was perfectly content to say what I thought others - whoever got the nomination - should do, but that I would not think of doing myself? Even if I wanted to play the coward's part, try to win an election by being all things to all people, the speech has been given, the whole country knows what I said. And the country knows something else as well: I did not give that speech, I did not say what I said, because I was trying to win anyone's vote. Like it, don't like it; agree with it, disagree with it - it is what I believe, what I think needs to be done. Vote for it, vote against it. There will be no room for confusion. What I say I'll do, I'll do."

"Or try to," a voice shouted out. "You have to get Congress to agree."

"Congress tends to agree with whatever the American people want. What they want, they'll decide in the election. Everything follows from that."

Every hand shot up, everyone halfway out of their chairs, eager, angry, swearing under their breath, desperate to be next. Julian, for his part, seemed relaxed, at ease, in no hurry. Everyone else was sweating with the tension they felt, the need to get something they could use; Julian seemed to grow stronger, fresher, the longer it went on. He took seriously the questions they asked, and seemed grateful for the chance to answer, to think about something he might otherwise have ignored. To Rachel Good, it seemed completely in character: he had that kind of curiosity. A question, instead of something to be handled and turned to his advantage, the kind of answer, the only kind, most people in public life knew or understood, was for Julian Drake a way to force to the surface of his mind something that, until he heard himself the answer he was giving, must otherwise have stayed hidden, something he had not known he knew.

"You're the Republican nominee for president," said a smooth modulated voice trained for television, "and America doesn't know anything about you. Why don't you tell us something about yourself. What do you like to do, what…?"

"Are you married?" interjected a young woman with the laughing eyes of a woman who hoped he was not.

"More than once?" inquired a balding, bespectacled round faced man in a rumpled suit with a voice that sounded like tires on gravel.

"Yes, what have you done all the time since you left Congress?"

"Lived a quiet life," replied Julian. He had caught the change of mood, the new interest in him as a person. "Read as much as I could; tried to learn what I could about the world; tried to learn what it means to be a human being. I studied; and no, I'm not married," he added with a quick glance back at the young, very attractive, woman who had asked. "But you never know what may happen," he remarked with a slight, disarming smile before he turned again to the crowd and nodded toward the next reporter with a question.

"What it means to be a human being? Is that what you said? What exactly did you mean by that?"

Julian's deep-set eyes seemed to grow larger, moving with lightning speed in a dozen different directions, as if searching among all the known possibilities for the one explanation that would make sense to someone who had not made the same journey and seen the same things.

"That is a very long question. Let me just say that, because of the time I had spent in Congress, the years involved in politics, I had an interest in how we had gotten to where we are, so I read everything I could about the history - our history - of the twentieth century. But if you do that, you are led back to the nineteenth century, and then back to the beginning, the early years of the Republic, the War of Independence, the Constitution. And I realized you could not understand anything about any of it - why Washington, Jefferson, Adams, Madison, all the rest, did what they did if you did not understand the way they thought about things. Who had they learned from, who were their teachers? You cannot understand what we were, how we began, you cannot understand the Declaration of Independence, unless you read John Locke. And when you do that," continued Julian as if he were talking to a graduate seminar instead of a room full of seasoned political reporters who were now listening in close to open-mouth wonder, "when you study Locke's Second Treatise on Government, you start to realize that he is following, and if you will, correcting, Thomas Hobbes. And then that both of them were making a conscious break with the ancient wisdom, replacing, or trying to replace, the teachings of Plato and Aristotle with a new teaching of their own. But the significance, the meaning of that, can only be understood if you begin to understand what the ancient teaching was. And so," he added with a sudden, self-deprecating smile meant to show that he knew this was nothing they had come to hear or had any reason to take seriously, "I was compelled, despite my obvious inability, to begin the study of those two impossible authors. Does that answer your question?"

Reporters shook their heads, shrugged their shoulders, certain now, if they had not been before, that they had never seen anything quite like it. Who else could give a speech like the one they had heard and win the nomination because of it, and then take a question that anyone else would have used as a chance to make a connection with what the great majority of the people in the country knew something about and turn it into a disquisition on what no one else either knew or probably cared to know?

"And you would be right in thinking what you must be thinking now," remarked Julian as if he knew what was in their minds before they could put it into conscious form. "There probably are not more than a dozen people in the country who have the slightest interest in this. But you asked me a question, and that is the answer." His eyes lit up, he tried, and failed, to suppress an impish grin. "It's not my fault. I left public life twelve years ago. I've forgotten how to lie."

It brought down the house, and what had seemed an exercise in scholarly irrelevance was turned in an instant into an example of wit and likability. Rachel Good was already convinced that everything Julian Drake said or did was planned in advance, that his mind moved so quickly that the moment he began to answer a question he knew what he would have to do to guarantee safe passage, how he could say what no one else would think, or know, to say and make it sound exactly what everyone would have liked to have said themselves. She watched the way his soft gray-green eyes moved, the cheerful, quick calculation, the keen sense of anticipation, as he called on one reporter after another. It was hard to believe he had not done anything like this in twelve years; hard to believe he had not been doing it all his adult life.

"What are the Democrats saying?" she asked, when she called her editor in New York after the press conference had finally ended.

Hobart Williams emitted a barrel-chested laugh. "The official version - they tried to be cute - is that….Here is the quote we're using, 'The Republicans finally agreed with us: none of the candidates for the nomination deserved to be president. They have nominated someone no one knows in the hope that everyone will forget everything they were saying before.' Privately they're worried. They saw what he did, they heard the speech. They don't know what the hell to make of it; no one does. I don't, do you?"

Rachel thought she did. "If he wins, it will be something bigger than a change of government, a new administration; it'll be something like a revolution. Listen to me, Hobart - he knew this was going to happen; he knew -"

"That he was going to be nominated? That's impossible. How could he; how could anyone -?"

"I don't know, but trust me, he knew. He isn't what you - what anyone - thinks he is. He isn't some new version of Sarah Palin, a new name, a new face, someone who comes out of nowhere and because of that, becomes the new center of attention, the only one anyone wants to talk about. Sarah Palin was an accident, a bad choice; Julian Drake has been getting ready, waiting for this moment, all his life. Don't ask me how I know this; it's just a feeling, an intuition, if you will, but I've never been so sure of anything. I know its true."

Williams asked the only question that really mattered. "Where is the story?"

"There isn't one; not yet, anyway," she admitted.

"No, not yet," replied Williams, thoughtfully. "But it isn't a bad way to begin. It's the biggest story in years: someone takes the convention by storm, gets the nomination with a single, remarkable speech, a nomination by acclamation. The other candidates don't even get to have their names placed in nomination; no one else is even considered. And no one knows anything about him. We'll need a whole profile done. 'Who is Julian Drake and why should he be president' - that kind of thing. Lots of stories in that," he mused aloud. "When did he first think he might one day run for president? That should give you room to work your way through that other business, whether he somehow knew what was going to happen. Try it. You're close to Louis Matson. Can you get an interview, one on one, with our new candidate?"

CHAPTER ELEVEN

"Who do you want to run with you? Who do you want to be vice-president?" asked Ismael Cooper quietly.

They were alone in the living room of the majority leader's suite. Louis Matson had just gone to bed. It was a few minutes past two in the morning. Julian had taken off his suit coat and loosened his tie. He sat slouched at the corner of the long, pale blue sofa, his feet on the glass coffee table. He was wide awake.

"I didn't answer that question, did I?" he remarked, staring up at the ceiling. "Everyone always wants to know what you're going to do next."

"When that reporter asked, you said you had not had time to think about that or anything else. That wasn't quite true, though, was it -?" Ismael got to his feet, went over to the bar and started to make himself a drink and then, with the glass in his hand, changed his mind. "It's too late - or is it too early?"

He shook his head at what he realized was not just an unexpected, but an incongruous situation. It was impossible, but it had happened; he was sitting there in the middle of the night discussing with someone who might actually become president what he wanted to do about the vice-presidency.

"I didn't mean to suggest...," he began to explain, and then stopped himself with a laugh. "This is the strangest business. I'm not sure if I'm awake or dreaming. We don't have anything, no staff, no campaign, and no plan for one. I don't even know if you want me involved."

"Only if you want to be," said Julian, with a quick, friendly glance. "I hope you do, because this isn't something I want to do alone."

"I'll do whatever you want," replied Ismael, with the simple dignity that made it a solemn promise.

Julian motioned for him to take a seat at the other end of the sofa, while he moved to the blue wingback chair directly across from where Ismael sat. They were now less than three feet apart, looking at each other eye to eye. Leaning forward, his elbows on his knees, his hands clasped together, Julian stared down at the carpet. The lines in his forehead deepened as his gaze seemed to focus on a small, diminishing point.

"I think we should take the governor," he said finally, looking up to see if Ismael agreed. But before Ismael could reply, Julian sat up straight and tossed his head back. "We have this much in common: neither of us could have been elected on our own. Although that may not be entirely true. Do you remember what Adlai Stevenson did in the Democratic convention in 1956?Instead of choosing his own running mate, he threw it open and let the convention decide."

"And John F. Kennedy tried to get the nomination, lost to Estes Kefauver, the senator from Kentucky. Had he won, become the vice-presidential nominee, he might never have had the nomination in 1960."

"Better not tell the governor that," remarked Julian with studied ambiguity. "I want him on the ticket - the others, the ones who ran in all the primaries, God help us if any of them ever become president - but I want him to be the choice of the convention."

"You want the convention -?"

"We throw the nomination open, let anyone who wants try to win it. This isn't 1956; the analogy doesn't hold. They'll all try to get it; they all want to show, they have to show, that what happened here tonight was an anomaly, something that shouldn't have happened even once and can never happen again; that take Julian Drake out of the equation and they would have had the nomination. That way, if I lose, they can blame me for the defeat and start running next time with the lead. They have to run, all of them."

Ismael was quick to point out the obvious. "Whoever wins, it isn't likely to be the governor. He doesn't have a single pledged delegate."

"Neither did I."

It made no sense but the look in Julian's eyes told him that there was more to it than what Julian had said.

"Do you want Louis to make the announcement?"

"No, let him sleep. He needs it. Besides, it works better if we do it now."

Ismael glanced at his watch. "It's already after two."

"Other than Louis, do you think anyone in this town is asleep? That reporter, the one Louis likes - Rachel Good - see if you can reach her. Ask her if she would like to do an interview."

Rachel Good was asleep. When the telephone rang, she reached for it, ready to slam it down on whatever drunk had reached the wrong room.

"Who the -?"

"This is Ismael Cooper," she heard someone say, a voice that in the haze of less than an hour's sleep seemed vaguely familiar.

"Ismael? What, why are you…?"

"Julian Drake asked me to call. We know it's late, but we were wondering if you might want a private interview, the first one he has given. There is something you might be interested in knowing. It is about the vice-presidency."

She was already out of bed, standing bare-footed next to the phone, switching on the light.

"Ten minutes, will that work?"

Julian greeted her at the door.

"It's good of you to come on such short notice. And I apologize about the hour," he said, as he showed her inside.

Ismael offered her a cup of coffee. With a grateful smile she took it and then sat down on the edge of the sofa, opened her notebook and took out her pen.

"Ismael mentioned the vice-presidency. In the press conference you said you had not had time to think about it. Have you now come to some decision?"

"Yes, I've decided not to decide."

She blinked twice in quick succession. "You have decided not to…?"

"I'm going to let the convention decide who the vice-presidential nominee should be."

Rachel Good looked across to Ismael as if she wanted him to confirm that she was not hearing things.

"But that means you could be running with someone who believes everything you said in your speech was wrong," she said, quickly recovering. "How can you reconcile what in some cases are diametrical opposites?"

"I don't imagine anyone will put themselves forward as a candidate who isn't willing to reconcile their views with mine," replied Julian with a shrug.

She searched his eyes, wondering if he could possibly be that naive, or that cynical.

"Both," said Julian to her astonishment. "What you were thinking: that I'm either a fool or a Machiavellian; that I honestly don't believe anyone would sacrifice his opinions for the chance at office, high office, or I believe that no one cares about anything else. It's what I would have thought," he said, gently, "if I heard someone say what I just said. In any event, everyone will now get to see what everyone thought they were going to see: a roll-call vote for the nomination."

"And you haven't told anyone about this yet? When are you going to make the formal announcement?" she asked, her pen poised to write down what he was about to say.

"A formal announcement? I just did; or, rather, you get to do it for me - unless you would rather not. I could hold another press conference, if you think I should," he said, a teasing sparkle in his eyes. "I wanted to give you the story first."

"But why…? Oh, I see, it's something Louis….Well, thank him for me." She got up to go and then remembered. "You can't just be neutral in this. Throw it open to the convention, let the delegates decide, but you must have a preference; there must be someone you would rather run with. Who is it?"

Julian moved close enough to touch her on the arm. "It would have been Louis,' he remarked, confidentially, "but I knew he would never do it."

It was only when she was outside, heading down the hallway to the elevator that she realized how deftly he had avoided her question.

All the candidates for the presidency had been asked repeatedly whether they would consider the second spot on the ticket if they failed to win the nomination. All of them had said no. With the announcement that the nomination for vice-president was being thrown open to the convention, all of them changed their mind.

"It's all they know how to do," explained Louis Matson, sitting in the back corner of the hotel restaurant having a late breakfast with Rachel Wood. "Even if they aren't very good at it," he added, rolling his eyes in a playful gesture. He was feeling better than he had in months, the effect, as no one had to tell him, of the sense of accomplishment, the knowledge that he had done something, something of importance, that no one else could have done. Whatever happened now was out of his hands.

"You're rather proud of yourself, aren't you?" Rachel lifted a cup of coffee to her mouth, took a sip, put the cup down and, vaguely conscious that she had not stopped to do anything with her makeup, dabbed her lips with a napkin. "I must look a fright; I haven't slept; I haven't even gone back to my room. This story just keeps going, building on itself, and…."

"And you've seldom felt so alive. Isn't that the truth of it?" asked Matson, with a look that seemed reflective of a deeper understanding, a deeper sympathy, than what she had normally seen on his aging, weathered face. "There is nothing like it - the sense of being in the middle of things. Especially something like this."

There were only a few other people in the restaurant. An hour earlier, you would have had to wait for a table. Everyone who had been up all night - and nearly everyone had - eager to find out what they might have missed, what was going to happen, what all the candidates were going to do with the nomination for vice-president now wide open. And then, an hour later, the restaurant emptied out as the delegates scattered to the meeting rooms where each delegation would try to decide who would be the best candidate for the vice-presidency and what their own votes were worth.

"Why did he do that, Louis? He must have asked your advice."

She was guessing, but she was certain it was true. There was not anyone else Julian Drake would have consulted.

"First I heard about it," replied Matson with a droll expression "was when I read it in your story this morning."

"That can't be true!" she blurted out, almost knocking over her coffee cup in her surprise.

"Let me tell you something," said Matson, leaning forward on his arms. He glanced from side to side as if to make sure no one was close enough to overhear and then, with a glance she immediately understood, insisted that what he was about to say was not only off the record but could never be mentioned to anyone else. "The only time Julian will ever ask for anyone's advice is when he wants them to feel they are someone he trusts, because whatever you think you have to say, he's already had the same thought himself. Watch him, if you don't believe me; watch his eyes, the way they look at you, as if he knows before you do what you're going to say. What is really fascinating is that look isn't one of boredom or disdain He doesn't look at you like you're wasting his time; it is a look of encouragement and approval, telling you that you're on the right track. It may take you a while to see what he saw right away, but he is sure you're going to get there. It's uncanny, is what it is. When he was a young student he must have taught his teachers."

Rachel peered at her old friend through puzzled eyes. She remembered how Julian had read her mind, telling her what she thought almost before she had become aware of it herself.

"You're telling me that he hasn't talked to you about this at all?"

"He talked to me about it this morning, after I saw your story."

"And? What did he tell you?"

"I can't tell you that. It was a private conversation."

She reached into her handbag and pulled out her notebook.

"On the record. The vice-presidential nomination. Who do you support, who do you intend to vote for? Who will the Michigan delegation support?"

"The governor of Ohio," replied Matson, as if the choice were obvious.

"On the record?" she asked, just to be sure.

"Yes, absolutely. And you can quote me on this as well: the governor will win on the first ballot and it won't even be close."

"Why? What makes you think that…? Oh, I see…."

"No, I don't think you do." A sly, knowing grin, barely visible at the left corner of his mouth, suggested something devious and secret.

"All right," she agreed, grasping in advance his negotiated terms. "Off the record."

"Not for attribution will be sufficient."

"Julian wants the governor. He won't say that publicly; he can't. Because of the way he got the nomination, he isn't in the same position as someone who has earned the right to tell the convention who it should nominate for the vice-presidency. Like Julian, the governor was not a candidate; he did not run in the primaries and he never announced his candidacy. If the convention were to nominate someone who came here with delegates they had already won, that might suggest that the convention had second thoughts about what it had done, that it was trying to make amends by giving to the candidate who would have been nominated had things gone through the normal procedure the only thing the convention has left to give."

With a doubtful look, Rachel rubbed her small chin.

"Exactly how is the convention supposed to know all this?"

Matson drank what was left of his coffee, shoved his plate aside, put a few dollars on the table for a tip, and started to get up.

"Because in about ten minutes - if you care to come and watch - I will be explaining to the Michigan delegation what I just said: that only by nominating the governor can the convention, can the Republican party, show that it stands behind the decision, the historic decision, we made last night."

Rachel reached across the table and held him by the wrist.

"Don't go, not just yet. There is something I need to know. Just between us. I promise I won't use it. I know what happened last night, that what you did was no accident. It did not happen because you collapsed. You faked the whole thing. No, don't bother - not with me," she said when he started to deny it. "All I want to know is when did you decide to do it and why?" she asked, with an intensity that made the question seem personal, something beyond the professional curiosity of a reporter.

"Julian asked me the same thing. The honest answer is I don't really know. It might have been the first time I met him. I think I knew that if I ever had the chance...." Matson scratched his head, laughing at his own incoherence. "When I read the speech he had written," he said, now, on the instant, suddenly quite sure. "I knew by the time I turned to the second page. I understood - I remembered - how different, how much better, he was than all the others. And I remembered…how old I am now, how I would never have another chance to do something that would…."

Rachel understood. But she wanted, she needed, a better explanation than what he had read in the first three or four hundred words of a speech, no matter how good that speech had been; a better explanation than what he remembered of the time he first met Julian Drake.

"You have to measure all that - what that speech brought back - against everything that has happened, the deep decline, the growing stupidity, of everything we do. Twelve years ago, Julian was better than anyone we had. But today! Hell, its like comparing, if you want to look at the other side, the Clintons, either one of them, to JFK or FDR. Read a speech by John F. Kennedy, there is something memorable in every line; read every speech Clinton - either one of them - ever gave and you won't find a line you would want to remember even if you could."

Matson shrugged his shoulders and turned up the palms of his hands, as if what he had just said must be as obvious to her as it was to him. Rachel shook her head, but not because she disagreed.

"There is something missing; something you keep leaving out. You haven't told me if he was in on it, if he knew what you were going to do. And," she added, before he could reply, "if he didn't know, what made you think he would go along with it, let you decide that he was going to be a candidate?"

"I didn't tell him; I didn't tell anyone," said Matson emphatically. "If I had, he would have been on the first plane back to California. He never would have done it. Never. This way he had no choice; and this way," he added, pulling back his lower lip in a look of shrewd calculation, "no one can ever accuse him of conspiring to steal the nomination. He is now the perfect candidate, the only one who did not want to be president. How did I know he would do it, take what I gave him, take it without objection? Because of what he did twelve years ago when he quit that senate race. His sense of duty, his belief in what we used to call fate. There is another reason - and you are never to use this, it's just something for you to keep in mind while you watch what he does as a candidate, and then when he becomes president. Julian Drake is quite simply the most ambitious human being I have ever known. You watch," he said when he saw the doubt in her eyes; "you heard what he said in that speech. He meant everything he said, and a good deal more," he added significantly. "This isn't going to be a presidency of small changes. You would have to go back to the New Deal, and maybe farther back than that, to find a precedent for the kind of things he'll want to do."

"He has to get elected first. He's been out of politics for twelve years; he hasn't run for office since. How is he going to handle a national campaign? Although given the way he got the nomination," she remarked with a quiet laugh, "he may not think he needs to campaign."

"You're laughing; maybe you shouldn't," said Matson in a way that suggested some prior knowledge of what the new candidate was going to do, a knowledge he immediately denied. "It's just a guess; a feeling, really. Whatever he does, it probably won't be what we're all used to seeing," he remarked as he got to his feet. "I have to go," he added with friendly reluctance.

With Rachel Good tagging along, Matson went directly to the ballroom where the Michigan delegation was waiting to hear what he had to say about what had happened last night, the nomination of Julian Drake and the now frantic rush of a half dozen different campaigns for the second place on the ticket. As he walked through the door, he threw back his head and laughed in triumph. Everyone was on their feet, clapping, their faces beaming with pleasure, whether because he had survived his collapse or because, as rumor insisted, he had staged everything to give Julian Drake the nomination, none of them could have said. Whatever the cause, the effect was all that any of them could have wanted. The other candidates had been all but forgotten. What no one could have predicted twenty-four hours ago had now taken on an air of inevitability, as if Julian Drake had been the only candidate they had ever really wanted. Louis Matson enjoyed every minute of it.

"Strange, isn't it? - How much better you sometimes feel after you have been ill than you did before!" he said, shaking his head at the wonder of it. "Almost as if," he added with a puckish grin, "you had never been sick at all!"

Not everyone understood what he meant; there were some delegates too new to politics to see everything through the eyes of a cynic, or the eyes of wisdom and experience, but there was not anyone who did not sense the eager confidence, the sheer excitement, with which Louis Matson spoke to them, the feeling that something of importance had happened and that they were part of it, part of something, moreover, that was just beginning.

"There is one more thing that needs to be done. Last night we nominated Julian Drake for the presidency. He has decided that because he had not been a candidate, because he had not run in any of the primaries, because he had not campaigned for the job, he should not dictate to the convention who the vice-presidential nominee should be. I understand his reason for doing this. I also understand that the best way to show that what we did last night we would do again, that if we now had a roll call vote the outcome would be the same, that we would choose Julian Drake over anyone else whose name was put in nomination, is to choose someone to run with him who also did not seek the office, someone who knows what it means to govern. The convention has been thrown open; you may vote for anyone you choose. The only vote I control is my own. I am going to use it to vote for the governor of Ohio." And then he added, with a look that seemed to cast doubt on the trustworthiness of anyone else who might be seeking the office, "Someone I know will always support the president he is elected to serve."

The reporters who were there began to shout questions. Matson flashed a smile at a few congressmen sitting among the delegates in the first few rows and then left through a back entrance, got on a service elevator and rode up to the chairman's suite on the top floor where a tumultuous meeting was already underway.

They were all there, the same wealthy power brokers who had been there two days before, the money people, the ones who had come to nominate someone who thought that government best that governed least, the ones who thought that money bought not just access but control. The only two people absent were the representatives of what a day earlier had been the leading candidates for the nomination. They had not been invited. The chairman, Reece Davis, was sitting at the head of the long conference table, fidgeting with his manicured hands, tapping his Gucci clad feet, seeming lost and confused under the baleful looks of a dozen pair of angry, unhappy eyes.

"What the hell are we supposed to do now?" wondered Conrad Wilson. "I'm the one who insisted that, given all we've done, all the money we've spent, we at least be informed what Matson was going to say in that speech of his. And now - this! We don't know anything about this guy, we...."

He did not finish. Louis Matson had come in, silent and, for a moment, unobserved.

"It was the greatest goddamn speech you ever heard, Conrad," growled Matson. "What the hell is your complaint? - That we finally have a candidate who deserves the office?" he asked, a corrosive grin on his sagging mouth and what seemed a warning in his eyes.

Davis started to say something, invite him to take a seat, something civil, polite, an attempt to give at least the appearance of being in charge. Matson ignored him. Patting the shoulder of each of those he passed, as if he had come to give them solace and support, he made his way to the empty chair at the opposite end of the table. Facing the window with its view of downtown and the river in the distance, he sat sideways, leaning on his left elbow. Tugging his tie into place, he pulled down the french cuffs on his shirt, and then slowly and quite on purpose stroked his chin as he turned his head and looked at each of their puzzled faces. Then he turned back to Conrad Wilson.

"You were saying?"

Wilson was in his early sixties, with gray hair cut close to disguise how far back his hairline had receded. He seldom moved when he spoke; he never gestured with his hands, his face was almost always a blank mask. It was a conscious effect, a way to keep anyone from knowing, or even guessing, what he really thought. He often held his chin with his forefinger and his thumb and spread the other three fingers in front of his narrow mouth. He was very good at cards, and very good at making money. It was only when it came to politics that he allowed his emotions to show, and then, when he found he was not in control, that he could not be in control, he forgot all the practiced lessons of restraint and his outbursts could be volcanic.

"You were saying?" repeated Matson, wearing a tight smile Machiavelli would have envied, the kind you only see when the game is over and you have lost.

"You lied to us!" screamed Wilson, his neck now seeming two sizes too large for his shirt. "You came to us, asked our support for whoever became the nominee, promised you would stay neutral, promised -"

"I didn't promise a damn thing. I told you I had only my own vote, and I didn't even use that. I didn't break any promises; I came here to give a speech. I couldn't do it. Julian Drake took my place, and after that....You were there, you saw what happened."

"I saw you take over the convention, change the rules, hand the nomination to someone we don't know a damn thing about!"

Matson gave him a strange, searching look. "In addition to everything else, you're a member of the New York delegation. What did you do, did you protest....?" He looked all around the table. "Did any of you object, any of you raise your voices against what the convention was doing, responding to what - tell me if you don't agree - was the greatest speech any of us has ever heard? Is there anyone here who honestly believes that anyone else we could have nominated would be a better president?"

There was a long, awkward silence.

"Well? Anyone?" asked Matson, daring them to say what was on their minds.

"You came to us - remember? You asked us to agree in advance to support whoever won the nomination," said Rufus Chambers who controlled a dozen different companies doing business around the world. "I asked what guarantee we had that if it was someone other than the candidates we supported - candidates who were known to us, candidates we had helped along the way - it would be someone we could trust."

He was staring at Matson through small, hopeless eyes. With round sloping shoulders and a mouth like a parrot's beak, he had the friendless look of someone absorbed in some private care of his own. He was always worried.

"You're right, what you said about that speech," continued Chambers; "but you're wrong about what it means. Don't misunderstand. It was a great speech - the way he delivered it; the immediate effect it had. If he had said two plus two is five, that the world is really flat - he could have said anything - and we would all have believed him, believed him until we recovered our senses and freed ourselves from the spell he casts."

Chambers looked around the room. Everyone was listening; everyone agreed.

"I read the speech this morning. All of you should do it. He can speak, he can write - even when I was reading it, alone in my room, the words, the language, catches hold of you, carries you along. But then you start thinking about what he is really saying. It is all about going back, recapturing the past, remembering what conservatism used to mean. It's the stuff for college seminars, what some people write books about. I know what it means to be a conservative: it means keeping government out of the way; it means free enterprise, competition; it means putting a stop to every attempt to penalize success. And now, thanks to you, we have a candidate who wants to do - what, exactly? Tax the hell out of us so everyone who does not want to pay for college can go at our expense! Read the speech, read it carefully. Everyone has a right to serve in the armed forces! Everyone. Sounds great. Very patriotic. But then, four years later, the bill comes due. And forget what is going to happen to the military, its ability to function, to do what we spend hundreds of billions of our money on each year, when you suddenly have a few million more recruits! No, this is a disaster! We came here to nominate someone we could trust and we nominate instead someone who thinks government can solve all our problems. I might as well become a Democrat!"

"Perhaps you should," said a voice that everyone now immediately recognized. Julian Drake was standing just inside the door.

It is one thing to vent your frustration in a private gathering of like-minded friends and acquaintances; it is something else again to show the same anger, or the same blunt confidence, in the presence of the person who is the object of your wrath, especially when that person is now quite possibly the next president of the United States. Without another word, Julian moved toward the head of the table where the chairman sat. Davis was on his feet, holding the chair. Dressed in a gray suit, white shirt and gray tie, Julian sat straight, one leg crossed over the other. He looked directly down the table at Rufus Chambers.

"You have to understand," began Chambers, tapping his fingers together, as if to underscore the serious thought he had given to their predicament, "that this is nothing personal. It's just that you were not what we expected."

Julian's eyes flew open, a smile darted across his mouth.

"It wasn't what I was expecting, either," he said in a self-deprecating tone that started to put everyone at ease. But he had not come to make them feel comfortable. “Don’t deceive yourselves. The speech I gave last night is only just the beginning. I did not come here as a candidate - that does not mean I’m going to leave here feeling grateful, much less indebted, for the nomination. I have the luxury of not owing anything to anyone, a luxury I am not going to give up. We can talk about that later. I came because Louis asked me if I would,” he said, suggesting that he otherwise might not have come at all. “If you have any questions, I’ll be glad to try to answer them.”

A woman laughed. “We’re sitting here while everyone else is trying to decide who they want for vice-president; sitting here, the financial backbone of the party, listening to you tell us that you don’t owe anything to anyone,” said Angela Murray in a waspish voice.

“And the question…?”

“The question is do you have any idea how much it costs to run a national campaign, a general election campaign for the presidency? Where do you think that money is going to come from, if not from us and the people who listen to us? - Small contributions of a hundred dollars or less from millions of right thinking, civic minded citizens? You don’t think you owe anything to anyone. Maybe not yet,” she remarked, her strident eyes shining. She spoke as if she were holding a pointer to a list of all the things to which everyone, whether they liked it or not, would have to agree.

Julian rested his left elbow on the arm of the chair and, holding two fingers against his temple, stretched his thumb beneath the line of his chin. He fixed her with a look of silk and steel.

“You seem to forget that there is a public system.”

She laughed even louder, a corrosive, patronizing laugh. The smile on Julian’s face went deeper into his eyes.

“The other side will never do that. Obama didn’t do it, which is how he won. You would be outspent by two or three billion, when you add everything up.”

“I won’t be outspent if I don’t spend anything,” he said in a strange, cryptic way, almost as if he were speaking only to himself. “You may be right,” he said, louder and more directly, “but money isn’t as important in a presidential race as it is in other contests.”

This was a thought none of the others in the room had ever had, and, for that reason, only deepened their suspicion that Julian Drake, for all his brilliance, was politically naive.

"You weren't a candidate; you didn't run a campaign. You have no organization, no one who works for you. We can help with that. We have the money; we have the people. We know everyone involved in all the other campaigns, all the major candidates who were trying to win the nomination. They're all available now. All you have to do is choose who you want. This is a major undertaking, something that requires hundreds, thousands, of people. You need a polling operation, media consultants, people who buy television time, people to do issue research, opposition research. You need someone to manage your campaign. You need -"

Julian held up his hand. "I'm sure that is exactly what I would do - if I had come here as a candidate, if I had won the nomination after a long campaign. That isn't what I am going to do now."

"But, you don't understand; you have to -"

Julian threw back his head and laughed, a deep full-throated laugh that enveloped the room, a laugh that seemed to carry a meaning no one could quite grasp.

"No, you don't understand. It's what I have been trying to tell you, the reason there isn't any need for money; the reason why I don't have to ask any of you for anything; the reason why, if I win the office, if I become president, I won't be under any obligation to you or anyone else. There isn't going to be a campaign; at least nothing like what everyone has come to expect. Things are going to be different, different from what they have been before," he added as he rose from his chair. "More than any of you can yet imagine."

CHAPTER TWELVE

Julian held his jacket tight around his throat and pointed to a gnarled wind bent cypress at the edge of the rocky cliff where a gray eagle had just swooped down to rest its wings from the harsh, snapping wind. A hundred feet below, the white surf beat with deafening repetitive noise against the steep-sided cove.

"Be grateful, the sun is out. It's the wind here doesn't let you forget the sea, that you have come to the end of the country, that there isn't anywhere left to go." He turned to Ismael Cooper who was holding his hand on his forehead to keep his hair from lashing his eyes. "Too loud to talk, isn't it?" he shouted, with an easy, careless laugh. He looked up at the high arching sky and then out to the thin flat line that divided the earth from the heavens in two only slightly different shades of blue. "I know," he said, in a voice tinged with regret, "we have to get back."

They walked along a narrow footpath through deep red ice plants that covered the sloping hillside, back up to Julian Drake's Big Sur home. Ismael waited in the living room, glancing idly at the bookshelves towering up to the two-story ceiling and the thick glass windows on the other side with their endless view of the Pacific. He had been here, along with Julian, for three days, three days in which they were supposed to be planning the fall campaign. It seemed now, as he ran his hand along a long row of books, the collected works of an author whose name seemed vaguely familiar but he had never read, that they had talked about almost everything else. Every time he tried to raise the issue, to ask what Julian thought they should do, Julian would say something about how that was no doubt important, and then start talking about something else.

"You don't seem to think this is real," he remarked, when Julian came into the room carrying two cups of hot coffee.

"Real?" he asked, with a slightly puzzled expression. He sat down in the chair he always used, heavily cushioned with thick round arms, and threw his legs up on the ottoman in front. There were three or four dog-eared books on the lamp table next to him.

"That you're a candidate, that you're running for president, that you don't have a campaign, that you haven't even decided who you want to run it!"

Julian held the cup of coffee in both hands, just below his mouth, warming himself from its heat. His eyes brightened and danced with amusement.

"We're not going to have a campaign. We don't need one," he said before Ismael could object. "We already have one."

"We already have…?"

"Our good and loyal friend, Reece Davis. What is his job supposed to be, if it isn't to elect Republicans to office?"

"There is a difference between a party organization and a candidate's own campaign," explained Ismael, wondering why he had to.

"I know that, but Davis doesn't. It's all taken care of. I talked to him before we left Cleveland."

"You didn't tell me you had talked to him," said Ismael, and then immediately began to apologize. "I"m sorry; it's really not my place to…."

"But it is…your place. Listen to me. You're the only person I can really talk to. Louis has other things to do. He's majority leader. He is going to have enough on his hands. And he won't have you to help him anymore. If I win this thing, I'll need you to be chief of staff. You wouldn't mind doing that, would you?"

"No, of course I wouldn't mind. I'd be honored," replied Ismael, with a sense of gratitude, but also a kind of foreboding. He knew enough about politics and government, enough about the way Washington worked, not to think that the presidency of Julian Drake would represent anything other than a seismic shift of power, a change of values that however much some might applaud, other would consider an attack on everything they believed.

"What usually happens after someone gets the nomination? - He replaces the party chairman with someone who will be loyal only to him. I told Davis I wanted him to stay on." Julian bent his head to the side and with his index finger began to trace a circle in the air. "He tried to hide his surprise, his astonishment. He was certain it was the end of his career, that everyone hated him and would never trust him again. He was the one who made the decision to ask Louis to chair the convention and give the keynote address. I thanked him for it, told him that even if the nomination had gone to one of those who came into the convention favored to win, it had taken courage to invite Louis, that it showed a real determination to broaden the appeal of the party; that he understood, as not many others did, that you can't win the presidency if you ignore everyone except a small minority that think you can solve all our problems by refusing to do anything about them. I told him that I was not about to run the same kind of campaign that everyone else had run, that I would decide myself what I was going to say and where I was going to say it, but that for the rest of it, I didn't think there should be two separate organizations. I told him," he added, with one last circle of his finger, "that it was his campaign, that he was in charge."

Julian looked at Ismael for a long moment. A thin smile slid along his lips.

"He thinks he owes me everything now. He thought he had come to witness his own execution; he left thinking that if he did everything right he might just live forever. All I have to do is think about what needs to be said and the best way to do it. If you haven't noticed, that is what we have been doing for the last three days, going over all these position papers you brought from Washington, tearing them all apart, going back to basics, trying to figure out where things started to go wrong. That's what I meant when I said you're the only one I can talk to - everyone else would think I was crazy, jumping around the way I do from one thing to another without any obvious connection between them. It's the way I work, the way things move through my head. It's only when I have to write things down on paper - that speech, for example - that everything starts to fall into place."

Julian put the cup of coffee on the table next to him and got up from the chair. He walked to the far end of the room and with his back to Ismael pulled down a thick book from a set of twenty maroon leather volumes on the second shelf from the top. Thumbing the pages until he found what he was looking for, he turned halfway round to look at Ismael and then read a few lines, but silently, to himself.

"Macaulay," he explained. "The speech he gave in the British Parliament on the last reading of the Reform Bill of 1832. No one reads Macaulay anymore; no one reads anything worth reading anymore. But Macaulay taught me how to speak. Why not? It's how Churchill learned. The reason I looked at it just now was to remind myself how much I had stolen, what I had taken from his peroration, when I was writing the close of the speech I wrote for Louis, the one I gave, the one that seems to have caused me all this trouble," he added with a glance full of guile and mischief. "Not the words; I didn't borrow any of them. No, the rhythm, the pace, the way that several phrases, several sentences, each begin the same way, the rhythmic repetition that, if you do it right, do it with the breathless speed with which Macaulay is supposed to have spoken, you turn prose into poetry, the kind of poetry that not only makes you listen, but makes it almost impossible to forget. Macaulay's speech, the way he ended it, those last few paragraphs - every time I read it my pulse begins to race. It becomes a part of you, something that reminds you what speech, human speech, can do."

Putting the volume back in its place, Julian began to pace back and forth, talking to himself in short bursts of incoherence, words that were not words at all, sounds that had no meaning. The quick abbreviations of thought followed so fast upon one another that the words by which to express them seemed to give only partial voice to what had already been relegated to an already forgotten past. He suddenly stopped in his tracks and stared at Ismael with such a terrific sense of accomplishment that Ismael was too embarrassed to even start to think of a reply, had he thought something in Julian's strange, disordered look required one.

"I used to talk to Louis about this. He's old enough to remember when speech was a power. He once told me, and I never forgot it, that the Second World War never would have been won without the ability Churchill and FDR had to speak. There was a difference between them and it fascinated Louis. It seemed to explain the decline he saw happening. Churchill started out before the radio, before your voice could be broadcast into millions of homes, before you had to make everything simple and easy to understand. He began speaking in Parliament when most members were educated in the classics and had time to read, when a major speech might last for three or four hours, when no one read the speech they were giving but had to speak spontaneously, or, as in Churchill's case, from memory. FDR, on the other hand, used the radio, spoke into a microphone from a room somewhere, talking as if he were having a conversation at the dinner table. He could give a speech in front of a large audience, or deliver a message to Congress, as he did that day the United States declared war on Japan, but they were all, by an earlier standard, short performances. And now, with television and the internet, three straight sentences are considered too long to cover on the news."

Julian stopped talking. Watching out the window the ocean shimmer bright silver in the long light of the afternoon, he became pensive and withdrawn. His mood changed from the bright excitement of the eager recitation of what he had once learned to a solemn sense of responsibility, the sudden awareness of a burden he could not longer ignore. He looked at Ismael as if he were sure he understood.

"What we do the next two and a half months will allow us to govern because there won't be any mistake about what it is I mean to achieve."

Julian stared into the middle distance, trying to capture and clarify the thought racing through his mind. He rolled his shoulders forward, crossed his arms and for a moment looked down at his shoes.

"You can't always tell the truth," he said, looking up; "not the whole truth, anyway. I said that everyone should be allowed to serve their country. I said it, and I believe it, and I am going to repeat it so often there won't be any doubt that, if I am elected, it is exactly what I am going to do. But it isn't because we need a larger army, and it isn't because it is a way to make it possible for more people to go to college. That is what everyone will concentrate on: how we are going to trade four years of service for four years of college. The truth is we would be better off if there were fewer people going to college. You know what I mean," he said when Ismael looked startled. "A kid who graduates from high school in France or Germany knows more, is taught more, than most of the kids who graduate from college here. Look at what used to be the high school curriculum a hundred years ago. My point is that we ought to be doing something about high school education. My point," he went on in a quieter, more reflective voice, "is that we are wasting too much time. Instead of four years of college, two years of technical training would be better for those who want to acquire the specific skills they need for the kind of jobs they want. In Italy, if you want to be a doctor or a lawyer, you go to medical school or law school right out of high school. College isn't the reason I want to bring into the armed forces as many children of the poor and disadvantaged as we can. If we have them for four years, they can be given the kind of education everyone should have: four years of discipline and training, four years part of an organization that teaches that nothing is more important than the country they are sworn to defend. And they will be better at it the more they know about the history and the form of government they are honor bound to protect. Four years to teach them that what they do is a lot more important than mindless pleasures and making money. And when they do go to college, they won't be going to have a good time; they will, at least some of them, go to improve their minds. It is the only chance we have."

"The only chance? I'm not sure I…?"

"To change what we have done to ourselves, become addicts to the need for constant contact, constant attention, the need to have something new to see or hear every few seconds, prisoners to the shifting images on a screen. Slavery used to mean forcible compulsion, physical constraint, something done against our will. Slavery now comes through our own choice, slaves to what everyone around us, all those voices on television and in cyberspace are constantly telling us what we want and what we should believe. But four years without that kind of self-indulgence, four years of what we used to understand by education, and we might have a generation that starts to remember what freedom was supposed to mean. But that is a reason that has to stay hidden. It is enough to talk about the need to give everyone, the children of the poor equally with the children of the rich, something like an equal chance," remarked Julian, pausing as if to consider the sound of a phrase he might later want to use.

"We have to go back tomorrow," Ismael reminded him. "We've spent three days here. Everyone is expecting some kind of announcement, what you intend to do, what kind of campaign there is going to be, who is going to run it - that kind of thing."

"I don't suppose we could just say I've decided to campaign the old-fashioned way, when presidential candidates sat on their front porch at home and talked to any reporter who happened to come by?"

"You could try that, but there would be at least a thousand trucks and cars blocking Highway 1 all the way back to Carmel, and probably a few dozen helicopters flying by to get pictures."

"I know," said Julian, glancing at the bookshelves and the glass walls and the two story stone fireplace. "If I'm elected, I'll never see this place again."

"You can always come out whenever...."

"What you said just now: the place would be overrun. It isn't as private, as secluded as it used to be, with all the tourists who think they have to see Big Sur, but....No, I couldn't do that. And besides, there wouldn't be time. There is too much to do, and I've never really liked vacations. But your question was what should we announce. Nothing. Just say we're ready. Let everyone figure out for themselves what we're doing, find out on their own that this isn't going to be like anything they have seen before. We have a press conference in D.C. day after tomorrow. That will give everyone a start."

When they arrived in Washington late the next afternoon, Ismael went directly to Capitol Hill. Louis Matson wanted to know everything that had happened.

"Happened?" laughed Ismael. "Nothing happened. We didn't go anywhere; we didn't do anything. The only people we ever saw were the secret service agents who were up on the road covering the place. Happened? Nothing at all, except a one-man tutorial on American history and politics that I could have spent three years in graduate school and never learned. I went out there to brief him, bring him up to date on the major issues in front of Congress. He doesn't have a television set, he doesn't own a computer, and as I told you the first time I went out there, he reads the papers - the Sunday Times - maybe once a month. And every time, as soon as I started talking, before I had two sentences out of my mouth, he would stop me with a wave of his hand, a look, and then proceed to give me his own analysis, the way he saw both sides of the question, whatever the question was. And each time he did it, I suddenly understood that I had not understood anything about it before."

Matson clasped his hands together behind his neck and with a knowing smile said he was not the least surprised.

"But what you did was still important. Even if he only listened to a few sentences, that would have given him everything he needed to grasp the thinking, the nature of the disagreement, of what has been going on here. What else? What else did he say? What decisions has he made. I know he wants you to be his chief of staff. I hope you said you'd do it."

"He talked to you about that?"

"Julian may be a lot younger, but if anything he's more old school than I am. He would not have asked you without first asking me if I would agree to let you go. Hell, I told him he'd be doing me a favor; I'd been trying to get rid of you for years," he growled, his chest heaving with laughter. "And then I had to admit - reluctantly, you understand - that I could not think of anyone better suited for the job. You did say yes, didn't you?" he asked, suddenly aware of the troubled look on Ismael's round, smooth face.

"I couldn't say no," replied Ismael, with a vanishing smile of no apparent enthusiasm. "How could I? I wanted to say yes, and I said yes, but the moment I said it I began to wonder, not if I would come to regret it, but if I would survive it. Chief of staff? I'm not even sure there will be a staff. He doesn't seem to think he really needs one. He has the idea that the White House is just another out of control bureaucracy, too many people doing too many things that aren't necessary. He likes to talk about Lincoln, how he fought and won the Civil War with two assistants and a half dozen cabinet secretaries. He talks about -"

"How Churchill wrote every word he ever spoke, and almost every directive issued under his own name. He's right. Hell, Harry Truman had a staff you could count on your fingers." Matson became serious. "With you as chief of staff, Julian just might be able to do it, have a White House that really works, instead of creating more problems than it solves. There is something else, though, isn't there, something that is bothering you? It isn't because you think there would be too much work; you've never been afraid of that."

Ismael slouched cross-legged in the upholstered chair, looking straight at Louis Matson. "It isn't that I'm envious; it isn't that I wonder what might have happened if I had not lost my seat in Congress and had one day been elected to the Senate. It is none of that. It is like trying to train with a runner no one can beat: you know you will never be able to keep up. The first night I was there, I could not sleep. After everything that had happened at the convention, all the excitement, all the running around, all the last-minute arrangements that had to be made, I thought I would sleep like a dead man, but I just lay there, everything that had happened running through my mind. Finally, about three o'clock in the morning I got up. I thought I might as well get something to read. Julian was already up. He had gone to sleep a little after midnight, and now, three hours later, he was at his desk, studying."

"Studying? Some of the stuff you brought for him to read?"

"No; he was reading Plato, trying, as he put it, to learn the secret."

"The secret?" asked Matson, leaning forward, more amused than surprised at what Ismael was reporting.

"The order of the world, and man's place in it."

"Did you really think Julian would be reading some mystery novel?"

"It isn't that. It isn't even that he was reading Plato. But here you have someone who has just been nominated for the most powerful office in the world, and he still thinks nothing more important than what he can learn from ancient dialogues written twenty-five hundred years ago. He said he first learned it from his father, and that it was the reason why his father gave him the name he had."

"His father named him Julian because of something Plato wrote?"

"I don't know. He wouldn't say more than that, and he seemed a little upset with himself for telling me even that much. It's strange, though, when you think about it. We've had presidents who have gotten in trouble because of women, and because of money, some have been guilty of crime and corruption, but we have never had one raise suspicion because he thinks studying the classics as important as affairs of state."

Matson started to acknowledge the point, but laughed instead.

"I just remembered something Kennedy said. He wrote it in his own hand on the typed text of the remarks he made at a White House dinner for all the living American Nobel Prize winners: 'There hasn't been this much intelligence gathered in a single room of the White House since Thomas Jefferson dined here alone.' And now, with any luck, we'll have Julian." He glanced at his watch. "Let's have dinner together. Then you can get over to the hotel to get ready for the press conference. I'll go home and watch it on television. Whose idea was it - yours or his - to hold it live?"

Ismael was on his feet. His gaze wandered to the white marble fireplace and the painting of the White House on fire in the War of 1812.

"Who else? Who but Julian would have insisted on that; who else but Julian would have thought it through, understood that if just one network agreed, all the others would have to go along?"

"Who did he talk to about it?"

"No one. He just put out a statement that he was going into seclusion for a few days and that he would be available for a live press conference at the Hay-Adams Hotel at six p.m. Everyone in America wants to see him; what reporter, what network, isn't going to show up?"

"It will be interesting to see who asks the toughest questions," remarked Matson, "the liberals who don't know what to make of him, or the conservatives, most of whom still can't believe he's the nominee." His expression became grim, defiant, and close to anger as he thought about what he had just said. "Damn it all to hell, do whatever you have to do, play every card we have. Don't let anything get started; don't let anyone start taking shots at Julian. Put the word out. Make all those know-nothings understand that Julian is no newcomer to the game, that he won't forget anything . Make it simple: those who help will be glad they did; those who don't will be destroyed. That should give the bastards pause."

Ismael remembered this last remark later that evening outside the entrance to the Hay-Adams Hotel when he suddenly found himself face to face with Conrad Wilson. Wilson was not happy.

"I've been waiting for you," announced Wilson with the impatience of someone used to having people wait for him. "I've called every day, I…."

"I've been out of town," Ismael started to explain. He looked around, worried that among the crush of reporters going inside he might be recognized and forced to answer some questions on his own. "And I can't talk right now. Julian is…."

"I know why everyone is here," replied Wilson, irritably, as they were both swept inside by the crowd surging through the open doors.

Ismael tried to be civil as Wilson insisted on following him down a side corridor that led to the front of the ballroom where the press conference was being held. When they reached the entrance, Wilson slammed his hand on the door.

"Just wait a goddamn minute!"

"Look, Mr. Wilson, I have things I have to do. I'm sorry I wasn't available to take your calls. I wasn't available to take calls from anyone. Why don't we get together in the morning; we can talk then."

"This can't wait. It's too important!" He looked both ways down the narrow empty hallway. "We've made certain decisions, the group of us, the ones - you were there the first time - that met with Matson, and then, later, after he had the nomination, with Drake. We just want him to know that we didn't mean anything by it. Some of what got said - some of what I said - was just our frustration, our surprise, that we didn't know anything about what was going on. We came there with certain expectations, and then we end up with a candidate about whom we didn't know anything. We didn't -"

"It's all right," said Ismael. "Don't give it another thought. Julian didn't take it personally. I've just spent the last four days with him. The subject never came up."

There was a double meaning in this, neither of which was lost on Wilson. He took a step back, studying Ismael with the kind of quiet anger that gives a real, if a transitive, pleasure to the one feeling it.

"It's up to him if he wants to ignore us; it's up to him if he wants to lose." The anger, once given expression, vanished from his face. He shook his head, not so much to apologize as to condemn the failure to control his own emotions. "That wasn't fair; it wasn't what I came to say. We've known each other for a long time. You know how much respect I have for Louis.

We don't always agree, but he's never lied to me, and I've never lied to him. What Louis needs to know - what the candidate needs to know - is that I managed to keep them all together. Rufus Chambers was the toughest to convince - he still thinks Drake's speech represents a direct attack on what we stand for - but everyone agrees that Drake is better than the alternative, that woman they have on the other side. We'll agree to spend whatever it takes - the independent organizations are already in place. All we need are some assurances."

"Assurances?" asked Ismael, his hand on the door. "I can't speak for Julian."

"All he has to do is give us some assurance that whatever changes he wants to make - whatever he says in public - he won't make any drastic changes in tax rates, he won't make it any more difficult for us to do business than it already is."

"I can't speak for Julian, but I know what he would say, the same thing I think he told you before, that -"

"I know what he said before!" Wilson fairly shouted. He grabbed Ismael by the arm. "But you tell him from us that he can't get elected without our help, and that even if he could he never could get anything through Congress if we oppose it. Tell him we can be the best allies he could ever have, or the worst…." The warning in his eyes finished the sentence. "Call me when you want to talk," he added cooly, and then turned and walked away.

The press conference began right on time, the exact moment the major news networks came on the air. Julian moved quickly from a side door, bounded up two steps to the raised platform and asked for questions while he was still adjusting the microphone on the podium.

"You won the Republican nomination, the convention chose the governor of Ohio as your running mate, and then you disappeared. Where have you been, what have you been doing, for the last week?"

"Sleeping," Julian shot back with a quick, irreverent grin that on the instant created a mood, an understanding, as it were, that nothing was off limits.

"Sleeping?" a voice yelled from somewhere in the back. "With who?"

"With whom!" Julian corrected to the delighted roar of hundreds of reporters. He pointed to a woman wearing thick glasses in the third row, a print journalist whom he remembered from his years in Congress. He glanced past her. "I won't have to worry about Jean McGregor's grammar," he explained.

She was on her feet, with a rakish smile all her own.

"With whom have you spent the better part of the last week? Was it, as we heard, Louis Matson's chief of staff, Ismael Cooper, planning the campaign?"

"Yes. Ismael and I spent a quiet few days at my home in California. And, yes, part of the time we discussed the campaign, although more about what we were not going to do than what we were."

Every hand in the room shot up; everyone wanted to know what he meant. Julian kept his eyes on Jean McGregor. He shoved his hands into the coat pockets of his dark, blue striped suit, and bent his head slightly to the side, the way he often did when he was about to say something he considered especially important.

"There isn't going to be a campaign in what has become the usual sense of the word. The party organization, under Reece Davis - whom I have asked to continue as chairman - will register voters, get voters to the polls, the sort of thing political parties have always done. But we're not going to do television and radio commercials, we're not going to advertise on the internet. I am not going to insult the American public by a thirty-second appeal to what they might feel. I am going to give speeches, and, if you like, I will have a press conference each week, conducted live, with no limit on the kind of questions you ask, and," he added with a significant glance, "no limit on the answers I give."

The press did not quite understand, or rather, they did not think he understood what he was saying.

"You're going to buy large blocks of time - ten, fifteen, minutes - and try to speak directly to the American people?" asked a television reporter who could barely keep from laughing.

"We're not buying any time, none whatsoever. I'll let all of you decide if the speech I am giving, or the press conference, is as much worth covering as a traffic accident somewhere."

"But the Democrats are already running commercials. How do you expect to compete - how do you expect to reply - if you don't run any of your own?" Julian nodded that he grasped the significance of what she said, grasped it and rejected it.

"It seems to me that a candidate for the presidency has an obligation to let everyone know what he, or she, thinks important; not just what position he has on various issues, but the governing principle that guides his conduct and his thought. One of the greatest dangers we face is something that most of us think not a danger, but a privilege and even a right: the way we entertain ourselves, the way others entertain us, with short, abbreviated images on electronic media that have taken the place of the written word. We don't read anymore; we watch, we listen, to a thousand different statements and think we have listened to everything there is to say on a subject. We have forgotten what it means to read and reason. Let me give you just one example: what we now call presidential debates. What are they but two hours of what, for all intents and purposes, are press conferences for two candidates. What are the rules? - Each candidate gets two minutes to answer a question about what should be the foreign policy of the United States toward China, toward Russia, toward the Middle East. The other candidate gets sixty seconds to reply. If that is a debate, what would you call what Lincoln and Douglas were doing in 1858 when they met seven times, each time in front of several thousand people who somehow managed to pay attention when the first candidate spoke for an hour, the other one spoke for an hour and a half, and the first one then had half an hour for rebuttal? We can now communicate instantaneously with anyone anywhere in the world. The price we have paid for this, for the technology that makes it possible, is that we have forgotten how to speak, or even how to listen. And so we watch the thirty-second commercials of candidates and think they have told us all we need to know. If the other side wants to keep doing this, that is their affair; but if that is the only way you can win, it is a little difficult to see why anyone would want you to."

There was a stunned silence. For a moment, no one knew what to ask. Finally, a network commentator, known to millions for his investigative reporting, stepped forward.

"You say you're not going to spend money on television commercials; you talk about the need to discuss things at greater length and in greater detail. Isn't it a fact, Congressman Drake, that the night after you won the nomination you met privately with some of the biggest contributors to conservative causes, a group that included Rufus Chambers and Conrad Wilson, both of whom just a few months ago were talking about spending more than a billion dollars if they had to, to elect a Republican?"

Everyone with a notebook began to scribble. The television cameras bore in for what seemed certain to be a pivotal moment. The candidate who had just announced a new kind of campaign had now been accused of still playing by the old rules, and, as a result, something worse: rank hypocrisy.

Julian did not hesitate, and in fact seemed to welcome it.

"Yes, I did. They wanted certain assurances; they wanted, if I understood what they were saying, an agreement that I would not really pursue what I said ought to be done in the speech I gave. I told them that the great advantage in getting the nomination the way I did was that I did not owe anything to anyone, and that whatever they thought they would be doing in the general election they would not be doing it for me. They did not all seem terribly happy about this. One of them even suggested he might just as well become a Democrat. I suggested he probably should. Next question?"

He started to call on someone else, but changed his mind and turned back to the reporter he had just answered.

"What you would really like to know is whether, despite that, those same people are going to help me; what you would really like to know is whether, operating as an independent political action committee, they will be attacking the opposition and telling everyone why they should vote for me instead. I have no way of stopping them, or anyone else, from doing whatever they want to do. All I can tell you is that anyone who does anything like that will never have a chance to talk to me if I'm elected. This has all gone too far; it has to stop. I'm not asking for financial contributions, and anyone who sends one will have it returned - or better yet, donated to a good cause: the Red Cross, or a home for retired journalists - I don't care."

"Then you're taking public financing? You'll be the only one to do so."

Julian's blue eyes flashed with the knowing confidence of the future foretold, the reaction he was sure to get with the single sentence he was about to utter.

"I'm not taking any money, public or private. Why do I need money?" he asked to their complete confusion. "Ismael Cooper over there," he said, point to Louis Matson's well-known chief of staff leaning against the wall on the far side of the room, "can arrange everything that is needed, and he doesn't seem to mind that he isn't going to get paid."

Aware that every eye was on him, Ismael raised his hands in mock protest. Julian had said nothing to him about this, but Julian was right: he not only did not mind, he felt strangely liberated.

"Politics," continued Julian with a chuckle, "like poverty, can be honorable, as long as you don't let it become a permanent condition. What do we need money for?" he asked, daring a response. "Are you going to stop reporting, stop asking questions, because the only time you'll see me on television is when I am giving a speech somewhere or when, like this evening, we share the stage together? But enough about how someone campaigns for the presidency. What do you want to know about how, if I am elected, I intend to govern?"

He searched the crowd as if he were looking for someone in particular, a suspicion that seemed confirmed when he settled on a young woman, one of the most liberal voices on cable television. Tall, thin, with boyish short hair and a ready smile, she had covered the Republican convention with a growing sense of astonishment. She liked Julian Drake more than she had liked any candidate in years, but she could not free herself from the nagging doubt that despite all his talk about a different, and older, kind of conservatism, he had some of the same backward beliefs as the reactionaries who would have burned her, a lesbian, at the stake.

"In your speech at the convention you made your opposition to gay marriage quite clear. Two questions: Do you still stand by those remarks? I ask this because, as we all know, you wrote that speech for the majority leader, not for yourself. And do you agree with the Republican platform in its opposition to abortion without exception, even the life of the mother?"

Nodding, Julian pursed his lips and looked straight at her.

"Fair question. You're right: I did write that speech for the majority leader, but I wrote it as if I were writing a speech for myself. I wrote it as a draft, a draft I assumed would probably go through a number of different revisions.

I had been asked to write a speech; I had not been told what should be in it. As to your first question, I think I have just answered it. I know you disagree. I don't mind that," he said in a kind, thoughtful voice; "I hope you don't mind it, either. We disagree. I gave my reasons. There is a difference, it seems to me, between private conduct and public custom. And while there are exceptions, it is generally a good rule that we not encourage what we could not possibly want everyone to do."

"I'm not sure I …?" she asked, seriously interested.

"If everyone engaged in same sex marriage, there wouldn't be anyone left to complain about it; there wouldn't be anyone left at all. There would not be a new generation to take the place of the old. But you also asked about abortion."

Julian looked around the room, wondering, as it seemed, how far he should go. But he was not wondering about that at all; he was thinking instead how much time had been wasted on an issue no one really understood.

"That is a long question. You want to know what I believe. The short answer is that I believe everyone is wrong. I am all in favor of a woman's right to choose. The question is how many choices does she get. She gets to choose in the first place whether she is going to have sex, she gets to choose in the second place whom she is going to have sex with, and she gets to choose in the third place whether she is going to engage in unprotected sex. Three choices before we even get to the question of abortion. There is an exception to this, of course: when she does not have any of those three choices because someone forces her against her will. There has always, as far back as you want to trace it in history and law, at least English and American law, an exception to the law against abortion for rape and incest, and to protect the life of the mother. There is an argument that is now being made that because life is a gift from God, we have no right to end a life just because that life was conceived in an act of brutal violence. An argument like that is nothing short of sacrilege. If life is a gift of God, do these people really believe that God would bestow this gift through the awful violence of rape? Is a rapist now to be seen as a messenger of the Almighty? Do they believe this is the way God gives life? - By forcing it on those who would prefer that conception come through an act not of violence but of love? So, no, I don't agree; there have to be exceptions.

"But that still doesn't answer your question. You want my view on abortion, whether it should be legal or a crime. My own view is that it should not be an issue. I don't think we should even talk about it. This, again, is a question that should be left private. It should not be made unlawful, the way a number of self-styled conservatives insist it should. But neither should it be treated as some kind of right, something without consequence. Leave the question to the woman who has to make that decision. There really is no reasonable alternative. But treat it with the solemn respect it deserves. The difference in all this is the question of whether we think everyone has a right to everything they feel like doing, or whether we think there is something more important, something worth the kind of sacrifice and effort I talked about before. The question, really, is whether we are going to be a frivolous, or a serious, people."

CHAPTER THIRTEEN

Rachel Good tried to learn everything she could about Julian Drake and his sudden rise to national prominence. She read everything she could find, all the coverage in the local papers when he first ran for Congress, the verbatim reports in the Congressional Record of the speeches he had given on the floor of the House, the interviews, the articles - whatever had been written about him while he served. Nothing she read told her what she wanted to know. There was something missing, something she did not understand, and so she flew out to Michigan, and in the small town a few miles out of Ann Arbor where Julian had grown up, talked to as many of his old friends as she could find. They all said pretty much the same thing. Julian was smart, well-liked, the quarterback on the high school football team, his only ambition, so far as any of them could remember, to play football in college. She talked to his high school coach, Clarence Philips who had just that year retired.

"Julian is going to be president," said Philips, as he offered Rachel a beer.

It was a hot, humid, August day. Rachel was glad to have something to drink. They sat under a shaded canopy on the back porch. The house, small and unpretentious, was on a well-tended half acre less than a mile from the football field where on Friday nights in the fall two or three thousand students and parents would come out to cheer on the local team, however many games they might lose.

"Julian president! I wish I could tell you I knew it would happen, that he would wind up doing something like this." Tall, with long arms and long legs, a short crop of graying red hair, Philips sat with his knees spread apart, twisting back and forth the ice cold bottle he held in his large, arthritic hands, thinking back thirty years to when Julian Drake was a scrawny kid with hardly any athletic ability at all. "Damnedest thing I ever saw," he mused, and then, embarrassed, looked at the well-dressed reporter from the New York Times, wondering if he should apologize.

"Damnedest thing you ever saw," said Rachel, drawling out the phrase with a glancing smile of encouragement. "You were saying…?"

"Yeah, damnedest thing. He couldn't run. When he was a senior we let him run wind sprints with the tackles, fat kids, most of them, who couldn't run much faster than he could. And he couldn't really throw - short passes, twenty, thirty yards, but anything farther than that, he didn't have the arm. Hell," he laughed, warming to the subject, "he really couldn't do anything. Except work at it more than any player I ever had. I mean, all the time, before practice, after practice, all year, summers, too. He was never going to be fast, he was never going to be strong, but within those limits, those physical limits, of what he could do, he was - if I can put it like this - damn near perfect. I said physical limits, because what that kid could do with his brain - I guess I shouldn't call him a kid anymore, should I? He knew more about the game… .I was the coach, but I used to ask his advice, what play he thought we should call, that kind of thing. But if you want to know how smart he was…." He noticed that Rachel, after taking the first drink, had not touched her beer. "Can I get you something else? Ice tea, something?"

"No, I'm fine," replied Rachel, shaking her head as she glanced at her open notebook. "I've talked to some of his friends. They all said he wanted to play college ball, but he didn't, did he?"

Philips knitted his brow. His shoulders, almost too wide for his body, heaved up as he sighed with nostalgia at what he now remembered. He looked at Rachel as if she were the one who should know the answers.

"Maybe that's why he is going to be president: he didn't know how to do anything except aim high. He could have played in college; some small college where football isn't the most important thing. He might even have made it at a place like Eastern Michigan, or Central Michigan, second level programs but good enough to play some of the majors. One of them - I've forgotten which - offered him a scholarship. He did not have any great natural ability, but he could do enough, and he ran an offense like nothing you have ever seen - but he wasn't interested. He wanted to play at Michigan State. I think he had dreams of being the starting quarterback, taking Michigan State to the Rose Bowl." He searched the curious eyes of Rachel Good. "You're trying to understand what he was like, how he turned out the way he did. All I can tell you is that from the time he was a kid the only thing he knew to go after was the highest thing there was. He went to Michigan State on his own, tried to make it as a walk-on. And this is the interesting part: when he discovered that he wasn't good enough, that he couldn't make the team, he didn't leave, try with some other school. He stayed at Michigan State, forgot about football, became a student and a pretty damn good one from what I was told. But if you want to know what kind of student he was when he was in high school talk to Fred Chaplin. He was the principal back then. He lives out on the lake, the other side of town. I'll call him if you like, tell him you're coming."

Chaplin was waiting in the driveway when Rachel arrived. He seemed nervous; his small hooded eyes looked away each time she opened her mouth to speak.

"I don't get many visitors anymore," he said in a quiet, self-conscious voice. In his late seventies, he seemed a shell of a man, shuffling along with the help of a cane, the tired, haggard look on his pale face proof of constant, debilitating pain. Rachel felt a twinge of discomfort , sympathy, for the effort with which he lowered himself into a threadbare easy chair that through years of use had lost most of its original shape.

"Philips said you wanted to talk to me about Julian Drake."

The use of the coach's last name, the way Chaplin still thought like a school principal, struck Rachel as a little depressing. Were we all prisoners of the categories in which we found ourselves? She did not like to think so.

"Yes, Mr. Philips said you would know more than anyone what Julian Drake had been like when he was a student in your school."

"Julian Drake," said Frederick Chaplin, speaking slowly and with great precision, "was the biggest disappointment I ever had in all my years of teaching."

He looked at Rachel with new-found confidence. He had surprised her, just as he had hoped. Something close to pleasure quivered at the corners of his thin, frail mouth.

"The biggest disappointment?" Quite on purpose, Rachel tried to look even more surprised than she was. "Why? What do you mean?"

The old man tapped the fingers of his right hand on the scratched wooden arm of his chair, the same way he must have done a thousand times before, years earlier, when he was calling some wayward delinquent to account.

"What would you call it when a student with the highest I.Q. you ever tested is perfectly content to get by with what wasn't much better than a B average?"

Out through a dusty sliding glass door, beyond a paint chipped wooden railing on the deck and a broken plank walkway to a small tattered sailboat tethered to the dock, across a small wind whipped lake, Rachel watched a young family sitting on a dock of their own begin their evening meal against the glowing background of a blood red sun, and for a brief moment wondered what it would have been like to have had children of her own.

"You think he should have done better?" she asked, vaguely, her eyes still on what was taking place the other side of the lake.

"Of course he should have done better," replied Chaplin with such sudden force Rachel immediately looked back, worried for half an instant that she might be reprimanded for failing to pay attention. "The highest I.Q. we had ever recorded, one of the highest I.Q.s ever recorded anywhere in the state, if I am any judge of it. Off the charts! That good, and he does B level work!:

"Because he was lazy, or because he was bored?"

"Neither. He was not lazy; he did everything he was asked to do. Bored? No, not in the usual sense," replied Chaplin, more forthcoming, more interested, as it were, than he had appeared to be before. "It's what all these psychologists with all their testing never understand. Julian was too intelligent. That is the key: too intelligent. What makes perfect sense to you and me, what comes easy to the normal student, I think sometimes was just the opposite for him. English, for example." Using both hands, Chaplin pulled himself up until he was sitting on the very edge of the chair. He leaned forward on his cane. "I read the papers; I watch some of the news. I saw the speech he gave; I watched that press conference. Everyone says he's the greatest speaker they have ever heard. They're right; he is. But he didn't know anything about English grammar. And if that was all that was taught in high school English he might have failed the class. The way it was taught then - even in grade school - diagramming sentences, identifying parts of speech, classifying everything as a noun, a verb, an adverb, an adjective, putting everything in the right category. He could not do it. I asked him - had him in my office - asked him why he couldn't. He said it was like looking at a solid white sheet, that when he was supposed to diagram a sentence his mind went blank. That is what I mean. He could not do the normal things; but he could do what no one else could do, he could write. He did not write by what he saw, he wrote by what he heard - the sounds, the voices, in his head. His English teacher asked me if Julian was religious. She wanted to know because she had read one of his papers - something about some work of literature he had been asked to read. She said it was one of the most searching, deepest, things she had read. You wanted to know what kind of student Julian was? Not a bad student, but - and there is no question about this - the only real genius I ever met. But you wouldn't have known it from his grades," he added with a sly grin, laughing at the world and all its misconceptions.

It was, it seemed to Rachel Good as she drove along the road toward East Lansing, the story of a misguided adolescent, the beginning of a life full of uncertainty and doubt, searching for something that would remain, at least for a while, always elusive. She was not surprised to learn that he had changed his major in college at least four times.

Albert Walsh propped his feet up on the corner of his scuffed and decrepit wooden desk in his small office on the third floor of the red brick building where the faculty of the philosophy department had been quartered as long as anyone could remember. The bookcases on the wall behind him were stuffed with the works of Kant and Hegel, Spinoza, Leibniz, Plato and Aristotle,

Descartes, Locke and Rousseau. Several of them, Rachel Good noted, were in German or French; others, a few, in bilingual editions which furnished the careful reader with an English translation along with the original Greek or Latin text. It was late morning, almost noon, but it was still summer and there were no classes to teach.

Walsh was now in his early sixties, but from the look of what he was wearing, a sports jacket with the elbows worn away, a button-down white shirt frayed at the collar, and a green and blue tartan tie, pulled loose from the unbuttoned top of his shirt, he must have looked much the same way a quarter century earlier when the young Julian Drake was a student in his class. It was not just that his clothing had not changed, except for the lines that dug deep at the corners of his eyes he did not look much over forty. Painfully thin, his cheeks were drawn so tight over his cheekbones he would have looked like a living cadaver had it not been for the almost unearthly brightness in his large, deep set brown eyes. Rachel had never seen anything quite like them, the way they seemed to burn with some inner fire of their own. He was all angles and sharp corners, elbows and knees, and the long fingers of a practiced pianist. Even when he was sitting still, he seemed in constant motion. Rachel liked him enormously. Everyone did. He was known, as she later learned, by every student who had ever been in one of his classes or even, just once, listened to one of his lectures, as simply "The Great Walsh."

"When you called, you said you were doing a story on Julian. How well do you know him?" he asked with such intense interest that before she knew what she was doing she was answering his questions as if he had come to interview her.

"I first knew him when he came to Congress, almost twenty years ago. Not very well, of course; I was a reporter, he was a freshman congressman. But even then there was something about him."

"Something about him; you knew right away that he was different, that he wasn't driven by the same kind of ambition, that he wasn't one of that breed that thinks only about the next election. You knew he had a future, and, reporter or not, you hoped he would have the chance. True?" he asked, his arms flailing in the air like some demented conductor who doesn't realize the orchestra has left.

"Yes," replied Rachel, laughing at the way this strange creature held her with his eyes. "You're right; he had that effect. You knew right away you were in the presence of someone different. But what it was, I'm not sure even now I understand."

"Easy!" exclaimed The Great Walsh, slapping the palms of his hands on top of his desk. "His mind was completely empty, the only thing in it ignorance - but ignorance of a very high order!" he proclaimed in a voice crackling with an electricity that made every word seem to have a life of its own. "Ignorance, profound ignorance, is the only guarantee of wisdom." He waved his hand in the air like someone batting flies. "You don't have to know Plato, you don't have to have read Rousseau, just look around at what goes on all the time, the stupid things people do and say. Well, it helps if you know Plato, if you know Rousseau. Then at least you have read the line, a line you find in both of them, that it isn't ignorance, but error, that causes all our problems. That's what I meant. Julian never came to anything with preconceptions of his own. He was never the prisoner of all the things we get taught, all the things, if I can put it like this, everyone else believes. Do you know what this is all about?" he asked, suddenly gesturing toward the contents of his small, cramped office. "What higher education was supposed to do ? It doesn't do it anymore, but that is another story. It was supposed to repair all the damage done by lower education, to liberate the mind, as we used to say, from all the nonsense we think it necessary to teach children - children of all ages, I might add. That was what made Julian different: he had somehow liberated himself. Or maybe he was just born that way. All I know is that from the first time he walked into one of my classes, the first time…."

Twisting around in his chair, Walsh lowered his head and looked at Rachel with the calm despondency of a man who wishes he could live all over again something he has just remembered.

"It was winter quarter. I was teaching Philosophy of the Law. Most of those who took the class were the pre-law types who thought the course might give them some advantage when they got to law school. You can imagine their surprise when I spent most of the time lecturing on Plato's Laws and Hobbes' Leviathan. It was winter quarter, the class met one night a week, three hours, seven to ten. It was the first night, early January, bitter cold, must have been ten below, and a snowstorm. Class was over. I had on my parka, heading out the door. Everyone else had gone, but Julian had stayed to ask a question. I started to answer, but the question went right to the heart of what I had spent three hours trying to say. Suddenly I saw things I had not seen before. We stood outside under a street lamp, the snow coming down; stood there for - I don't know - thirty, forty minutes. That is what he could do: listen with a completely open mind, listen to the way things were seen twenty-five hundred years ago, seen in ways so different as to be almost unintelligible to anyone who believes in the things we believe today, listen as if there was nothing unusual, nothing even difficult to grasp about it, and then ask a question that went to the very heart of it. You came here to ask me what he was like as a student. I wouldn't know. Julian wasn't my student; it was the other way round."

Leaning back, his arms dangling over the sides of the chair, Walsh's silent laughter echoed soundless in the narrow, high-ceilinged room.

"'Julian taught his teachers.' It is a line from a Roman historian, Ammianus Marcellinus, written in the fourth century to describe that other Julian, emperor of Rome for less than two years. 'Julian the Apostate,' as he used to be called." He turned to Rachel, a strange secret in his bright, incandescent eyes. "It's who he was named after. His father - do you know this? - taught history, ancient history, at Michigan for years. I think he and Julian were close."

Rachel thanked him for his time and got up to leave.

"Will he win?" asked The Great Walsh. "Could we really be that lucky?"

There was only one person left to see, the girl - the woman now - Julian had supposedly been in love with, a girl, from what Rachel had been told, who had been every bit as bright as Julian. Rachel's first attempt to reach her had been a failure. Joli Wharton had nothing to say about Julian Drake and had no desire to talk to a reporter, whether from the New York Times or any other paper. That had been the whole of their telephone conversation. She had been polite but her refusal had been final and emphatic. Her refusal suggested to Rachel Good that there was a better story there than she first had thought. What was the reason, what was it that after all these years Joli Wharton still wanted to keep secret? Rachel caught an afternoon flight to Chicago.

The cab pulled up in front of the University of Chicago Hospital. Rachel told the receptionist that she was a reporter for the New York Times, there for a meeting with Dr. Wharton. Her credentials as a reporter were obviously in order; her manner, which she had learned to use with effect, suggested a woman in a hurry without any time to lose. The receptionist gave her directions to Dr. Wharton's office and sent her on her way.

Steeling herself against the protest she fully expected to receive, Rachel knocked on the door.

"I know you said you didn't want...," she began as the door swung open. A woman, tall and willowy with striking almond-shaped eyes, was looking at her, starting to laugh.

"You're the reporter, the one who wants to talk to me about Julian, and, from the look on your face, no one told you. That says something good about us, doesn't it?" she asked in a dark, silky voice.

"No one told me...?"

"That I'm black. What else did you think? But, please, as long as you came all this way, come in, come in."

Wearing the white coat of a physician, Joli Wharton looked every inch the dedicated doctor. If she was a little heavier than when she had known Julian, she was still remarkably fit and, with cheekbones the envy of a fashion model and tight, glistening skin the color of ebony and bronze, still remarkably beautiful. She got right to the point.

"I didn't want to talk to you because while no one thought anything of the fact that Julian was white and I was black when we were in school, and together, there are still a lot of people out there who would use it, or try to use it, against him now. The same ones, the 'birthers,' who fantasize that Obama was born somewhere else and isn't a citizen. But you're here, and you have been told that Julian and I were once a couple. And that's all you're going to know," she added, inviting Rachel to sit down.

In addition to a desk and chair, her office was furnished with a small sofa, two light blue easy chairs and a coffee table. The walls were covered with pictures and diplomas. On a shelf at a right angle to her desk was a framed photograph of two young women in their early twenties and a younger, teenage, boy.

"I'm married, have a wonderful husband - he's also a physician - and three great children. I haven't seen Julian in it must be nearly twenty-five years. There is nothing I can tell you. I'm not part of his story."

Rachel set her handbag next to her on the sofa. She gazed one more time at the pictures on the wall, pictures mainly of Dr. Wharton with her family, pictures taken at different places in the world, vacations, travel, the occasional escapes with her husband and children from the taxing responsibilities of medicine.

"Not part of the story," she replied, as her gaze came to back to Joli Wharton sitting quietly and cautiously expectant on the edge of the easy chair the other side of the coffee table. "You may be the most important part."

She reached inside her handbag for her notebook, chancing that she could ease her way into an interview. Wharton shook her head.

"I won't talk to you at all, on the record. I won't tell you anything about Julian or anything else, unless you agree not to use it."

Her soft eyes had a distant, wistful look. There were things she remembered that still had a value. She waited for Rachel to say whether she would agree to her conditions and, as Rachel immediately understood, hoped she would. She wanted to talk about Julian, and, if not desperate to do so, would have been disappointed if she could not. Rachel shoved the notebook back in her bag.

"I'm trying to write a background piece, a biography, something that will give everyone a better idea what he is like, who he really is. I covered him a little when he was in Congress. I've known Louis Matson for almost forty years; I knew he asked Julian to write a speech. I had not known - no one other than Louis had ever known - why, twelve years ago, he had suddenly withdrawn from a Senate race he was almost certain to win."

"His sister," said Joli Wharton, staring straight ahead. "Her husband murdered her, and then killed himself."

"Her husband…? Then you were in touch?" she asked simply.

"A few times," she explained reluctantly. "After what happened to his sister, he called. A few other times. He always knew he could talk to me. We had been close once; I don't think he was ever close with anyone quite like that again."

"He was in love with you; you were in love with him."

"Oh, I was in love with him all right, really in love with him," replied Joli with a strange, rueful smile. “You know how we met?” she asked, looking at Rachel with the kind of excitement the memory of it still produced. “I was in my first year of medical school, here, at Chicago; he was in his first year of law school. It was late in the afternoon, at the end of November, just before Thanksgiving. I was walking down a long hallway from the library. There was a place there I liked to study. There was no one around, and then, suddenly, from around the corner, Julian appeared. I was wearing a long, dark coat that came down to my ankles, and I wore my hair up and I had on one of those wool hats that covers your head down to your ears. And Julian steps right in front of me and with those blue smiling eyes of his asks me in all seriousness whether I am Tahitian! I'm not very dark, and my eyes had a certain shape, and he thought I must be Polynesian. So of course I had to give him a practiced look of complete indifference - I thought my heart was going to thump right out of my chest, - and said that yes, of course I was, as any fool could tell, and that I had swum all the way across the ocean because the weather was so much nicer in Chicago. He did not bat an eye. He just looked at me and said, ‘I'm glad you made it. Would you like to go for coffee?’ And we did. And, yes, I fell in love with him and it took all of about five minutes. But no, Julian never fell in love with me. Julian has never been in love, really in love, with anyone. I'm probably as close as he ever got. Haven't you figured him out yet? Don't you understand? Nothing was ever enough for him, nothing will ever be enough for him. I don't mean what you probably think I mean. Julian wasn't one of those guys who doesn't fall in love because he always has to have something, or someone, new. He isn't - he never was - someone who has to have everything: wealth, power, fame, reputation. He wanted more than that - or less.”

She drew her hand over her mouth, wondering how to explain to someone who had not known Julian then what he had been like.

“I loved medical school, everything about it: the long hours, the endless study. I was going to be a doctor; there was never any doubt in my mind what I wanted to do. Julian hated law school. He did not want to be a lawyer; he had no interest, only contempt, for the idea of joining some firm where everyone is a specialist and the only thing important is how many billable hours you have each year.”

"Then why…?"

"He had to do something, and a law degree lets you do a lot of things. He did not know what he wanted to do - except study. He came to Chicago as a law student, but he spent half his time the other side of the street, the other side of the Midway, sitting in on classes - graduate seminars in history, politics, philosophy, whatever he thought might be interesting, whatever he thought might teach him something worth knowing. He seldom went more than once or twice. Nothing, or almost nothing, was ever what he was looking for. Almost nothing, because he did find someone who taught political philosophy, a professor who had been here for years. I've forgotten his name, but Julian thought he was the only real scholar, the only one with something serious to teach. This is the University of Chicago!" she said with a sudden, irresistible laugh. "And Julian thought there was only one teacher here worth listening to! He was probably right," she added, shaking her head, "but I couldn't tell you why. Only Julian could do that."

"You were in love with him, and…?"

A subtle smile creased the corners of Joli Wharton's full mouth.

"You're wondering, because of what I said - that I didn't think he had ever fallen in love with anyone; you're wondering, because he never married, whether…? No, that much I can tell you. He had more passion than anyone I had ever known. But then, when it was over, it wasn't that he regretted what we had just done; he didn't feel guilty, or think we should have waited; nothing like that. And it wasn't like some one-night stand where all the guy wanted was to get you into bed and once he had you could not wait to get away. Julian and I practically lived together, at least for a while."

She studied Rachel for a moment, trying to decide whether she had said enough. Rachel did not try to argue the point, and, more importantly, had the face of an older woman who could keep a confidence. Joli Wharton had never talked about Julian with anyone, and now she wanted to tell everything. Nothing she said would find its way into print, but it might give a greater depth, a sense of understanding, to the story that, with or without her help, was going to be written.

"We would make love, and it was all-consuming, the kind you read about in novels: the earth moves, you can't - you couldn't - stop if your life depended on it; and then, when it was over, Julian thought of other things. It might be ten at night, it might be three in the morning, it didn't matter. He would kiss me, tell me I should get some sleep, and then, before I knew it, he was out of bed, back at his desk, studying, but never any law book, never anything for class, always something deeper, more profound, ancient history or philosophy, something that suddenly he had to get back to. There is more to it than this. Even if we had not made love, even if he was back at his place, sleeping alone, however late it was before he finally slept, he did not sleep for more than three or four hours. Every morning, he was up by four-thirty, leaning on both elbows, his head bent down over an open page of Aristotle or Plato, or Hegel or Heidegger, something only he thought important."

Joli Wharton folded her arms and stared across the room to the windows that looked out across to the gray buildings in the quadrangle, the old vaulted library with windows like cathedral glass and tarnished electric light chandeliers that provided as little illumination as the candles in a medieval monastery, the library where, if she had not liked to study there, she might never have met Julian.

"Julian was not meant for this century," she said finally, her gaze still on the window and what she saw there of her own distant past. "The world is too small. He should have been born in ancient Rome or Athens, when everything seemed possible, before everyone was thought to be happy and content with a well paying speciality, doing the same thing over and over again every day. I told you that I was in love with him," she said, turning slowly back to Rachel Good. "Which was the reason I said no when he asked me to marry him."

"He asked you to…? And you said…?"

"It is what I said before: I was in love with him; he wasn't in love with me. He asked me to marry him. It was something he thought he should do. No, it wasn't that. I wasn't pregnant. Julian was always preoccupied with the question that hardly anyone ever asks themselves: how he should live. Not what he should do, how he should make a living, what kind of occupation. He asked me to marry him, and it was like finding yourself in the middle of a problem in geometry, part of a possible solution; not a number, but close enough. There was always passion with Julian, but there was never romance." She paused, as if she were suddenly not sure, or rather, that suddenly she was.

"No, that isn't right. Julian was full of romance, but not the kind that involves another person. He was not in love with me; he was in love with all these dreams of his own, the things he thought worth doing, things he thought could not happen anymore. He read Homer and imagined himself Achilles; he read Seven Pillars of Wisdom - read it more than once - and wished he could have been Lawrence of Arabia. You should have seen him when he talked about what it must have been like, living when things like that were possible, the way his eyes seemed to take in all the world, the excitement he felt. I used to tease him, call him my Don Quixote, but he was more serious than that. He understood the way the world had changed, understood it and kept trying to find a way to bring it back, make the world what it used to be before everything got mechanized and everyone wanted to think the same way as everyone else. It used to make him a little crazy, how everyone seemed to think everything had gotten so much better, that science and technology had made a better life for everyone. He thought we were all insane. And the thing was, when I was with him, listening to the way he talked about the future and the past, I agreed with him. And to tell you the truth," she added in a voice softening into laughter, "I still do. Maybe I should have married Julian. After all, who knows? But I didn't, and it was all because I thought in my youthful ignorance that he lived so much in his own mind, had so many dreams, romantic dreams, of what he wanted to do, that if I married him he wouldn't stay with me, stay with me when I became a doctor and had to stay in one place, that he would not be able to live with that sense of confinement, that limit, that limit of time and place on what he could, on a sudden, decide he had to do. I was a fool for that. Don't misunderstand," said Joli Wharton, her eyes shining with the memory of what had not happened, the bittersweet nostalgia for a life she had not had. "I love my husband, but…there was never anyone like Julian."

CHAPTER FOURTEEN

Hobart Williams leaned back in his chair, his hands locked together behind his balding head. He was not without sympathy for Rachel Good's dilemma.

"You're right; you can't use what she told you. Hell, you can't even use most of what she said. You know the rules. But you can still use what you learned from her about what he was like: young, driven, with dreams of his own; someone who did not know what he wanted to do, someone who - and you can use this - 'should have been born in a different century' - not the phrase, not the quote, but the general observation, this sense - and she was not the only one to have it - that he had his own way of looking at the past. Sure. Why not? It's what he said in that speech of his - going back to what conservatism used to mean. I mean, look, it's a start. We wanted a profile, what Julian Drake did before he became the only person anyone seems to want to talk about, what he was like, who he really is, who -"

"Who he really is?" exclaimed Rachel, with a doubting laugh. She sat sideways on the chair in front of Hobart Williams' desk, her left arm slung over the back of it. She could not count the number of times she had sat in that same chair, going over whatever she had been able to discover in whatever story she had been asked to cover. But this time felt different. There was more at stake.

"It's been three weeks since the convention," said Hobart, shrugging his shoulders in a gesture of his own confusion, "and with every poll that comes out he increases his lead. I just got the results of the latest one we've done. It'll be the lead story in tomorrow's edition. He's at damn near sixty percent! Three weeks ago no one had ever heard of him, and now he's running better than anyone since - I don't know - LBJ against Goldwater in '64, Nixon against McGovern in '72. You weren't at his press conference, the one in D.C. The television ratings went through the roof! The son-of-a-bitch has changed everything. He was right: he doesn't have to campaign the way everyone else has done; he doesn't have to go anywhere to get an audience; he doesn't have to stage events. All he has to do is announce a speech or a press conference and everyone stops whatever else they're doing to watch."

Hobart stared out the window, down the glass canyons of the New York streets. The soft, pudgy fingers of his left hand beat a slow, steady rhythm on the padded arm of his cream colored upholstered chair.

"How many times were we told when we were young reporters; how many times have I repeated the same thing, given the same advice since I became an editor: 'follow the money.' It always made sense; it was always a good place to start. Greed, ambition - they were always joined at the hip."

Turning away from the window, he reached for the cup of coffee he had not touched in hours and, too caught up in what he was thinking, did not notice it had gone cold. He took a sip, put it down and searched Rachel's eyes as if she must by now have discovered the answer to a question he had not yet asked.

"The money," he said, as if to remind her what was in his mind. "The guy doesn't have any. He has enough of his own, I guess, to get from place to place. He doesn't have any campaign money. He isn't taking the public money he could have used; he isn't raising - he won't accept - any money from anyone else. Okay, when it comes to money he's like Caesar's wife - above suspicion. Or is he? Is this all some kind of massive fraud?"

"Massive fraud?" asked Rachel. She was not surprised that Hobart was raising the possibility. It was his willingness to look at a story from every angle, especially if it was an angle no one else had thought of, that had made him a great journalist.

"Sure. Why not? Look at what he's done, look at the effect. Why does everyone think he's different, better than anyone they've seen, the great new hope? Sure, he can give a speech, and he has the kind of charisma that works on television. People love to watch him, love to see the way he handles questions, the humor, the wit, the intelligence. But it is this refusal to take money from anyone, public or private, that has made him seem unbeatable. It makes him seen untouchable, someone who will never owe anything to anyone, someone who - and this is what a lot of people don't yet seem to understand - is willing to serve, but doesn't really want the office. He is the perfect reluctant candidate, willing to win or lose as the people decide, and - this is really priceless - almost, as it applies to him, indifferent as to the result. It must just kill those other bastards who tried to get the nomination, how much they wanted it, all the things they would have given up to get it, including whatever integrity they still had left, and this guy doesn't even steal it from them, he gets it as a gift, a gift he doesn't even want. Or did he?" he asked with a sudden sharp, inquiring look. "You're close to Louis Matson. Was any of this…?"

"I don't know when he decided to do what he did. The only thing I know for sure is that Julian Drake did not know about it. There is no story there."

"It's part of the story you're writing now," he reminded her. "I know Matson is a friend of yours, but…."

"All right, I think Louis staged the whole thing. A lot of people think he did. And he'll tell you - he told me - that almost from the first time he met him, when Julian first came to Congress, he thought Julian should be president. But he'll never admit he didn't suffer a collapse; he'll never say that he faked it so Julian Drake could give that speech."

"But you think he did?" asked Hobart, just to be sure. "Interesting, because that would help make the case."

"What case? What are you talking about?"

Hobart smiled, shook his head, then looked depressed. He tapped his fingers, sighed, reached for the cup of cold, stale coffee, picked it up, then put it down.

"The case, the case," he repeated, turning his head from side to side. "'Nothing is what it seems.' 'If something sounds too good to be true, it is.' The usual timeworn, but time tested, rules of reporting, the hackneyed, trite expressions, not so much of method but attitude. Attitude!" he repeated, a cynical grin weaving its way across his drooping heavy lined mouth. Jumping forward, he dropped his forearms on the desk and, careful not to hit anything, pounded his clenched fists in a brief staccato. "If Matson knew all along what he was going to do, wouldn't he have made sure that if Julian Drake got the nomination he would have all the support, all the financial support, he needed? Yes, I know," he said, growing more intense, more convinced that there was a story here, "Drake isn't taking any money from anyone. But everyone knows - he said it in the press conference - that he can't stop anyone from spending money on his behalf, that he can't do anything about what some political action committee decides to do."

"No, that's not right," objected Rachel. "He said he would never talk to anyone who did."

Hobart raised an eyebrow.

"Why do you have to talk to someone you've elected when the reason you elected them is because you know what they're going to do?"

Rachel threw back her head and laughed.

"From the start he's made, from what's he said so far, it doesn't sound like the kind of thing people like Rufus Chambers and Conrad Wilson - that crowd - would be much inclined to support!"

"Sometimes you support someone because you want him to win; sometimes you support someone because you want the other side to lose." Like a seasoned gambler calculating the odds, Hobart slowly and methodically spread his fingers and began to tap them together. "They're already doing it, running commercials in the dozen states likely to decide the election. That story will be in the paper tomorrow, along with the latest poll results. Julian Drake is running way ahead nationally, but its closer in the states that count, and millions are being spent in those places on ads attacking the other side." He narrowed his eyes, concentrating hard. "They never mention Julian Drake, never give a reason why anyone should vote for him. It's all about making her unelectable. Vicious stuff, some of it; libelous if you were dealing with a private individual. Now, the question is - and I know what Drake said at the press conference - is this all simply happenstance, or planned, orchestrated, from the beginning? Did they know, did they understand, that no one who was seeking the nomination could win in the general election? Did they decide that only if they had an outsider, someone they could portray as an independent, someone above politics, would they have any chance of winning the presidency? Or rather - and this is the point - stopping a Democrat from getting it? If Julian Drake wins, won't that be the effect? The question is whether the effect has a cause, and, if so, what is it? Was it just the inspiration of Louis Matson, acting all alone, or was there something else involved, a conspiracy, a lie like nothing else we have ever seen, a candidacy that was never anything but a fraud?"

Rachel Good looked at him as if he were half insane. Hobart knew that look, he had seen it on her face nearly every time he had tried to show her what she might be missing.

"Okay," he relented, "you know Louis Matson a lot better than I do. If you tell me he wouldn't be involved in something like this, okay…, but, still, there has to be more to this story than this."

"Why? It's perfect the way it is."

"Perfect?"

"We haven't had a convention in fifty years in which there was fight for the nomination. When was the last time - maybe the Democrats in 1972. But everyone knew that it would be McGovern. But the old days, before we had all these primaries and someone wins a majority of the delegates before the convention convenes, hardly anyone still living remembers when someone gave a speech that sent everyone into such a frenzy of excitement that they forgot everything except how much they wanted the one who gave that speech to be their nominee. Hell, Hobart, when was the last time anyone gave a speech at a convention anyone would even want to remember? Julian Drake is what no one expected, and though they did not know it, what everyone was looking for. I'm older than you are. When I was a freshman in college, JFK was president. We used to skip class so we could watch on television whenever he was holding a press conference. Guys who had never been to

Massachusetts starting speaking like they had been born and raised in Boston; girls all wanted to look like Jackie Kennedy. Kennedy was different - younger, smarter, with that wonderful wry humor, generous, self-deprecating. There is a number that tells everything. He won in 1960 with 49.6 percent of the vote; when he was killed three years later, almost seventy percent insisted they had voted for him. Things like this happen, not very often - not very often at all - but they happen. The case, as you put it a moment ago, the case isn't about some right-wing conspiracy, a shrewd appraisal of what might be the only chance for the Republicans to win; the case is about the American love for what seems new, and, strange as it may seem, the American love for the language. Or maybe it isn't so strange. Having lived for years now in our sound-bite incoherence, Julian Drake comes along and we suddenly realize what we have been missing."

Like a metronome measuring time in the ordered segments of a closed system, Hobart's round, balding head moved slowly from side to side, and in the same rhythm tapped his fingers on the desk. And then he stopped and looked at her, completely still.

"And what do you think would have happened if Kennedy were running today? We remember the charm, we remember the speeches, but what he was doing - the women in his life - wouldn't be treated the way it was then when no one reported on the private lives of politicians. Now it's damn near all anyone wants to know. That is what is missing here. There is nothing about his private life. Yes, I know - that girl he knew when he was in law school, the woman who told you things you promised not to use. But since then? Never married, never engaged, doesn't, so far as we know, see anyone now. He isn't gay. So what is he - a priest? Hell, he's not even Catholic! I mean, everyone has someone, or wants someone. Are you telling me he's really that different? There has to be something."

Rachel remembered something Joli Wharton had told her, something Julian had said late one night, years before, when they were both still young enough to take things seriously.

"It isn't like giving up food or drink. You won't die if you never have sex."

"No, but neither will you find many like-minded friends," replied Hobart, with a droll expression that did not quite hide the lively sparkle in his tired eyes. "Well, why don't you ask him, ask Julian Drake what he has against sex?"

"Ask him? When? I've been trying to arrange an interview, but...."

"Ask him at the debate. The first one is set for next week. There will be three reporters asking questions. You're one of them."

"I'm...?"

"The request just came in, last night, before you got back. I said I couldn't answer for you, but that I was pretty sure you would be willing to do it. I hope it was all right to say that. I think you're the first reporter we have had asked. I'm told that Drake insisted on it. Not you by name, you understand - though I suspect he knew you would be the name they chose. He insisted that there be at least one reporter who wasn't affiliated with television. He seems to have the idea that we still do a more serious brand of journalism," he said as a thin smile edged its way across his mouth. "So go ahead, destroy his last illusions, ask him what he has against sex, what he has against what everyone else seems to think the only way to real happiness."

This, a chance remark, a rather uninspired commentary on a fairly minor difference in the way someone has lived his life, began to take on a life of its own. In the days leading up to the first of what were supposed to be three nationally televised debates Rachel Good found herself coming back again and again to that single question. Sex, like ambition, had at it's center the desire for recognition, the acknowledgement by someone else that you were worth something; worth, at least at the moment, more than anyone else. There was also the desire for immortality, if not in the literal sense of living forever, the foreseeable future: the lasting fame that comes with high office, in the one case; the continuation in the lives of the children who, after that instant of joyful agony, you leave behind you, in the other. Nearly everyone in politics seemed to want both, fame but also children. Was that the secret of Julian Drake's astonishing gifts, that untrammeled by the same carnal desires that most men, in or out of politics, never thought of controlling, he could concentrate all his thought and energy on the greatest prize of all? And if that were the case, what did it really mean? He had not done anything that suggested that he was even ambitious in the usual, political, sense of the word. Was he, as she had insisted to her editor, what everyone had been waiting for, or was he, in a way she did not yet understand, dangerous, a danger, if in no other way, to what everyone believed?

The first debate was held in southern California on the campus of UCLA in an auditorium in which the audience had been as evenly divided as possible between Democrats, Republicans and political independents. Each candidate was given two minutes for a brief opening statement. Madelaine Shaw did what candidates almost always do, thanked the sponsors of the debate, thanked the university, and thanked the audience that was sitting there and the millions more who were watching at home for giving her the chance to share with them her hopes for the country and what she knew they could accomplish together. In forty seconds time, she described growing up in a middle-class family, her term in the Senate and her service as secretary of state. She looked forward to this and the other scheduled debates and the chance to show the important, even crucial, differences between her and her opponent. She spoke in a calm, confident, friendly voice, every word memorized, rehearsed, tested for it's likely response. It was, in other words, predictable, dull, and safe. The rule, as all the experts agreed, was to get through the debates without making the kind of egregious error that could destroy a candidacy. It was a lesson she had not needed to be taught. There was always a reason not to take chances.

Julian Drake did not seem to want to do anything else. Instead of opening with an expression of gratitude for what everyone had done to make the debate possible, he opened with an apology for something he had not done.

"Before we start I want to apologize to Secretary Shaw," he said, turning toward her for just a moment before looking back at the camera. "I don't watch television, and so I haven't seen the kind of things that have been said in commercials produced and paid for by an independent political action committee. The things that are said about Secretary Shaw in many of these commercials are, so far as I know, not even close to the truth. I had nothing to do with them. After the convention, after I was nominated, I met at their request a number of wealthy donors. All of them had been backing other candidates. I told them I wasn't interested in their financial help and that I wasn't going to change anything in what I said or in what I believed to win their support. At a press conference I tried to make my position as clear as I could. I said, and I am saying here again tonight, that should I become president no one involved in this, no one who put up so much as a dollar for this kind of scurrilous television campaign will ever be given so much as a minute of my time."

Smiling in disbelief, Julian shook his head.

"Would you really give up your vote, give up your right to use your own intelligence, your own good judgement, because some paid for idiot on television tells you some made up story about how the election of one candidate or the other will destroy civilization or blow up the world? What kind of people do they think we are? And so tonight, in front of all of you, I apologize to Secretary Shaw for my failure to convince these people - the people who did this - that I meant what I said, that the only communication they will ever have with me is the off chance that I might read part of something they may hire someone to write as an op-ed piece in the New York Times. Let me close by saying - and I hasten to add that I mean this only figuratively - that if it were up to me I would have anyone who did this taken out and shot."

There was a stunned silence. No one knew quite what to say. The moderator, Richard Cromwell of public television, who, along with Leonard Rosenthal of CBS and Rachel Good had spent hours preparing and organizing the questions they were going to ask, was so startled that he suddenly turned to Madelaine Shaw and blurted out: "What do you think of that? Is there anything you want to say?"

The cameras had caught her in open-mouthed astonishment. There was no time to consider, no time to craft a carefully scripted response of the sort she had spent days rehearsing, no time to calculate the effect on the various constituencies into which with precise analytical measurement the electorate had been divided; all she could do was close her eyes and leap. But then, just as she started to answer, Cromwell added, "Will you make the same pledge - promise that if you're elected you'll have nothing to do with anyone associated with the various political action committees responsible for the television commercials attacking Congressman Drake?"

For an instant she froze. Her eyes, distant and remote, moved left to right and back again, reading some hard-earned lesson from the pages of her own biography, searching for the words, the right combination of phrases, that would allow her to make a promise that could always, later, be reinterpreted.

"If anyone were to run the kind of things against Congressman Drake that have been run against me, commercials full of half-truths and lies, commercials that engage in the worst kind of character assassination, then, yes, I can assure you, they certainly would never have a chance to talk to me, or, I might add, have access to anyone in my administration."

"But you wouldn't have them taken out and shot?" asked Julian, with a quick, bright smile.

It brought down the house. Even Madelaine Shaw had to laugh.

"No, but it's tempting, isn't it?" she asked, with the friendly confidence of a competitor who knows what being a candidate is really like.

"Leonard Rosenthal has the first question," announced Cromwell in his pleasant, easy going voice.

With a thick, bulldog neck, a tight, quarrelsome mouth, and small, deep set grey eyes that looked out at the world with what seemed inveterate suspicion, Rosenthal had a voice like a nervous tick, a kind of itching scratch, the words coming a few at a time, a short staccato, each separated by a brief flash of his eyes, sometimes followed by the kind of sudden thin-lipped smile one might see on the grim face of an executioner who took pride in his own efficiency. But he was at heart a kind and sensitive soul who tried with a series of shrugs and mournful sideways movements of his head to apologize for the impression he more than anything wished he could control and change. He glanced down at the first of the questions he had written out, then shoved the list aside.

"My question is for Secretary Shaw. Congressman Drake just apologized for what others have said against you - political action committees over which he has no control. I noticed you did not apologize to him. Isn't there something odd about that?"

"Odd?" she asked, not certain what he meant or where the question was going.

"Yes, odd; because the ads attacking you are coming from sources over which he has no control, but the ads attacking him - ones that suggest that 'We don't know anything about him' - I think that is the line used in all of them - are paid for by your campaign. At the end of each of them you say you 'approve of this message.' These ads seem to suggest some dark conspiracy, that Julian Drake is a kind of Manchurian Candidate, controlled by alien forces trying to take over the country. My question, again, is whether you think you owe Congressman Drake an apology of the sort he just gave you?"

Madelaine Shaw leaned forward, closer to the camera, closer to the millions watching, waiting for her response.

"I have been in public life for more than forty years, from the time I first worked as a volunteer in a presidential campaign, through my years in the Senate and then as secretary of state. Everything I stand for, every position I have taken, every bill I introduced, every bill I voted for, every speech I gave, every article I wrote - all of it is there, a matter of public record. There are no questions, no serious questions, about what I believe, what I would do as president. The same thing cannot be said about the other side. If you are going to run for the presidency, if you are going to ask the American people to entrust you with the most powerful office in the world, the people have a right to know everything about you."

She held both hands, palms up, evenly balanced, and then, as she spoke, raised one while, at a corresponding rate, she lowered the other.

"You have to weigh these things against each other: what you know about one candidate, what you do not know about the other; what one candidate has done consistently through long years of public service, what the other candidate did, once, twelve years ago, and then disappeared."

"Disappeared?" asked Julian, when Rosenthal gave him chance to reply. "That's right, I did; I disappeared from Washington and all its endless bickering. I did not disappear from life. I spent the better part of the last twelve years like the rest of you," he went on, looking directly into the camera, "living my own, private, life; doing what I could to raise two children, doing what I could to become a better man and a better citizen. That may seem like disappearance to someone who spends all their time running for office, trying to figure out what everyone else thinks so they can claim to think the same thing, but then there may be something to be said for trying to learn all you can, including, most importantly, how to think for yourself."

Cromwell turned to Rachel Good for the next question.

"This question is for Congressman Drake. Secretary Shaw has said that American support for Israel is unconditional, that when it comes to our policy in the Middle Eat we should never do anything that endangers the security of

Israel. Is this also your position, and if not, why not?"

Julian narrowed his eyes into a look of intense concentration. His chin came up a slight fraction of an inch.

"A president of the United States has one, and only one, unconditional obligation, and that is to pursue what is in the best interest of the United States. That may, or may not, be consistent with support for Israel - or any other nation. I understand that some believe we should never do anything that Israel doesn't want. A president doesn't have the right to think that way. We do not elect someone president to let the leader of another country - Israel or anyone else - decide what our foreign policy should be. It would be well to remember that without American assistance - the decision made by President Truman in 1948 - Israel would not have become a nation. We owe Israel what we owe every other country: the honesty of our opinion and respect for theirs, nothing more and nothing less.

"You asked what my policy would be in the Middle East. I will answer with a single word: disengagement. What happens in the Middle East has to be decided by the people who live there; it cannot be decided by us. What have we done? - Destroyed Iraq in retaliation for an attack with which they were never involved, created hatred that will last for generations, and worse even than that, created in this country a belief that we somehow have the obligation to sacrifice the lives of thousands, tens of thousands, of our own sons and daughters, and spend ourselves into bankruptcy every time some new force arises that threatens what we erroneously think our interests in the region. This country has to decide something no one talks about: are we going to be an empire or a republic, a country that believes it has to use military force to impose its will, or a country that leads by our example, the example of what a free people can do of its own volition."

Shaw saw her opening, and with catlike cunning tried to take advantage of it.

"I'm sorry that Congressman Drake doesn't think that we, and our closest ally, Israel, face serious danger from the rogue nations and terrorist organizations in the Middle East. If he had been paying more attention to what is going on in the world, perhaps he might have noticed that there are every day threats against Israel's very existence, threats to wipe Israel off the face of the map, and that the same people making these threats would destroy the United States if they were given half a chance. This is a dangerous world we live in. We aren't living in the 18th century anymore. It doesn't take weeks to cross the Atlantic; it's only minutes once a missile is launched."

Cromwell started to ask the next question, but Julian interrupted.

"Despite what the secretary seems to think, the United States cannot solve every problem in the world. We cannot fight other people's wars. Ask yourself this question: What good have we done in the Middle East?" Turning away from the camera, he faced Shaw directly. "Do you really think that a civilization that has been in existence for almost fifteen hundred years is suddenly going to give up everything it believes, discard everything they have been taught, because deep down they really want to be just like us? Do you really think that you can bring them into what we like to call the modern age by bombing them into submission? What have we really accomplished, except to make us more enemies than we had before? Thanks in no small measure to what we have done there, much of the Middle East is now involved in civil war. Isis, which is all anyone seems to want to talk about, is not a state, it is a movement, and you are not going to stop a movement - you will only help it grow - by attacking it as if it were a conventional military force. The people of the Middle East have to decide what they want and whether it is worth fighting for."

"So you wouldn't do anything to help Israel?" Shaw shot back. "You wouldn't do anything to help keep the peace in the Middle East?"

"Keep the…!" exclaimed Julian with a look of astonishment. "There hasn't been peace in the Middle East since - you tell me! Since oil was discovered . And Israel - Israel will always be given our help against invasion or attack; but this is not a one way street. Israel has its interests and we have ours. Serious friendships require serious respect for the integrity and intelligence of the other side. It requires at a minimum that you do not attempt to influence the domestic politics of the other country. That is really all I am going to say about that."

Shaw was up on the balls of her feet, her eyes shining with all the certainty of a quick victory.

"It was the Republican Speaker of the House who invited the Israeli prime minister to address Congress on why the treaty with Iran should be rejected. You are the Republican candidate for president. Are you now trying to distance yourself from what your party did?"

Julian Drake seemed amused. He scratched his ear, paused, smiled, shook his head and then threw up his hands.

"I'm not a Republican," he said as if the fact were obvious. "And I'm not a Democrat. I'm a citizen of the United States who in the most unlikely way imaginable finds himself the nominee of one of the two major political parties. I did not seek the nomination; I never promised anyone anything to get the nomination. When someone does something they should not have done, I don't look to see which party they belong to before deciding that they should not have done it. Yes, I know, it's true, I served several terms in Congress as a Republican, but for the last twelve years, living in California, I have been a registered Independent."

Rachel Good could almost hear Louis Matson laughing. Julian had just changed the political dynamics of the race. He was not just the nominee of a party, he was what the great majority of Americans liked to think they were themselves, someone who would decide every issue on the merits and party be damned. But how much of this was instinct and how much calculation, how much a reflection of who Julian really was and how much the work of a remarkable, Machiavellian, mind? One thing seemed certain, after everything she had learned about him: whatever the reason he did something, he understood the effect. She could see it in his eyes, the silent laughter as he waited for Madelaine Shaw to try to turn the attention back to herself. And the strange part was that he was watching like someone who had seen it all before, that he somehow knew in advance each unfolding scene, that he had, in a sense, written it all out, thought through all the possible variations, all the possible responses, and was still writing, making whatever last minute adjustments were needed, and doing it all with such effortless speed that he seemed, as he stood there watching, to be doing nothing at all.

"I can understand why Congressman Drake would like to distance himself not just from the Speaker but from the Republican party. No one has ever said he was not intelligent."

Lifting an eyebrow, Julian nodded, the slight gesture by which a teacher might approve the effort of a struggling student. Shaw smiled and nodded back, and then, before the moderator could ask the next question, went on the attack.

"You were a Republican member of Congress, you ran as a Republican for the United States Senate, but as soon as you were out of office, the moment you were out of politics, you changed your mind, decided you didn't want to be a Republican anymore and became an independent?"

Julian smiled, gently, without indignation, without any sign that he at all resented the implied suggestion that he had never believed in anything except his own advancement, that he was, and always had been, the worst sort of political opportunist.

"There were two young children I had suddenly to raise. I wanted them to learn to think for themselves; I did not want them to be influenced by what I believed. I did not want them to look at the world through anyone's eyes but their own. I wasn't there to teach them to become Republican or Democrat or anything else; I was there to teach them what I could about the history of this country, the great things that had been accomplished whether by a Democrat like Thomas Jefferson or a Republican like Abraham Lincoln. The last thing I wanted them to do was to look at this country and its history from the point of view of a partisan, one of those misguided people who think that nothing his party does is ever wrong and nothing the other party does is ever right. Does that answer your question?"

There was nothing Shaw could say. She turned to the moderator and waited for the next question.

"I want to turn to domestic issues," announced Cromwell. "It is estimated that the Social Security system will go bankrupt in the not too distant future. What would you do to save it?"

"The system is not going to go bankrupt. It isn't going to happen. I can assure the American people that the system will remain viable," replied Shaw. "There are certain things we may need to do, including raising the age of eligibility, the age at which someone can begin to draw benefits; and we may have to increase the amount on which the social security tax is paid. But the system will not be allowed to fail. Fixing Social Security will be among the first things I do as president."

It was the same answer she had been giving from the day she first declared her candidacy; it was the same answer nearly everyone who was a serious candidate, not just for the presidency, but for the House and Senate had been giving for years. Cromwell turned to Julian Drake, expecting a similar response.

"Congressman Drake - Do you have any different plans for Social Security?"

"I wouldn't raise the income limit on which the Social Security tax is imposed; I would abolish it. Let's understand what Social Security was meant to do; let's understand, to use a phrase many conservatives like to use, the 'original intent.' It is not, and was never meant to be, a savings program. You do not pay into some private account where your money earns interest. It is what the name Social Security suggests: an insurance program. Everyone who earns a salary, everyone who works for an hourly wage, has part of that money withheld. You can pay into the system for forty years, but if you die before the age at which you are entitled to benefits you collect nothing. We all pay so that those of us who survive into old age will have enough to live on. If everyone lived to be ninety, if everyone lived long enough to collect benefits, and to go on collecting them, the system would have collapsed years ago. We keep raising the rate of taxation, keep asking people to pay more and more of their income - unless they make a great deal of money and then we ask them to do nothing. You ask what I would do. Simple. Remove the limit on the income that is taxable. There is no reason why someone making ten million dollars a year does not pay more than someone making a hundred times less than that amount. Remove the limit, and, if you do that, you can then reduce the rate that everyone pays and even do something no one seems to have thought of before: eliminate the tax altogether on the working poor. In other words, eliminate the upper limit and institute a lower limit. One other thing: start counting as income on which the tax is paid not just salary and wages, but investment income, stock options, every form of wealth someone receives. That, it seems to me, is the best way, the only way, to conserve one of the most important things we have ever done together as a country."

"Do you really think you could get Republican support for something like that in Congress?" asked Cromwell, astonished at what he just heard.

"Once they understand that it is the business of conservatives to protect and defend the basic institutions of the country; once they understand that this is the best, if not the only, way to restore the original intent of one of the most important programs we have by which to ensure that our citizens have a decent level of support as they face the hardships of old age," insisted Julian, with a stern, determined glance.

"Secretary Shaw, do you want to respond?" asked Cromwell, eager to hear how she would handle what seemed an attempt to outflank her on the left. "It would seem that, as between the two of you, Congressman Drake has the more liberal position."

"I think it simply underscores how long he has been away, how remote he is from the way his own party - even if he now claims he isn't really a Republican - has tried to privatize everything, including Social Security. He doesn't seem to understand that the Republicans in the Congress, the Republicans he thinks he can persuade, are the same people who keep talking about private accounts, letting everyone invest the money that would go into Social Security in the stock market. Congressman Drake may think the rich should pay more, but most of the people he thinks he can persuade believe instead that everyone should pay less. He doesn't seem to realize that they don't all love F.D.R.; he doesn't seem to realize that most of them would like nothing better than to repeal everything the New Deal, and not just the New Deal, everything any Democratic president, ever did."

Julian Drake seemed to grow taller as he raised his chin and stared straight ahead.

"Just because they won't listen to Secretary Shaw doesn't mean they won't listen to me."

A single sentence, but delivered with such inner certainty and confidence that it seemed the statement of an essential fact, established, as it were, in advance of the event. No one watching had any doubt that somehow it was true, that somehow, inexplicably, Julian Drake could foretell the future.

CHAPTER FIFTEEN

Rufus Chambers tapped three fingers on the lamp table next to his chair, stopped, then did it again, but harder, faster than before. His small, childlike mouth twisted back and forth. Hidden behind thick folds of mottled skin, his fierce, calculating eyes stared at the television set in angry disbelief.

"I told you, I told everyone," he said in a harsh, unforgiving voice. "I told you what a mistake this was; I told you at the convention, I told you after that goddamn speech of his, after I read it the next morning, read it in the clear light of day, that Louis Matson had screwed us all."

Chambers turned to look at the two other people in the room. Conrad Wilson and Angela Murray had both been there with him when, with stunning arrogance, Julian Drake had told them that he had no need of them or their money, and, worse yet, that what they had heard in that speech of his had been only the beginning of what he was going to do if he got elected.

"You believe me now; believe me, now that it is too late to do anything about it?"

They were gathered together in Rufus Chambers's mid-Manhattan office. Chambers, or rather one of his many companies, owned the building, one of the tallest in New York. Central Park stretched out in the distance, a long dark rectangle lit by the lights that on four sides marked out some of the most desirable, and most expensive, real estate not just in New York but in the world. Chambers owned some of this as well. He would liked to have owned all of it, but then he would have wondered if he could have gotten it at a better price.

"I did what we agreed on," remarked Wilson in a sullen voice. "I saw Matson's guy, told him - it was just before Drake held that first press - that we could work with him, that we weren't asking for anything, didn't expect anything, that all we wanted was an assurance that whatever else Drake did he wouldn't make any major changes in the taxes we pay. Cooper said he couldn't speak for Drake. That was the only response; nothing, not a word, since. So my question is why are we spending all this money trying to defeat a candidate that, after what we have just watched, after what Drake has now told everyone he wants to do, we should probably be trying to elect? Hell, he makes her look like the voice of reason."

"Let me be very clear about this," said Chambers, measuring his words. "Julian Drake is a danger, a danger to the country, a danger to us.'

"The question," insisted Angela Murray, with a quick artificial smile that only underscored the sinister look in her heavily made up eyes, "is what do we do about it, how do we fix this?"

Wilson had never understood why Rufus Chambers always wanted her included. She had failed in every position she had ever held. The apparent ease with which she constantly rattled off facts and figures, which seemed to impress so many others, seemed to Wilson a screen behind which there was a complete and total absence of any serious thought of her own.

"Fix this?" he asked. "This isn't like being the head of some company. You can't just fire a bunch of people; you can't just get rid of somebody you don't like."

Her eyes, mean and defiant, flashed with condescension.

"I am aware of the difference between business and politics. I am also aware of the similarities. We can't fire him. That does not mean we can't get rid of him."

Wilson regretted he had come. He could have watched the debate in the comfort of his penthouse apartment two blocks away on Central Park West, but Rufus was an old friend and Rufus had been fairly insistent. Still, if he had known this woman was going to be here ....

"Get rid of him? And just how to you imagine that might be possible? What are we going to do - start running ads attacking him, try to elect Madelaine Shaw instead?"

"That wouldn't be the worst idea," suggested Chambers. "You can work with her. She wants to be president; she doesn't care what she has to do to get there." He got to his feet, stood with his hand on the top of the chair, and looked directly at Wilson. "How bad could it be? She isn't going to do anything, she isn't going to try to make any real change. It's all cosmetic, all these detailed proposals she makes. No one seems to understand this. All those endless details. They give people the sense she's doing something, that it's all important, but it's never anything that tries to change the way things are done. It's always a little bit more, a little bit less; small, incremental, making things easier for the middle class, showing how she is going to save a family of four a few dollars on their energy bill, or a few hundred on the cost of tuition. She'll make some minor changes in the tax rates. Julian Drake? He thinks that instead of the backbone of the country, the rich are a danger to the republic. She wants to make the military more open to women; he is going to make service in the armed forces almost compulsory. She wants to be president," remarked Chambers with a shrewd glint in his eye, "but he wants more than that. He wants to remake the country, take it back to what he thinks it was supposed to be. He doesn't understand anything about the modern world, about the way things have changed. He doesn't understand that the past is the past and the less we think about it the better."

"If you believe the latest polls, it doesn't seem that too many people agree with that. Let's face facts. There isn't anything anyone can do to stop him. He's going to win. It is as simple as that," said Wilson.

"That's too simple," remarked Angela Murray with the quick, nervous insistence that sent shivers up his spine.

Wilson hid his irritation behind a bland smile of indifference. "Too simple?"

"Yes, because even if you were right - which I don't think you are - that he can't be beaten, that would be all the more reason to make sure that he wins by the smallest margin possible. What could be worse than a huge mandate that would allow him to claim support for all the crazy things he wants to do? Congress would have a hard time resisting that kind of popular support. So, no, I don't think we can afford to sit by and do nothing, especially when there is so much we can do."

"So much we can do?" asked Wilson, throwing up his hands.

"Yes, absolutely, if we start right away." Her voice, harsh, brittle, determined, and emphatic, nothing in it to suggest even the slightest doubt she was right. "What did you just hear? What was Shaw asked to apologize about, what did she refuse to apologize about? -Commercials attacking Julian Drake, ads suggesting that no one really knows who he is. We can do more than that. We don't have to raise questions; we can give answers. We don't have to suggest the country doesn't know enough about him to elect him president; we can tell the country who Julian Drake really is."

"And by that, I take it, you mean what you invent about him, what you can think up to fill in the blanks, interpret, or rather re-interpret, things he has done, things he has said?"

She glanced toward Chambers, gave him a knowing smile, and then turned back to Wilson.

"Rufus understood what that speech meant, what Julian Drake was really saying, and that is what we need to do now: show everyone what it means when he says he wants to take the upper limit off the income taxed for Social Security, what it means when he talks about giving four years of college for four years of military service, what it means when he insists on withdrawing from the Middle East. We need to tell people that Julian Drake wants to tax everything everyone earns, that Julian Drake," she went on, becoming more strident with each word, "wants to make poor people join the army before they ever have a chance to go to college, that Julian Drake doesn't care if withdrawal from the Middle East puts Israel at risk and gives terrorists the freedom to launch attacks on our homeland. So, no, Conrad, I don't think there is nothing we can do. And that leaves out the question of whether we shouldn't be thinking of how to put an end once and for all to what, as Rufus was just saying, is perhaps the greatest danger the country has ever faced!"

"Rufus didn't say that!" protested Wilson. "He said Drake was a danger; he didn't say he was the 'greatest danger' the country has ever faced. But that's your problem, Angela," he said with contempt, "you always take things to extremes. That's what you're doing now. How we 'put an end once and for all to…' What? What are you saying? - That we should have him killed, assassinated?"

She cocked her head and with cold resentment looked right through him, and now, for the first time, Wilson understood that nothing was beneath her, that there was not anything she would not do, that right and wrong, that the rules of civilized behavior had no meaning for her. The only allowable measure of anything was her own immediate advantage. She would kill you as easily as look at you. He gave her a look that would have withered anyone else and started to get up, ready to leave. Rufus Chambers stopped him.

"The issue we have to decide is whether we stop attacking Shaw and do something else instead; the question is whether we change sides," he said in a calm, quite voice, trying to draw Wilson back into the discussion. "If Shaw wins, we can claim some credit, and if she loses we will have at least cut Drake's margin and given our friends in Congress a reason to resist what he tries to do."

Wilson felt as if he had wandered into an asylum. The shortest distance between two points was now a circle.

"We'll look like complete hypocrites if we do that," he tried to explain. "After months attacking the Democratic candidate, we're going to attack the Republican! After spending millions, tens of millions, telling everyone why Madelaine Shaw would be the worst thing that ever happened, we're going to spend millions more telling everyone we were wrong, that Julian Drake would be even worse?"

"Exactly!" shouted Angela Murray, jabbing her finger, as thin as a stiletto, in the air. "That is precisely what we ought to be saying: that we knew she was bad, but now, like the rest of America watching that debate we learn that Julian Drake isn't who we thought he was. We took him at his word when he said he was a conservative; now we discover that it was all a lie, that he doesn't want to conserve anything, he wants to tear down everything we have built up. He doesn't want to reward success, he wants to punish it!"

"Jesus Christ! How much longer do I have to listen to this?" muttered Wilson, wishing he could scream.

He rose from the thick cushioned chair, shoved his hands into his pants pockets and moved the few steps to the sliding glass doors that opened out to a balcony overlooking the park. He pushed the doors open and took a long, deep breath of the cool night air. Looking across to the other side of the park he could see the lights of his own penthouse patio, flickering like the signal of something he had once wanted more than anything: to be someone not just wealthy and powerful, but someone everyone wanted to go to for advice and counsel. He had never wanted to be at the center of event; he wanted to control things from a distance, to work his will through the agency of other men's ambitions. Nothing got done without money. Once he had enough of it and showed a willingness to spend it, nothing would get done without him. He turned from the open door and the night air and the magic of Central Park and his now vanished dreams.

"Did you really mean what you said before, that question you suggested, that we should be thinking how to put an end - 'once and for all' - to the 'greatest danger the country has ever faced'? Because if you did," he said, measuring his words, "I think now would be a good time for us to go our separate ways."

"Separate ways…?" asked Rufus Chambers, baffled by what he thought an obvious exaggeration. "Angela didn't mean -" But she cut him off.

"I meant exactly what I said. When you face a threat you deal with it."

Wilson stared hard at her, a dark warning in his eyes, and then looked at Rufus Chambers whose mouth hung half open in astonishment.

"It's all right, Conrad," was all he could think to say. "She doesn't mean it literally; it's just an expression. She's angry; we're all angry, but no one is seriously suggesting…."

But Conrad Wilson was not sure of that, he was not sure of it at all. The only thing he was sure of, and he had to wait only three days before he was sure of this, was that despite his vigorous objection, despite the argument through which he had patiently explained the mistake they would be making, the commercials that had been running against Madelaine Shaw were suddenly pulled off the air and a new campaign of suggestive half-truths and startling accusations was unleashed against the candidate that until the first new commercial appeared everyone thought they were supporting.

Rachel Good raised an eyebrow. "You're not surprised? Not surprised that some of the wealthiest people in the country, people who were supporting you, are now supporting your opponent?"

She studied Julian Drake, waiting for his response. He was just as polite, just as friendly, as he had been the few times she had spoken to him before, but she had the feeling of something reserved, held back, kept secret to himself. She reminded herself that in just a few brief months he had gone from a forgotten former member of Congress to the most famous public figure in the country; gone from a one-time only speech writer for the Senate Majority Leader, sitting alone and anonymous at the back of the Michigan delegation, to someone almost certain to become the next president of the United States.

"The last time you and I had a chance to talk at leisure," said Julian, ignoring for a moment the question she had asked, "we were sitting on a couple of folding chairs in the ballroom of that hotel in Cleveland after a few of the candidates had spoken to the Michigan delegation."

Julian sat in the middle of a long, cushioned sofa. His legs were crossed and his arms folded across his chest. He was dressed formally in a dark blue suit, white shirt and striped tie, but leaning back, his head bent at an angle, he had the relaxed, almost languid air of someone who had no other place he had to be and nothing he had to do. A faint smile flickered like a well lit candle at the corners of his mouth. His eyes brightened at the memory.

"I suggested you might visit me sometime in Big Sur. If I had known what was going to happen, I might never have left."

There was a trace of irony in the warmth of his voice, but it was not clear what that irony concerned. Rachel thought it worth pursuing.

"Would you really have rather lived your life in seclusion, would you really rather not be president? You didn't have to accept the nomination. No one forced you to say yes," she reminded him with a searching glance.

Julian's eyes filled with laughter. He bent forward, daring her, as it seemed, to challenge his next remark.

"Read the record of the proceedings. I didn't say anything. The convention nominated me; or, rather, as we both know, Louis Matson nominated me and the convention, which perhaps did not know what it was doing, was perhaps driven a little mad by its own momentary enthusiasm, which perhaps to this day doesn't know what it did, shouted its agreement. No one asked me if I would accept the nomination, no one remembered the usual formalities; the convention went crazy, nominated someone whose name hardly any of them even knew - and all I did was watch!"

"You didn't turn it down!" she said, challenging him back.

She was sitting in a pale green Queen Ann chair, her notebook open on her lap. A thick, plush, oriental rug, woven in dark threads of red and blue hundreds of years ago in some forgotten Persian village by the gnarled hands of an old man half blind with years of fine close work, lay unnoticed beneath her shiny black high heel shoes. A silver service and two china cups and saucers waited unclaimed on a low, oblong table between them. With a practiced hand, she poured herself a cup, stirred in cream and sugar, took a sip and then carefully placed the cup and saucer back on the table.

"I hoped you might want some," remarked Julian, in an idle, careless voice.

"You're not having any?" she asked, glancing at her notebook. This was the only private interview Julian Drake had granted. She had written out the main questions.

"I drink too much of it as it is. And, besides, it's a little late for me."

"A little late? It's only nine o'clock."

Julian looked like he wanted to laugh. He started to explain what he meant, but then thought better of it.

"A cup or two after I get up," he said, vaguely.

He placed the palms of his hands flat on the cushion seats on both sides of him and turned his head toward the windows and the White House, bright and shiny in the morning sun, the other side of Lafayette Square.

"Do you know the history of this place, why it's called the Hay-Adams Hotel?"

Rachel began to tell him what she knew about the once famous pair of 19th century Americans whose names, and whose houses, were now linked together in what had become a successful commercial enterprise, but Julian was still staring at the place that now almost inevitably would become his new residence, or, as he sometimes complained privately to Ismael Cooper, his future four-year prison.

"No, I'm not surprised," he remarked, his gaze steady and unmoved. "What you asked just a little while ago about people who were spending millions trying to defeat Madelaine Shaw now spending more than that trying to defeat me." He turned toward her, slowly, shaking his head with the weary amusement of a spectator who has seen the same performance played by much better actors. "What else could they do after that debate two weeks ago? The only wonder is they did not start going after me the day after the convention. Have you ever noticed how often in politics people insist that someone did not really mean what they said when it isn't what they expected to hear? It is the arrogance of commonplace minds. As to the other question," he went on, throwing back his head, "would I really prefer to live a life of seclusion than be president - that isn't the simple question you might think it is."

Julian gazed down at the rich blue and red carpet. A cryptic smile made a brief, furtive appearance and then, as quickly as it had come, vanished completely. He looked at her now with a scholar's doubting eyes, as if were deciding how far he could go, how close to the truth he should get.

"I would have told you that I would much prefer a private life, had you asked me six month ago; but now, after everything that has happened, the question answers itself. There isn't a choice; there is nothing to be done except follow wherever the road may lead. Everything is in the hands of fate."

"You could have said no," she reminded him again, pressing for an answer as to why he did not. "You could have said no, and you didn't."

"At that point it was out of my hands," he objected. "What excuse could I have given? That I didn't think I was qualified, that someone else should have the nomination? You were there. Do you think I should have just stepped aside, made a polite refusal, told Louis he didn't know what he was doing? I'll tell you exactly what I thought when he did what he did, when the convention, when twenty-thousand people went wild with excitement - that it all made sense, that it was exactly the reaction I thought that speech could have. The night I wrote it I imagined what it would be like, what it would be like to stand in front of a convention made up of people who thought themselves conservative and did not really know what it meant, people who had never been taught what a conservative government could really do, people who only knew what they had been told: that instead of the best protection, government was the greatest threat to the rights they prize. Don't misunderstand, I never thought that I would end up giving that speech myself, but as I wrote it I imagined how it could be done, how something intelligent could be said, said in a way that everyone could see for themselves where we had gone wrong and how we could remedy our mistakes. And then, when I was giving that speech I was reliving the moment, writing it again, seeing in my mind's eye everything that would happen, the reaction, the applause, the rising chorus of approval, the demand to hear more."

"That seems to have been what Louis thought as well. When he read it he knew you should be president." Rachel looked straight at him, pausing long enough to give the question she was about to ask the significance it deserved. "Is that when he decided to fake that collapse, so that you could take his place and give the speech yourself?"

"I'm sure Louis has told you as much about that as he's told me. But - and I think this is the question you and a lot of other people want to know - is when did I know what he was going to do, if in fact his collapse wasn't real. I didn't. I did't know I was going to be giving that speech until he was lying on the floor and he told me I had to do it."

Rachel Good had never quite believed that. She had become convinced that from the moment he began to write that speech he had somehow known exactly what would happen.

"But you knew - you must have known - that Louis would know as soon as he read it that he could never give it and that you were the only one who could. And if you knew that," she went on, pushing herself forward on the chair until she was perched on the very edge of it, "you must have known that he would try to find a way to make it happen, arrange things so you could give the speech at the convention and what you imagined when you wrote it would actually happen."

A kind of hard shrewdness, not quite concealed by the friendly smile on

Julian's mouth, came into his eyes.

"I have a certain belief in fate, but I'm not clairvoyant. But you didn't come here to delve into the strange origins of my nomination...."

Rachel had no choice but to nod a reluctant agreement. She moved back into the deep comfort of the chair and glanced down at her notebook.

"After you got the nomination, why did you decide not to run a campaign in the traditional sense, no television commercials, none of the normal campaign appearances, no staff, not much of anything, really, except speeches, each one different from the others, and the press conferences you hold every week?"

Julian hesitated. He searched her eyes, making sure she had not forgotten the condition under which they were speaking.

"I understand, this is background only, nothing will be attributed to you."

" I promised you an interview the night at the convention when I gave you the story about letting the convention decide who the vice-presidential candidate should be, and I am sorry I have to insist on this."

"Speeches, press conferences, but no interviews, only this one and it has to be a secret. What is the reason for all this? No one has ever run for president this way."

"Wouldn't that be reason enough?" asked Julian, laughing. His eyes were alive with the sheer temerity of what he had done, defied the conventional thinking that had made politics so utterly predictable and banal. "There is a reason. What is the effect of all these political campaigns conducted through thirty-second ads? They change the way people think. Everything is reduced to an attitude, a simple-minded opinion: cut taxes, cut spending, save the environment, create jobs, stop terrorism, make America strong, make America great. It's what Orwell was writing about in 1984 - a world in which everyone speaks in slogans. And at one level everyone knows it. Listen to what all these self-styled experts say about candidates and their campaigns. The only question is the measured reaction to the different words and phrases in a debate. It is a recipe for stupidity. Everyone sits around trying to find the exact word that will produce the most favorable response. We have forgotten how to speak, what it means to make a reasoned argument, what it means to think sequentially. This is the reason why I am doing this, why there are no slogans, no mindless commercials. I'm not going to be the clown in someone's badly written comedy. I am going to assume that there are still some people out there who want a president who is going to treat them with the serious respect they deserve, and that means, as someone once taught me, always to talk as if there were someone in the room who knows more than I do. Because if you believe that, you will treat everything with all the intelligence you can. I am doing what I am doing as a candidate because that is the way I intend to govern. Everything is going to be public, nothing is going to be private. That is the reason why, with this one exception, I won't give interviews in which the public is not involved. I make this one exception because it is the only way I can give you the kind of background that may help you explain to your readers the reasons for the things that are happening."

"Everything public?" repeated Rachel as if to assure herself that she had heard right. "Except what you regard as private."

"If you mean…, then, yes, you have a point. My niece and nephew have enough to do without having people show up at all hours of the day and night asking what they think of all this."

"I didn't mean that. You're the biggest story in a generation. No one has ever done what you have. They don't even make movies about something this improbable. You're probably going to be president and no one knows anything about you. All we have is what could be written on a half sheet of paper, a one paragraph biography."

"You mean, 'Who is Julian Drake?'" he remarked with a dismissive glance. "Everyone knows what I intend to do if I'm elected. It's all there in the speeches I've given, in the answers I've given to all the questions reporters have asked. I know. You want to know - because you think the public wants to know - about my personal life. What if I told you I've never really had one? What if I told you," he said with a soft undercurrent of laughter in his voice, "that from as early as I can remember all I have ever wanted to do was learn about the world and my place in it?"

"You raised, you helped to raise, two children!" objected Rachel.

"It would be more accurate to say that they helped raise me. I did not teach them anything; we learned things together. They helped me see the world with the child's eyes that, like everyone else who thinks he has grown up, I had lost. When I say I've never had a personal life, that doesn't mean that there haven't been people I have cared about; it doesn't mean that I haven't had my share of disappointments. It doesn't mean," he said, pausing to smile in a way that suggested a confidence, 'that I never wanted to get married."

"Joli Wharton. She told you. Yes, it makes perfect sense that she would. Did she tell you…?"

"Everything," replied Julian. He shook his head at what he must have seemed like, all those years ago, the strange intensity that had both attracted and discouraged the women he had known. "What she told you isn't all true. I really was in love with her. Marriage wasn't just something I thought I should do."

With three fingers of his left hand he scratched at his eyebrow and tried to think how to explain what he had not fully understood at the time. If he had gained any clarity in the vast retrospective of what was now half a lifetime there was always the question how much of what he remembered was the wishful work of his own imagination. Pressing his fingertips together over his mouth, he sat there for a moment, pensive and, as it seemed to Rachel, a little lost.

"I was always talking about what I thought important things," he remarked, coming back to himself, "things that had no obvious bearing on what it takes to live day to day, things that had no relation to what most people are concerned about. I did not care about the things most people care about. All I wanted was to learn, to find someone who could teach me. What kind of woman would have wanted to marry someone who half the time did not know where he was or what time it was, someone more interested in what was going on - and I mean to put this in the present tense - twenty-five hundred years ago in ancient Athens than in what was going to happen tomorrow." With a bashful grin, he added, "Not to put too fine a point on it, I was a complete disaster, a hopeless romantic unwilling to be a prisoner of the present. Which is probably the reason I was so devastated when Joli wouldn't marry me. She thought - she told me - that she didn't think I was really in love with her; she told me she didn't think I could ever really be in love with anyone. I knew then I was never going to have a normal life, that I was always going to be a kind of outsider, that whatever life I had would be lived largely inside myself."

Suddenly aware that he had gone much farther than he had wanted, disclosed more about himself than he had ever intended, Julian looked at Rachel, acknowledging the skill with which she had brought him to talk about things he would never have talked about on his own. He looked at her with the wry respect of a player who too late learns he has lost. He became confidential.

"It's your face. I knew a lawyer who almost never lost a case at trial. A judge said it was because he had a face like a sworn affidavit. All you had to do was look at him and you were sure you could trust him. Joli told me she told you things she shouldn't have, and now, despite that warning, I've done the same thing."

"I'm obviously not as persuasive as that lawyer: I couldn't get either of you to talk on the record."

"That isn't the point, though, is it? You got both of us to tell you things we never would have told anyone else." Stretching his right arm along the back of the sofa, he turned on his hip and with what seemed genuine curiosity and an equally real doubt, asked, "Does it help? Do you know someone better when you know some of the personal details of their private life?"

It seemed an odd question. In any event, the answer was obvious.

"Yes, of course it helps." With a reporter's instinct, she turned it into a question of her own. "Wouldn't you want to know as much as you could about the background of someone you were going to entrust with an important office?"

"Do you mean," he replied with a quick, eager glance, "someone I was thinking to ask become secretary of state? No, I wouldn't. What conceivable difference would it make whether they had a happy childhood or had ever been in love? I know nothing about your background, where you came from, what you wanted to be when you were a young girl, but I trust you to keep your word. I wouldn't have done this with any other reporter. Part of it is that Louis knows you and trusts you, but I make my own judgments. Why do so many people seem to trust me, someone just a few months ago they had never heard of? We trust others because of judgments we make from almost the first moment we hear someone or meet someone. I didn't fall in love with

Joli Wharton because of the things she told me about herself, I didn't fall in love with her because she was going to be a doctor, I didn't fall in love with her because she was black and beautiful and exotic; I fell in love with her the first time I saw her. It is as simple, and as profound, as that. All this analysis, all this endless asking questions, all this search for causes - it is the mystery of existence, and instead of asking how something came to be we ought to be grateful for what it is."

A broad smile shot sideways across his mouth, a triumph over his own impatience, as he laughed away any thought that he might ever be able to explain that what nearly everyone else took so seriously was so comically wrong.

"Next question?" he said, springing forward, ready to get back to specifics.

Rachel glanced at her list, but when she looked up, Julian was on his feet, walking to the window. He shoved his hands deep into his coat pockets and leaned against the casement with his left shoulder. With a wistful expression in his eyes, he studied the scene: not just the White House the other side of the square, but the perspective, the way it looked from this one very particular location.

"I used to come here for breakfast, when I was in the House," he said, looking back to Rachel, sitting straight and alert in the shadows of the elegantly appointed sitting room. "Not very often, but once in a while. I would sit there, in the restaurant down on the first floor, watching well-dressed lobbyists talking seriously among themselves or with some congressman or senator, explaining how some bill would either save the republic or destroy the American economy, and I would wonder whether any of them knew where they were, if any of them knew that this hotel in which they carried on their lucrative trade was once two separate, but joined, houses built for two of the most extraordinary men this country has ever known. John Hay - do you know this? - was one of the two young assistants to Lincoln. Hay and the other assistant, Nicolay - the White House staff, if you will - wrote one of the few biographies of Lincoln worth reading. Hay went on to become one of the greatest secretaries of state we have had. Henry Adams, almost forgotten before he had a chance to make any mark of his own, along with his brother, Brooks, the last of the line that began with John Adams, his son John Quincy

Adams, both of them presidents, then Charles Francis Adams, the son of John Quincy, ambassador to Russia and then, more importantly, ambassador to Great Britain during our Civil War. What was left for a fourth generation Adams to do, with all that history running in his veins, all that second-hand experience, all the stories told by all his old relatives, but become a historian himself, probably - though most of our academic historians would doubtless disagree - the greatest one we have had."

Julian's eyes moved slowly, and, as it were, reluctantly, back to the window and the White House and all the history he remembered, history in which, so far as he could tell, few others had an interest.

"Adams and Hay became lifelong friends," he said, continuing his narrative as if there was some reason that made it important, a reason she would soon come to understand. He gave her a look that seemed to suggest that it was somehow the key to understanding him and what he was trying to do. "Adams, never part of what was going on around him, content to be an observer; Hay, driven to try to make some difference in what he saw as the coming madness of the world, everyone, like their friend Theodore Roosevelt, intent on making America a power to be reckoned with, an industrial giant with a military force that other nations would not only respect but fear."

Julian stared down at the hard polished floor, the side of his face burnished bronze in the sparkling light of the morning sun. The other half, the side closest to where Rachel sat silent and waiting, dark and brooding, as closed to any scrutiny as the other half seemed open to the world. When he turned to look at her his eyes now seemed burdened with regret, a sense of something already lost, the knowledge that what he wanted to accomplish was more than he could ever achieve, that for all the hope and promise, all the bright dancing dreams of the future, it would all end in failure. Then it vanished, that haunted look of a future known before it happened, vanished so quickly that it would have been easy to think it had never been there at all.

"Hay and Adams, the lives they had, the things they knew," he remarked with cheerful seriousness. "What they both saw coming! The law of acceleration - that is what Adams called it - the increasing rate of speed with which through science and technology the world, and especially America, was moving. This, remember, was at the end of the nineteenth, the beginning of the twentieth, century. No one was going to be able to control it! What Adams did not understand - or perhaps he did - was that the time would come when no one would want to, that the time would come when we would all become the prisoners - the willing slaves, if you will - of the science and technology that seemed to promise that with each new discovery, each new breakthrough, each new invention, we would be closer to a golden age in which everyone could have whatever they wanted and would be happier than anyone had ever been. We forgot that the only important question is what kind of people we are, what kind of people we want to become." With a taunting grin, he added, "Write that. Say that you asked me for a list of the most important books I have read and that among other long forgotten things I mentioned The Education of Henry Adams as something that everyone who wants to understand this country and how it has changed should read. That by itself might be enough to cost me the election."

Rachel seized on the suggestion. "And what other books would be on that list?" she asked, as she turned the page in her notebook.

Julian ignored her in a way that made it seem he was not ignoring her at all. He had not finished what he wanted to say; he had left out something essential.

"It started the First World War, it started this century long series of wars and revolutions, technology, industrialization, everything changing, never anything stable, the only constant the fear that you might not keep up, that you might fall behind, that someone else, some other nation, might through some new discovery, some new development, become more powerful and that you would lose your independence and become a client state in another nation's empire. Without any thought what we were doing, without stopping to ask what kind of country, what kind of people, we would become, we became a world power with an empire of our own. That is the issue, the question that needs to be addressed: Should the United States be an empire or a republic? If you are an empire there is no end to the power you think you have to acquire, and like every empire that ever existed every citizen will think the same thing: that whatever you have, you have to keep acquiring more." Julian gave Rachel a long, searching glance. "And what chance do you think I have of convincing anyone of that?"

CHAPTER SIXTEEN

Julian Drake leaned against the grey stone casement of the window, his arms crossed over his chest, staring at the White House glowing in the darkness of a cold November night the other side of Lafayette Square. It was a little before ten o'clock. The polls were closed on the East coast, but they were still voting in California.

"You want to hear a great story?" he asked, smiling at something he had not thought of in years.

Ismael Cooper was struck by the calm quiet of Julian's voice, how utterly composed he seemed. Anyone else would have been wild with excitement, knowing that it was just a matter of minutes before every television network declared the election as good as over.

"Sure, go ahead. Tell me a great story. This may be the last time I won't feel obligated to applaud and tell you it was the greatest goddamn story I ever heard!"

Julian turned toward Ismael slouching in the soft comfort of the sofa half a dozen steps away.

"I imagine we'll both have enough to do without worrying about applause," he said, drily. "You may know the story," he remarked with an air of indifference, turning back to the window. "I wonder what it is like over there. Almost everyone in politics, national politics, has had the itching eagerness to be president. They imagine what it would be like to run, to win, to hold the office. How many of them ever wonder what it would be like when it is over? How many of those who actually got there - how many presidents - gave any thought to what it was going to be like the day they have to leave? Some of them, some of the best - Lincoln, FDR, Kennedy - died while they were still president, but the others…? How many of them haven't wished they could do it all over again, certain that after what they have learned they could do it better? And whatever their mistakes, whatever their failures, they're probably all convinced that history will decide that they could have been one of the great ones if only they had not been stopped at every turn by a senseless opposition. The verdict of history! They forget that history has to be written and that there isn't anyone anymore who knows how to write it!"

"You were going to tell me a story - a great story is the way I think you put it," remarked Ismael, laughing in advance as he tried to anticipate the way Julian would somehow manage to connect this long digression with the story he had not even started to tell.

Julian's eyes flashed with recognition. "When Louis was working as a young assistant to Bob Griffin he had a friend, a Democrat, who was working for Phil Hart, and that is how Louis heard it. A few years after Harry Truman left office he spoke at the Jefferson-Jackson Day Dinner in Detroit. The Democratic national committeeman took him around for the few days he was in Detroit. On the last night, before he said goodbye to Truman at the hotel, he told him what an honor it had been for him; that, like everyone else, he had never forgotten how on election night in 1948, when everyone thought he had lost the election to Dewey, Truman had gone to bed like it was any other night and woke up the next morning to discover that he had been elected to another term; how everyone remembered the huge smile on Truman's face in that famous photograph in which he is holding up the front page of the Chicago Tribune with the headline: 'Dewey Wins!'" Julian tossed back his head and rubbed his hands together, relishing the story he was about to finish. "Truman looked at him for a moment and then, as if he were revealing a deep secret, said 'I'm an old man, and old men have to get up in the middle of the night to take a leak.'

"So the whole story - the one everyone believed, the legend of a president so calm, so confident, going to bed, sleeping through until morning - was a lie. Or was it?" asked Julian, the sparkle in his eyes growing brighter, and deeper, with each word. "Years later, years after Truman told this story in his hotel room, David McCullough wrote a biography of Truman. Truman did not get up in the middle of the night to take a leak; Truman never went to bed. With reporters camped out in front of his house in Independence, Missouri, Truman turned out the lights, went out the back door to an alley where a car was waiting to take him to a hotel outside of town where along with some of his closest advisors he spent the night getting the returns. Now," said Julian with a sudden, sharp look, "what did we learn from this? That Truman told a lie? He didn't. He did not say he got up in the middle of the night to take a leak; he said that old men do that. Did Truman ever say that he went to bed that night? Everyone just assumed he had. It is the difference between telling a lie and not telling everything you know about the truth. It is the difference between knowing the facts and understanding what the facts mean; and knowing, more importantly, which facts have any meaning at all. And that is the reason why there are no more historians, none worth reading. They can assemble facts, they can fit them together the way a child puts blocks back into empty spaces, the way a child in India strings beads on a chain, but give you a sense, a feeling, of what someone was really like, how they thought, why they acted how they did, why they made one decision instead of another - ! They can't do it because they never had to do any of what they are trying to describe, and they have never been close enough to anyone who has, never been close enough to understand what someone in a position of power was trying to do. Read a historian today - What is it but hearsay, what someone else said, what someone else wrote, about people and events."

Julian checked his watch. Twenty more minutes. He shook his head, burdened with the knowledge that his life was about to change, and, changing, would never change back. He looked down at his black polished shoes, clenched his teeth and then, shrugging his shoulders as if there were nothing more to be done, slowly raised his eyes.

"Tell me," he said, turning to Ismael who was sitting, fascinated, on the other side of the room. "Something I've always wanted to know: How did you get your name? Why Ismael? Were your parents religious?"

"Would you like to trade? It isn't the nicest thing you can do to a child, give him a name that will make him an object of ridicule on every playground and in every classroom until he is out of school."

"And an object of serious appraisal and regard when his classmates are old enough to think for themselves," Julian replied with a broad, generous smile. He moved away from the window and took the chair at the end of the coffee table closest to the end of the sofa where Ismael was sitting. "Was it the Bible, or Moby Dick?"

"Moby Dick," laughed Ismael, with a look of wonder and no inconsiderable pride in his small, round eyes. Even now, after all these years, he remained a little astonished at how his name had been chosen. "It was an act of defiance by my mother; gentle defiance, let me add. She loved my father, but my father was a direct descendant of James Fenimore Cooper, and, as if that weren't enough, taught English and American literature. He had it in his head to call me Fenimore. She would have done anything for him, and he knew it - but not that. She told him he could choose the name if it was a girl, but she was going to name a boy. He damn near died when she chose Ismael. She told him that, one, she thought the name pure elegance, and that, two, she could have named me after Moby Dick's author and called me Herman. There are certain benefits. When someone asks what they should call me, I can answer 'They call me Ismael,' and can tell immediately if they are a serious reader. The usual reply is to ask me to spell it."

Ismael Cooper leaned back and studied Julian with a new interest.

"Your father taught ancient and medieval history at Michigan. I remember something...."

He paused to let Julian fill in the blank, but Julian stayed silent, daring him, as it were, to try the hazard of his own memory. A vague recollection of something he had once heard mentioned began to become clearer. His mouth tightened as he moved from doubt to something close to certainty.

"Julian, the emperor, the one who tried to destroy Christianity, the one who tried to bring back the ancient gods of Rome. That was your father's...?"

"Yes, but that was not the reason."

"Not the reason?"

Julian laughed. "It wasn't because of what Julian tried to do; it was because of what Julian was, perhaps the greatest mind since Plato and Aristotle, in some ways the last great mind of antiquity, the student who even as a boy taught his teachers."

"I used to hear the same thing said about you," said Ismael, with a searching glance. "When you were in the House, when everyone - and not just Louis - thought you would one day wind up being president. They all thought you the smartest guy they had ever met."

Julian smiled with regret at the world's mistake; and then, quick as light, his eyes opened wide and the smile, changing, flashed with a kind of gleeful self-mockery.

"No one who thought that ever read Ammianus Marcellinus!"

"Ammianus…?"

"The Roman History of Ammianus Marcellinus. What I said a moment ago, that there aren't any historians worth reading today. Ammianus Marcellinus was a great Roman general when the Roman Empire was on the very verge of collapse. He knew Julian, served under him, understood him in a way few others ever did. And the care with which he writes! He lived through the greatest change that had taken place in the long history of Rome, the change from a martial empire in which the gods were in the service of the state, to an empire guided and controlled by a religion that disparaged the very things - discipline and courage - that had made Rome great, a religion that was as ruthless as any secular power when it came to those who refused to consent to what it taught or stood between it and power. Marcellinus wrote the history of Rome, but he wrote it after Rome was finished, weakened by Christianity to the point that everyone understood that it was only a matter of time before the barbarians would come. I only wish there were someone like him now to write our history, the decline and fall of the great nation we could have been."

"Could have been? You don't think…?"

"That we're a great nation anymore? There is a difference between power and greatness, a difference between strength and wisdom. All we talk about is freedom; all we have done is make ourselves slaves, slaves to what in an older tradition were called the needs, the desires, of the body. No one talks about the soul, or the mind; or if they do happen to mention the mind it is in the context of the need to train enough good minds so we can lead the word in technology, innovation. Did you ever read Plato? - Julian, emperor of Rome, spent all day on the business of the empire, governing and making war, and half of every night writing letters, messages and orders, commentaries, even dialogues, all concerned with what he wanted Rome to become again. And then, after all that, every night a few hours studying, reading Plato in a way scarcely anyone now would know how to do, remembering everything, each word, each sentence, noticing how the meaning changes, realizing the importance of each character, seeing it all as if he were there himself watching every gesture, hearing each turn of phrase, noticing how the conversation always leaves out something of importance, how every dialogue abstracts from something essential and how that becomes the key to understanding what is really at issue. Julian filled his head up with this, understood it as well as he understood himself. Everyone who has ever read The Republic, if they remember nothing else remember two things: the story of the cave and that strange suggestion that the only remedy for the evils of the world is if philosophers become kings or kings become philosophers. Julian was exactly that, a philosopher, that rarest of all human beings, a man who could see straight into the heart of things, and who, because of that, knew how to conceal what he saw."

With a look of thoughtful cynicism, Julian brooded for a moment over what, as he well understood, no one else knew, much less cared about. For most people ancient history began and ended with their grandparents, if it extended even that far back in time.

"Julian became emperor in 362 A.D. and died - was killed - twenty-two months later. The world was full of him then, loved by those few fortunate enough to know him, those like Ammianus Marcellinus who lived to write about him, and hated as few others have ever been hated, by the priests and apologists for Christianity as the apostate who was certain to spend eternity in Hell. And now, today…?" A strange, fugitive smile creased the corners of his mouth. "Julian did not want to become emperor, but he knew that if he did not, Rome would be ruined and he would be destroyed. He did what he had to do, arranged things so that it would seem that the army had forced it upon him. Do you see the genius in that, the double deception involved? He would have preferred a private life, studying Plato, to a life in politics. He pretended to be a Christian so he would be left alone. Constantius, the emperor who had killed, among others, his own brother, Julian's father, decided he could trust Julian precisely because he had no political ambition.

"Julian did not want power, power was thrust upon him. He had never been a soldier and became one of the greatest commanders Rome had known. Suddenly, Julian seemed a threat, which meant Julian was in danger. If Julian had not been a scholar, he would not have been given power in the first place; if he had not been a scholar, someone who could grasp in an instant what most people could never understand, he would not have known what to do when power was given him. And now, in a sense, history repeats itself, doesn't it? If I had not read, and studied, certain great writers of the past; if I had written nothing more than an ordinary speech...."

The sentence went unfinished. Whatever had happened in the past, whatever Julian had done to start the chain of events that had led to this, there were limits, limits of chance and opportunity, to how much of the future could be written in advance. Dreams of greatness, almost always the stuff of tragedy in the end, were, despite that knowledge, irresistible when fate made plain the need. Suddenly restless, tense, unable to sit or stand still, Julian began to pace nervously around the room. He laughed at his own discomfort.

"I wish it would not happen; I wish that the telephone would ring and instead of the loser's call of congratulation someone would tell me that I lost." He flashed a quick, self-deprecating grin. "And then I wish I did not have to wait two months, that I could start tonight, just walk across the street and begin all the work I want to do." He stopped at the window and gazed again at the White House. The lights were on in all the windows. "They're all watching television," he said, with a careless shrug. He looked back at Ismael. "You and I may be the only two people in the country who aren't."

"Do you want me to turn it on?" asked Ismael. "It feels a little strange, not knowing."

"Remember Harry Truman."

"I remember what you told me."

"Remember how much credit he got for seeming to be that much in control of himself, that confident in what would happen."

"And what should I tell the press when they ask what you were doing, how you spent the evening of your election to the presidency?"

Shoving his hands deep into his pockets, Julian gave him a rueful, sideways glance.

"Tell the truth; tell them we spent the evening in conversation. Tell them we talked about politics, tell them we talked about Roman history, tell them…." Julian's eyes suddenly brightened. "Tell them we discussed certain passages in The Roman History of Ammianus Marcellinus."

"You don't really want…?"

"Sure. Why not? Even if it wasn't true, it would be a good thing to say. There might be a few people who, when they hear that, will want to know what possible relevance something like that could have," remarked Julian, with an ambiguous smile. "Someone once wrote a remarkable line about Nietzsche, that he 'sought by a new beginning to retrieve antiquity from the emptiness of modernity and, with this experiment, vanished in the darkness of insanity.' It is not impossible that someone may someday write something similar about me. But don't worry, that day is, I think, still a long way off. In the meantime…. Did you ever read Nietzsche? The last philosopher. Really. There is no one after him. Some say Heidegger, but without Nietzsche, Heidegger is impossible. Nietzsche questioned everything about modernity - and antiquity as well. Modern science, the religion of the modern world, what everyone believes will solve all our problems, what has in fact created most of the serious problems we have - Nietzsche said it was 'one way to see the world,' i.e. not the only way, not the best way."

Julian was speaking faster the longer he spoke, the words coming now in an endless flow, speaking as if he were all alone, listening to himself say things he would never say in front of anyone else, the private, late night musing of a solitary soul. Ismael had come almost to expect it, the way that on a sudden some otherwise random, unremarkable thought would lead to a long digression into things that no one beside Julian knew anything about or had the slightest interest in hearing. He was, thought Ismael, like a character out of Shakespeare, forever explaining things to people who, if you read the plays, existed only in his mind.

"Science," continued Julian, "is the prejudice of the modern age. It is fascinating the way everyone thinks that if you can trace things back to a beginning, instead of trying to understand the end toward which something is made to move, you have everything you need to know. Science looks back and insists that the only scientific, that is to say knowledgeable, men in antiquity were some of the pre-Socratics philosophers like Democritus who thought the world was made up of atoms and that atoms were organized by chance. Socrates, and those who came after him like Plato and Aristotle, were by that reckoning garrulous fools who did not understand anything. What does science tell us about the human condition? - That we evolved from lesser species. Evolution. No one seems to notice that evolution and revealed religion share a common belief in a beginning. No one takes seriously the possibility - which was more than a possibility for every important thinker - that there is no beginning, that the world is eternal." Julian started to laugh. "If I had said that in that speech I gave, the only thing certain is that we wouldn't be sitting here, waiting to find out if I have just been elected president of the United States."

The telephone began to ring with a lonely, strident insistence. They looked at each other, certain, each of them, what it meant. Standing straight, his shoulders square, Julian picked up the receiver and listened in silence.

"You conducted yourself with grace and courage. You have much to be proud of. I hope we have the chance to talk things over sometime in the next few weeks. And thank you, thank you for your kind words of encouragement."

He put down the telephone and for a brief moment stared down at it, pondering what he had heard.

"She's more interesting when she isn't working off someone else's script, when she isn't trying to convince everyone that she's exactly what they want." He looked at Ismael with mock despair. "And now I get to go downstairs and try to convince everyone that they haven't made the worst mistake of their lives."

He started for the door, hesitated, and then turned around.

"There was something in her voice. She was forcing herself to sound cheerful, confident, only interested in wishing me well. But, my God, this has to be devastating for her, the one thing she has wanted for years, the chance to be the first woman elected president. And now, to have it all taken away, the last chance she'll ever have. The years, the effort, the constant, unremitting attacks, the.... I kept hearing in the back of my mind the words of Adlai Stevenson when he lost the second time to Eisenhower: 'I'm too old to cry and it hurts too much to laugh.'"

Julian glanced at the clock on the mantelpiece. It was ten minutes past ten. He took a deep breath. "Are you ready for this?"

The hotel ballroom was jammed with people, but unlike other election nights when those who had worked on the campaign came to celebrate, eager to cheer all the expressions of gratitude of their candidate, all the glittering promises of how, thanks to them, the future was going to be so much better than at least the recent past, the room was filled with reporters, come to cover an event. It was the culmination of a campaign that had, in ways most of them still did not quite comprehend, depended on their willingness, their eager willingness, to convey directly to the public whatever Julian Drake had wanted to say. There had been no organization, no fund-raising, and certainly no speechwriters; there had been no 'ground game,' no effort to recruit thousands of volunteers to go door to door convincing people of what they had already heard directly from the candidate on television or the other electronic devices that had become almost as much a part of them as their own eyes and ears. Julian began with what Rachel Good, standing at the back, thought might have been ironic.

"I want to thank all of you for your honest reporting, for the way that through the questions you asked you allowed me to talk directly to the American people about the problems we face, the problems we now, together, need to solve."

Few things give greater encouragement to enthusiasm than victory, even if, or perhaps especially if, it is a victory in which you have played only a minor part, if any part at all. The press had come almost to idolize Julian Drake. He had given them unprecedented access, had never failed to answer a question, even when they had been, as some had been at the beginning, hostile and even disrespectful. He had met them, as he had promised, at least once every week, and he had never once stopped their questions because of time. He was something new in their experience: a candidate who thought their questions deserved a serious response and because of that was more than willing to admit his ignorance when he was asked something he did not know. When it happened, when he could not answer someone's question, he always came back to it at the next press conference, after he had had a chance, as he put it, "To remedy some of the deficiencies of my education." They saw him as someone different, someone with wit and charm and an uncanny sense of what was relevant and what was not, what was at the heart of things and what was merely errant chatter. They saw in him - and this was the key to everything - someone who when he spoke seemed to be speaking directly, if not exclusively, to each of them. They were, almost all of them, in the conventional sense liberal in their politics, but more than half of them voted for him, and most of those who did not did not much mind that he won.

"What did you think, what passed through your mind, when the networks first declared you the winner?" asked an earnest young woman, batting her eyelashes as she struggled to control the nervousness in her voice.

"I'm afraid I wasn't watching," replied Julian, with a quick, apologetic glance. He had not wanted to make her question seem unimportant. "They say that in 1948, Harry Truman went to bed and woke up in the morning to find that he had won an election everyone thought he would lose. I didn't go to bed," he added to the laughter of the crowd. "But I knew I would learn the result soon enough."

"Well, if you didn't watch," yelled someone, "what did you do? Did you call anyone, talk to anyone? Weren't you the least bit concerned about what might happen? Didn't you think there was at least a chance you might lose?"

"Losing was a hope I never quite gave up," replied Julian, with a look that seemed to invite a challenge. "But I'm not going to say with Sherman that if elected I won't serve," he said, laughter in his eyes. "Make no mistake. I am honored that the people of this country have given me their trust. That trust is a sacred responsibility." His expression was now serious. He searched for the words to convey some sense of the burden he felt. "I did not seek the office, I never thought myself as someone indispensable, but now that it has happened all I can promise is to devote myself, heart and soul, to what is in the best interest of the country. This will require sacrifice and effort, not just from me, but from all of us. This country can do great things again, but only if we believe, as we used to believe, that great things are worth doing; only if we believe, as we used to believe, that it is not what we have that is important, but who we are; and that it isn't wealth or fame, but human excellence, that is worth pursuing."

CHAPTER SEVENTEEN

Clutching the collar of his dark coat tight around his throat, Julian bent his head against the snow swirling in a glistening haze as he trudged along a Paris sidewalk soft as a white Persian carpet. The lights from the windows of the shops and restaurants, the muffled sounds of the voices inside, dozens of dinner table conversations, the passing sideways glimpse of eager faces, the quick easy laughter, the silent smiles, the sudden graceful gestures, the shared intimacies of friends and lovers, the polite familiarity of aging married couples, all of it part of the inherent charm of the place. Paris, anytime of the year, but Paris a week before Christmas was irresistible.

Julian walked fast, laughing at the way he seemed to be following his own breath, visible in the frigid air inches in front of his face. He passed the tan stone facade entrance to Notre Dame, glowing with a melancholy warmth in the lights that surrounded the ancient cathedral from below. There were other people on the street and once or twice Julian could feel the look, sense the surprise, and then the quick decision that they were wrong, that it could not have been who for a brief moment they had thought it was. Crossing the bridge to the Left Bank, Julian continued on his journey, threading his way through the narrow streets until, a few blocks from the Sorbonne, he found the building he was looking for. He climbed a narrow decrepit wooden staircase to the third floor where two doors faced each other across the landing. One of them was open, just an inch or so, but enough to tell Julian that he was expected.

A short hallway led past the only bedroom to a large book-lined living room that was also the library and study. An old man was sitting at a desk positioned sideways to a double-window through which Notre Dame could be seen on the other side of the river half a dozen blocks away. Marcel Dubose looked up from the book that lay open under a bronze lamp light on the desk. His lips, pressed tight together, gave the impression of great concentration. A few wisps of gray hair covered a small and almost perfectly round head, and the skin sagged a little beneath an unremarkable chin, but, along with most of the other features of his face, this was background, the vague outline of what might have been remembered had you never seen his eyes, eyes that seemed to be a reflection, a mirror, if you will, of the closest thing to perfect reason anyone had ever encountered. It was impossible to know their color, whether to describe them as blue or brown, or green, or any other single shade; they were every color, and every depth, drawing you deeper the closer, the longer, you looked. Those eyes told you that Marcel Dubose understood things few others could even begin to learn, and that if you were just willing to admit that everything you thought you knew might be wrong, he could help you find the truth.

"Julian!" he cried, taking both of Julian's hands in his own. "How good of you to come!"

Marcel Dubonse spoke English with barely a trace of a French accent. Despite his rather fragile appearance, he had a rich, cultured voice that filled the room with such a sense of comfortable self-assurance that it would have been impossible for someone of intelligence to want to be anywhere but here, in this small Paris apartment, on a cold winter night, listening to whatever he might care to say.

He motioned for Julian to take one of the two slightly shabby armchairs that sat opposite the window and the desk. There was a small table with a lamp between them. A half dozen leather bound books, each with numerous scraps of paper marking pages waiting for another reading, were stacked beneath a white lamp shade.

"I was a little surprised....No, that's not true," he said, shaking his head in mild disapproval at beginning with a well-intentioned lie. "I thought I might hear from you; I certainly hoped I would. Perhaps a letter, a telephone call. I knew you were in Paris, but I couldn't imagine you could ever get away. Everyone now knows who you are - your picture is in all the papers, meeting with the French president and other European heads of state - Julian Drake! Soon to be president of the United States! And all those security precautions! How did you ever manage it?"

Julian glanced around the room, remembering the times he had been here before, sitting in this same chair, listening to the quiet, unhurried voice of the wisest man he had ever known. Everything was exactly the same, nothing had been moved or changed, the furniture, the few pictures on the walls, the only difference the books on the lamp table, the ones Marcel Dubose was reading now.

"It wasn't that difficult," he replied, his gaze on the near wall where in an old black and white photograph a younger Marcel Dubose was standing with two other young men, obviously students, all looking as old and serious as they knew how. Even in his twenties he had the same, astonishing eyes. "I left the hotel by a back entrance," he explained, with a brief, rather modest smile. "When no one expects to see you, when no one is looking for you, no one really notices if you happen to pass them on the street. A few people seemed to think I looked familiar, but decided I could not be who they thought I looked like."

"So you hid yourself in plain view - like certain writers we used to discuss when you were here."

"Like Machiavelli, say things that seem so outrageous nearly everyone will think you don't really mean it?"

"Yes, precisely," said Marcel Dubose, his eyes bright with recognition. "I have missed our conversations, our late-night ventures into ancient and largely forgotten things. I still give my lectures at the Sorbonne, but that isn't quite the same as having someone with whom I can talk. But never mind that now. I want to tell you that I am not surprised, what has happened; not surprised that you've been elected president," he said in all seriousness. "Yes, I know - it is extremely surprising, the way it happened. But not surprising that it should have happened. Anyone who has ever known you would know that."

He reached across and gently patted Julian's arm and for a moment searched his eyes.

"Whatever you intend to do, you'll need to do it right away. American history, I don't need to tell you, is full of this example, although everyone seems to have forgotten it. Roosevelt's Hundred Days, the first few months after you come to the office, that short period of time when the country wants its new president to do well and when everyone is too stunned by what has happened to have any thought about any alternatives, when there hasn't been time for any serious opposition to form. This isn't just the American experience. Remember what happened when Julian Caesar was murdered, or rather remember that anything could have happened, that if Brutus and the others - if Cicero - had had a better idea what to do, the republic might have been restored."

A shrewd smile crossed his pale lips as he waited for Julian to pick up the thread, to continue, as it were, the conversation that had begun between the two of them years before, the conversation that though frequently interrupted had never been abandoned.

"A republic or an empire," replied Julian, nodding in agreement that this was still the issue on which nearly everything else depended.

"When you called to tell me you were coming, I found the passage in deGaulle's memoirs I wanted to make sure you knew." He took a book from the lamp table and opened it to the page he had marked. "This is from de Gaulle's account of the meeting he held with John F. Kennedy when Kennedy visited France early in his presidency. It is about what Kennedy was planning to do in Vietnam.

"'John Kennedy gave me to understand that the American aim was to establish a bulwark against the Soviets in the Indo-Chinese peninsula. But instead of giving him the approval he wanted, I told the President that he was taking the wrong road.'"

Marcel Dubose looked up. "Without the Soviet empire, without the Soviet attempt to dominate Europe, there might not have been an American empire.

Perhaps - though we can never know - if the Soviets had been content with only Russia, the Americans might have lost any desire to involve themselves in Europe and other places. That is a separate question from whether, having decided to expand its power throughout the world, it made sense to do what Kennedy wanted to do. de Gaulle, who knew something about Indo-China where the French had suffered a humiliating defeat, tried to warn him in words which can only be described as prophetic, and not just for what happened in Vietnam, but for what is happening now, today, in the Middle East.

"'You will find,' I told him, 'that intervention in this area will be an endless entanglement. Once a nation has been aroused, no foreign power, however strong, can impose its will upon it.' Then de Gaulle told him point blank what would happen. 'I predict that you will sink step by step into a bottomless quagmire, however much you spend in men and money.'"

Marcel Dubose slowly closed the copy of de Gaulle's memoirs and held it for a moment in his lap as he thought about the lessons that should have been obvious to everyone and nearly everyone had ignored. He shook his head, put the book back on the table and turned to his guest.

"It is the virtue of Americans, and it is the vice of Americans, to believe that everyone wants to be like them. It is the reason for their remarkable generosity, their willingness to come to the assistance of people, of nations, that need their help; it is the reason why they think that anyone who doesn't share their belief in the rights of the individual, who doesn't believe that democracy is the only legitimate form of government, is the embodiment of evil. It is the reason why no one in America has the faintest understanding why nothing you do in the Middle East will ever work. It is the reason why, despite, or perhaps because, so many American politicians talk so glibly about Sunni and Shiite, none of them understands what Islam means." A sudden, bright smile crossed his mouth. "All of them, except one. You know better than anyone what I mean."

"I remember what you taught me," replied Julian, grateful for the chance to remind him how much he owed to the time they had spent together.

"It is easy, too easy, to get sidetracked by those who want to make a religion, their religion, more acceptable to what the modern world demands

- toleration, everyone free to think or believe anything they like. But what is toleration if not the insistence that you ignore the truth and encourage error? What is toleration if not the admission that you don't believe in anything, that one belief is as good as any other, that nothing is worth dying for? This is possible only if you believe that religion, that faith, is a purely private affair. Islam has never believed that, never allowed that. Neither, remember, did Christianity when Christianity, for more than a thousand years, dominated Europe and the West. The Inquisition ought to be sufficient proof of that. How could the Church, God's voice on earth, tolerate any teaching other than its own, how could it do anything except stamp out heresy whenever and wherever it could? The early Christians, the most devout Christians there ever were, were more than willing - eager! - to die for what they believed. Hundreds of years before Mohammed was born, Christians gladly went to their death, martyrs to the faith, rejoicing that they were leaving this 'vale of tears' for eternity in heaven. That is what Christianity and Islam share at the core - the belief that life is nothing more than a test, a way to determine who deserves salvation, life in heaven, life in paradise, life forever, life that begins only with death.

"Islam took seriously the Christian teaching. If everything depends on the crucial question whether you have embraced the true religion, if the question is whether you will live forever in the joys of paradise or the torments of hell, then it would be intolerable not to do everything within your power to bring this truth to everyone. These misguided historians of ours sometimes talk about the toleration extended to Christians, to unbelievers, when Islam ruled all of North Africa and Spain. There is some truth in this. There was a kind of toleration. Christians were given three choices: convert to Islam, pay a poll tax, or be executed. Some no doubt paid the tax. It was substantial. Most converted, or pretended to."

Folding his arms over his thin, sloping chest, Marcel Dubose crossed his right leg over his left and began to swing his foot back and forth. A smile danced across his mouth.

"It isn't just the question of what you believe; it goes to the nature of religion. We forget our own history; we think that history is our history, that everything that has happened has led to us, the present moment, the modern time. We still believe, despite all the evidence to the contrary - the wars, the genocides, the revolutions of that most violent of all the centuries of which we have any record, the twentieth century - that history moves in only one direction, that we are, somehow, always making progress, that our lives are and will always be getting better, that each generation builds on the others. We may be dwarfs, but we stand on the shoulders of all who came before and, as someone once put it, we can do more than giants ever could. You will forgive me if I remind you what you have heard me say more than once before: the world is completely mad.

"There is more to it than this," he went on, nodding twice to emphasize the importance, an importance he knew Julian understood, of what he was about to say. "It is the question what Islam really means, why it has such a hold, why so many are willing to martyr themselves for their belief, why American seem so incapable of understanding what is going on. We in the West, even most Catholics, think that religion, faith, belief, is a matter of conscience, what each individual chooses to believe. It was what the Reformation managed to accomplish: everyone could think that they could have a relationship, a direct relationship, with God. No need for a Church, no need for a priest, no need for a common authority to tell you what you needed to do for your salvation. Read Kierkegaard to see what happened as a result, how easy it became for everyone to make all kinds of accommodation with the requirements of the world, how success in the here and now became part, an important part, of how God would judge you. Islam has never thought anything like the same way. There is no room for individual choice - in anything. Islam is the closest thing we have to our own antiquity, before the modern experiment by which the state and the individual were seen as two things separate and apart. Simple formulation: in modern democratic countries anything the law does not prohibit is permitted, in ancient Athens, or ancient Rome, in the writings of Plato and Aristotle, anything the law does not require is prohibited. The distinction is lost among us; we have forgotten all our own beginnings. When we see those same things, that same teaching, among Muslims we think it backward, barbaric, the ignorant practices of people who have never been allowed the kind of education that would liberate them from their prejudices.

"Islam controls everything, every aspect of the lives of believers.

Everything, even the hand you use to perform certain bodily functions. We look at this, we read the Koran, and see a kind of regimentation that seems the very antithesis of the freedom we all claim to prize. A Muslim looks at America, or looks at France, and what does he see? What is the result of our much vaunted freedom, the freedom we insist he should want as much as we do, and, more than that, insist it is what he really wants, deep down inside, if he were only free to express himself? What arrogance! What does a Muslim see? - A people devoted to mindless entertainment, to violence, to sexual exploitation, a people without religion, without faith, without the ability, or even the desire, to distinguish good and evil, a people who in the name of toleration proclaim sodomy a legitimate alternative to the natural relation between men and women. We say we believe in freedom. They ask, freedom for what?

"But leave all that aside. What really is the nature of our complaint? That they engage in acts of terrorism. We bomb them, destroy their countries, kill hundreds of thousands, and then, when their governing class has been eliminated, hundreds of thousands more are killed in civil wars that inevitably follow. And then we think that if only they were democratic.... Do you know how ignorant we are? We refuse to believe that democracy isn't what everyone wants to have. It is beyond our comprehension that there can be no democracy in a Muslim country. The law is not, and can never be, what a majority might happen to want; the law is what the Koran - the word of God - says it is. So we attack them, overthrow their governments, insist that they believe, like we do, in the rights of the individual, insist, in effect, that they stop believing in what they have believed for more than a thousand years, and call them barbarians when they take up arms, or try to take up arms, when we go after them with planes and tanks and all the advanced weaponry of our more civilized way of life!"

Julian had listened with an intense interest. He disagreed with nothing that Marcel Dubose had said. The question was not whether it was true, whether the West continued to misjudge Islam and what it meant; the question was what could be done about it.

"deGaulle gave Kennedy advice that Kennedy did not follow. And Vietnam ended up exactly as deGaulle had said it would. But deGaulle did something himself that we should probably do now. He ended the French control of Algeria, did he not? And that, if I remember what I have read, almost started a civil war at home."

"You're wondering if the same thing would happen in America? Algeria was considered part of France. Generations of French settlers had made it their home. You have nothing like that kind of connection with the Middle East, except, in a sense, Israel. That isn't the problem you face. The problem is -"

"That I'll be accused of running from a fight, accused of letting the terrorists win, accused of inviting an attack."

"You may well be preventing one. Why do they hate America, why do they hate the West, if it isn't because we refuse to leave them alone? But," he added, with a shrewd look in his eyes, "you're not worried about what anyone is going to think about what you've done. You didn't get elected president because you wanted applause. You are going to try to do something no one else would even think of, much less attempt. And it wouldn't stop you - it won't stop you - if you knew you were almost certain to fail. You have to convince a country that what it most prizes isn't worth having, that wealth isn't an end in itself, that....I read some of the things you said. You're right of course - human excellence is the only thing worth pursuing. But most people still think that means the ability to make money."

"It won't be that difficult," replied Julian. He seemed to dismiss the objection as a matter of at most minor importance. He glanced around the small dimly lit room, laughing quietly at the contrast with the stunning luminosity of Marcel Dubose's remarkable mind. "Remember the discussions we had, just last year, about the French Revolution and all the things that brought it about," he remarked, as he got up and walked over to the window.

Through the slow falling snow, across the sharp sloping green metal roofs of the buildings that stretched a tangled mass down to the Seine, he watched the way the ground lights bathed the cathedral, built nearly a thousand years before, in a golden haze, while he watched in his mind the generous and inept Louis XVI and the faded remnants of the aristocracy of France play their appointed parts in a drama that, once it started, nothing in now more than two hundred years had been able to stop. He turned back to Marcel Dubose sitting quietly in his chair.

"Everyone now thinks it was the greatest thing that ever happened. No one remembers what was lost. A well-intentioned, dull-minded king, a stupid, greedy and utterly useless aristocracy, taxing the poor to starvation and death, and a new voice in the world, an echo of Rousseau, preaching the new religion of human brotherhood and equality; a religion that destroyed every sentiment of respect for the differences between what is better and what is worse, that destroyed every belief in order and authority, that brought into being mass democracy and then, because someone had to govern, Napoleon, and after him, the constant back and forth between anarchy and tyranny."

"But, Julian - do you really think we can go back? Remember what we studied, remember what Plato and Aristotle wrote. City-states in which everyone knew, at least by second-hand report, everyone else, ten thousand citizens. Athens, when Socrates was alive and Pericles controlled things, had a population of more than three hundred thousand, but that included slaves and foreigners who were allowed to stay for a limited period of time and without civic rights. That would be considered today nothing more than a large town or small sized city. Everything has changed. It doesn't affect the truth of what the nature of a human being is, but the conditions under which we live are so different, the enormous volume and density, all the people who have to have some means of existence. Someone could give a speech in an assembly in Athens and change what Athens was going to do. Even in Rome, with its empire, someone like Cicero could make a speech and the world, if I can put it like this, would listen. But now....?" He started to laugh. "But I forget, that is exactly what you did, isn't it? - Gave a speech that changed everything. Still, you understand my point. The world has changed; we cannot go back."

A smile like the triumph of duplicity, a smile like an open secret, slipped across Julian's mouth.

"It depends on what you want to restore, what you want to preserve, what you want people to remember. And, besides, if everything moves in circles, going forward is going back. It is one of the things you helped me see, years ago, when I first came to Paris and we began our long conversation. Phaedrus, that dialogue in which Plato writes about writing, that anything well-written can be started, and ended, anywhere, that perfect writing is like a perfect sphere."

"Yes, but he understood by that the necessity to read things more than once. You cannot know what the beginning really means until you have read something all the way through."

"And even then," remarked Julian, with laughter in his eyes, "if it is one of Plato's dialogues you would not yet have understood very much. Every night, for a few hours, I put everything else aside, and concentrate on trying to grasp more firmly, to see more clearly, the real meaning of what he wrote."

Marcel Dubose looked down at his small hands with their thin white parchment fingers. His mouth trembled, twitching at the corners with the eagerness of his thought. He looked up with a strange, pensive stare.

"Like a second Julian. Just three blocks from here, the place where Julian spent winters when he was with the army -"

"Almost seventeen hundred years ago."

"When the army made him emperor."

"When Julian managed things so that the army would force him to do what he could not appear to do on his own."

"Yes, precisely," agreed Marcel Dubose, "if you read between the lines of what our historian, Ammianus Marcellinus, wrote almost that long ago. It was a perfect life."

"Killed when he was, what, thirty-two or thirty-three?"

"But did more, understood more, than almost anyone ever has."

"Agreed, but only to a point. Because had he lived, think what he might have achieved, how much would have changed. Instead of Christianity and the fall of Rome, the restoration of the ancient gods and a world that believed in life instead of death. If Julian had lived neither Christianity, nor any other religion that taught weakness instead of strength, would have survived. Instead of slavery to the delusion of a false equality before God, there would still be respect for the freedom of the human mind. I don't flatter myself that I can be a second Julian, but I have tried to live the way he did, trying to learn more about the world - the way the world is ordered and the way in which we, as human beings, have our place in it. And that, really, is the reason I was so desperate to see you again. There isn't anyone else I can talk to, no one else would have any idea what I was talking about, no one who would think an interest, a serious interest, in ancient thought more than a strange eccentricity. Don't misunderstand. I won't hide the fact that instead of playing golf, or watching sports on television, like most of our recent presidents, I study the serious works of the human mind, but I have to do it in a way that makes it sound like something everyone would like, if not to do themselves, then to have their children grow up wanting to try."

"In other words, you plan to be ironic - not the way most people think the meaning of the word. Ironic in the sense of saving others from the embarrassment, or the anger, of their own limitations; saying things that nearly everyone will believe means something of which they readily approve. The way Socrates always spoke, or, more to the point, what Winston Churchill once said to Stalin: 'The truth is too precious not to be attended by an accompaniment of lies.'"

"Yes..., ironic, if you will, but not with you. I will write you letters. Only when I write do I find I can really think. Sequential thought comes only at the point of a pen. Keep what I write, show it to no one. Never mention to anyone that I have written anything at all. When I am finally done with politics, give the letters back, but if something happens to me do with them what you think best. Burn them, or pass them on to someone, if there is anyone, who might benefit from them. More important than any of that, when you get a letter from me, write back to me, if you would: keep this conversation of ours alive. There is nothing more important than keeping alive the best thought we have. Here," he added, reaching inside his jacket for his pen. "This is how to address things so that no one but me will ever read them."

Marcel Dubose took the sheet of paper on which Julian had scribbled down the private address he could use. Nodding his agreement that he would do exactly as he had been asked, he folded she sheet in half and placed it inside his own pocket.

"We began talking about Islam and the way we have failed to understand it," he said, never doubting that Julian would want him to go back to the central thread of the conversation. "Machiavelli was a great admirer of Islam, the discipline it imposed, the willingness to use force, the way in which every aspect of life was controlled by a single, undivided authority. Christianity had no chance against that kind of organized militancy. Constantinople had just recently fallen. The rescue of the all but forgotten works of Plato and other Greek writers made possible by the Medici and their money was the beginning of the Renaissance. Islam was triumphant; the Church, under Pope Alexander VI, the Borgia pope, and his son, Cesare, had become through treachery and murder utterly corrupt. Machiavelli understood - and no one remembers this - that Christianity was in its death throes. A new religion was needed. If it had not been for the Reformation, if it had not been for Luther, the Church might have been transformed, turned into an agency of encouragement for the life we have instead of an imaginary kingdom of heaven.

"Machiavelli writes somewhere that a religion lasts between 1667 and 3000 years. He wrote in the early years of the sixteenth century, which means that Christianity had only a hundred years or so left. Machiavelli wanted to establish a new religion, and, in a way, he did - a religion in which everyone worships the acquisition of power. It has been a great success. Look at how many have abandoned Christianity. What has been the result? We have no religion, in the traditional sense of the word. Religion is dead. Nietzsche understood this. God is dead, everything is permitted. Julian wanted to restore the ancient gods of Rome, because without that belief the Roman people would never feel the necessity to sacrifice themselves and what they owned for the greatness of Rome. But Nietzsche - which means all of us in the modern world, in the West - had nothing he could restore. You know - I remember we discussed that line, so awful in its significance, that Karl Lowith wrote: 'Nietzsche sought by a new beginning to retrieve antiquity from the emptiness of modernity and, with this experiment, vanished in the darkness of insanity.' That line still haunts me. It puts a stop to every hope, it confirms every feeling of despair, about our future. Modern science has become the only thing we take seriously, and modern science, and the technology it has created, seems destined to destroy not only whatever we have left of civilization, but what it means to be a human being. And so, my friend," he added with a gentle, benevolent smile, "now that you are about to become president of the United States, what do you intend to do about it?"

There was a long silence, a profound quiet in the room, expressive of a cheerful confidence, a self-assurance that had nothing to do with any estimate of the chances that success would follow the attempt, whatever that attempt might be. It was instead the certainty that the attempt itself was what was important, that it was not what you were able to do that counted, but what you were able to be.

"I remember Lowith's line," said Julian, as he began to move around the room.

His words had the distant sound of someone speaking to himself. There were times when Marcel Dubose could not quite hear, which did not mean that he did not understand what Julian was saying. He could imagine easily enough what he missed.

"Not that long ago I repeated it to someone, repeated it with the suggestion that it might end up my own fate, driven mad by the world's insanity, the doubt I sometimes have about whether the ancient thought I think so valid, so important, has any meaning, whether it might be only a delusion, proof of my own disordered mind that what everyone finds so obvious, so clear and convincing, is to me in every respect entirely false."

Marcel Dubose laughed. His eyes, dazzling in their brilliance, seemed to move in a dozen different directions at once. His small, perfectly shaped head bobbed from side to side with a child's eager delight.

"Yes, precisely; that is the choice we have left: either the world is insane or we are; or, rather, the world is completely insane and we are not entirely crazy. It is the strange fate of human beings, the reason why we are sometimes said to be the playthings of the gods. No one possesses wisdom; the best of us, the very few of us, Plato, Aristotle, a handful of others, who alone warrant the name philosopher, that is to say lovers of wisdom, love what they do not have. Philosophy is not the possession of wisdom, it is the quest, the constant, unending search for it. Only God has perfect wisdom, but God, as Plato understood, is nothing more than another name for Reason."

Julian cocked an eyebrow. "Yes, precisely," he said, repeating, quite on purpose, the phrase Marcel DuBose had used. "God is reason, the world has an order, and we are all somehow a part of it, part of the order, a participant in reason. Yes, precisely," he said with a quick, eager smile. "It all seems obvious: there is a nature, an order, if you will, that defines what each of us should be. The question is why it isn't obvious anymore."

"It was never obvious to everyone. Remember what Plato wrote in the

Laws: 'We do not hold, as the many do, that preservation and mere existence are what is most honorable for human beings; what is most honorable is for them to become as excellent as possible and to remain so for as long a time as they may exist.'"

"I know the passage; I understand what you mean," said Julian, stopping in front of the window to look again at Notre Dame in the middle distance. "And I know the danger implicit in what he says, what can happen to someone who doesn't seem to agree with whatever those who have power happen to believe. Just a few lines earlier, he writes that what all human beings have in common is the desire 'To have things happen in accordance with the commands of their own soul - preferably all things, but if not that, then at least the human things.'" Julian glanced over his shoulder at his old friend and teacher. "What a ridiculous race we are, wanting power over everyone and everything - as if we knew what to do if we had it!"

"Yes, but there are some of us - Julian, for one - who did know what to do with power -"

"And because he knew it, did not want it. He took it, arranged things so he would have it, because he had no choice."

"Because Constantius would have had him killed. Yes, but that wasn't the only reason, was it? Even if his life had not been in danger, he knew that no one else could rule as well. That knowledge brings with it an obligation, because no matter how important the pursuit, the search, for wisdom, for philosophy, we are, all of us, human beings and we have a duty to look after one another, to do what we can to make us better than we are."

"Better than we are," agreed Julian, nodding emphatically. He turned around, his back to the window, a look of the utmost seriousness burning in his eyes. "Better than we…." A smile shot across his mouth. "Everyone, almost everyone, when Plato was alive and now as well, preservation, 'mere existence,' is what they think most about. How make them think instead that other things are more important. Plato thought you would have to get rid of everyone over the age of ten to have any chance of creating a citizenry capable of living the way we should."

"That is not entirely impossible," remarked Marcel Dubose, lifting his chin in a way that suggested a kind of eager malice, a dismissal of any false sense of decency. "What other reason did Moses have for keeping everyone in the desert all those years - so no one who remembered Egypt would be part of the new citizens of the Promised Land. Why else did he kill everyone - thousands - who attempted to oppose him? I said, not entirely impossible," he remarked as Julian was about to object. "You can't do that now. Too many people, and where could you take the others? There are no hidden places anymore. But the point about the children is not without relevance. It is worth remembering, a president does not just execute the laws, he doesn't just recommend changes, and he is more than the commander-in-chief. He is, if he wants to be, and if he knows what he is doing, the spokesman for what the Americans would like to think they are. We're talking about the Laws. Remember the passage: Others consider someone educated who is trained in trade or commerce, but 'we mean rather the education from childhood in virtue, that makes one desire and love to become a perfect citizen who knows how to rule and be ruled with justice.' From childhood - That, surely, is an argument a president can make. Speech is everything. What do you want your citizens to be like, what kind of people should they be? Remember what your civil rights leader said, that memorable phrase, that speech Martin Luther King, Jr. gave some fifty years ago, that hope, that expectation, that one day 'our children will be judged not by the color of their skin but the content of their character.' Isn't that the point you have to make? Character, what it should be, why that is the most important thing for any human being, what kind of person, what kind of citizen, he can be."

Julian had thought of another line from the same dialogue. "'It is possible to persuade the souls of the young of just about everything, if one tries.'"

"That line comes, remember, just a little after Plato makes two observations which seem to me of supreme importance. First, when he writes, 'Surely it is necessary that one who takes delight in things becomes then similar to the things he takes delight in, even when he is ashamed to praise them....' And then, because this leads to the question how to lead them to take delight in things they would not be ashamed to praise, he insists that 'an audience should be continually hearing about characters better than their own....' I remember reading somewhere that you can always tell what kind of people you are dealing with if you know what it is they look up to."

"You read that in Machiavelli," said Julian without hesitation. "Everyone looks up to something or someone. 'What the Lord praises, everyone praises.' I think that was the line."

"I was a young man when John F. Kennedy became president. Every young man, and not just in America, wanted to be just like him."

Two hours later, when Julian was walking back to his hotel, he stopped at the side of the river where, a few blocks past Notre Dame, it flows back together after passing both sides of the island, and remembered the other nights he had come this same way, other nights spent with Marcel Dubose in the most serious conversations he had ever had. He wondered whether, after tonight, he would see him again or, as seemed more likely, this would be the last time. He felt what he thought Julian, the ancient Julian, must have felt when, having become emperor, he knew that he would never see Paris again.

CHAPTER EIGHTEEN

Louis Matson sat back in the gray leather chair he had been using since the day he was first elected to the Senate, and nearly burst out laughing. He still thought party chairmen the dullest, least interesting people on the planet, and Reece Davis in particular a mindless mechanic, all charts and numbers, one dimensional and that dimension not much more than a thin veneer of habit and ambition, someone for whom self-knowledge began and ended with the title he happened to hold. Davis, the chairman of the Republican party, kept a picture of Lincoln on the wall behind his desk that seemed to suggest a direct line of succession from the beginnings of the party before the Civil War to the present day. They all did that, everyone, or almost everyone, who held any kind of office. It was greatness by association, every new member of Congress, every lunatic elected in a spasm of popular anger and hostility, another Henry Clay, another Daniel Webster; every new president, however incompetent or morally reprehensible, another Roosevelt or Kennedy, another Washington or Jefferson. They held the office, they had the title, what reason to think themselves less able than any of the others who had held it before? Louis Matson remembered the stories about Richard

Nixon, talking in the middle of the night to the White House portrait of Lincoln, searching for the reason why he was being forced out of the office he had spent a lifetime trying to get; Nixon, driven crazy by his own failures, talking to Lincoln as if the office itself had somehow made him Lincoln's equal.

Matson gripped the arms of the chair and told himself to concentrate. He had to be careful. The medicine his doctor had given him to control the increasing pain had sometimes a disorienting effect; his mind would start to wander, turning his attention from one seemingly unrelated thing to another, straying from a normal, logical sequence into a labyrinth of different, disordered thoughts, a kaleidoscope of shifting images. He did not have much time left, perhaps only a few months. He squeezed the arm of the chair, clenched his teeth until his jaw began to shudder, and then let go. He took a deep breath, closed his eyes, took another, opened his eyes and looked around. The long, rectangular room, as familiar as the face of an old friend, seemed suddenly alien and strange, a place that had lost its meaning, like a home that, put on the market, becomes again a house, a property, someone else will soon occupy. He picked up the telephone and told his secretary to send in the chairman. He had made him wait ten minutes, the same ten minutes Davis had been late when he had come to see the majority leader months before.

Leaning on his elbows, his fingers spread wide apart, three of them pressed against each other, the tips of his index fingers against his nose, his thumbs right below his chin, Louis Matson watched in silent amusement as Reece Davis hurried into the room. Suddenly, as if he had never seen it before, he stopped in front of the painting of the White House on fire in the War of 1812. Shaking his head, he looked at Matson, certain he would understand.

"Some of those people we had in Cleveland - some of those who used to give millions to the party - they'll tell you privately they wish something like that would happen again. Makes you wonder - doesn't it? - what kind of people we have to deal with."

"A couple of months ago," replied Matson, without any change of expression, "someone came in here, looked at that painting, and said exactly that, that it wouldn't be a bad idea to burn the White House down to the ground."

"Unbelievable!" remarked the chairman, as he settled into a chair in front of Matson's desk.

Months ago, the day before yesterday, it did not matter how much time had passed, Davis would not remember what he had said. It was a common mistake to think politicians insincere, or even inconsistent; they simply said what they thought others wanted to hear. You might as well accuse a mirror of lying when it reflected different things back to different people.

"You asked to see me," said Matson, sitting back in his chair.

There was a glint of irony in his half-closed, drooping eyes, the residual habit of an endless curiosity, the interest of someone who, without any particular desire to help with whatever problem you might have, and in fact a desire to avoid if possible any involvement at all, wanted to know which among the various stupidities you might this time have committed.

Davis bent forward to the precise degree to which Matson had leaned back. Matson placed both elbows on the arms of his chair. Davis rested his forearms on Matson's desk.

"Julian Drake would not be president if it weren't for what we did," he began, a solemn, practiced complaint in his solemn, practiced voice. "He'd still be somewhere out in California, if it hadn't been for that speech he gave, that speech you were supposed to give, the speech I asked you to give. He wouldn't be president if I hadn't convinced everyone in the party - and not just the candidates and their millions of followers, but the money people, the -"

"Some of whom spent considerable amounts of money trying to help the other side."

"Yes, that's no doubt true," conceded Davis, with a brisk nod of his head. "But everyone else went along, everyone else stayed loyal. I didn't do all of this myself, of course, but....They stayed loyal, did what they could for his election, and, thanks in part to them, he's president."

"I know that," said Matson. "I know he got elected. And I also know he got elected without any help from anyone. He didn't raise money, he didn't spend money, and he didn't -"

"It's been almost a month since the inauguration, almost a month," said

Davis, trying, and failing, to control his frustration. "A month, and I can't even -"

"You can't remember a better inaugural address, is that what you're trying to say?" interjected Matson, more than ready, eager, to pretend he did not know what had Davis, and half of Washington, so angry and upset. "I've heard them all, going back to Eisenhower when I watched it on television with my seventh grade class. The only one you can compare it to is Kennedy's - don't you think? They both talked about the need, the importance, of sacrifice, of doing what is necessary for the country, the responsibilities, and not just the rights, of citizenship."

"Yes, yes, terrific speech. Everyone said so. But then, after that…nothing, not a word from the president, not a word out of the White House. Hell, some people have started to wonder if he's even there, if anybody is there. Ismael Cooper is chief of staff, but if anyone else has been hired, if there is anything like a White House staff, if there are any presidential assistants, it is the best kept secret in town. I can't even get a telephone call returned. Reporters are calling me all the time, people are asking me all the time - 'Where is the president, what is he doing, what is happening over there?' What am I supposed to do, what am I - what the hell am I - supposed to say?" cried Davis, as he threw up his hands and raised his eyes to the ceiling. "Every day a new rumor, and the rumors stranger all the time - No one has seen the president, no one has seen his chief of staff. Next thing, the tabloids will start reporting that aliens have kidnapped the president! Even serious journalists are saying Ismael Cooper never leaves the White House, that the White House is his new home, that -"

"That isn't a rumor, that's true. Ismael has taken up residence. He lives there now. Why shouldn't he live there? Knowing Julian, he won't have time to sleep."

Astonished, Davis started to say something, but Matson stopped him with a look. He picked up the phone and on his private line put in a call.

"Ismael, I'm sitting here with our good friend, Reece Davis. He tells me he can't get anyone over there to return his calls. He wants to know what he should be saying to everyone who keep asking what is going on, why no one has seen or heard anything from Julian - I mean, the president." He listened in silence for a moment. "Okay, I'll tell him: Six o'clock tomorrow evening."

Matson hung up the phone and for a moment did not say a word. A thin, subtle smile slipped across his heavy mouth.

"Have you noticed? They're all trying to talk like him now." The smile moved to his eyes, became cunning and sly, filled with a deeper knowledge of the vanity of things. "Not Ismael," he remarked, removing any possible confusion. "Everyone else. Those mindless one-liners everyone used, the constant repetition of the same few meaningless words, the unfinished sentences, the fragments of abbreviated speech - the way everyone running for office learned to talk before, the way they had to talk to get something they said on television. Who is going to do that when everyone now thinks everyone should speak like Julian Drake?" His tired eyes flashed with the light of an agreed understanding, the certainty that, even if he had not thought of it before, Davis would share the same belief. "They'll all fail, of course; they'll talk themselves stupid. But it isn't what anyone does now that matters; it is what the next generation thinks it wants to be, what those just starting out think they have to learn, what they think they have to be good at. It is what they look up to, who they want to be like. If you're a college student and you think you might one day want to run for public office - if you think that one day, in the far distant future, you might want the chance to run for president - who do you want to be like? - Julian Drake, or one of those half-educated fools he defeated? Julian is going to be a great president. He already is, and if you aren't yet ready to believe that - though you were there, sitting two rows back, at the inauguration - wait until tomorrow evening when Julian - when President Drake - holds his first presidential press conference, televised live to the nation."

By the time Davis left the majority leader's office, news of what would be the first presidential press conference of the new administration was all over town. The announcement that it would be held in the East Room, instead of the White House briefing room, and that it would be broadcast live to the nation made it seem all but certain that after nearly a month of silence something major was about to happen. What else could Julian Drake have been doing, how else explain the astonishing secrecy that had drawn a curtain over what the president was doing? All the major newspapers sent their best reporters, all the networks, all the cable news shows, sent the reporters who had covered

Julian Drake during the campaign. The East Room, the room where Teddy Roosevelt's children had once ridden their pony, where other, less exuberant presidents had presided over the most important public functions, was crowded to capacity. The air was electric, the sense of anticipation intense, everyone's mind concentrated on only one thing: what was going to happen when Julian Drake entered and made whatever announcement he was to deliver. Louis Matson, who had come to watch, sat on a chair in the back row, and, though everyone recognized him, no one thought to so much as say hello.

Precisely at six o'clock, Julian Drake, dressed in a dark blue suit, light blue shirt and maroon striped tie, walked from a door at the side directly to a podium and three microphones. Louis Matson had already turned to watch another man in a dark suit move quickly away from the podium and vanish behind the crowd the other side. He had seen the same thing countless times before, but he still marveled at how deftly it was done, the impeccable timing with which a secret service agent, at the exact moment the always anonymous voice of another agent announced, "Ladies and gentlemen, the President of the United States," at the exact moment that every eye turned toward the side from which the president was about to enter, walked from the opposite direction, placed the official seal of the United States on the two brass hooks on the front of the podium, and then, without breaking stride, turned and, just ahead of the changing glance of the crowd following the president, disappeared out of view. It was a magician's sleight of hand, done in plain sight where anyone could see and no one ever did. Sleight of hand, seeming to do one thing while you were doing another, that was not just a magician's trick, it was what lay at the heart of the difference between those who could, and those who could not, play the politician's game. And now, unless he missed his guess, Julian would show a more practiced hand at the art than anyone had yet thought possible.

Julian Drake stood at the podium, smoothed his tie with his right hand, and then, with the same hand, brushed the back of his head. He looked around the crowded room, the glistening faces of hundreds of journalists and reporters caught in the bright lights of television.

"This is the first of what will be a regular weekly occurrence. I will hold a press conference once a week, broadcast live. Now, who would like to ask the first question?"

There was a stunned silence. They had come expecting a major announcement, some accounting of what he had been doing and what he was planning to do, and he had nothing to say?

"Ms. Good?" he said, pointing toward Rachel Good sitting to his left in the first row.

"You have been in office nearly a month," she said, as she jumped up from her chair. "This is the first time any of us have had a chance to ask anyone anything. There isn't anything you want to announce? Nothing you want to say about what new legislation you might be about to propose, nothing about whether you are really going to ask Congress to do some of what you said in the campaign you would try to do?"

"I intend to ask Congress to do everything I said I was going to try to do. In fact, I've just done it. Everything I talked about, every legislative proposal I mentioned, has, as of three o'clock this afternoon, been put in final form and transmitted to the Speaker of the House and the Senate Majority Leader."

"Everything? You're asking Congress to authorize unlimited enrollment in the military, anyone who wants to join, anyone wiling to serve four years, and in exchange, their college education paid for?" asked Rachel Good with a slightly baffled expression.

"You seem surprised," replied Julian, amused by her reaction. "It is what I said I would do if I were elected. Did you think I wouldn't keep my word?"

"No, it isn't that; I just didn't think - I think everyone thought - that this was something you might try to do gradually, instead of all at once, that -"

"There are some things that, if you try to do them gradually, piece by piece, never get done at all. This is something that has to be done all at once. It has already been done. I have instructed the joint chiefs of staff to change the criterion so that any citizen between the ages of eighteen and twenty-one can join. I am asking Congress to appropriate the funds necessary to support this increase in the size of our military. I have no doubt they'll do what has to be done."

"That won't be the only cost!" someone shouted. "There is still the question of how to pay for the four years of college."

Julian shook his head, dismissing what others thought a difficulty.

"Any college or university that fails to provide a four-year education at no expense to returning veterans will no longer receive federal funds for any purpose whatsoever. They give scholarships to athletes, full rides to men and women who play games. They can certainly provide the same thing for men and women who have given four years to the defense of their country. They're not even being asked to do that much. They aren't being asked to provide board and room. Just as we did with the G.I.Bill after the Second World War, the government will provide the necessary living expenses."

"You would really cut off funding for, say, scientific research, if a university refused to do this?" asked an incredulous young reporter from one of the more liberal cable news stations.

"In the proverbial New York minute," replied Julian, without even that much hesitation. "I said over and over during the campaign that the question isn't how much we have, it isn't how long we can live; the question, the only serious question, is what kind of people we are, what kind of people we want to be."

The room had come alive. Dozens of reporters were on their feet, waving their hand, trying to get the president's attention.

"What have you been doing the last month? Why was there so much secrecy?"

With a shrewd, guileful smile, Julian seemed to ponder the question, or, rather, to consider which among several equally improbable answers he should give.

"There was no secrecy. That would suggest there was something someone wanted to hide. It was not secrecy; there was nothing to report. You want to know what I've been doing for the last month? - Trying to think through the alternatives about how we can best achieve the changes we as a country have to make, changes that are necessary to restore in their proper relation liberty and restraint. Do you remember Edmund Burke, the great British conservative, who observed that 'liberty without wisdom and without virtue is the greatest of all possible evils; for it is folly, vice, and madness, without restraint.' And then," Julian continued, quoting from memory with the ease of someone reading from the printed page, "Burke, having defined what real liberty requires, describes how those with the responsibility to govern should approach the problem: 'A disposition to preserve and an ability to improve, taken together, would be my standard of a statesman.'

"Notice that unlike those who are all one or the other, all for changing everything, or all for changing nothing, Burke combines the two. What change is necessary? Change that is in the way of making a restoration, a return, if you will, to the original understanding of things. A country is like a building. With the passage of time the building decays, crumbles, and repairs have to be made to save it. But what kind of repairs? - Those that, so far as possible, follow what the original architect intended when he designed it. That is what I have been doing the last few weeks: thinking through how best to start the work of getting us back on the path we were meant to follow, the path that leads to the kind of freedom Washington and Jefferson and Lincoln understood, freedom to pursue, not whatever we happen to want to do, freedom to do what as reasonable human beings we know we should."

"Who has been helping you? Who, besides Ismael Cooper, whom we all know is your chief of staff, is part of your team?" asked a gruff-voiced reporter who had been covering Capitol Hill since Ronald Reagan was president.

Julian scratched his head and stared into the middle distance. "Team?" he repeated as if there was some deeper sense to the word. "There is no team, there isn't going to be any team. I was not elected president to speak someone else's words, and I was not elected president to prepare legislation I had not drafted, or at least outlined, myself. There aren't going to be any speechwriters, there aren't going to be dozens of White House staff. Ismael Cooper doesn't mind working long hours, and I don't need that much sleep. And besides, I have the invaluable help of an endless supply of secretaries who take down every word. You wanted to know what I was doing the last month - thinking, and putting those thoughts on paper, dictating everything that needed to be said, everything that the Congress needs to begin its own work."

Julian stopped, ready to take the next question, but then changed his mind. There was something more that needed to be said.

"We waste too much time. We waste too much time because we are always too much in a hurry, running from one thing to the next, always busy doing something, whatever that something is. We have forgotten what it means to concentrate on one thing, to take our time with it, to go slowly, reading, if you will permit the analogy, one word, one letter, at a time. There is a story told of Socrates that he once stood in the same spot, did not move, from dusk till dawn, lost in some thought of his own. None of us is Socrates, but consider what we could do if we could concentrate on our own work, whatever that work might be, for even an hour without interruption."

The room went silent. No one knew quite what to make of it. Was it really possible Julian Drake really believed he could run the government almost alone, that he did not need more than a single assistant and a little secretarial help?

"Yes, actually, I do. What you must be thinking. The regular, routine business of the government is run by the various executive departments and agencies. There has been a tendency over the last half century to concentrate more and more of the power into the White House. That movement will now be reversed. The cabinet secretaries will now be responsible for their departments and directly accountable to the president. Though with important differences, the government will be similar to cabinet government in Great Britain. Cabinet secretaries will meet with me at least once a week, and all of them will be invited to express their views on every question of public policy that has to be decided, and, whenever it seems appropriate I will appear before the Congress and take any questions any member might care to ask."

"Any question any member might care to ask?" asked a balding, middle-aged newspaper reporter, reading back what he had just jotted down in the spiral notebook he held in his hand, reading it as if he could not quite believe what he had just written. "Anything - any question - whatever any member of the House or Senate decides to ask?"

"Do you think I should treat the members of Congress differently than I treat members of the press? Is there any question you have asked that I have refused to answer? How else would you suggest we open a clear channel of communication? It doesn't strike me as very helpful spending all our time responding to rumors, and allegations, about what someone is supposed to have said. That is the stuff of tabloid television, it isn't the kind of public discourse that promotes the efficient conduct of the public business. Others may, if they will, hide behind the anonymity of unnamed sources; there isn't going to be any question about what I say and what I do. And there won't be any confusion about what I mean. I will explain my intentions, and I will do it directly with members of Congress and, through press conferences like this, directly to members of the public."

A woman in her thirties, tall and willowy with bright, ambitious eyes and a flashing, artificial smile, a woman men found irresistible and other women despised, stood like a lead actress taking a curtain call. There was something thrilling in her voice, and an unexpected intelligence in her question.

"A few moments ago, you quoted Burke. 'The ability to preserve, and to improve.' And you talked about a restoration. There are those who would ask why we should be in any way limited by the past, why we should not be free to decide for ourselves what kind of future we want to have. How do you respond to them?"

"How would you know what kind of future you want unless you know what kind of past you have had? You cannot remedy a deficiency unless you know, not just what that deficiency is, but how it came into being. There is a more fundamental question: How do you know something is a deficiency, unless you have a standard by which to make that judgment? One example: In the ancient world, in both Rome and Athens, to say nothing of the Persian Empire, or of a great many other places since, few people thought slavery wrong. We fought a civil war to end slavery here. What reason did we have to do that? Where, and how, did we learn that slavery was an evil, that slavery for some was incompatible with freedom for others? Lincoln based the case against slavery on the Declaration of Independence, on what you might call the organizing principles of the American republic, the belief, the insistence, that all men are created equal. Everyone talks a lot about the Constitution, what it does, or does not, allow. The Constitution does not interpret itself. What do the words mean, how are they to be read? Lincoln thought the Constitution had to be read in light of the Declaration. It is the Declaration, not the Constitution, that is primary. The famous beginning of the Gettysburg Address, the speech every schoolchild once had to learn by heart, 'Four score and seven years ago,' - that does not refer to 1789, when the Constitution was ratified; it refers to 1776 when the Declaration of Independence was signed.

"There is another speech of Lincoln's, the Young Men's Lyceum speech, given years before he became a national figure. He insists that the country cannot be held together, that it cannot survive, that, far removed from the founding generation, without any memory of their own about the Revolutionary War and the sacrifices that were made, ambitious men will try to become powerful and famous by trying to destroy what had been built, to change," he added with a significant glance at the reporter who had asked the question, "what had been done, and so put their own mark on the future. The answer, the way to preserve what had been achieved, the way to protect the American experiment in free government, was to establish what Lincoln called a 'civic religion,' a belief, as strong as any religious creed, in the sanctity of the Declaration and the principle of equality of which it speaks. In a marvelous phrase that only Lincoln could have formed, he told his audience that 'every mother should whisper to her newborn child' and repeat every day, the words of the Declaration, make them the first words the child ever hears, and in that way make the Declaration part of the very being of every citizen. The strongest, and perhaps the only real beliefs, we ever have are those we are taught before we have the ability to doubt or question what we are taught."

"You're not suggesting something like that now?" asked a thin young man with rimless glasses. Trained to the constant, changing movements of a computer screen, his eyes did not stay fixed on anything for more than a second or two at a time. Julian looked right at him. The reporter looked away, then looked back, then, immediately, his gaze shifted again.

"Mother reading the Declaration to…?" he mumbled, shaking his head.

"If you're suggesting that it probably isn't possible, you are probably right," said Julian, with a look meant to encourage confidence. "But that only proves the necessity of doing something that will help remedy the deficiency in what let us call our civic education, doesn't it?"

Unbuttoning his suit coat, Julian stepped to the side and rested his left arm on top of the podium. The young reporter was three rows back. Julian talked to him as if they were alone in the room.

"Have you noticed how much you can tell about someone by who they look up to, who they would like to be like? You see it all the time, don't you? Kids on a playground, trying to be like the player - whatever sport is involved

- they idolize. Young men, young women, starting their careers, almost always there is someone they admire, someone they hope one day to be like. We all do this, try to imitate those who have done, and done well, what we ourselves hope one day to do. When you were just starting out, a young reporter, I imagine there must have been someone - a broadcaster, a journalist, a writer - someone who set the standard you wanted to meet. We do this as individuals. The great question - Lincoln's question, and not just Lincoln's - is what do we look up to as a people, who do we admire, who among those who have led us do we revere? Who, to be more precise, would we want our children, and our children's children, to honor? Who do we want to hold up as models in our public life? Everyone who happened to hold an office, even if it is the highest office in the land, or those, and only those, who brought distinction to the office in which they served? The answer seems obvious. And that is the reason why, among the other things I am asking Congress to do, I am requesting that we get rid of one holiday and replace it with three others. I am asking that President's Day be abolished, and that we go back to what we had before, a separate celebration of the birthdays of Washington and Lincoln."

"You said three holidays!" a voice shouted from the back. "Washington, Lincoln - who, which president, is the third?"

Louis Matson had long ago given up trying to guess what went on the mind of Julian Drake. He had told him that he wanted to get rid of a holiday that honored all the presidents, everyone who had held the office, treating as somehow equivalent the better and the worse. It was, for Julian at least, important to remind each new generation what greatness meant, to set an example to be followed, to honor the best of the best, the greatest presidents the country had had. Washington, who won the War of Independence, who, as first president, established the standard of even-handed justice and dedication to the public interest; Lincoln, who saved the union and, in that famous phrase of his, gave a new birth to freedom. Julian had not said anything about a third president who deserved to be remembered the same way.

"Franklin Delano Roosevelt."

For a moment, no one knew what to say, or quite what to ask. Julian Drake had not been nominated by the Democratic Party and yet he wanted a national holiday to celebrate the birthday of the president whose work Republicans had been trying to dismantle for well over half a century! It was stunning, unbelievable, beyond anything anyone would have thought possible, even from someone everyone was already convinced was not just unpredictable but essentially unknowable. Louis Matson had a feeling, a certainty, really, that the third addition, the decision to include Roosevelt had only just been made, that sometime after Julian told him what he was going to do, restore the two holidays so the memory of Washington and Lincoln would not be buried in the obscurity of an abstraction, a holiday honoring the office, he suddenly remembered that something more needed to be done. It might have occurred to him just now, when he started to explain what he was going to ask Congress to do.

"Not Teddy Roosevelt," someone asked, just to be sure. "Franklin Delano Roosevelt?"

"The third founding," said Julian, without a moment's hesitation. Washington, the first founding: the new nation, the new constitution; Lincoln, the second founding: the Civil War to guarantee we remained one nation, one nation in which freedom was the equal birthright of everyone. Franklin Roosevelt because with the industrial age, the age of large concentrations of private power - big business, big labor - the government took responsibility for the material well-being of all our citizens. Franklin Roosevelt because he saved democracy when other countries, faced with the problem of industrialization, took the road of either fascism or communism; saved us from the anthill existence of people condemned by totalitarianism of whatever kind to live their lives as the unthinking parts of a machine. No one, before or since, has had as great an influence on the way we live, or on the way we think about what government should, or should not, do."

CHAPTER NINETEEN

They were all there, every conservative commentator, every conservative critic, every conservative who thought himself an intellectual, every politician who identified with the conservative cause, all of them part of a movement that had suddenly found itself confronted with a president who insisted they had forgotten what conservatism really meant. They sat at tables of ten, two thousand men and women, their voices a constant cacophonous hum in the cavernous ballroom of the Mayflower Hotel. It was one of those annual events in which one speaker after another tells his audience what they already know and proves to everyone, audience and speaker alike, his own profound intelligence.

Dinner had been served, dinner had been eaten, bottles of wine had been opened, glasses had been emptied, glasses had been filled. One conservative writer, author of several books that, if they had said very little, had said it well, remembered a line from Disraeli, spoken at the end of a dinner when the champagne was poured, "At last, something warm!" It brought a smile to his face, but he thought better than to repeat it out loud for fear that he would have to explain to the others at his table who Disraeli was. Three tables away, in the second row from the dais in front, Angela Murray sat next to Rufus Chambers, insisting in a loud voice that it had been a waste of time to come.

"We all know what you think," said Conrad Wilson from the other side of the table. "You've made it clear before that -"

"You saw what he did in that press conference last week! - A holiday for FDR! I told you," she hissed. "Rufus warned all of us. He isn't a conservative - he's worse than any Democrat we could have elected. He's -" But, suddenly, she was interrupted by a voice booming over the loudspeakers: "Ladies and Gentlemen, the President of the United States."

They were all on their feet, and if it was not with the kind of wild enthusiasm they might have shown for one of their own, one of the candidates who had sought the nomination, with polite respect and even, some of them, friendly interest.

Julian Drake had already broken with tradition by arriving only in time to give his speech. Ismael Cooper had explained in a way that left no room for argument that the president always worked during meals and would therefore not be available for dinner. Julian walked in now without stopping to shake anyone's hand and without so much as a wave to the crowd. He stood at the lectern, looked down at what would have been his speech had he brought one with him, smiled to himself, and then, with the smile still on his face, looked up.

"You would like to know what kind of conservative I really am, how far back in the past I am willing to look for guidance as to what we should do in the future, or, rather, what we should do now, to make the future more consistent with the ancient principles on which this country depends not just for its prosperity but for its continued existence. How far back in history do I look? - To our first historian." The smile grew broader, more confident, the look of someone eager to share something he knows you will find every bit as fascinating as he. "That first historian that I know all of you have read more than once, that historian from the day you first read him, you keep going back to read again - Herodotus, who by telling us about something once done in Babylon tells us something about ourselves. You look confused," he laughed. "Let me explain."

There was something in the way Julian Drake told a story that made you, while you listened, think it one of the most interesting things you had ever heard. It was, in a way, the difference between listening to an unusually dull accountant read a page of Shakespeare and watching Lawrence Olivier play the part of Henry V. Julian was talking about a Greek historian dead for twenty-five hundred years, someone that perhaps not more than a tenth of his audience had ever heard of, and perhaps not more than a tenth that number had ever read, and he had them all thinking that this was a writer they really ought someday to read.

"According to Herodotus, it was the best law the Babylonians ever had, the law that made Babylon strong and united, one city instead of two. Every city, every nation - including especially our own - is in constant danger of becoming divided against itself, two cities instead of one: the city of the rich and the city of the poor, each of them doing everything it can to dominate, and even destroy, the other. But Babylon, ancient Babylon, not only kept the two cities in balance, but managed to knit them together. They did it with women."

There was a quickening of interest, everyone more alert, the suggestion of a woman's involvement, provocative, sensual. Julian caught the subtle change of mood, the heightened sense of expectation. He treated them with an immediate digression that seemed to teach moderation.

"It seems a strange, and perhaps barbaric, practice to use women as a means of solving a social problem, a tribute, perhaps, to the ignorance of an ancient age which still thought in terms of duties instead of rights. But, if the ancients were far from perfect, we in the modern world have problems of our own, and if we cannot follow exactly what was done in the past, we might still have something to learn if, looking deeper, we look beneath the surface of what an ancient writer wrote.

"It was quite remarkable, ingenious, even - dare I say it? - Machiavellian, the way some unnamed lawgiver gave the law that saved Babylon from the kind of discord and division that almost always leads to civil war. With a single, stunning, alteration in the way marriages were arranged, the rich lost some of their wealth and the poor became almost well to do. Marriages were arranged, not by parents interested in what was best for their families, the way it was done for generations among the titled nobility of Europe, but by the workings of a free market - a kind of capitalism, if you will - in which those who could afford it were able to buy exactly what they wanted."

He had them now, everyone eager and attentive, waiting to hear the wonders that could be brought about by the marvelous workings of a system of free enterprise in which success, instead of punished, was rewarded, not with more money, but with the love of a woman.

"An auction was held," explained Julian, suppressing a smile at a secret his audience could not wait to hear, "an auction unlike any you have heard of before, an auction in which men paid for women…and women paid for men. Once each year," he continued, hurrying on before they could react to this outrageous remark, "all the women of marriageable age were paraded out in front of all the men who were ready to marry. The bidding began. The most beautiful woman brought the highest price, a price that only the richest man could afford to pay, a price that had no limit beyond the buyer's wealth and desire. The women were auctioned off until all the women anyone wanted to pay for were gone. The next step was the work of genius. The money paid for those more desirable women now became the inducement by which men who had not been able to buy the more desirable women were willing to take the women who were left. Instead of men paying for women, women, in a manner of speaking, now began to pay for men. Men bid, not what they were willing to pay, but what they were willing to take. Each woman - and I am sorry for putting it like this, but this is what they did - each woman, as she got uglier, brought a bigger price, a dowry that, for the ugliest of all, was equivalent to what the richest man had paid for the most beautiful woman, an amount, according to Herodotus, staggering in value."

Raising his arms, Julian turned up his palms and shrugged. "It was - not to put too fine a point on it - redistribution, but redistribution that, instead of breeding resentment, passed unnoticed. The wealthy got the women they desired; the poor, who took the women the wealthy did not want, got their money. This reduced, if it did not eliminate, the disparity of what they had and in that way removed the principal cause of dissension and distrust. Babylon remained one city instead of two. What happened later," added Julian, with a warning glance, "when Babylon was conquered and its ancient laws abandoned, proved, at least for Herodotus, how sound the reasoning had been. The rich, who could now do whatever they wanted, became richer still; the poor, driven to desperation, sold their daughters into prostitution, a trade practiced just outside the gates of the city from which they were now excluded."

No one seemed quite certain what to make of it, whether their reaction should be curiosity about a strange, long-forgotten custom practiced for a time by a long-forgotten civilization, or resentment, the growing suspicion that Julian Drake was in the most oblique way imaginable questioning the very measure of their success.

"It would be easy to dismiss the ancient custom of an ancient city as irrelevant to the problems of the modern world. No one arranges marriages like that anymore. Women are not put up for auction; men do not participate in a bidding war. And if it is true," he added drily, "that women sometimes marry more for money than for love, and that men have sometimes found marriage to a woman from a wealthy family more desirable than marriage to a woman from more meager circumstances, there is a difference between what someone does in their private life and forcing everyone into the same practice. Better to leave to random chance the result of how each of us decides to live. Be compelled to buy or sell at auction the marriage we wanted, or had, to have? What could ancient Babylonians have to teach us about the meaning of human freedom?

"Everything, if you want the truth; everything, if you believe with Herodotus, and not just Herodotus, that a city, that is to say, a country, cannot survive divided against itself; everything, if you are willing to admit the possibility that human nature does not change, that the questions that have to be answered, the problems that have to be solved, if human beings are to live together in a tolerably decent way, were the same in the past as they are today. Engraved on the American coinage are the words, in Latin, 'Out of many one.' The need to keep a people united did not vanish with the advent of American capitalism. The war between rich and poor, whether in ancient Babylon or modern America, is always there, waiting to erupt, and the only way to stop it is to stop anyone from becoming permanently rich."

There was a rumble of discontent, an almost universal expression of displeasure. Several people sitting at tables in back got up and left. Dozens more shook their heads in angry disagreement. Julian seemed to enjoy it. He became even more serious.

"The Babylonians understood this, and passed a law to prevent it. Plato understood this, and explained why it happens. When 'wealth and the wealthy are honored, virtue and good men are less honorable," insists Socrates in the most famous dialogue Plato wrote. What is honored is practiced, what is not honored is neglected. When that happens," said Julian in a tone that suggested that nothing was more important, instead of 'men who love victory and honor, they finally become lovers of money-making and money; and they praise and admire the wealthy man…while they dishonor the poor.' The result is always the same: 'Such a city, not being one but of necessity two, the city of the poor and the city of the rich, dwelling together in the same place, ever plotting against each other.'"

The more serious conservative writers sat forward on their chairs, intrigued that Julian Drake could quote Plato off the top of his head, but more astonished that he would insist on the evils of acquisition to an audience in which even those who were not rich themselves admired , and envied, those who were, and do it, moreover, by using something first reported by a Greek historian. They were intrigued, others were appalled. What did - what was his name? - Herodotus, what did Plato - someone they remembered only philosophy majors read in college - have to do with anything that mattered? The world had changed, the world had become more enlightened. Everyone knew that. Everyone, at least everyone with a brain, knew that capitalism, and only capitalism, could provide, could protect, freedom, and everyone knew that capitalism - free market economics - could only survive if everyone continued to be rewarded for their success.

"You wanted to know what kind of conservative I am," said Julian. "Someone who believes in the importance of remembering the important lessons of the past. I did not become president to tell you, or anyone else, what you might like to hear. I did not become president to encourage you, or anyone else, in the false belief that nothing had to change. I did not become president to shy away from reminding you that what too many of us now think irrelevant: the greatest minds of the past were as familiar to the Founders we claim to revere as the names of today's well-known entertainers are to us. Herodotus, Plato - Jefferson, Adams, Hamilton, Madison - the authors of the documents that have ordered our existence as a nation, did not just read them, they studied them - in the original Greek

"You wanted to know what kind of conservative I am - The real question is what kind of conservative are you. It is no answer to say that this, or any other country, can, or should, be held together by giving everyone an equal opportunity to become rich; that everyone, or almost everyone, will be content with the knowledge that because others have started with next to nothing and managed to get rich it is possible for them to do so as well. It is no answer, because the question, strange as it may seem to our modern, all too modern, ears is whether becoming rich is really good for anyone. The question, the real question, is what kind of people we should be. We are what we look up to, what we honor above everything else. We honor what we have been taught is important, what we have been taught to believe. Plato - yes, Plato - wrote in another dialogue that 'the most well-bred dispositions usually spring up in a home when neither wealth nor poverty dwell there. For neither insolence nor injustice, nor again jealousies and ill-will, come into being there.' A well-bred disposition meant in ancient times, and should still mean now, a well-ordered soul for whom nothing is more important than doing everything he or she can to protect and preserve a well-ordered city, a place, a country, in which the public is always more important than anyone's private interest; a country, a civilization, in which the wealthy compete among themselves to see who can provide more of what will benefit the public; a country in which, as Herodotus once taught, redistribution is seen not as an evil, but a virtue, a way of producing the kind of moderation that, by preventing the war of rich and poor, makes out of many, one, a single people which understands that the measure of success is not how much you have, but how you choose to spend it. This, to say no more, is the ancient wisdom that, for those of us who wish to follow the highest teachings of the past, we need to follow."

Julian Drake looked one last time at his audience, nodded briefly, whether to underscore the significance of what he had said, or simply to indicate he was finished, that there was nothing more to say, then turned and left as quickly, and as decisively, as when he arrived.

There was little applause, much confusion, and a vague sense of disappointment. The president called himself a conservative, but after what he had just said, the word had a meaning not just different from the way most of them had understood it, but completely alien from everything they believed. There were exceptions, mainly among those who had gone to the better universities and, in protest against the prevalent liberalism, had studied Burke and Churchill, and even some of the ancients, but there were also a few who, without having read anything of serious importance about politics and history, had sufficient intelligence, and were sufficiently fair minded, to recognize a tour de force when they saw it.

"He's right. Everything he said." Conrad Wilson rested his elbows on the table. All around him people were leaving. The ballroom was full of muffled noise. He looked across at his old friend, Rufus Chambers. "You have to admit it, the argument he makes....It may not be what we want to hear; we wouldn't have heard it from any of the other candidates, the ones we wanted to win, but I can't honestly say we - the country - would be better off if they had. He's right. That's all I can say. I was wrong." He shook his head, deploring his own failure to grasp from the beginning how different Julian Drake was from all the other politicians with whom he had come in contact. "He's right, the country can't...."

Everyone else had left the table and headed for the exits. Angela Murray was on her feet, ready to leave, but when she heard this she sat down again and pulled her chair closer. She looked at Wilson as if he had lost his mind.

"That's truly philosophical of you, Conrad," she remarked, her black painted eyebrows arched high above her piercing, unforgiving eyes. "Philosophical - that is the word, like that goddamn Julian Drake, trotting out all his old quotations from books no one has ever read. So, what now, exactly? - We're all supposed to be like good students in our freshman year, giving back to our instructor what he has just told us about the rise and fall of some forgotten civilization? Aren't you a little old, Conrad, to start acting the repentant schoolboy, promising to study harder, promising to learn your lessons, promising -"

"Oh, shut the hell up, Angela!" shouted Wilson, becoming angrier with every vicious, sarcastic word she spoke. "Why can't you admit that the country is in trouble, that things can't go on like this much longer. He's right, damn it! We are two countries - two cities - the rich and the poor. He's right when he says its nothing short of delusional to think that we can solve the problem by this stupid insistence that everyone has an equal right to get rich. It's a lie - everyone doesn't have an equal chance. And even if it were true - what then? - You'd still have rich and poor. Remember what he said - the rich become arrogant and demanding. That's a pretty damn good description, don't you think?"

"You're overreacting," insisted Chambers, trying to calm them both down. "You're right, Conrad: he knows how to give a speech. No one else I know of could have talked about the things he did - talked about Hero... whatever his name is, - and Plato, and held his audience. Even if no one knows what he is talking about, even if none of us....He doesn't let you doubt for a moment that he knows, that he's read - and understood - all those dead writers he's so fond of, and that everything they say, all of it, makes perfect sense to him. But, Angela is right as well. He isn't a conservative, not the way we have always understood the word. What he said at the beginning - that marriage auction he talked about - redistribution, that is what he is all about. He wants to destroy the rich, take away everything we have earned. The only difference - the only difference I can see - between Drake and the Democrats is that he thinks the rich should be grateful that they won't have their lives ruined by money!"

Angela Murray's narrow, pinched face twisted up with rage. She held her thin, bony hands tight together as if it were the only way to stop herself from beating them on the table.

"I told you months ago, I told you both, what a threat he was, what a danger to everything we believe." She gave Chambers a hard, determined glance, challenging him to decide whose side he was on. "He wants to destroy us - Isn't that what you just said? What do you do when someone wants to destroy you, what is the only choice you have when someone lets you know it is him or you?"

Wilson shot out of his chair, shoved it up against the table, and put both hands on top of it. A long stare, silent contempt for the ease with which she was willing to contemplate the worst crime imaginable, said more than the spoken word ever could. He turned to Rufus Chambers.

"No more! You understand me? We're finished. I'm done with all of it," he said, as he let loose his grip on the chair and sent it rattling against the table. He started to walk away, but there was something else that had to be said. He leaned close to Angela Murray. "And if I ever hear of anything that even suggests you actually mean to carry out this mindless threat of yours, I won't wait a minute to tell the White House what you're planning. You make a threat like that, Rufus here can visit you in prison."

It was the way she looked at him, the hatred in her eyes, the absence of the slightest sign of conscience, the cold calculation of her own advantage, that sent shivers up his spine. It was not just the loose language of angry frustration: she meant what she said. Julian Drake was a threat to everything she believed, everything she had spent a lifetime trying to achieve. Worse than that, he threatened to change the value of who she was, turn her from a woman whose enormous success was envied and admired into an object of disdain, a woman whose only claim to attention was the kind of wealth Julian Drake would teach everyone to despise.

The ballroom had emptied out, the room full of empty tables and the desolate noise of quick moving part time waiters taking away, an armload at a time, smudged half-empty glasses and dirty dishes with half-eaten dinners. Outside, on the street, bundled up in cashmere coats and expensive furs, the privileged and the powerful stood with democratic patience waiting for a cab or their private drivers. Inside, in the dark recesses of the hotel bar, dozens of different conversations were going on all at once, all of them, like a jazz concert, variations on a single theme: What was Julian Drake really trying to do? Louis Matson thought it obvious.

"Teaching the country how to think," he replied, when Rachel Good asked what he thought. "The speech at the convention, the inaugural, tonight - Forget the details, forget the things he wants to do. That's important, extremely important - but it's the speech itself; not just what he says, but how he says it. He talks about things no one talks about anymore. You know - you've heard it often enough - all these witless politicians talking about what 'history' requires, what 'history' will say - when they know about as much history as the average fourth grader. Julian talks about specific things that happened and the forces set in motion and how they helped shape the world in which we live. He traces - there isn't anyone alive, not anyone in public life, who could do this - the whole history of human thought; he shows - like he did tonight - how some of the problems we face have been faced before. He ties everything together, makes everyone see - with a clarity they never had before - the reasons for whatever difficulties we have. But the key," he added, leaning across the small table where the two of them were sitting, "the key to everything about him is that he always speaks as if he were speaking to people who, if anything, know even more than he does. He is teaching a whole generation how to speak, how to reason; he is teaching all of us how to read. And he's doing it in a way no one seems to notice. Look around you," he insisted, nodding toward the well-dressed crowd. "What do you think they're all talking about? - How he is going to screw them out of their money."

"Can I quote you?" asked Rachel, with the teasing cynicism he could never quite resist.

"Quote me? - I wish you would." He reached for his glass and after a long, slow drink, suggested she should do more than that. "Tell them, tell your readers, that 'the Senate Majority Leader insisted that the president's remarks were long overdue, that is was time someone had the courage to remind everyone that conservative doesn't mean let the rich get richer and the devil take the rest.'"

Smiling into his glass, Matson took another drink. He became, suddenly, quite serious and even somber. Shoving the glass to the side, he gave Rachel a look that seemed to raise a doubt, a question.

"What?" she asked, reaching across to touch him briefly on his thick heavy hand. "What is it you want to say? You know you can tell me anything."

"Off the record, just between you and me," he remarked with an earnest, almost boyish sense of expectation. He did not have to wait to hear her response; he had known her longer than he had known anyone else and trusted her in way he had not trusted anyone else. "I'm leaving the Senate, resigning my seat."

She was shocked. For one of the few times in he life, her emotions got the better of her. The Senate was everything for Louis Matson; he had no other life. There could only be one reason he would leave.

"How long…?"

He had not expected this. He had forgotten that his age was more apparent to others than it was to him, and that the first thought anyone would have who heard he was stepping down was that death could not be far away. He started to deny that there was anything wrong, but remembering that she was as good a friend as he had ever had, one of the very few people he really liked, he laughed at how little reason he now had to lie about this or anything. But such are the habits of a lifetime he could not free himself entirely from the long practice of duplicity by which he had for so many years kept himself in power.

"Who knows, a few months, a few years - unless I get hit by a car. I don't know how much time I have, but I know its time to go - at the end of this year's session when we all go home for the summer recess. Enough time to get through Congress what Julian wants done."

A dozen different questions flew into Rachel's head at once, all of them about the prospects for passage of the radical legislation the president had proposed. Suddenly, none of it seemed important.

"A few months, a few years - that isn't what you were told, that isn't the reason you're going to quit. You haven't got a few years, do you?"

Louis Matson looked past her to all the bright, shining faces gathered round the bar, cheerful in the ignorance of their own mortality, death still an abstraction, far as yet from becoming personal.

"I've had a long run," he remarked, his eyes still fixed on the crowd. "I've nothing to complain about." A solemn smile on his face, and something, a kind of rare ferocity, in his gaze, he looked again at Rachel. "I gave the country Julian. What more could anyone do than that?"

"What more could anyone do than…? What are you saying, Louis?" asked someone behind him.

He knew who it was before he turned around. The voice was too much like the sound of shattering glass to belong to anyone other than Angela Murray. He tried not to wince.

"Is it true - what I've been hearing - that you are doing all you can to get the Senate to approve that absurd bill that would open the military to anyone who wants to join, and then pay their way through college?"

"No, it isn't true," replied Matson, without any change of expression. "Not true at all. I won't put through the bill without amendment."

Angela Murray's sharp chin came up a defiant half-inch. "Amended? - Killed, you mean."

"Hello, Rufus; I didn't see you standing there," said Matson, who remained sitting where he was.

Chambers nodded toward Rachel who smiled back, politely, and as from a distance. All her attention was concentrated on Angela Murray.

"You were saying something about amending the bill," said Chambers, hoping to keep Angela from saying anything that he, at least, might regret.

"Yes," drawled Matson. "It involves too many people, too much money. We're going to have to cut the thing in half. We're going to limit the program. No men, only women, will be eligible."

Angela Murray's mouth fell open. "Only women? What in the….? You're not-"

"Serious? Sure, why not? Men are always what women want them to be." He cast a quick, passing, but for all that, disdainful, glance at Chambers. "Don't you agree, Rufus?" He looked again at Angela. "If you want to change what we think important, change the way the next generation sees the world, what better place to start than with the women, eager to serve their country, willing to sacrifice, women who would rather fight for something important than to think themselves important because of how much money they happen to have. But I see you don't like the idea," he said, raising his glass as if to confirm and celebrate an agreement. So, out of respect for your wishes, I'll withdraw my amendment and do every damn thing I can to pass the bill in the form the president, Julian Drake, first sent it to the Hill."

CHAPTER TWENTY

"I thought that went well," remarked Julian, drily. His eyes danced to a music of their own as he sat back, clasped his hands behind his neck and stared at the ceiling. "I know why it's called the Oval Office, but I don't know why it was built like this in the first place. Do you think it was because someone had the idea that the president is the central figure in the Great Republic, and America is the center of the world? Look at it: nothing ever ends, and everywhere you look a new beginning. Why don't you ask someone over at the Library of Congress. Someone there should know."

Ismael Cooper slouched deeper into the cream colored sofa that, along with its opposite twin, sat at a right angle to the president's desk, the one that had belonged to Theodore Roosevelt, a dozen steps away. He made a mental note to make the call, but not now, tonight, sometime next week after he had taken care of the other hundred things he had to do.

"No, seriously, I thought it went as well as I could have hoped," insisted Julian, trying hard not to laugh. "No one booed, - no one hissed; there was no great stampede to the exits."

"No, you're right - no one did," agreed Ismael, with a mocking smile, an attempt to play the critic of a performance in which he found no fault at all.

"They were all too astonished to do anything except sit there and wonder if you had completely lost your senses."

"Everyone else is crazy - why not me?" Moving forward, he planted his elbows on the desk and folded his hands together just below his chin. "It's true; I can prove it: What distinguishes us from the other animals? - Reason. But none of us has reason in its complete, or perfected, form. Philosophy is the quest for wisdom, i.e. the question for something we, none of us, possesses. All of us then are, in some degree, less than completely rational, which is to say that we are all irrational, or, in other words," he went on, his voice getting louder until he pounded both hands on the desk and jumped to his feet, "we are all of us stark raving mad!"

His eyes full of laughter, he seemed so confident, so sure of his own powers, that though he might not be immortal, he was invincible: Nothing could ever touch him because the strength he had depended on himself alone.

"How long do I have?" he asked, suddenly coming back to himself. Ismael glanced at his watch.

"Half hour - if he is on time."

"He'll be up. Why shouldn't he?" Julian turned to the windows behind his desk and looked outside. "The Arabs were more interesting before they became rich with oil, living in the desert, sleeping under the stars, living under the strict surveillance of a religion that instilled from birth belief that everything - everything without exception - was to be done in compliance with the same set of rules, that there was no forgiveness, no second chances, for anyone who failed in his obligations. That was the secret - it is still the secret - of their power. Christianity - what is not prohibited is allowed. Islam - what is not permitted you may never do. It isn't that difficult to see which religion men are more likely to die for." He turned back to Ismael. "Then they got rich and became, too many of them, corrupt; used their money to buy the armies, the weaponry, the secret police, to keep - or try to keep, because it was never entirely successful - everyone else in line. But outside the gilded palaces and the air-conditioned buildings Islam kept its hold, and those who taught it to the faithful kept their influence."

Julian shook his head. There were other, more immediate matters, he needed to talk about. He moved around to the front of the desk and leaned back against it. A tight-lipped grimace took an instant's possession of his mouth. He seemed to be struggling with a doubt, how best to bring together in expression what, in the normal run of things, no one else would have thought to connect.

"I should have quoted Rousseau," he remarked, looking across at Ismael. "'What will become of virtue when one must get rich at any price?' And then, 'ancient politicians incessantly talked about morals and virtue, those of our times talk only of business and money.' And then, instead of quoting Plato - that must have seemed the height of ignorance to that crowd - one last thing from Rousseau, the dagger in the heart of those who, like most of us now, think comfortable self-preservation the highest achievement of man: 'With money one has everything, except morals and citizens.'"

His hands shoved deep in his pockets, Julian began to pace back and forth, a smile like that of an eager conspirator edging its way along his lower lip.

"Citizens - that is what we are missing, what we have to have. And that is what we'll get with four years in the military, four years of a martial education, four years taught the importance of discipline and service. When they go to college, they won't still think making money the purpose of what they go to learn - If we can pull it off! I wonder…."

"You wonder?" protested Ismael, sitting forward, his hands on his knees. "Forget those people tonight, they wouldn't have voted for you if there had been any other possible choice. Forget Rufus Chambers and that crowd - I can imagine what they're talking about tonight. They can't stop this. There is enormous public support; everyone - almost everyone - thinks it's a great idea: Instead of free tuition, the old G.I. Bill - education paid for as part of the debt owed to those who serve their country."

Julian gave Ismael a long, worried, look. "Support for now, but later… after they calculate the cost, the kind of taxation; when they start to realize what I'm really doing…"

He moved closer, patting Ismael on the shoulder as he passed in front of him. He plopped down on the far corner of the sofa and loosened his tie.

"I should have quoted Rousseau," he announced again to his own, vast amusement. He tossed his head, considering what the reaction might have been. "Citizens, ancient virtue, what Machiavelli, what Rousseau both wanted to do - what that other Julian, the one my father named me after, wanted to do....I wonder - do you think, could someone imagine, that nearly two thousand years later someone would want to be like him? Do you think Julian...?"

"The emperor, that Julian -?" asked Ismael, at first astonished, and then surprised that he had not seen it before. It was all there, right in front of him: the same unquenchable desire to learn, the endless curiosity, the same ability to hide, in plain view as it were, what he really thought, the same mastery of misdirection.

"Like Julian, the emperor of Rome. Who wouldn't want that? Both a philosopher and a warrior, able to see things no one else could see, grasp in an instant what everyone else could spend a lifetime trying to understand and never get. Become emperor and start to change everything because no one could challenge what you knew you had to do - save the country, the empire, restore the ancient, martial virtues by resurrecting the ancient, martial gods. Be like Julian? - Yes, if only I were able."

There was a long pause. Julian tapped his fingers on his knee.

"Julian wanted to destroy Christianity. It wasn't because he believed in the ancient gods of Rome. That was not the question. The question was what everyone else believed. The Greek gods, the gods of Hesiod and Homer, what were they, what did they represent, except the various forms of human excellence, the pattern, the model, the perfection of what we can be: courage, wisdom, prudence, speed of thought, power, grace, even vengeance. The Roman gods - victory, discipline, greatness - Christianity replaced them all with one god, one teaching that insisted that this life was nothing but hardship and suffering, that what had been thought human excellence was mortal sin, that the only life worth having was the life that waited for the weak and obedient on the other side. Julian tried to change all that. Julian failed. Julian was killed, killed in battle with the Persians, perhaps by one of his own soldiers, a Christian who thought Julian the enemy of God.

"Christianity ruled the empire, and, not many years later, the empire was destroyed. And now, well, what is it we worship? God is dead. Everyone knows the phrase; how many know what it means? God is dead. Everything is permissible. Everyone is free to do whatever they wish. Which means that every choice is equal to every other. God is dead. The gates of hell and the gates of heaven have both been permanently closed. What is left, nothing, except 'spirituality,' which is nothing more than the vague and somewhat embarrassed admission that something is missing, a sense that there should be something more to our existence than the daily repetitive work of earning a living. The 'emptiness of modernity' - we no longer even remember the words. After the war - the Second World War - existentialism was all the rage, the belief in nothingness - a third-rate philosophy that had at least the merit of thinking the emptiness of modernity an issue worth trying to deal with. And since then - what? Nothing, not so much as a regret that we no longer think anything serious. Philosophy, except in a few places, taught as history, the irrelevance of former times, or logic, the means by which to engage in mathematics and science. Religion? - We believe all religions are the same, which means nothing," exclaimed Julian with a sharp-eyed glance as hc suddenly got to his feet and once again began to walk around the room.

"Means nothing?" asked Ismael, who thought from the abrupt way he had stopped that Julian's mind had turned to something else. "You were saying that -"

"Means nothing, if it doesn't mean that there isn't any religion we believe in, because -" He saw that Ismael grasped the point, that a religion that tolerated others did not believe in itself. "What are we left with - what do we worship now? - Money, only that. It is the measure of everything we do. Think someone a success - how much is he worth? What I said tonight - it won't have any effect on that audience; they aren't going to change their minds. But I wasn't speaking to them, I was speaking to the country. Everything we do here has to be done with just one thing in mind: the effect it will have on what people look up to, what they think the best way to live. And part of that, an important part of that, is what they think I look up to, what the president honors."

Julian stopped at the side of the enormous, handcrafted desk, the one that had first been used a hundred years before, when the belief in America's greatness, its "manifest destiny" to lead the world, had first become an accepted article of the American creed. He rapped his knuckles on the same polished shining surface where Teddy Roosevelt had once taken pen to paper in his effort to convince Congress and the country of the absolute necessity to expand American power. Julian remembered the phrase, the perfect expression of Roosevelt's belief in what a president was in a unique position to do.

"The 'bully pulpit' - T.R. was right, but its more than that. And he knew it. Everything he did - every time he spoke in public - all energy and even exuberance, the way to show strength, determination, eager always to do battle. It isn't just what a president says; it is what he does - how he conducts himself; again, what he honors, what he lets everyone believe he thinks important. Even when he doesn't," he added with a quick, piercing glance.

He stood next to Teddy Roosevelt's desk, his desk now, stood still as stone, staring straight ahead, lost in some thought of his own. There was a slight movement of his head, a kind of quiver, then his eyes opened wider, flashing with recognition.

"Yes, precisely," he announced, turning to Ismael. "Music."

"Music? What about it?"

"It was half of education - Plato…, never mind. Music, the kind of music, how it helps form the soul, brings harmony, if it is well-ordered. Let the press know, when they ask how the president spends his time, or how he does his work - tell them that I always have music on - classical music. When they ask for something more specific - tell them I prefer classical piano, and that I listen more than to anyone else, Glenn Gould playing Bach. I never get tired of it."

"They'll ask what other kind of music you like. What popular music. What should I say?" Ismael leaned forward, trying to hear everything Julian, who sometimes in his eagerness to say everything on his mind not only hurried through the words but whispered in a way that was at times inaudible, was telling him.

"Just tell them classical is all I listen to, and then add, as if this is a concession to what everyone else must like, I also like jazz. Then announce that there will be a free concert on the White House lawn every Saturday - start it with the New York Philharmonic. And then," continued Julian, intrigued by the possibilities, "we'll have, every week or so, a White House event with someone famous, a great pianist, or a great jazz musician."

"How soon do you want this to start?" asked Ismael, as he got to his feet. It was almost time for the president's next meeting, the one that was on no one's schedule.

"Immediately. As soon as it can be arranged. There is something else we can do," added Julian, gesturing for him not to leave just yet. "Those we honor for their contribution to American life. Don't make any announcement about this, don't mention it at all, but we are only going to honor those who have made serious contributions - men and women who have done something great and lasting: physicists, educators - if there are any left - great classical composers. No more actors, no more movie people - no more athletes. This is the highest award we give. It should go only to the most serious people, people who have given us a better insight into the human condition. The Medal of Freedom should be our version of the Nobel Prize."

He nodded twice, a sign he was finished, that Ismael could now take whatever steps were necessary to see this was done. And then he added something that made Ismael stop in his tracks.

"Julian, the emperor Julian, ruled for only twenty-two months. I wonder if I'll have even that long. Anyway - what time is it? I have that other meeting."

"It's almost twelve-thirty."

"See if the ambassador is here. Have him brought to the Cabinet Room."

"You don't want to meet with him here?"

"No," he replied. His glance went to the well-worn cover of an old monograph that lay undisturbed and alone on the desk. "The ambassador and I have too much work to do."

"Do you want me…? asked Ismael, tentatively. He had been told nothing about the meeting with the Saudi ambassador.

"No. He won't be bringing anyone. Better if it is just the two of us." He pulled his tie back in place and buttoned his coat. "There is still one thing we all look up to, isn't there?" he remarked, as Ismael opened the door on his way to get the president's late night guest. "The stars, the stars in the heavens, what first gave us the thought that there was an order to the world and that the order did not occur just by chance."

Ismael had the feeling that Julian had more he wanted to say, that something important followed from that otherwise almost commonplace observation, but there was not time. One thing Julian would not tolerate was being late. The meeting had been set for half past midnight. The ambassador was waiting in the outer office, formal, polite and mystified.

"This seems a strange time to be…summoned -"

"Invited, Mr. Ambassador," Ismael corrected.

"We're not going into the -?"

"The president thought it would be easier to work in the Cabinet Room," explained Ismael as he led him down the hall.

Nuri Feisal stopped him.

"I've been the ambassador of Saudi Arabia for almost ten years," he said in the clipped British accent he had assumed since his days at Oxford. "I've never been asked to come to the White House before in the middle of the night. Do you mind my asking what is going on? There isn't any international crisis that I'm aware of. My government has not been apprised of any problem that might require immediate attention. So why, Mr. Cooper, this sudden request for…?"

"The president has his reasons. All I can tell you now is that he thought it best that the meeting be kept as private as possible."

"So he thought that something after midnight….Tell me, Mr. Cooper - is it really true, what they say, that he never sleeps?"

"No, it isn't true. He just doesn't get that much of it. He is always awake at this hour."

Feisal rolled his eyes in mild amusement and followed Ismael to the door of the Cabinet Room.

There were just the two of them, the president and the Saudi ambassador. Julian was sitting where he always sat, in the middle of the oblong table around which two dozen people could comfortably sit. Directly opposite, a chair had been pulled out. A white legal pad, a fountain pen, a glass of cut crystal and a silver water pitcher had been placed on the table. The lights had been dimmed so that only the center of the room was lit. Everything around them remained in shadow. When Feisal, dressed in a dark suit, had taken his chair, Julian nodded toward the pen and paper.

"In case you want to make any notes."

Feisal smiled his appreciation.

"I have a pen, but thank you, Mr. President."

He paused, searching for the right way to begin. It was a habit, the brief hesitation that gave the impression that he never said anything without thinking first. Diplomacy, he seemed to say with each small, meticulous gesture of his hands and eyes, should never be in a hurry. Caution, careful deliberation, postponement, delay, anything that gave one time, because time settled most things that action usually only made worse.

"I heard your speech tonight at the Mayflower, and I must say it was one of the most interesting things I have heard from an American president."

Julian studied the ambassador with a look of amused incredulity. "'Interesting,' as in 'you must be crazy to give a speech like that to an audience that hated every word?"

Feisal was smiling before he knew it. "Yes, well, I suppose you could put it like that."

"But you were really there? I wish I had known. Instead of quoting Plato in front of people, most of whom have never read him and barely remember the name, I would have quoted Averroes and Alfarabi in the knowledge that there was at least one man in the audience who not only studied both but once wrote about what he had learned."

"How…? You couldn't possibly have….?"

With a knowing look, Julian reached inside his jacket pocket and pulled out the monograph with the faded gray cover. He held it up, examining the front as if the title itself signified something important.

"'Studia Islamica,' published thirty years ago by - let me see: 'G.P.Maisonneuve-Larose' in Paris, the paper you delivered to a meeting of the Middle East Studies Association, a paper entitled 'Democracy in Islamic Political Philosophy.'"

Nuri Feisal grinned broadly, exposing a fine set of perfectly white teeth. In his early sixties, but easily mistaken for forty-five, his face was evenly balanced with dark brown, almost black, deep set eyes, black close-cropped hair and a brisk mustache under a slightly hawkish nose. Women often stared at him in the street, a fact he noted and approved, and ignored.

"I don't know how you happened to come across that," he said, in a voice suddenly modest and self-effacing. "I doubt more than six copies were ever printed."

"Which only proves how good it is. That isn't just my judgment; it is what I was told by the man who sent it to me. He was there, when you gave the paper, in Paris, all those years ago. Marcel Dubose, an old friend, whom, I gather, is an even older friend of yours."

"Marcel...! Yes, but I didn't realize..., I didn't know. But it all makes perfect sense. You studied with him, in Paris -"

"Not exactly. I lived in Paris for a while, almost ten years ago. That's when we met. I went to a lecture he gave. And I knew right away that it was a turning point, that he could show me the way, help teach me - if I can put it like this - how to read."

"I was in Paris just last month. We had dinner. He didn't say anything about....But, no, of course he wouldn't. He sent you my little monograph. He must have had his reasons."

Feisal's eyes were alive with curiosity, fascinated by what Marcel Dubose had done, fascinated even more that Julian Drake had the depth of understanding that allowed him to appreciate how remarkable, how unique, Marcel Dubose really was. It was unusual - unprecedented, really - for an American president to mention, much less quote, Plato, but that was something any serious graduate student could have done. But understand, grasp the meaning, read, as Marcel used to say, not just what Plato wrote but what he did not write, learn to find the missing thought, read a dialogue as if you were there yourself to witness all the gestures, the silent expressions, that give a different meaning to the spoken word - it was astonishing. More than that, it was the basis of a trust. That monograph, that paper he had once, in his youth, delivered was something he never spoke about. There was a danger in what he had done, raising questions about what others thought the essential teaching of his own religion.

"Not everyone would approve of what, in my careless days as a young scholar, I tried to write."

Julian thumbed through the first few pages until he reached the beginning of the second part of Nuri Feisal's long forgotten critique of ancient Muslim thought.

"Careless days of a writer who even then knew better than to be careless in what he wrote. 'Of the falasifa' - the philosophers - 'two have addressed the subject of democracy directly: Abu Nasr al-Farabi, who died in 950, in various of his writings, and Ibd Rusd, who died in 1198, in his great commentary on Plato's Republic. Both discuss democracy as a corruption of the virtuous regimes.'" Julian looked up. "I haven't read Alfarabi. I have read Averroes, but not in Arabic."

"The translation by Ralph Lerner of his commentary on the Republic is almost as good as reading it in the original."

"Tell me if I am wrong. Alfarabi and Averroes - the two greatest philosophers in the history of Islam - thought Plato's political philosophy the 'true philosophy.' Is that not what you wrote? And - let me find the place. Here, you quote Alfarabi - and it reads very much like what Plato wrote - who says of democracy that, 'Everybody loves it and loves to reside in it, because there is no human wish or desire that this city does not satisfy.' And you write, in describing what these two philosophers thought, what they, along with Plato, considered democracy's weakness: 'Democracy promotes to honor those who lead the people to freedom and to the things that would satisfy their passions and their desires. The guiding principle -' And this I found remarkable, '- is not that of excellence or virtue but rather the wishes and whims of the citizens. The citizens are equal, no man thought to be better than any other. This, for Alfarabi and Averroes, is detestable and contrary to reason. All that can be said in favor of democracy, and it is something, is that precisely because it allows everyone to live in any way he chooses -' How did you put it? - 'from this great variety of human natures and ways of life, it is possible that, in course of time, men of excellence, including even philosophers, may grow up in it.'"

"Yes, that's what I wrote…all those years ago, but…."

"And you still study - Alfarabi, Averroes…Plato?"

"Privately," replied Feisal, his eyes full of nostalgia. "Like you, alone, late at night. Am I correct?"

"Late, early….As soon as Marcel Dubose sent me this, I put everything else aside and read it straight through, and then I read it again, slowly, until I was sure of what it meant. The summary - Albarabi's summary of Plato's philosophy: the attainment of happiness is through 'A certain knowledge and a certain way of life. This knowledge,'" continued Julian, quoting from memory to Feisal's delighted surprise, "'is knowledge of the substance of each of the beings: this knowledge is the final perfection of man and the highest perfection he can attain.' This knowledge, this final perfection - what only a philosopher in the true sense, someone like Plato, could ever hope to achieve -"

"Or know enough to want to achieve," interjected Feisal before he remembered that he was in the White House talking to the president. He started to apologize. Julian stopped him with a look of impatience. The conversation - the dialogue - was everything.

"If democracy is, to say no more, questionable in the judgement of the greatest Islamic philosophers, it is impossible under any reasonable interpretation of Islam itself. Am I correct? Does this not follow from what you wrote? Here, near the end - 'According to Alfarabi, every being "is made to achieve the ultimate perfection it is susceptible of achieving according to its specific place in the order of being."'"

The monograph in his hand, Julian stared into the middle distance, a look of wonder in his eyes. Slowly measuring each word, he repeated what he had just read.

"Your translation? - I envy you, able to read this in the original. But my point," he said, with sudden energy, "or, rather, yours…."

"Alfarabi, I think you mean."

"Both, not just the teacher, but the student. The next line: only a few have the capacity to 'grasp the primary intelligibles,' only a few 'capable of happiness.' Everyone else lives by opinion, persuasion; everyone else, the 'majority of believers,' accept what they are told by those who give the law, 'a divine law that directs them to some form of knowledge of the truth.' Then - and this explains everything - 'What philosophy renders intelligible by demonstration, divine law represents by means of "corporeal and political things." Religion is the instrument by which these representations are made.'

"Democracy has no place in Islam, because, if I follow what you write, the Sharia, the divine law, provides for everything needed, all the rules of conduct. Shiite political theory takes this a step farther: there is no role for the participation of the community in legislation. Once there is divine legislation or inspiration through a descendant of Ali, every other opinion is, by definition, unenlightened and superfluous. And, you add, even though Sunni political theory allows for participation, it has to be within the framework of the Sharia. In other words," concluded Julian, as he placed Feisal's monograph on the table, "anyone who thinks Western style democracy can be made to thrive in the Middle East is totally insane?"

The dark eyes of Nuri Feisal glittered with silent laughter. He tapped his slim, elegant fingers together, studying Julian the way he might have tried to find in the face of a long lost friend evidence of what he must have experienced in all the time that had passed.

"Do you know - except for Marcel Dubose - this is the first occasion on which I have had the chance to have a conversation, a serious conversation, in - what? - thirty years. And even then, when I was still that young scholar who wrote what you were so kind to read, there really wasn't anyone who thought what I was doing anything more than a waste of time, a strange diversion, an attempt to understand ancient texts that could have no possible relevance to anything important for the present. And now, of all people - you!" He struck the side of his head with two fingers twice, then, again, a third time. "Of course! That is why he mentioned it. Julian. Julian the Apostate. Marcel asked me if I had ever read him. I had to admit I had not. He said I should, that for more than the obvious reasons I might learn something useful. Useful! A word he never uses, never cares about. I hardly noticed. Only now, looking back....Another Julian! " He bent forward, his elbows on the table. "I read a little about him, after Marcel..., something Alexandre Kojeve wrote fifty years ago. Enough to know that...." There was something in the way Julian was looking at him that made him let the rest of it go unfinished, something that told him that Julian knew what he was going to say. "We are not going to be dealing with half-measures, are we, Mr. President?"

Julian leaned toward Feisal. "Only Ismael knows you are here. No one will ever know what we have talked about. When I read what Marcel Dubose sent me, I was certain I could talk to you - in private; talk about things I could never speak about in public."

"Every being made to achieve its ultimate perfection."

"Not just that."

"I know. How can I help? Of what service can I be?"

"Half the people in this country, and more than half the members of Congress, think the only way to fight terrorism is to fight against it on the ground, where it starts."

"Yes, and every time you bomb another city, another village, every time you inflict more casualties, the anger, the hatred, grows. It won't stop, Mr. President. Islam won't allow it. I needn't tell you - you know already - that every Muslim, everyone who believes, believes Islam is the word of God, the true word of God. We know the truth, we know God's meaning - we cannot tolerate error," explained Feisal, with a subtle smile of honorable duplicity. "These American politicians, arguing about whether to call it 'radical Islamic terrorism!' Read the Koran. There should be no confusion. The central teaching: all the world, everyone, is destined to come to the true belief. There may be secular elements who try to water it down, suggest that, like what happened to Christianity, Islam has become more - how shall I put it? - willing to accept the modern world. And it is - but not by those who are really devoted to the faith. And, I have to tell you, even what you might regard as the more moderate among us still think of you - the Americans, the West - as at war with Islam and all we believe, think of you the way we did of the Crusaders, come to take our lands, everything we have, everything we believe, away from us. That is why -"

"The Crusaders!" laughed Julian with raised eyebrows. "We both know they came to take back what was taken, what had belonged to Christianity before Mohammed was born."

"And belonged to the Romans, and the Persians, before Christ. History, when it comes to what someone wants, is all a matter of choice: look back to where your grievance first began, not to when you first took what had once belonged to someone else."

Struck by the phrase "matter of choice," Julian rubbed his chin. History, not as a necessary progress toward the present, the present the culmination of everything that had gone before, the highest achievement, the perfection, of the human race. Choice, no one would admit it now. History, a process that gave meaning to time, gave meaning to the lives of people who had to think themselves part of something else, and not accountable for their failure to live as if their life had its own meaning in the miracle of their existence. Choice, what else was life if it was not that?

"The Crusaders, think what would have happened if the Christians had not tried to take back what once belonged to them. No mathematics - and therewith no technology - without Arabic numbers. And, on the other hand, if Islam had not driven out the Christians and taken Constantinople, no one would have brought the works of ancient Greece - the works of Plato - to Florence, and without that, without what the Medici and their money made possible, the Renaissance would never have happened."

"Without mathematics, without the Renaissance....Yes, but then is the modern world such a great improvement? Are we any wiser, any better off? Who do we have who rivals Alfarabi or Averroes, to say nothing of Plato and Aristotle."

"I don't disagree, but this is the world in which we have to live, the world we have to change." The fingers of Julian's left hand began tapping a slow, methodical beat, measuring the intervals of a long line of thought. "There are three things I am going to do, three things in which I need you to act as an intermediary. Gradually, over the next several months, all the forces we have in the Middle East will be withdrawn. There will be no residual forces, no trainers, no special forces, no air support - nothing. There will be no American presence. We don't like to think of ourselves as an empire, but since the Second World War that is what we have become." There was a hard edge to his voice, contempt for the refusal of others to look things straight on, to see things as they really were. "You will remember - you've read Thucydides - what Pericles said, how it may have been unjust for Athens to acquire an empire, but it would be dangerous, and perhaps fatal, to give it up. But he also warned in that same speech that it could cost them the war if they tried to make their empire bigger, greater, than it was. And when Rome became an empire, what did Augustus do? He drew back and confined the empire to a defensible limit. The American empire - this notion that we have some obligation to bring democracy to the world - our real obligation is to lead by example, become the kind of republic we were meant to be. The American empire - we need to draw back."

"So you would leave the Middle East," said Feisal, studying Julian closely.

He knew he could trust him. That was no longer even a question. There were not half dozen people in the world - men like Marcel Dubose - who had the kind of mind that could follow - or would think it important to follow - the difficult, and sometimes hidden, teaching of the greatest philosophers, the only ones who deserved the name, who had ever written. And now, to his amazement, he had discovered that Julian Drake, the American president, was one of them. This was a revelation; it was also a great danger. Whatever Julian Drake might decide to do, it was certain to be revolutionary. Great success, or great failure, it would have to be one or the other.

"That will remove the cause of most of the resentment, most of the hatred, most of the incentive that has driven so many to join organizations devoted to your destruction. But it will not remove all of it. Too much has happened, too many people have been killed, too many have gained power in the struggle against the West. We have too many conflicts of our own, too many governments have been overthrown, too many rebellions have been suppressed. We are filled with bad memories and live too much on promises of revenge and retribution."

"The second thing, the second part, is whatever assistance, civilian assistance, economic aid, that might be needed to help rebuild what we helped destroy: schools, hospitals, roads, bridges, housing. The third thing - and about this there is no room for discussion - we cannot withdraw, we cannot leave, without a clear understanding that terrorism is now your problem, not ours."

"Our problem…? How do you mean this? In what sense does it becomes ours?"

Julian looked across the table with a strange reluctance, regretting the necessity of what he had to say next.

"It will be our policy that any attack on the United States will be considered an act of war by whatever country in which any terrorist who commits such an act has most recently resided. If someone from Yemen attacks the United States, we won't go looking for someone hiding in Yemen, we will go to war against Yemen. If Bin Laden were alive today, we would go to war against Pakistan. That is what I mean when I say it is your problem. I want you, as the

Saudi ambassador, to inform the other governments in the region that this is what I will do. It's their job to make sure it doesn't happen, their responsibility to stop any terrorist organization from operating in their territory. We're not going to be there - we're leaving. They will have no one now to complain about, no one to blame. There isn't any Great Satan, threatening their way of life. They are going to be left alone to solve their own problems however they decide. They leave us alone and all will be well. If they don't, they will, I assure you, have reason to regret it."

"You're taking quite a chance. How many of those governments do you think can really control what goes on inside their borders? Yes, I know...they haven't had much reason to try." He paused, considering the possibilities. "It might work. And it's hard to see how it could be any worse than the situation as it now is. It will give us more leverage - with certain of the other players in the region - the argument that the Americans are leaving, that they won't be back, unless...." He suddenly thought of something. "But will it work here? You'll be accused of abandoning your allies in the region, accused of giving up the fight against terrorism, accused of-"

"Of everything imaginable. Unless it works. Now, tell me something more about Alfarabi and Averroes. Is it true that when Alfarabi describes the best regime, he avoids any conflict with Islam and the religious authorities by avoiding any reference to God, revelation, the divine law or miracles?"

"It is always necessary to avoid the appearance of disagreement with what those in power, whether a tyrant or a whole people, believe - is it not?"

CHAPTER TWENTY-ONE

It used to be said of Lyndon Johnson, when he was majority leader in the Senate, that he knew every senator's secret wish and secret fear and how to use that knowledge to his own advantage. With one long arm thrown around the shoulder of a senator whose vote he needed, he would jab him in the chest with a crooked finger, telling him all the torments of hell he could expect to receive if he voted the wrong way, and all the rewards of heaven if he would only agree, just this one time, to ignore what the people in his state might want and do what, deep down in his heart, they both knew was the right thing. "The Treatment," as it came to be called, did not always work, but those who resisted it were few and far between. The Senate under Lyndon Johnson did its work ,and did it with something close to clockwork efficiency. But Lyndon Johnson was dead and gone and the Senate was nothing like the same place. Louis Matson could only shake his head at the loss of all sense of responsibility, the unwillingness of senators to give any thought to anything beyond what their vote on a given issue might cost them in the next election.

"You never used to have to worry about this kind of thing. If you were an incumbent, you might, once in a while, find yourself with an opponent in the general election you had to take seriously, especially if it was a year like 1964, when LBJ was facing Goldwater and everyone knew he was going to win in a landslide, or 1972, when McGovern was going to drag down the Democrats when he got buried by Nixon. But have to worry about what someone in your own party might do, worry about a primary for Christ sake! That stuff just didn't happen. And now - hell! - that's all these idiots think about. Julian's been in office - what? - almost four months, and all that legislation, all the things he wants to do - everything we should do - it's still here, sitting in committees, everyone too goddamn scared of what might happen, not to the country, but to them! I can't bring anything to a vote; I don't have enough votes to get it through, and I'm not going to try until I do. Jesus H. Christ! It's that goddamn ..., it's those same goddamn people: Chambers, Murray, that whole crowd of mindless, self-important fools who think that because - usually through no fault of their own - they became billionaires they're smart and everyone else is stupid. They think they got stiffed at the convention. They didn't like it. Instead of one of those wind-up dolls, those straw-stuffed politicians, they get - Christ, this must have damn near killed them - Julian! And then what? - They decide to back the other side. They lose again. And then what do they do? - They keep running a campaign, fill the airwaves with all these warnings about how if Julian Drake gets his way, if Congress gives him the legislation he wants, America will be bankrupt and all our rights taken away!"

Matson was angry, as angry as he had ever been. And he was enjoying every minute of it. Gesturing with his hands, gesturing with his arms, shaking his head in disbelief, and with every swearing word laughter, loud laughter, in his voice. He had not felt this good in months. The anger, the sense of engagement in a rightful cause, made him forget the discomfort and, if only for the moment, banished from his mind all thought of his own, not too distant, death. He was still alive. Better yet, he had a reason to keep on living, however short a time he might have.

"Well, for Christ sake, Ismael, what the hell are we going to do about it?"

They were sitting in the ornate comfort of the Senate Majority Leader's office. Ismael Cooper had come at Matson's invitation. It was half past six in the evening. Outside the window, the sky had a fiery reddish glow, adding warmth to the plush silence of the thick carpeted room, and a deeper meaning when the silence was broken by speech. Matson reached for his glass, half full of whiskey.

"I'll get it done," he sighed. "Don't know how, but I'll get it done." He looked at Ismael, sitting in a pale green upholstered chair the other side of his desk. "I promise."

"There is great support in the country…."

"Oh, Christ! - Don't tell me….You know better than - It doesn't matter what the country thinks. The only thing that counts is what these people I have to deal with think they might have to fear - someone in a primary with more money than anyone has ever seen to spend against them. Remember The Wizard of Oz - the tin man, the straw man, the lion without courage? Take all of them together and you have the perfect description of most members: no brain, no courage, no heart!" Matson laughed. "That's not bad. So now I get to be the wizard, make everyone think I've got a power I don't. Well, I've done that often enough."

Pausing, Matson bent his head to the side, a question in his tired eyes. It seemed to take all his attention, and for a moment Ismael thought that, though he was sitting right in front of him, he had forgotten he was there. Matson had always done this, slipped away to some thought of his own while someone else was speaking, but somehow still listening enough to comment immediately on what he had heard.

"You're going to take my place," announced Matson, suddenly. Ismael had no idea what he was talking about. "Here, in the Senate, when I'm gone. This summer, that's when I'm resigning. The governor - who wouldn't be governor if it weren't for me - is going to appoint you to fill the vacancy. After that," he remarked, grinning at the look of helpless wonder in Ismael's mild, modest eyes. "After that, you're on your own, when you run for a full term, forced to defend all the awful things you helped Julian Drake do to the country."

There was no reaction, nothing in the way of a reply to the gentle needling about what he could look forward to. Ismael had not gotten past the first, all too stunning, announcement that Louis Matson was leaving, and that, without a word to him, everything had been arranged so he could take his place.

"I can't…," he said, stumbling over the words. "And why would you…why are you - leaving? Why resign from the Senate?"

Matson took a drink and ignored the question.

"What do you mean, you can't? You can, and you have to. There isn't anyone else, no one I would ever trust to fill the seat. Next to Julian, you're...."

"That's the point. I can't. I promised Julian - I promised the president that I would serve the full four years, and I won't break my word."

"I know you gave your word. But Julian won't need you after this summer."

"Julian won't...? You talked to him about this?"

"I told him I was leaving, and that you were the only one I thought should take my place. He said he could not agree more. In fact," he added, "he said he had once told you the same thing."

"In Cleveland. I remember. He told me....But that doesn't change anything. He can't - the president can't do everything by himself. It isn't that I think myself irreplaceable," he added quickly, "but, my God, do you have any idea - you can't know - what it is like working with him? There is never any stop; the only thing I think he really hates is rest." Ismael thought better of what he had just said. "No, I can't explain it. There is constant motion, but all of it so grounded, so connected, that it doesn't seem like anything is moving at all. I told you, when I came back after that first trip out to California, when he wrote the speech you wanted, that you get the feeling, the impression, that he takes in everything at a glance, but now, after what I have seen, I understand that it isn't that at all. He takes things in, all right, faster than anyone I've ever been around, but the secret isn't just the quickness of his mind, it's the study, the constant study, of everything involved. He knows the details - I mean the smallest details - of everything he does. When we were drafting the legislation that was sent to the Hill, he would remember every change we made, every period, every comma. That is what he does, that is who he is: a student, always learning, always trying to find out more. But - and this is more important than anything else - for all his eye for detail, he has an even better eye for what is essential. You start talking to him about something not right on point, his eyes go cold. When it comes to time, he is the most ruthless human being I've ever known."

"Ruthless? That seems a strange way to put it." Matson sipped slowly on his drink. "Ruthless," he repeated, rolling the word round his tongue as he rolled the ice round his glass. "Yes, I've seen that in him. Never in the way he acted toward another person; always toward himself. That discipline he has.

It's why everyone thinks he's an enigma: they've never seen anyone quite like him. They don't know whether it is real or not, and, if it is, what it means."

"Enigma? Someone who doesn't want, or need, the same things other people want. I wonder if they will think him that after the next move he makes."

Matson put down his drink and leaned forward on his elbows. "Next move? What next move? What is he going to do now? What has he -?"

"I can't say," replied Ismael, his small, round eyes shining with the certainty that, for one of the first times, he knew something Matson did not. "'It's all a question of what we look up to,' - that was the way he put it," added Ismael, with an eager, purposely ambiguous smile, as he rose from the chair and said goodbye.

Matson was left in a state of amused impatience, anxious to learn what Julian was going to do next, but sharing some of Ismael's apparent pleasure in the secret he would not tell. Standing outside, waiting to catch a cab, Ismael thought about the remarkable thing Matson had done, arranging things so that he, who had once lost his seat in the House could now become a member of the Senate. Then, as a cab pulled up, he remembered that his old mentor and friend lived alone. He waved off the driver and went back inside to invite Louis Matson to dinner. He found him slumped over his desk, gasping for breath.

"It's nothing," he insisted, in a harsh, choking voice. He reached for the top right hand drawer, but his hand was shaking and Ismael had to open it instead. There was a pill bottle, which he quickly opened, took one out and put it directly into Matson's mouth. Matson swallowed it and then sank back down into his leather chair.

"Don't - not to anyone, especially Julian. Never! - You understand? Not a word - I'm all right; I'm not dead yet."

Those last four words told Ismael all he needed to know, the reason Matson was going to resign, the reason for the urgency to settle on his replacement. The only thing that could be done now was to follow the old man's lead in whatever fiction he wanted to invent. Death was an intimacy on which no one not involved should intrude.

Ismael took Louis Matson home and did not leave the senator's side until almost midnight. He listed to all the stories Matson wanted to tell; stories, some of them, he had never told before; stories about the secret lives of politicians he had known and, some of them, despised; stories, a few of them, about men he had admired.

"It's what we do, isn't it?" he asked at one point, far into the night. "Tell stories about what we have done, what we have heard. When you think about it, that's really all we do, tell stories, give an account, give some meaning to what goes on around us; explain what - if we were ever to tell the whole, unvarnished truth - is just the result of chance. Nixon, Johnson - devious bastards, both of them - but Nixon was the better man. No one believes that now: Watergate, impeachment, resignation in disgrace. But in 1960, when the Democratic machine in Chicago stole the election for Kennedy, Nixon refused to allow an investigation. He thought it would hurt the country to have a contested election for the presidency. Johnson - the reason they called him Landslide Lyndon was because it took some stuffed ballot boxes from down in Duval county, where more votes were cast than they had voters, to get him elected to the Senate from Texas with fewer votes than almost anyone in history.

"No one remembers anything anymore, and what they think they remember they have all wrong. Jerry Ford, everyone joked about how awkward, how stiff he was, a mediocre congressman from Grand Rapids who could put you to sleep before he had finished two sentences. But next to Woodrow Wilson he was the best educated president in the twentieth century: University of Michigan undergraduate, Yale law school. And then you have Jimmy Carter, that sanctimonious son-of-a-bitch. He could lie to your face and then deny he ever did it even when you proved it! Let me tell you a story. Years ago, back in the seventies, maybe a year before Carter became president, when no one knew who the hell he was. I was working for Bob Griffin and I had a good friend who was working for Phil Hart. Griffin is a Republican, Hart a Democrat, but they got on great together. Anyway, my friend tells me about this young woman, tall, blonde, great looking. She was working for someone running for Congress, if I remember right. She tells this friend of mine that the guy she is working for doesn't have a chance and that she's been asked to join the presidential campaign of this guy, the governor of Georgia, Jimmy Carter. Well, my friend starts to laugh, asks her why she wants to jump from one sinking ship to another. So she tells him she knows some of his people who are running things. She tells him that Carter and his people have figured out that what the country wants more than anything after Nixon is someone who tells the truth, and so Carter comes up with this line about how he'll 'never lie to the American people.' Worst hypocrite I ever knew. Least trustworthy bastard ever held the office, except maybe Clinton."

Matson kept talking, each memory bringing back another. It seemed to Ismael that he was trying to knit together all the most important things he had done, all the most important people he had known, connecting everything on a central thread by which chance would be removed and something like fate take over. Finally, sometime close to midnight, his voice fell to a whisper and then, a short while later, his voice fell silent and he was asleep. Ismael was not sure what to do: cover him with a blanket and leave him there, in his chair, or wake him up and help him into bed. Nor was he sure, either way, whether he should leave him there alone in his apartment. He could not stay there with him; he had to get back to the White House. He wondered if he should call an ambulance to take him to the hospital, which is where he ought to be, but Matson would never forgive him if he did that. He called Rachel Good instead.

"I know its late, but I'm over at Louis Matson's place and -"

"Is he all right?" she asked. Her voice told Ismael that she knew.

"Yes, but he's asleep in his chair, and I'm not sure what to do. I was with him in his office. I left then decided to go back, and when I walked in, he…."

"I'll be right over. Can you wait until I get there? It shouldn't be more than twenty minutes."

She was there in less than fifteen minutes, full of assurances, insisting there was no reason for Ismael to stay, that she could take care of everything.

"I'll sit here with him, and when he wakes up, I'll make sure he gets to bed. In the morning, I'll get him to his doctor." She gave Ismael a look of intense curiosity. "You know, don't you - that he's dying? Cancer. I don't know how long he's known - he would not tell me that - but quite a while, certainly before he sent you to find Julian Drake and ask him to write that speech he never intended to give himself."

"Never intended…? Did Louis tell you that?"

"He didn't have to. I knew it - maybe almost as long as you did." She glanced across the small darkened room, crowded with books and papers, to where Louis Matson slept in his chair. "I would have married him, years ago, if he had ever thought to ask. He thinks I'm only making it up when I tell him I would have gone out with him if he had only asked a second time." She laughed quietly, and with regret. "I didn't want to seem easy, so instead I seemed, to Louis Matson's then surprisingly innocent eyes, impossible."

It was nearly one in the morning when Ismael drove up to the White House gate. The guard, a black officer who moved with the agility of a man half his enormous size, greeted him with a knowing grin.

"The president asked if you wouldn't mind stopping by. That is the way he put it, just like that: 'if you wouldn't mind.' And no, it doesn't matter how late it is," he added, his large eyes luminous with the sheer pleasure of proximity not just to power but to someone who deserved to have it. "Whatever time it is, one thing you can always count on, he's still working. Good evening, Mr. Cooper," he said, waving him through.

One o'clock, two o'clock, three in the morning, time did not matter; or, rather, time was the only thing that did, time in which to work, to study, to finish, if you could, what you set out to achieve, what, in this instance, you had promised the country you would try to accomplish. Sleep was darkness, sleep was death, sleep and death both necessities, but nothing, neither one, to look forward to, not while there was still time to do something important, something that gave meaning, that justified, if you will, the fact that you had been born.

Ismael found Julian in the small room just off the Oval Office where presidents and their vice-presidents sometimes met for lunch and where Julian worked at night. He was wearing khaki pants and an oxford shirt with the sleeves rolled up. He never went into the Oval Office without a coat and tie. Ismael started to say something, but Julian, hunched over the table, held up his left hand while he finished scribbling what he was writing on a long white lined pad in front of him.

"There," he said, still holding the fountain pen in his hand. "Not too bad."

He looked up at Ismael, so eager to tell him what he had been doing that he did not notice the worried expression, the deep distress, in his eyes. He fumbled through the pages of a notebook in which he jotted down things he wanted to remember: bits and pieces of conversation, a line or two, sometimes whole paragraphs, from something he had read.

"Here it is. Why are you still standing there? Never mind. Sit down, listen to this. I was trying to think about a way to explain, to describe, how we have changed, how we see things differently - well, to be blunt about it, how we have become less intelligent than we were." His eyes danced from side to side, moving quick step through everything he knew he was going to say. He often took delight in the absurdity of things. "I remembered reading somewhere - or maybe someone once told me - that Kennedy's favorite books were Lord Melbourne by David Cecil and Pilgrim's Way by John Buchan. I've read them both. Melbourne was prime minister in the first years of Queen Victoria. She was still just a girl. Melbourne - Do you know this? - was Charles Lamb. His wife, Lady Anne Lamb, is the one who ran off with Byron. Melbourne had to live through the disgrace of it, and - this is what is remarkable - he did it in a way that made him one of the most admired men of his time. The other book, Pilgrim's Way….I'll come back to that in a minute."

Leaning back, his elbows on the arms of the chair, he stroked the side of his chin. He seemed to draw back inside himself, as if to consider more fully exactly what he wanted to say, or, rather, what he had learned.

"I looked it up, Kennedy's favorite books; I knew there had to be more than just the two. There were close to two dozen, nearly all of them histories: biographies of Lincoln, John Quincy Adams, Henry Clay; the speeches of Daniel Webster. And not just American history, Gibbon's Decline and Fall of the Roman Empire, all seven volumes - Do you think anyone reads that anymore? - And Churchill's biography of his ancestor, The Duke of Marlborough." Julian flashed a smile full of nostalgia. "When I was in law school, at Chicago, I used to sit in on classes in the graduate school. There was one teacher who taught me more than all the others combined. He had been there when Leo Strauss was still teaching. He told me something I never forgot. Strauss never discussed in class any current political events. He taught political philosophy: Plato, Aristotle, Machiavelli, Hobbes, Locke, Rousseau, Nietzsche - those were his contemporaries. The only time he ever spoke at any length about a contemporary was in 1965 when Churchill died. He came to class - a seminar on one of Plato's dialogues - and, reading from two paragraphs he had written out by hand, said among other things that Churchill's Marlborough was the greatest work of history written in the 20th century. I've read it, twice, four volumes, two thousand pages, and it was one of Kennedy's favorite books. And his favorite work of fiction? - The Red and the Black, by Stendhal." Julian threw up his hands and laughed. "Gibbon, Churchill, Stendhal, the speeches of Daniel Webster. And now? But wait," he said, reaching for a large, paperbound book that lay on top of an official looking report. "Pilgrim's Way. There is a reason I wanted to come back to it," he mumbled, as he thumbed through the pages, looking for the passage he wanted to read to Ismael.

"Buchan studied classics at Oxford at the end of the 19th century. He knew almost everyone who played an important part in British politics through the 1930s. At the end of it, after everything that had happened, the First World War, or the Great War, as if was called - after all the changes, after all that science, applied science, had produced, his nightmare, as he put it, was not a return to 'barbarism, which is civilization submerged or not yet born, but to de-civilization, which is civilization gone rotten.' And what is a civilization gone rotten? Listen to this: 'In such a world everyone would have leisure. But everyone would be restless, for there would be no spiritual discipline in life. Some kind of mechanical philosophy of politics would have triumphed, and everybody would have his neat little part of the state machine. Everybody would be comfortable, but since there could be no great demand for intellectual exertion everybody would be also slightly idiotic. Their shallow minds would be easily bored, and therefore unstable. Their life would be largely a quest for amusement.'"

Julian looked at Ismael and shook his head, as if there was nothing he could do but laugh at the insanity of the world. But there was also, just beneath the surface of that apparent surrender, a kind of eager defiance. Faced with a problem few others knew existed, a problem that, to the contrary, nearly everyone thought a mark of progress - the comfort, and the diversions, the modern world provided - he had a clear understanding of what needed to be done.

"This was written in 1939! Kennedy read it. It was one of his favorite books. Listen to the kind of future he read about: 'It would be a feverish, bustling world, self-satisfied and yet malcontent, and under the mask of a riotous life would be death at the heart….Men would go anywhere and live nowhere; know everything and understand nothing. On the perpetual hurry of life there would be no chance of quiet for the soul. In the tumult of a jazz existence what hope would there be for the still small voices of the prophets and philosophers and poets? A world which claimed to be a triumph of the human personality would in truth have killed that personality. In such a bagman's paradise, where life would be rationalized and added with every material comfort, there would be little satisfaction for the immortal part of man. It would be a new Vanity Fair, with Mr. Talkative as the chief officer on the town council.'"

Julian stopped, weighing in the balance the last line he had read. "Mr. Talkative….Yes, that's good. But, now, listen to the way it finishes, what it says about what has happened: 'The essence of civilization lies in man's defiance of an impersonal universe.' - Even with his critique, as devastating as it is, Buchan remains under the influence of modern science - 'It makes no difference that a mechanized universe may be his own creation if he allows his handiwork to enslave him. Not for the first time in history have the idols that humanity has shaped for its own ends become its master.'"

Carefully, as if in respect for what a serious author had written, Julian put down the book, setting it, not exactly where it had been before, on top of an official-looking report, but just next to it. He picked up his fountain pen, tapped it gently against the pad on which he had been writing and shook his head again.

"That is what Kennedy read - along with those other works of history. And what does this generation of leading politicians read? I found a list of Hillary Clinton's favorite books, almost all of them fiction, and, with the exception of The Brothers Karamazov, which she read in college, all of it contemporary stuff: mysteries, thrillers, popular fiction. The only history, Citizens of London, about prominent Americans who played a part in the Second World War. Two political memoirs, one by George Bush, the other by John McCain. She apologized, in one story, for never have read Proust, mistranslating the title so that instead of 'Remembrance of Things Past,' it became something like 'Remembering Time Lost,' so she could then joke that she had never found the time!

"Buchan was right: There aren't many serious people anymore. Well, perhaps we can do a little to change that. It's what I have been working on," he explained, nodding toward the scrawled pages on the desk. He stood up and stretched his arms and then crossed them loosely over his chest as he stared down at what he had written. "The universities teach each new generation what they should know, what the universities think they should know. The interesting question is who teaches the universities. Where is it they learn what they teach?" He gave Ismael a shrewd, penetrating glance. "Set up a dinner, make it a public event, honoring the leading institutions of higher education. Say it is for the top fifteen or twenty - the number doesn't much matter - but include the presidents of all the major private universities - Harvard, Chicago, Yale, Princeton - all of them, especially those who have expressed their unwillingness to do what we're asking public universities to do, give four years tuition for four years service. In addition, invite...."

Ismael was looking down at his hands, his mind somewhere else.

"What is it?" asked Julian, feeling suddenly quite guilty for not having noticed earlier that Ismael was preoccupied with some problem of his own.

"Louis," replied Ismael, slowly raising his eyes. "He has cancer, he's dying. I left his office, then decided I ought to invite him to dinner. He was almost in a state of collapse. I took him home, and he talked, talked about a lot of things...."

"He told you he wants you to take his place when he leaves, this summer; that he had talked to me and that I agreed there was no one else?"

"Yes, but I don't....As I say, I took him back to his apartment, and, finally, he fell asleep in his chair, and I called Rachel Good - She told me she would have married him, years ago, when he was first in Congress. I never knew they were - or had been - that close. She came at once. She's staying with him tonight. I don't know how long he's got, but it can't be very long."

When Julian only smiled, Ismael was not sure what to make of it. Julian understood his confusion.

"He won't die before he's finished here, before he has managed to get through Congress everything we have asked for. Someone told me once - a nurse, a doctor, I don't remember - that people in nursing homes seldom died when they had a birthday coming up. It was something to look forward to, something they could still achieve. He won't die, not so long as he still has work he think important that he hasn't finished." He looked at Ismael with a different sympathy. "He made you promise not to tell me, didn't he? Remember something: if it was the other way around, if I were dying, Louis would have never forgiven you if you hadn't told him. If he remembers the promise, he'll remember that he felt honor bound to force you to make it, and that you had no choice but to do what you have done. Now you better get some sleep."

Nodding his appreciation, Ismael got up to leave. His eyes drifted to the book that John F. Kennedy had liked so much, and then, almost by chance, to the document that lay next to it. "FBI?"

"Yes. It seems that some of our friends - Chambers, Murray - may not be content with just spending half their fortunes trying to stop what we're trying to do," he explained, tapping his finger on the thick, blue cover. "Strange, though, when you think about it. What better way to guarantee passage of something you oppose than to assassinate the president responsible for it?"

Ismael was thunderstruck. For a moment he could not speak.

"I wouldn't worry much about it. There are always people out there making threats."

"Not people like Rufus Chambers and Angela Murray." Suddenly, he thought of something. "Chambers, Murray - but not Wilson?"

"He isn't mentioned. But it's all just talk. The only reason there is a report is because I asked Justice to see if any laws were broken by the kind of expenditures that were made during the campaign. Someone ought to be prosecuted for that."

"May I - take it with me, read it myself?"

Julian tried to suggest that it was not worth his time, that there were more important things to worry about.

"I read pretty fast," Ismael reminded him in a tone of voice so determined that it was, even for Julian, difficult to refuse.

"All right," he agreed, reluctantly; "but remember, this is confidential.

Nothing gets said about this to anyone. And besides, it may become useful."

"Useful?"

"We'll see." And with that, Julian picked up his pen and started correcting what he had written.

CHAPTER TWENTY-TWO

More than surprised, Conrad Wilson was astonished when his secretary hurried into his office to tell him that Ismael Cooper was waiting to see him. No one had called, no one had made an appointment, and, more to the point, no one had asked him to come to Washington to see the president's chief of staff. Cooper was here, just outside, and that meant that whatever Cooper wanted was urgent. He had not seen him since the night he tried to talk to him just before Julian Drake's first press conference in D.C.

"Show him in," he said, finally. "No, never mind; I'll take care of this." He got up from the glass and grey steel desk and walked to the hand wrought double doors made of polished brass and shadowed Venetian glass. He pushed them open, just in time to see the expression of cold anger on Ismael's face. He forced himself to sound pleased to see him.

"Ismael, this is a surprise. Are you in New York for…?"

Ismael walked right past him and, with an air of importance that was unusual for him, settled into a tall, narrow cushioned straight back chair in front of Wilson's desk. He did not bother with the view from the eightieth floor over the park; he did not so much as glance at the half dozen French Impressionist paintings that lined the wall. He opened his briefcase, dropped a thin document on the desk, and just sat there, staring straight ahead, waiting for Wilson to get back to his chair. Wilson felt like someone who, accused of a crime he did not commit, begins to doubt his own innocence.

"What is this?" he asked, trying to appear carelessly indifferent.

"It's an FBI report. I read it last night. My first thought when I finished was that you should read it today."

"You want me to…?" He slid his fingers toward it, slowly and with reluctance, then pulled his hand back. "This concerns me exactly how?" Tilting his head to the side, an equivocal look in his grayish blue eyes, Wilson studied Ismael closely. "What is it you think…? You came all the way to - ?"

"Read it, damn it, Conrad! It won't take long," insisted Ismael with such sudden anger that before he knew what he was doing Wilson opened it to the first page and began to read. Three lines into it, his mouth fell open.

"Good God! - I don't believe…." He shook his head, bitterly and with reproach. "I should have known...I should have…"

He leaned forward on his elbows, holding his head between his hands, reading with growing interest and concern about what appeared a conspiracy that, at least by implication, seemed to suggest his involvement. As his concentration deepened, the speed with which he read increased, matching in its own way what, the moment he finished, was a rush to judgment.

"I had nothing to do with this! Nothing! So if you have -"

"Your name isn't in there," replied Ismael, his gaze withering in its contempt. "Should it be?"

"No! Of course not; I just thought….Yes, I see. You assumed because I know them, because we have been involved together politically, I must have known about - this! But I didn't!"

"You just said you should have known. Should have known what? - That your friends and associates, Rufus Chambers and Angela Murray were planning the assassination of the president?"

Wilson looked out the window, out across the park, suddenly remembering the night in Rufus Chambers's office, just a few blocks away, when the three of them had watched Julian Drake on television, remembering the ease with which Angela Murray had said it, the absence of all conscience, the question of someone's life or death no different than a simple calculation of profit and loss.

"Angela I believe, but Rufus…? I don't care what this says, he couldn't… unless….She has a hold on him. I don't understand it, I've never understood it. He tries to reason with her, to get her to tone things down, but in the end - whatever she wants, he doesn't try to stop her." Wilson shoved himself back from the desk. "Why are you here? What is it you want from me?"

"It's very simple: I want you to stop it."

"Stop…? How? You think I just have to ask, call them up, invite them over, tell them the FBI has been wiretapping their phones, listening to their conversations?" He glanced again at the report. "They haven't done anything: they haven't taken any action. All you really have is talk, talk abut what they want to do - what she wants to do - and the different ways it might be done."

Ismael listened with a blank expression and then pointed to the report.

"I want you to give them that. I want you to tell them that it doesn't matter whether there is enough to prosecute. If they don't do exactly what I want them to, every news source in America will have a copy. Perhaps they can explain how it was only talk, that they never really meant to do anything; perhaps they can explain to the shareholders in their various enterprises, to their boards of directors, that their idea of looking after the best interest of their companies was to spend their time planning - 'talking' - about the best way to assassinate the president of the United States!" shouted Ismael, as he rose from his chair and stared hard at Wilson. "Now, call them both, tell them that something has happened, that you have to see them right away, tonight!"

"I'm not sure they're in town. I haven't spoken to either of them since the night -"

"They're in town. After what I read last night, trust me, we're always going to know where they are. Call them. Do it now. They'll come, and when they do, give them that report and tell them they have only one way out."

Five minutes later, Ismael was on his way back to Washington. Two hours later, at seven o'clock, Rufus Chambers and Angela Murray arrived, doing nothing to hide their irritation at what Murray in particular thought a summons. She had barely sat down when she started venting her displeasure.

Wilson stopped her with a look.

He had begun to understand more clearly the situation in which he found himself. He was not the one in trouble; he had nothing to fear. Ismael Cooper, and through him, the president, were not threatening him with any kind of reprisals for anything he might have done; he was being asked to serve as an emissary, to deliver in no uncertain terms an ultimatum which, if his two former friends - that was how he now thought of them - chose to ignore it, would mean their complete destruction. The more he thought about it, the more he thought about what it would to do to Angela Murray, a woman he had come, not just to distrust, but to despise, the better he felt. It was all he could do to control his exuberance.

"Can I get you something to drink?" he asked. A smile full of subtlety and malice cut quick across his lip. "You might need it."

He moved across to the paneled bar and poured himself a drink. Holding it in his hand, he stood for a moment, admiring the way the sinking sun bathed the park in such rich colors, the trees turned orange under the soft scarlet sky. He sipped on the scotch and water, studying the way the two-story glass wall made everything below seem smaller and less significant. It was what he used to imagine as a boy, laying on the summer grass, wondering what it must be like to ride across the sky on one of the clouds that drifted overhead. It was strange, he thought to himself, how good he suddenly felt, how relieved, and all because he was the one about to deliver, and not receive, news worse than death.

"Ismael Cooper came to see me," he announced, in a calm, steady voice. He waited to see their reaction. There was not any, just two blank faces. "He wanted to show me something," he said, walking back across the enormous well-lit room to his desk. "Are you sure you wouldn't like something? As I said...."

Rufus Chambers looked at Angela Murray. They were sitting at opposite ends of a sofa under the French Impressionist paintings Wilson prized more than anything he owned. Angela did not look at him. Her attention was concentrated on Wilson's bizarre behavior: first, the demand that she drop everything, cancel her plans for the evening, and come to his office, and now this constant harping on the need - her need, according to him - for something to steel her nerves against what he had brought them there to tell them. She had had enough. She got to her feet.

"I don't really care what Ismael Cooper wanted, and I certainly don't care about whatever it is you want to tell me. Just say it, so I can get back to what I was doing."

Wilson lifted an eyebrow. "More planning about how you intend to kill the president?" he asked, with a shrug so casual that there could be no mistake that, if he did not know everything, he knew enough. Angela sank back down onto the sofa.

"What are you talking about? Is that why Cooper…? Whatever he thinks he knows, he doesn't….What's that?" she asked, as Wilson pulled open a drawer and took out the FBI report.

"Something Cooper wanted me to give you."

Her eyes flashing with rage, Angela just sat there, her knees pressed tight together. Chambers grabbed the report out of Wilson's hand and started to read, first one page, then another.

"They listened to what we…, tapped our phones, heard everything we talked about…?"

He stared at Angela. "Congratulations! You've finally done it. You never thought anything like this could happen, that you were too smart, too goddamn powerful, that you could get away with anything - And now! Now we're both going to prison!"

"You're not going to prison," said Wilson, "although God knows you should. What were you thinking, Rufus? We've known each other a long time; we practically started out together. You're the last person I would ever have thought….It's her, isn't it? What you see in her, what kind of hold she has on you, how she could ever convince you to get involved in something like this, I -"

"Oh, shut up, Conrad!" cried Angela. "You wouldn't know what to do with a woman even if you found one who wanted anything from you but your money. Just say what you have to say. Cooper gave you this report. So they were tapping our phones, listening to what we said . So what? - If there was evidence we ever did anything except talk about some fantasy, we wouldn't be here, listening to this patronizing shit of yours; we would be under arrest, charged with a crime."

"You're right, Angela," he replied, with an eagerness that surprised, and then alarmed, her. "There isn't any evidence that you did anything, nothing that could be used to prove a conspiracy. But that doesn't really matter. They have all they need."

"All they need?"

"All they need to convince you to do the right thing."

"And what, please tell me, is the right thing?"

"You - and that means both of you - are to stop this orchestrated campaign of yours against what the president is asking Congress for. You're to stop all the television ads, all the threats to spend money against any congressman or senator who doesn't vote against him, all the promises of money and support to any candidate who does what you want."

Chambers let out a sigh of relief. His shoulders, sagging under the burden of all he had been caught doing, straightened up. The color came back to his face.

"That's easy; that won't be a problem. Consider it done."

Angela did not share his willing enthusiasm. With more self-knowledge, she had a deeper suspicion of other people's motives.

"There's more, isn't there. They want something else. But they can't have it, they can't have anything. You've already said they can't prove anything. There isn't anything to prove. So why should we - why should I - give a damn what they want?"

"Because if you don't do what they want - if you don't stop what you have been doing - if you don't publicly change your mind," he added, pronouncing each word as if were a court's final sentence, "and announce that after reconsideration you have decided that the president is right, that everyone, every Republican, every Democrat, should join together and vote for everything the president has asked Congress to approve - if you don't do that, and do it by the end of the day tomorrow, every newspaper, every television station, everyone will have their own copy of this report. Everyone in America will know what you said, how you were caught on tape planning the assassination of the president."

Rufus Chambers went white; Angela Murray choked with rage. Conrad

Wilson sipped quite contentedly on his drink.

"You know, I may be wrong, but I have the impression that Cooper - and I imagine Julian Drake as well - are almost hoping you don't do it. After this gets out, what effect do you think your opposition to the president will have?"

She wanted to scream. Her eyes filled with fire. She stamped her heel on the marble floor, a quick, hard beat that echoed like a canon shot in the high-ceilinged room.

"I won't be blackmailed, I won't!"

"What you call blackmail, others might call justice." Wilson's lip curled back in stern disdain. "You have until five o'clock tomorrow. And, as I say, I don't think they really care what you decide to do."

Angela Murray was five feet six, but she had mastered the art of looking down her nose at much taller people. She tried that now, but Wilson, who had never liked her, now did not fear her. She might still be thought one of the two or three most successful, which in America meant powerful, women in the country, but he knew she was about to become either a laughingstock, if she suddenly changed sides, or a national disgrace if she did not. His only response was to shake his head and smile.

When they were alone in the elevator, Angela, staring straight ahead, listened with growing impatience to Rufus Chambers and his endless complaints.

"For God's sake, Rufus, are you really so stupid you don't see we've won?"

Rigid, erect, her thin shoulders held tight as a soldier on parade, she turned her head just far enough to let him see, not what he expected - the look of disdain that so often traced her disappointment in something he had done or said - but something close to sympathy. He had missed the point, had misunderstood the significance of what had just happened. She was smarter, quicker, than he was. He was not sure she always had better judgement, but she was always a little ahead of him, could see things a little earlier than he could. She could run circles around nearly everyone he knew. But for the life of him, he could not see that they had won anything.

"Won? What are you…?"

"They don't know anything. Take me to dinner. They don't know," she repeated, in a strident voice. He still did not understand. "Don't you see?" she said, squeezing his wrist in her hand. “They think all we did was talk.”

‘But that is all we did - talk!”

She looked away. “That’s all you did, Rufus; that’s all you ever do,” she remarked, as the elevator came to a stop and the door opened on the ground floor. “Now take me somewhere nice for dinner, and then take me to bed, and I’ll show you things you never imagined.”

Ismael had not told Julian that he was going to New York, or what he was going to do when he got there. He had acted, in part, out of anger. He was furious with Chambers and Murray, with the whole crowd of people who thought money the only measure of things that counted and, because they had more money than anyone else, were entitled to decide how everyone else should live. It had reached the point where they believed that, more than buying and selling candidates for office, they could toss them aside, get rid of them, the way they would any other product that was no longer serviceable. Wilson had at least the intelligence to know when he was wrong. You could talk to him. In one respect he was like some of the better members of Congress, a man who wanted to do the right thing even if he did not always know what the right thing was. Ismael was not sure what to tell Julian, or whether to tell him anything at all.

He found Julian in the president’s private office, hunched over a legal pad on which he was writing in his indecipherable scrawl, a dozen handwritten pages stacked neatly on the far left side of the desk. Still wearing the same shirt, his hair tangled from all the times he had run his fingers through it while he tried to find the right word, he had not yet shaved.

“You’ve been here all…? You haven’t left; you’ve been working on whatever it is you’re doing - since last night?”

Cheerfully confused, Julian glanced around as if to make certain that he was in fact where Ismael said he was.

“Has it been that long?” He ran his hand along his lower jaw, grinning at how rough it felt. “I guess you’re right. What’s missing one night’s sleep? I’m finally finished.” He laid aside the fountain pen, leaned back in the chair, took a deep breath and then slowly let it out. “I’m a little hungry. Give me a minute. I’ll take a quick shower and then, if you’ll join me, we can have dinner and you can catch me up on what you’ve been doing all day in my - absence!”

Brimming with confidence in the success of his achievement, what he had worked on for close to sixteen hours straight, he sprang to his feet like someone well-rested about to start a new day. He pointed to the handwritten pages on the desk.

"After dinner, I'll dictate this to whichever secretary is on duty tonight. Then I'll be ready - to give a little lecture of my own, to teach the teachers, so to speak; though some, maybe most, of these higher officials of the higher learning, have never themselves taught - or perhaps even read - anything serious."

They had dinner downstairs in the White House mess where staff usually ate; but there was scarcely any staff under Julian, and there were just a few people, five or six, sitting over coffee at three or four different tables. They all stood up, or started to, when Julian walked in with Ismael, but with a lifted hand and a brief sideways movement of his head, he let them know it was not necessary. He and Ismael took a table in the far corner. Ismael, famished, ordered a steak; Julian asked for a tuna sandwich. "And a cup of black coffee," he told the steward.

The steward, who had become a familiar friend, looked doubtful.

"The chef is threatening to quit, Mr. President. He doesn't think you appreciate his talents."

Julian seemed to take it under advisement.

"Tell him that it is precisely because I appreciate his talents that I am saving him for a special occasion - when I invite to a formal dinner all my political enemies and, like the Borgias used to do, have them poisoned."

"He'll be glad to know that, Mr. President," said the steward with just the whisper of a laugh.

A few minutes later, when the steward brought the sandwich, Julian asked if the chef had made it himself.

"Yes, he did."

"Did you tell him what I said?"

"I did, Mr. President."

Julian shoved the sandwich across the table to Ismael.

"Would you mind taking a bite?" he asked, and then immediately pulled it back and took a bite himself. "Tell the chef its almost edible. Now," he went on, as the steward, smiling to himself, left the table, "where did you go today? New York, unless I miss my guess. It's what I would have done."

"What makes you think - ?"

"If you had been here, you wouldn't have waited until eight o'clock in the evening to see me. That means you weren't here. And if you were somewhere else for the whole day, you were out of town. And if - well, if I had read that FBI report, if that was all I knew - I would, in your place, have at least considered taking some direct action, letting them know that I was on to them, that they had been under surveillance, that they could not get away with it. That would have been my first thought."

"Your first thought - not your last?"

"I don't know. Eat your steak. Don't let it go cold. Who did you see?"

"Conrad Wilson."

"That makes sense. He's not named, presumably not involved, but close to the others. Do you think he was approached, asked, but refused?"

"No; that much I'm sure of. He didn't know, but he thinks he should have known"

"With the result that he was willing to help. What did you ask him to do?"

Listening to Ismael describe what had happened, what he had demanded of Wilson, what Wilson had promised to do, Julian took a few more bites of his sandwich and then pushed it aside, half unfinished.

"Angela Murray is the one, not Chambers, not anyone else. I saw it in her eyes that first time I met her, in Cleveland, the morning after I had the nomination. Three husbands, three divorces, head of one of the biggest high tech companies before she turned forty-five, ruthless, efficient, hated and feared by everyone who worked for her. 'Eyes like dollar signs and a mind like a cash register,' is the way someone who served on her board of directors described her. He was wrong. She isn't after money, the money is just a means; and she isn't after power, not in the usual sense."

Julian stroked his chin, thinking about what he had just said. He started searching Ismael's eyes, as if inviting him to consider with him the validity of what he was about to say.

"Most people take what they can get, settle for a workable arrangement in which others get something too. There isn't really any choice. Unless, like

Angela Murray, you start out with, or somehow acquire, more money, more power than almost everyone else. You don't think about how to get a better job, a better house, a better life. You try to bend everyone to your will. You have all this power, you have this position in which you dominate thousands, tens of thousands, of lives, a position in which you - at least you tell yourself - can dominate a good part of the country's, and not just the country's, but the world's economy. And you know something else: You know you're a good deal smarter than everyone you deal with. That is the great revelation that comes when you reach a position like hers - how utterly commonplace, how average, are the other people who hold positions like yours. And then, when you start meeting governors and senators - even presidents," he added, laughter in his eyes, "then you know that the world is full of fools. She wants her way in everything, and anyone who gets in her way is, by definition, expendable.

"She was second in command at that company of hers when her predecessor, who had started it twenty years before, suddenly took his own life. There was a rumor that she had something on him, that she threatened to expose him, and that he killed himself to avoid the scandal. It wouldn't have had to have been anything he had actually done. She's perfectly capable of inventing something, doing it in a way that everyone would believe it was true. She is as lethal as anyone I've ever met. She's everything I could have hoped for."

"Everything you could have...?"

"Part of the fiction we call life," replied Julian, scratching his smooth shaven chin. "A perfect villain - well, almost perfect - someone easy to blame, someone no one would want to win. 'Lucky in the friends you have.' That may be true; but in this business it is your enemies you want to be lucky with. But she won't do it - what you told Wilson to ask. She'll never say she's changed her mind, that she now supports what I am trying to do. She would rather be dead than do that. They'll stop the organized campaign, stop the television. No one will notice. She won't have anything to explain. She knows I won't do anything, beyond what, thanks to you, we have done already. Don't underestimate her. For all that flashing arrogance of hers, she's a fairly shrewd judge of other people. She may not even know she knows it - everything with her works on instinct - but she understands that we're not going to go public with what they were caught saying. She thinks I'm above that sort of thing. It's one of the reasons she hates me as much as she does."

"I told Wilson that they had until the end of the day tomorrow."

"She'll tell him they agree. That gives her more time."

"More time?"

"More time to figure out what she wants to do next - whether she wants to go forward, whether she wants to draw back, wait to see what happens, decide later if she can afford to take the chance, arrange for my assassination." Julian shrugged off Ismael's worried glance. "It wouldn't be difficult. It isn't like she would be doing it herself. She wouldn't even have to ask - just tell someone - her head of security - someone who doesn't have to have everything spelled out, that she has a problem with the president, and the problem has to get resolved. When you get right down to it, it's a wonder it hasn't happened more often. It can happen…to anyone,… at any time. Now, let's talk about something more important. The invitations to the university presidents….?"

"They went out this morning, before I left. A week from Saturday. 'Dinner with the president,' that's all they were told."

"Congress - next Monday. Remind the Speaker what we discussed. It's an open forum. The Speaker presides: he calls on those who have a question they want to ask. Members of both the House and Senate sit wherever they like, the same way they do at a state of the union address. Remind him its his job to keep order, and remind him that I don't want any planted questions. They can ask whatever they want. Tell him that I insist he call on at least as many of those, of whichever party, who are most opposed to passage of our legislation! Tell him," he added with a chuckle, "that he should announce that one of the rules is that anyone who wants to heckle can do so - if they have the wit to get away with it. This will be on live television, so I doubt anyone will stay away. It is to our advantage to have a packed house. Things are livelier that way, and, more importantly, it is easier to be serious, to say serious things in a serious way, where there is standing room only. You better call him. When I spoke to him yesterday, he didn't seem to think I meant it, that I was coming to answer questions, that I wasn't coming to make a speech."

Ismael took a deep breath, and held it for a moment. He did not doubt the Speaker had been incredulous. Herbert Douglas lived for the House every bit as much as Louis Matson lived for the Senate. He knew every arcane rule backwards and forwards and could trace a procedural precedent with all the interest and care of a biblical scholar tracing the lineage of an Old Testament prophet. A Question period might be well and good for the British and their backward ways, but the American House of Representatives had its own, better, way of doing things. He was wise enough to know that he could not refuse a presidential request; that did not mean that he had to like it. Ismael winced at the prospect of the conversation he knew he had to have.

"It won't be that bad. I told him that I knew I was breaking new ground, but that despite his best efforts, efforts which I admired, I thought I should give him all the help I could to get this legislation passed. I told him that we probably had only this one chance to do something for which, he more than anyone else, would be given credit in the history books. And I told him, finally, that we both owed it to Louis Matson to do what we both knew Louis wanted to cap his long career. Douglas is a rigid disciplinarian, but he has a sentimental streak. He would never admit it, but he loves Louis like a brother."

CHAPTER TWENTY-THREE

No one quite believed Julian Drake was going to do what he said he would. It was nothing short of madness to allow any senator or congressman to ask any question they felt like; madness to let others dictate the issues the president would discuss. From a place high above in the gallery, Rachel Good thought the madness all on the other side. Had not everyone seen for themselves what Julian Drake could do with an audience? Had they not watched any of the press conferences in which the more hostile the question the better he performed? All the eager chatter, all the noise, suddenly stopped and the silence made a sound of its own as Julian entered from the side and, instead of the podium below where the Speaker presided, took a wooden chair in the well. He had nothing with him - not a notebook, not so much as a scrap of paper - nothing but his own mind and memory to remind him what he might want to say. Speaker Douglas reminded everyone why they were there.

"Are there any questions for the president?" His voice bore a strange resemblance to a rusty, slow closing gate, a voice that made speech itself seem an imposition, something he would just as soon avoid. He glanced around the crowded chamber. "Does anyone have a question?" he repeated, glaring at the failure to get on with the task at hand.

Suddenly half the audience was on their feet, clamoring for the chance to be first to speak. There were at least a dozen senators begging to be recognized. A thin smile slipped unnoticed across the jagged contour of the Speaker's lower lip. He called on the senior congressman from Ohio.

James Michael Marshall was a no-nonsense conservative, fervent in his support of military spending and fanatical in his opposition to taxation.

"Two questions, Mr. President," he asked from the center of the sixth row from the front. "How do you plan to pay for this enormous expansion of the military? And how do you expect the military to retain anything like the efficiency it needs if it has to train, every year, millions more recruits than it has before - millions more, if I may so, than it is ever going to need?"

Julian, on his feet, waited for the congressman to finish.

"How are we going to pay for it? The same way we did in the Second World War when virtually every able-bodied young man was brought into the military: by adjusting the tax rates to meet the need."

There was an audible groan from part, a sizable part, of the audience. Julian held up his hand.

"To meet the need. The phrase was deliberate. When your house is on fire, you do what you have to do to put it out; you don't fix a price beyond which you are not willing to pay."

"Unless the house can't be saved!" shouted another member of Congress from somewhere in the back. "After that, anything you spend only adds to the loss!"

"I take it, then, you don't think the country worth saving?" Julian shot back. "You think - you believe - it better to save your money, spend it on - what, really? - than spend what is needed to make this country what we want it to be? To meet the need. Let us suppose that each year we have three or four million young men and women who want to join - three or four million willing to give four years to the service of their country. You want to know what it will cost? - Less than what it costs if that same number are unemployed, if that same number never gets a proper education, if that same number, or anything like that same number end up using drugs and committing crimes and we have to pay the cost of keeping them in prison."

"Is it not true, Mr. President," asked a congressman from Florida, "that you recently said at a dinner here in Washington that you believe in redistribution? Isn't this project of yours simply another way to justify the kind of tax increases on the rich that - I have to tell you - many of us believe will destroy the American economy?"

"You understand me well," he replied with a bright smile. "It does provide a justification, though I don't believe that either increasing the revenue needed to do important public works, or opening up military service to any citizen who wants to join, needs any justification. I have spoken about the proposal for four years service; I don't think I need to go over the same ground again. The reduction of the disparity between rich and poor in this country is of paramount importance. We cannot go on like this, two nations instead of one. The case against redistribution is worse than false, it is fraudulent. Every tax, every dollar government takes in, is the subject of redistribution: from the individual who paid it to whatever we then spend it on. What do you think happens when we buy a new plane, or a new ship, or a new tank? The only question is where we get the money, who can best afford to pay, the money that we then distribute among whatever things the country has to have."

This was so far beyond what anyone who considered himself a conservative expected to hear that they just sat there, too confused to think what they might ask next. Julian asked for them.

"But isn't this asking, in effect, for a standing army? Isn't that something we, as a country, have always opposed? A standing army is made up of professional soldiers who know no other life. Other countries with democratically elected governments require their citizens to undergo military training. In Israel, and in many countries in Europe, everyone has an obligation to serve. We do not go that far: no one will be forced to join."

"Of course they will!" a liberal congressman from Colorado shouted. "These won't be the sons or daughters of the rich; they'll go off to their private Ivy League schools and never serve a day! What you're proposing isn't fair - it puts the burden entirely on the poor!"

Unbuttoning his suit coat, Julian placed his left hand on his hip. He looked across several rows to the congressman, nodding twice to acknowledge the serious issue that had been raised.

"You're right: it is unfair that some start life with more advantages than others, that some never have to worry about anything and others have to worry if they'll have enough to eat. The question isn't whether life is unfair; the question is what we can do about it. How many of us grew up dreaming of great adventures, of doing something heroic, something we thought worthy the respect of others? That will give everyone the chance to take part in something important, to serve their country, and then, having learned what has meaning and what does not, spend four years learning something more."

"But after four years, when they all go to college," asked Lenore Fitzsimmons, who represented a district that included Ann Arbor, "won't that change the college experience? I mean, all these older students...."

Julian rubbed the back of his neck, and for a moment stared down at the floor. Raising his eyes just high enough to look at the congresswoman, he tried to suppress a grin.

"Good God, I hope so," he said, bursting into such good-natured laughter that everyone was smiling before they knew why.

"You hope...?" she said, caught completely off guard.

"It might make college more serious than it has been; it might mean that the library would become as important as the football stadium; it might mean that students would stay up studying, instead of drinking, until midnight. It might mean - though this is probably too much to hope for - that the universities would start to take themselves seriously again, remember that they were created to teach people what a civilized man or woman needed to learn to become an independent, cultured, human being. They might start to worry more about empty heads instead of empty stadiums."

He started to wait for the Speaker to recognize someone else, but looked again at the congresswoman and added, "That is another reason why you should support this: It will force the universities to start thinking of their students as adults who are there for something serious, not children who need to be entertained. After the Second World War, and the passage of the G.I.Bill, millions of returning servicemen were suddenly back in school. After what they had been through, they had perhaps a better sense than most others how important it is not to waste the little time we have. Does that answer your question?"

The Speaker was not paying much attention to the questions or the answers. He was preoccupied with a game of his own: which member of Congress to call on next, who among the four hundred thirty-five he either owed a favor or wanted in his debt. That was one game; there was another: how many congressmen could he call on before he called on a senator? It was not very often that he had a chance to show the members of the Senate what he thought of them and all their preening arrogance.

"Congressman Jenkins," he announced, looking past the half dozen or so senators who were waving their arms in a futile attempt to attract his attention. "Do you have-?"

"I think it's time we gave someone from the Senate - outnumbered as they are - a chance," interjected Julian in a calm, civil voice. "I see the majority leader is on his feet."

The artful use of makeup, a little black dye in his ragged hair, and a long afternoon nap, concealed, at least from a distance, all the signs of illness. Louis Matson could barely stand, but his voice was still strong and commanding. He spoke in a sharp cadence, breaking off the words in a precise staccato.

"Mr. President, a number of stories have recently been published that you intend a complete withdrawal from the Middle East. These same stories suggest that the United States will no longer involve itself in the affairs of that region. This would constitute a major, some would say a revolutionary, change in what has been our policy for the last half century. Are these reports true, and, if they are, why do you think what is tantamount to disengagement would be in our best interest?"

Julian buttoned his jacket. For a brief moment, he kept his eyes on Matson, acknowledging with a look of unmistakeable gratitude, more than the importance of the question, the bond between them. A broad, sweeping glance gave notice that what he was about to say would mark a turning point, a new departure from how things had been handled in the past.

"The question we have to ask is why we were in the Middle East in the first place. The British and the French had strategic interests there in the 19th and the beginning of the 20th centuries. The British wanted to protect their route through the Suez to India and other places. The French had established colonies in Syria and North Africa. Our interest in the region began in the 1920s when British and American companies began to develop the petroleum that had suddenly become a vital necessity for industry and the automobiles that began to dominate, and make possible, our new way of life. We needed the oil and we became dependent on it. Without it, as we discovered when OPEC imposed an embargo in the 1970s, the American economy would be in danger of collapse. Twenty years later, when Iraq invaded Kuwait, we went to war, according to the Bush administration, because this threatened our access to the oil we needed. Everything we did in the Middle East, all the investment, all the military assistance to regimes which, to put it as diplomatically as I can, did not share our interest in a democratic way of life, was because of oil. They had it and we needed it. We do not need it anymore. We now produce more than we need; instead of buying from other countries, other countries now buy from us.

"Oil is why we went; it is not why we stayed. We stayed because after 911, after we were attacked we wanted to retaliate for what had been done to us. We were attacked by a group based in Afghanistan; we invaded Iraq instead." Julian shook his head at the colossal stupidity, the mindless ignorance behind this misjudgment. "We were told we had no choice: Sadam Hussein had 'weapons of mass destruction.'"

Julian paused to let everyone remember how that phrase had been used, how it had been repeated over and over again like the war chant of a blood-crazed tribe; how it had been repeated, later, by every critic eager to remind the country that no such weapons existed.

"No one seems to have considered that if Sadam Hussein had really had weapons of mass destruction, the one thing that would have guaranteed their use was the very invasion which we supposedly had no choice but to make. Who in their right mind would have sent the Army, the Marines, the Navy and the Air Force into harm's way if they really believed that someone not only had 'weapons of mass destruction,' but was trying to obtain - and might have already obtained - nuclear weapons; someone who, pushed to the wall, faced with an invasion he could not otherwise defeat, would be perfectly willing to use them? 'Weapons of mass destruction,'" he repeated with derision. "That was never the reason; that was an excuse. What was the real reason we invaded a country that had nothing to do with what happened in New York? - Because we believed it was our place to give direction to the world. We believed that we were the first nation in the history of the world that could become an empire and make the world better by our domination. We invaded Iraq because we thought we could turn Iraq into a new America, a model of democracy and progress that would, by its example, bring the Middle East into the modern world. We disbanded their army, disbanded their government, and tried to build something for which they had no experience and no tradition. We took down a tyrant and left in his place organized incompetence and utter chaos. With nothing to control them, the two sides of Islam started civil war. Terrorism, first directed at themselves, became a way to organize their hatred against the outsider, the invader. Terrorism became a way to fight against those who, in their minds, threatened what they prize more than anything in life: their religion - Islam, as they understand it. We can stay there for a thousand years, and the fight will never end. We will always be seen as the infidel, the crusader, the enemies of God. The Middle East has to determine its own fate. Democracy cannot be imposed with the barrel of a gun. Only the people of a country can decide what they want.

"We do not need their oil, and we cannot solve their problems. What we can do is remove, so far as is in our power, the source of the grievances they have against us, the reason why instead of a country they look up to, we have become a country they hate: our presence, the military force by which have tried too often to make them into an image of ourselves.

"But, you ask, how control terrorism, how prevent another 911, how stop those who will, despite a withdrawal, still seek to kill our people? By redefining the enemy. By insisting that every country is responsible for any attack launched against us from anyone trained in their territory; by declaring that any country who fails to do this is in a state of war, that we will retaliate not just against those who attack us, but the country they came from."

There were shouts of protest from every corner of the room; dozens leaped to their feet, demanding to be heard.

"If we withdraw, if we don't have forces on the ground, the terrorists will have a free hand!"

"You wish to prevent terrorism? - Our presence encourages it," replied

Julian, and immediately turned to someone else.

"We'll be abandoning those who stood with us; we'll be abandoning everyone who wanted democracy!"

"Democracy - freedom - has to come from within. And democracy, free elections, need I remind you, has often meant the victory of those who hate us most. No, all we do by remaining there is give support to those who argue there has to be a Holy War, a fight to the death between Islam and the West."

"But you would have us withdraw from the world, give up our leadership, let the Russians, or the Chinese, take our place!"

Julian smiled in a way that told them that there was something he had not told them. He stood there, his eyes eager, alive, full of confidence, and, what seemed inexplicable, full of daring.

"'Withdraw from the world'? Yes, exactly; that is precisely what I propose we do. It is the way in this still new century of ours to lead the world to places it has never been, lead by our example, lead by our achievement. Let others waste their time in petty quarrels, fighting over who is the best defender of whatever they claim to believe; let other nations argue over a few square miles of disputed territory; let other people look for other reasons to kill each other - America has other things to do. America will explore the stars; America will lead the world in the serious exploration of space. I am tonight asking Congress to embark on the greatest adventure in human history; I am asking everyone in this country - I am asking us - to give up our lives of private pleasure and devote ourselves to something that will change the world, something that will lift our eyes, lift our minds, lift our hearts to what is above us. I am asking for a space program that will dwarf anything ever thought of before."

"You want us to go to Mars, you want -?" a black congresswoman from Los Angeles started to ask. "You want -?"

"Mars is just the beginning," replied Julian, with complete self-assurance. "We're going to go everywhere."

"We still have to live here, Mr. President," she insisted, her thin face rigid with emotion. "And a lot of my people are suffering. They don't have jobs. Some of them, if they make it out of high school, can't afford to go to college. We're in trouble, Mr. President, and I don't see how this new space program is going to help."

"I said this was going to be the greatest adventure in the history of the world; it is also going to be the largest public works program in history. Hundreds of thousands, millions, of people are going to be employed. This is not something we are going to hand out to bid; we're not going to privatize space. Everyone who wants a college education, everyone who cannot afford it - those kids in your district - everyone willing to give four years to the service of their country - they won't be unemployed; they will have more than enough to do. Everyone who wants to work, everyone who has - or who wants to learn - a skill, will have a place in this, the greatest enterprise on which we, or anyone else, has ever embarked." He glanced around, his gaze stern, determined, and hopeful beyond measure. "This is who we are, this is what we do, this is what America is all about - We build, we explore, we create, and we do it in a way that makes every generation proud of the one that came before. We dare things no one else would dare at all. We do not ask how we can get something done. We ask only how soon we can start!"

There was a roar of approval, bedlam everywhere, everyone suddenly on their feet, shouting, clapping, pounding one another on the back, slapping each other on the shoulders, mad with enthusiasm, certain, somehow, that what none of them had given a moment's thought to before they heard Julian Drake speak the words, had been what they had wanted, what they had been waiting for, all their lives.

"I'm afraid I've used up the hour you were kind enough to give me," said Julian, when the cheering finally stopped. "If you want me back - next week, next month - I'll be glad to try again to answer any questions you might have."

Julian never stayed to shake hands with well-wishers or engage in idle small talk with those who wanted to be seen with him. He was almost to the door when he noticed Rachel Good among the reporters who rushed forward, shouting questions. Suddenly, he stopped moving, but just long enough to invited her to ride with him back to the White House. As soon as the car door shut behind them, he started to explain why he had done what he did.

"What do we look up to? The question should be what we are still capable of looking up to? Nothing, except the stars themselves. Space - exploration -

the great project, one that requires sacrifice, discipline, the willingness to take the long view."

Rachel was sitting opposite him in the long limousine, trying to catch up to what he was saying as she fumbled for her notebook and pen. The president was looking out the window, watching the lights of the city slide by, seeing, as it seemed to her, something else altogether: a vision of what he hoped to bring about.

"A long view," he continued, "what none of us may live to see, and what, for that very reason, is worth all the sacrifices that have to be made." Suddenly, turning back from the window, he looked at her as if he knew she understood how important it all was. "It took a hundred forty years for the French to build Chartres, almost that long to build Notre Dame and St. Michel, a tribute to God - and a tribute to themselves, to show what they could achieve. What are we to be known for, how will we be remembered down through the ages? What can we imagine, what can we take strength from, what will give us that feeling of immortality that Christians once found in the promise of eternal life, what give meaning to our existence? - The private houses of the useless rich, golf courses and athletic stadiums? Or that this was the generation that turned its attention to the greatest exploration in the history of the world?"

They reached the White House, but Julian was not finished. With Rachel trailing behind him, he kept talking as he moved at a quick, steady pace inside to the Oval Office. Leaning back on one of the sofas, he folded his arms and crossed his ankles. It was not clear to Rachel, who sat in the middle of the sofa opposite, that he even knew she was there. His eyes, burning with an intensity all their own, seemed to move in every direction at once, a movement that had the odd effect of making him seem almost immobile, his mind somehow detached from his senses which were left to do their own, separate, work.

"Something to look up to," he said repeating the phrase which seemed so central to his thought. "We started out a republic, grateful for, and dependent on, our separation from all the evils, the political ambitions, of the old world, of Europe. We were that City on a Hill Reagan liked to talk about, a beacon of hope to the rest of the world. But even then it was nothing more than a hope of our own, a dream, a myth of our own devising. We were never content to live with what we had: there was a whole continent to conquer. We thought ourselves a republic and, like ancient Athens, wanted an empire. We wanted he continent - all of it, including Canada, which we tried to take in the War of 1812, Mexico in 1848, and then, at the end of the first century of our existence as a nation, Cuba, the Philippines, everything we could get our hands on in the Pacific. And then, with the wars of the twentieth century, we became, along with the Soviet Union, the dominant power in the world; and now, today, responsible in our own minds for everything that happens. It is the nature of things, part of what we are, this need we have to expand our power, expand our reach, nothing ever enough, always this need for more. It is the way that we - most of us - forget our own mortality; the way we ignore the requirement, the specific excellence, of our own nature. It is too late; we can't go back. Science, modern science, which we thought would make us free has forced us to live with its requirements, the need to keep finding something new. The only chance we have is to use it for something that will make us interested in something more serious, more lasting, than the comfort of our own self-indulgence. The reaction tonight…."

His eyes stopped their endless movement. For the first time, he looked across to where Rachel sat, pen in hand.

"You saw it, you heard it. I may be wrong, but it seemed to me this was, quite without knowing it, what they, and the country, have been waiting for. Now," he said, as he got to his feet, "tell me what you know about our good friend, Louis. I know he's dying. Is there anything you think I can do?"

CHAPTER TWENTY-FOUR

"I know this is ludicrous, a complete waste of time," explained Julian, as he finished pulling up his tie. "But, you have to admit, it is really quite irresistible: talking to people who because of their positions think themselves every bit as intelligent as what those positions once used to mean."

Ismael rattled the ice in his glass and sank lower in the green overstuffed chair. The president's bedroom, everything clean, neat, and orderly, was so well-insulated that the bare whisper of a voice could be heard wherever in it you happened to be.

"Did you read it - what I wrote?"

"What you wrote that night, a week ago, when you stayed up all night? Yes, of course I read it."

"And…?"

Ismael shrugged his shoulders and took a long, slow drink. He put it down on the lamp table next to him, pursed his lips and for a moment did not say anything. It was not that he was reluctant to tell Julian the truth; it was not that he had found anything to criticize or that he thought needed correction.

"Have you thought that it might be better if instead of English you spoke in Greek?" he asked with a droll expression.

Lifting his eyebrows, Julian acknowledged the wisdom of the suggestion. "My Greek isn't that good."

"Who would know?" replied Ismael, with a dry, searching glance, a reminder, as if one were needed, that what Julian had written, the speech he was going to give that evening, was as far from the interest, or the capacity, of his audience as it was possible to go.

"Which would be a good reason to do it - to teach them their ignorance."

"Which, I take it, is the reason…?"

But the mention of Greek reminded Julian of something he thought he could use.

"Years ago - remember 'Love Story,' the movie about a college girl and college boy who fall in love. The boy is from a wealthy, established family; the girl from a working class home. His family opposes the marriage; the girl dies of cancer at the end. The people who were making the movie decided that it would be better if they first had a best-selling book. Someone knew someone who taught at Yale. What does this have to do with anything?" he said, laughing at the look of helpless wonder on Ismael's face. "Its what the author, Eric Segal, who taught classics once said, a remark no one would have noticed if he had not been thought to have created a story that had nothing whatever to do with the classes he taught. I think I'll use it tonight."

Two dozen university presidents, with their wives and husbands, along with another two dozen assorted university provosts and deans - the American academic establishment - were seated together for a White House dinner at which, they had been told, the president would make a few remarks about the state of higher education. What they got instead was a lecture that invited them to forget everything they thought they knew. Julian began with an observation that put them at their ease, but should have put them on their guard.

"I am reminded for some reason of a dinner held here at the White House more than half a century ago for all the then living American recipients of the Nobel Prize. President Kennedy - and he wrote this in his own hand on the margin of his prepared remarks - said that 'there hasn't been this much intelligence gathered together at a dinner in the White House since Thomas Jefferson dined here alone.'"

There were bright smiles and cheerful laughter everywhere. Comparing their presence with a dinner for Nobel Prize winners guaranteed their confident strict attention.

"I used to believe, when I first read what President Kennedy had said, that with his usual charm and grace he was putting things in perspective, reminding an audience knowns for its intelligence that there had been men in public life who had some considerable intelligence of their own. He had in fact something deeper, a more profound lesson, in mind for those with wit enough to understand it: Instead of the progress we all believe has marked our history, there has instead been a significant decline. There were more than two dozen Nobel Prize recipients at that dinner, but for Kennedy, Jefferson was as good - no, better - than all of them combined. Kennedy knew more about Thomas Jefferson than we know about Kennedy: He knew what Jefferson had read; we have forgotten - if we ever knew - that among the dozen or so of Kennedy's favorite books were the seven volumes of Gibbon's Decline and Fall of the Roman Empire. Kennedy knew something else as well, that when Jefferson read all the works of Plato and Aristotle, the histories of Herodotus and Thucydides, all the most important works of ancient Greece, he read them, not in some translation, but in the original Greek.

"We don't read what Jefferson read, even in translation, and as for anyone reading Greek - recall what someone who once taught classics at Yale - but became famous for other reasons - once said about a Harvard - and not just a Harvard education: that it used to be necessary to know both Greek and Latin to be admitted, and now you did not need to know either one to graduate. We call this progress, this getting rid of dead languages, this escape from everything old and ancient, this ardent, single-minded devotion to every form of innovation. Which raises a question, a question we all should ask: Does history have any use?"

Dressed in a dark suit and solid color tie, an easy, gentle smile on his face, Julian studied his audience of distinguished academics with a look that challenged them to show they deserved to be taken as seriously as they thought they should. It was not a look they were used to, a look most of them had not seen since they were children in school: the look of someone who could tell you why everything you ever thought you knew was wrong.

"The question is what does the past have to teach us, we moderns who think we stand at the end of history; we moderns," he added, with quick, flashing eyes, "who have inherited all that science can teach. Why should we bother, why waste our time, learning what others, burdened with ancient prejudice, thought about the world? Is it not better to concentrate on the future, better to consider how we can use the technology that has made us able to conquer time and space, better to conquer, and therewith change, nature, better to improve the conditions under which we live? Better, in other words, to continue the way we have been going, better not to think too much about how we have gotten to where we are, better not to wonder what it was like when the human race was still young and, instead of through aging, half-blind, eyes, saw everything with clear and unobstructed vision?"

Pausing long enough to let them wonder where he might be going, what it was he was trying to tell them, he looked one way, then the other, with a determined gaze.

"We think ourselves newer than the past, as if an old man were newer than a child. We are the latecomers, clinging to existence, the only dream left the empty dream of a long life and comfort. Old and infirm, we are too weak in spirit to dream of anything that might risk everything. The memory of the time when the human race was young, that time when everything was questionable and we still knew how to ask questions, that time when we relied on our own intelligence instead of assumptions given to us by other, earlier generations, has vanished in the fading memory of our own senility. The present is older, much older, than the past. We are older, much older, than the Greeks. We, who like to call ourselves modern, are the ancient ones."

Sitting at a table near the back, Ismael watched the reaction of an audience mesmerized by what they heard. Some of them sat with their mouths half open, astonished by the way that in two short paragraphs the president, of all people, had somehow managed to turn everything upside down. Ismael had read what Julian had written, but the words sounded different in Julian's different voice. What had seemed on paper too arcane, too removed from what was most on the minds of this, or any other contemporary audience, suddenly seemed the only thing you wanted to hear about. The voice, Julian's voice, had a quality no one else could rival, a voice that made you stop whatever you were doing and listen.

"But the present, some of you may object, is the product of the past. History is nothing if not the record of the progress that has been made. Whatever the Greeks, or the Romans, whatever any nation or civilization, may have accomplished is next to nothing in comparison with what we have been able to do. Everything that ever happened was building to what we have now. Everything. All the wars and revolutions, all the slaughter, the blood and hatred, all the selfish short-sighted ambitions of vain politicians and greedy men of business: what were they but the means by which to move history forward to its appointed goal? - a goal described in different ways by Hegel and Marx, but first discovered - or invented - by Rousseau: the perfection of the human race, the natural right of everyone to live as he thinks best, the proud achievement of the 20th century, the century of the common man, the century of unsurpassed, of unprecedented, scientific progress, the century of mass murder and genocide, the century that was built on the history, and the idea of history, of the 19th century, the century," Julian went on, speaking faster with every word, "the century of the 'overproud Europeans,' who were, in the judgement of the most insightful mind of that century, 'stark raving mad!'

"There were those," said Julian, his voice become once again conversational, "a few who saw it coming; a few who with their knowledge of the past - the ancient past - understood what was about to happen, how the world, or more precisely, the West, had lost its reason. In 1825, Goethe not only foretold the coming barbarism, but insisted 'we are already in the midst of it.' Writing to Karl Freidrich Zelter, he remarked, 'Nobody knows himself anymore, nobody comprehends the element in which he resides and operates, nobody comprehends the material with which he works…Wealth and alacrity are what the world admires and what everyone strives for. Railroads, express mail services, steam ships, and every possible way of facilitating communications are what the educated world wants in order to overeducate itself, though as a result it persists in mediocrity. Of course it is also the result of universality that an average culture becomes base.'

"Goethe closed by observing that the 19th century would be characterized by 'quick-witted people who, equipped with a certain adroitness, feel their superiority over the masses even if they themselves are not capable of what is highest....We will, together with perhaps just a few, be the last of an epoch which will not return very soon.'"

Julian was speaking without a note. The only copy of the speech as he had written it out was in Ismael's inside jacket pocket. That, it seemed to Ismael as he sat watching, was what struck everyone so forcibly: that the president could speak with this kind of eloquence and quote from memory long passages from a letter Goethe had written almost two hundred years ago . Had they been less impressed with the manner, they might have wondered whether Goethe's prediction of what would constitute success in the future applied to them.

"And they did not return, those few, the last of an epoch; they are not even remembered, footnotes in the unread books of writers who view the past from the perspective, the all-too narrow perspective, of the present, recording, if they mention at all, the warnings and the misgivings about what had happened as the distorted imaginings of men who failed to grasp the great lessons of the French Revolution: that there are no essential differences, no important distinctions, between one man and another, that everyone has a right, a natural right, to freedom and equality. Instead of a difference in what men aspire to, a difference between what was noble and what was base, everyone was now seen to be driven by the same desire for self-preservation and the kind of comfortable existence produced by an 'invisible hand' that, through the wonders of the new science and an instinct for acquisition that was no longer regarded as a sin, could provide material abundance for everyone. Rousseau, though he more than anyone helped bring about the French Revolution, understood that this meant the loss of what was most important in the interest of what was easiest to obtain: 'Ancient politicians invariably talked about morals and virtue, those of our time talk only of business and money.'

"And now? What do we think of the contrast between what the ancients talked about and what today dominates the discussion? We know nothing about it. We take for granted that money and business are the only things that count and refuse to believe that this could ever seriously be questioned. The only history taught in our universities is the history of humanity, a history that is for all intents and purposes, to quote Goethe again, 'merely the continuation of the history of animals and plants.' It is the history of evolution, of modern science altogether: the attempt to find the end of things in the origin of things, the attempt to find the meaning of things in the meaningless motion of matter, the principle of the pre-Socratics, the Atomists like Democritus, the history of random chance that somehow leads to a grand design, an infinity of minuscule parts forming and reforming themselves into an intelligible whole, guided by something unknown: the many gods of Hesiod and Homer, or the one god of Christianity. It is the history of the higher mathematics, the world converted into the handmade work of numbers, numbers by which nature is not so much discovered as forced into the useful, and usable, pattern of human design. Nothing has a nature; there are no unchanging and unchangeable beings. There is no human nature, only a drive to become different than we are, with the result that the nature of the human being has become endlessly perfectible. History has a meaning after all."

There was a dead silence in the room, the only thought anyone had what Julian might say next.

"We know nothing of this: it happened before our time. It happened in the past, four hundred years ago, in the 17th century, when the belief in an ordered universe was replaced by the new science, the belief that what was rational, the world as we know it, is the result of forces that are themselves not rational at all. The principles of the new physics became the principles of the new politics. The discovery of the best regime - those 'superb palaces built on mud and sand,' as Descartes described it - on which the ancients expended so much useless genius, was abandoned in favor of the search for a reliable political order, one built on the secure foundation of the irrational, i.e. the passions, and specifically the desire for self-preservation. The aim was no longer human excellence but a tolerably decent regime of satisfied wants and limited ambitions. Building on the same principle - the desire for self-preservation - Hobbes taught the necessity of the Leviathan, the single ruler who, being of one mind, would eliminate the chance of civil war, while Locke taught the necessity of republican government in which everyone had an equal voice in how best to preserve their lives, their liberty, and their property. Both involved a lowering of the horizon, what it means to be a human being, the only thing important now life itself. It produced, in the words of Rousseau, men without morals who cared only about money. It produced, in other words - us!

"This is the origin of the world in which we live, an origin that was new precisely because it was a conscious break with the past. We cannot know our own beginnings unless we know that as well; we cannot understand modernity, the world as it is now, unless we understand antiquity. We cannot understand Europe and the West, we cannot understand America, unless we understand what Athens was, unless we understand what Athens meant. At the end of the 19th century, Nietzsche, according to one of his most profound students, 'sought, by a new beginning, to retrieve antiquity from the emptiness of modernity and, with this experiment, vanished in the darkness of insanity.' But if it is impossible fully to recapture, impossible to return to what once has been, it is still possible to read ancient authors and try to understand them, not as we understand ourselves today, but as they understood themselves.

"The place to start is with language itself, the way in which ancient words have become burdened with modern meanings. The Greek word 'arete' translated as 'virtue' does not mean what we mean by virtue: a woman's virginity or the love, hope, and charity of the Christian gospels, but something that implies a different sense of man's place in the world, man's place in the natural order. Arete, or virtue, means the specific excellence of a thing. It means that everything, including especially the human being, has something toward which it is inclined by nature. It raises the question: what is the specific excellence of human beings; it raises the question whether there is a specific excellence of human beings. It remains for us to discover what it is. Thomas Jefferson understood that, but then Thomas Jefferson read Greek, even when, or perhaps especially when, he dined here alone."

And then, without another word, without waiting for applause or any other sign of approval, Julian nodded twice for emphasis, flashed a modest smile, and left. There were other things he had to do.

"Do you think I went too far?" asked Julian, his eyes shining with the knowledge of what, as he well understood, no one else would consider a triumph. "I should have gone farther still, spent an hour and a half - I once heard Marcel DuBose lecture that long on the first words of Plato's Republic: 'I went down.' They did not know what to make of it, did they?" He cast a sideways glance at Ismael who was trying to keep up as Julian bounded up the stairs to the residence. "That should teach them that they don't know everything, teach them something of their own abysmal ignorance." He stopped at the top of the stairs, and with a rueful look, shook his head and dismissed the possibility. "They'll tell each other that it was 'interesting,' and that will be the end of all discussion. They're always talking - God, how I hate the phrase - about the need to 'think outside the box.' They don't know what the box is; they don't know what thinking means."

"Then why did you bother? What was the point, unless it was to convince them what most of them already suspect: that you're the enemy of everything they believe?" asked Ismael, genuinely curious.

"Precisely! That's exactly what I want. Because then, whether they are even aware of it, they'll start moving toward me."

"I'm afraid I don't…."

"They'll make what they think are small concessions. What will they take away from tonight, what will they remember? - that a case can be made for learning Greek. They won't remember anything else. They'll remember what I said about JFK and what he said about Thomas Jefferson. They will decide, because it will now seem like the only intelligent thing to do, that they should at least consider bringing back Greek and Latin - not as a requirement, but as something to made available to that no doubt small number of students who might have an interest in ancient things. They won't think anything of it, and it will be the only thing they will ever do of any real importance."

Grasping the railing behind him, Julian raised his chin. His face glowed with an inner certainty that has banished all doubt. There was no past to remember or regret, no future to look forward to or fear, only the present moment, a moment in which time did not exist.

"I did it - traced the movement of the thought that first defined, and then changed, what we are - because I could. It doesn't matter whether anyone agrees. If I don't say what I know to be important, if I don't do what I can to tell the truth of things, to find the light, we will never leave the darkness that most of us do not even know we're in. I know what will happen. We are not going to turn back and become that city on a hill; we're not going to become again a small republic in which everyone knows everyone else. We're too big, too dependent on the science, the technology, we invented. But we can change the way we spend our lives, give them the meaning that comes with involvement in a great project - the exploration of space, of our world, of the universe - that has the virtue of lasting as long as the human race itself. But that by itself won't keep the most important thing alive: the ability of some small number to free themselves, to think through everything with their own, unassisted reason. That is why this seemingly small thing - teaching Greek for those who want to learn - is more important than anyone might care to believe. Come with me, I'll show you something."

He led Ismael to a private room just off his bedroom. From a shelf above his desk he pulled down in quick succession three slim volumes.

"This is a line from the final chorus of Sophocles' Oedipus Rex: 'Where, where is the mortal who wins more of happiness than just the seeming, and, after the semblance, a falling away?' That is one English translation, here is another: 'man after man after man, O mortal generations, here once, almost not here, what are we, dust ghosts images a rustling of air, nothing nothing, we breathe on the abyss, we are the abyss, Our happiness no more than the traces of a dream.'

"You would be forgiven if you wondered whether these were translations of the same poem. The jacket on the second volume says that it goes 'beyond the literal meaning of the Greek to evoke the sense of poetry evident in the original.' In other words, it isn't what you would be reading if you could read the original! And what might that be? The same line was translated by Martin Heidegger, translated into German. In English it reads - This is unbelievable! - 'What man has in him controlled and ordered being-there than he requires to stand in appearance and then, having done so, to incline (namely from standing-straight-in-himself)?'

"If you assume that Heidegger had a much more profound understanding of Greek - of language altogether - than those who have attempted to translate Sophocles, or the other Greek classics, what hope do we have of recapturing what the world looked like through the eyes of those like Plato and Aristotle whose vision was not obstructed, distorted, by two thousand years of changing and therewith false interpretation and belief? If you think the translation of Sophocles, of the Greek poets, anything but a true reflection of what Sophocles, of what the poets, said, look at the various ways Plato's dialogues have been translated. Until the translation by Alan Bloom, literal, like they should all be, you are more likely to read what the translator thought Plato should have said than what Plato meant."

Julian put the three volumes back on the shelf and dropped into the chair behind the rosewood desk. There was a single window in the room, to the right of where he sat, and through it he could look out over the roof of the West Wing to the lights of the city beyond.

"Tomorrow the talk will be all about what the House and Senate are going to do this week, whether the votes will be there for what I've asked, or whether my entire presidency will come down in ruins."

Far from worried, Julian seemed almost amused. This is not to say he was not intensely interested. It was a strange dichotomy, or it would have been had Ismael not become used to the way Julian could detach himself from everything that was going on around him. It sometimes seemed as if Julian was both the central character, and the main audience, for a play, a play that was at one and the same time a tragedy and a comedy. There were dozens of congressmen, and a fair number of senators, driving themselves crazy weighing in the balance the wishes of their constituents, the various private interests and contributors on whom they relied for support, and what some of them at least thought would be best for the country. Julian thought their distress nothing short of laughable.

"What are the numbers, the latest count? - The House first."

Ismael had been on the telephone almost without interruption the last several days. He knew who was in favor and who opposed, and, more importantly at this stage, what it would take to convince those who had not made up their minds to vote with the president.

"Two hundred ten in favor; two hundred five against."

"Twenty undecided - or rather twenty who say they are. We only need eight of them. What about the Senate? I know Louis has been working. Does he have the votes we need?"

"Almost."

"How short are we?"

"Forty-six to forty-four, ten undecideds or not willing to say."

"All of them, or almost all of them, up for re-election next year. They know what will be done against them if they vote with us. They know they'll probably have a primary fight, and against someone who may have more money than they can raise. The same thing with most of those in the House."

Julian's gaze drifted toward the window and the clear night sky. He tapped his fingers on his knee, thinking what he should do next.

"There isn't a state, and only a handful of congressional districts, where there isn't a sizeable majority in favor of this. They're all afraid of the money, what could be spent against them. And we know where it comes from, don't we? We have to show them they have nothing to fear. Invite them, all of them, everyone who has not yet come out in favor of the bill, members of the House and Senate. Tell them I want to meet with them, that I want to give them a chance to ask me anything they want about the bill and what it is intended to do. And tell them that it won't be a one-sided conversation, that the leaders of the opposition, in both the House and Senate, are being invited as well. Tell them I'm looking forward to the debate."

Julian tapped his fingers the way he had before. His eyes narrowed as his concentration became more and more intense. Clenching his jaw, he pressed his lips tight together as he stared down at the floor. Then, suddenly, he raised his head and looked at Ismael as if he must know already what he was about to say.

"Invite Murray and Chambers. Tell all the others they're coming too. Tell those two what we're doing, that we are going to debate the bill in front of the undecideds, and that in the interest of a fair and open debate they are being asked to help make the case in opposition."

Ismael looked doubtful.

"After what I told Conrad Wilson to tell them -"

"They'll come. They did exactly what I said they would. They pulled everything they were running on television, but they certainly haven't changed their position. They'll come. Angela Murray will think it proves she was right, that it was all a bluff, that we don't have any evidence, and that

I'm now so desperate that I've been reduced to debating her as my last best chance to get a majority. She won't be able to stop herself. Stand on an equal footing with the president, go head to head in front of an audience made up of the very people - the senators and congressmen - she thinks she has the power to control. For someone like her, someone who thinks she is smarter than anyone else - it is irresistible!"

Ismael was even less convinced than he was before that this was a wise thing to do.

"Even if you're right, even if she thinks she can win, or even hold her own, in a debate with you, she -"

Julian held up his hand. He was already thinking ahead to what was going to happen.

"Everything she says will be accompanied by the silent threat of the money she and the others have at their disposal. You watch. She'll tie it all together. She won't just explain why she doesn't like the bill, she'll explain why they have spent millions - and will spend millions more - to make certain nothing like this ever gets passed."

"Then why give her the chance, why invite her at all?"

"Because without her opposition I might lose."

CHAPTER TWENTY-FIVE

Standing at the entrance to the East Room, Ismael greeted each arriving congressman and senator. He had become a keen observer of the idiosyncrasies - the strange manners, the sometimes peculiar speech or the off-key voice - that characterized so many members of both the House and the Senate. He took a particular interest in the small details that usually went unnoticed. There was the matter of how they dressed. Senators wore more expensive suits; congressmen almost never wore anything that had not been bought off the rack. The Senate was made up of millionaires, some of whom owned more houses than they could count; the House was full of small town lawyers and big city politicians who could barely keep up with the mortgage payments on the only house they owned. Grasping the sleeve of everyone he greeted, Ismael let the feel of the fabric tell the story.

If his sense of touch allowed him to distinguish a congressman from a senator with his eyes closed, his memory for the words and phrases with which other, earlier, observers had described their own contemporaries, gave him a vocabulary which often came unbidden to his mind. Greeting a congressman who had for thirty years always avoided doing or saying anything unpopular, he almost laughed out loud, suddenly recalling what Teddy Roosevelt had once said about the average legislator with whom he had to work - "smooth oily, plausible and tricky." Those two words - "smooth oily" - seemed to take him inside the machine, that marvelous assemblage of five hundred thirty-five interchangeable parts, in which money was energy and no one much cared for what purpose it was used, so long as the machine, the process, never stopped. The danger, as Ismael understood, was that the machine would become overloaded and come, finally, to a stop, no one any longer able to comprehend, much less solve, the problem of governing a nation of such increasingly divergent interests and such enormous size. Ismael decided he had read too much Henry Adams and, shaking hands with the last invited congressmen, touched the sleeve of his own, well-tailored, suit.

Everyone was there, everyone except Angela Murray and Rufus Chambers. Ismael wondered, not if they would come - he had caught the tone of vindication in Murray's voice on the telephone - but how late they would be. It would not be more than a minute or two, just enough to make the point that no one, not even, or, in this instance, especially a president, could set their schedule. Three minutes late, Ismael pretended not to see them as they started down the hallway. He began to close the door.

"Did you think we weren't coming?" asked Angela Murray, with a brittle smile that bragged insincerity. "Sorry we're late," she added, as she breezed past him.

Looking worried, Rufus Chambers stopped to say something, but, changing his mind, reluctantly followed her inside.

The East Room had been turned into a conference room. There were two rows of chairs on each side of a long table for the members of Congress. Four chairs stood at the far end, two of which had already been taken by the House minority leader, who was opposed to the president's proposal, and Senator Rivers of Texas, who had made it clear he would oppose anything proposed by the man who had stolen the presidency from him. When Murray and Chambers had taken the two remaining seats, Ismael nodded toward the secret service agent at the other side of the room who immediately opened the door behind him.

Julian moved quickly to the head of the table. Following behind him,

Rachel Good took a chair off to the side. As soon as he was settled in his chair, Julian cast a long measured glance down the table.

"You look concerned, Ms. Murray; even, perhaps, a little worried. Did you think this meeting was going to be strictly private, that something as serious as this would be kept from the public? After all the money you and your friends have spent on television, you surely can't object to having this discussion in public."

There was nothing in her demeanor, nothing in her reaction, to suggest that she was the least disturbed, nothing but a change in the intensity of her gaze so slight as to be imperceptible by anyone who had not himself been the unfortunate recipient of her wrath. It was deep inside her eyes, a speck of light which, like a solar flare, had to be looked for to be seen. But Julian noticed. She sat rigid and erect, leaning forward on her elbows, her chin resting on hands folded over one another, her thin, tapered fingers interlaced.

"How can I help you, Mr. President?" I know you would like me to tell everyone here that I - and everyone I represent, which includes some of the most successful business people in the country - have changed our minds, that we have seen the light, that we now understand that what you are proposing won't bankrupt the country, won't require the kind of taxation that will not just threaten, but destroy, the country!" Her head shot up, the corners of her small mouth curled down, she started to say something in anger, but caught herself in time. "No, Mr. President; if anything we oppose the bill more than we did before. The more we study it, the more we see what is involved, the more we find wrong with it."

"And the more the country learns about it, the more the country finds right with it," Julian shot back. All his attention was on her; the others were an audience.

She could feel it, she was used to it, the center of attention, the focus of the conversation. She dismissed the president's remark as simply irrelevant.

"The public thinks in generalities, in favor of anything that appeals to their imagination - the exploration of the universe, what they have seen in a movie! - in opposition to whatever might cost them jobs or money. The public -"

"The public no doubt has good instincts," interjected Rufus Chambers to her obvious displeasure. "The public no doubt wants to do the right thing. But their elected representatives, who have to decide what is best for the country - you haven't convinced them that this is the right thing to do. Isn't that the reason we're here today? Because there isn't enough support in Congress? And doesn't that suggest that the better policy would be to offer some concession, reach some kind of compromise that -"

"Compromise? Compromise on what?" demanded Murray, shaking her head.

"Compromise on the number, and the qualifications, of those who are allowed to enter the program," he replied, in a cold, emphatic voice. "It isn't a bad idea to give those who can't afford it a chance at a better opportunity. The president isn't asking that anyone be given anything for nothing; he's asking that we make some decent return for the service of our veterans."

A scornful smile slipped across her closed tight-lipped mouth. She turned back to Julian.

"Is that all you're asking - a 'decent return'?"

Ignoring her, Julian responded to Chambers instead.

"On a great many things, I would agree with what you just said. Without compromise we couldn't exist as a free people." He pulled his head sharply to the side, the way he often did when something suddenly entered his mind. "Someone told me, when I was in my first term in the House, that it is always a mistake to think something is a question of principle, because, he explained, there are always two principles involved - 'yours and the other fellow's', was how he put it. I accept that. It is necessary to compromise, to take account of the legitimate concerns of those with whom you have differences. But there are times when it is necessary to do something of such importance to the country that it simply cannot be subject to compromise. This isn't a question of how large our military establishment should be. If it were, it wouldn't matter if you wanted a higher or a lower number, we could reach an agreement somewhere between what each of us had initially proposed. The question we now have to ask, isn't how big or small we want the military to be, but what should be the nature of citizenship in the greatest democracy the world has known. Should it be the freedom - some would say the license - to do whatever anyone likes, except the right to serve their country? It is the question whether everyone, or only those who can afford it, has the right to the education they need and of which they are fully capable."

"A 'decent return!'" muttered Angela Murray, angrily. "Everyone can join the armed forces, everyone can have four years of college paid for by the government! And you don't think this will …! We've been summoned here because you think you can win a debate, show everyone you're quicker on your feet. It's the only hope you have left. But you will never get the votes you need," she insisted, speaking slower and more emphatically with every word. "You'll never get them because everyone here knows the price they'll pay in the next election if they let themselves be tricked - seduced - into something that will bankrupt the country!"

Julian looked at her as if to make certain she was really serious, shook his head, incredulous at what he had heard, and then shook his head again.

"Bankrupt the country! That's what you keep saying. All those mindless commercials of yours: families worried how they're going to pay their bills, worried that - how did those paid for actors put it? - 'bankrupt our children's future with his…' That's me, of course - 'crazy schemes.' Bankruptcy means the inability to pay, Ms. Murray. But I notice that when your company is trying to attract investors you talk about America as the wealthiest country the world has ever seen. The question a lot of people are asking is, wealthiest for whom? - Not for that supposedly typical family of four in that commercial of yours. Worried about bankruptcy? Run an ad with the family of a CEO of a Fortune 500 company worried about how they're going to pay their bills. You really expect me to take you seriously? Are you going to tell the people in this room - are you going to tell the people who are going to read what Rachel Good will be writing in the New York Times - that unlike other countries, unlike France and Israel, that have some form of mandatory service, the United States alone can't afford it, that we'll go bankrupt if we try? You're not worried about bankruptcy; you're worried about taxes. You're not worried about whether we can pay for what we need; you're worried about what it might cost you. Why you - and those who think like you - call yourselves conservatives defies explanation. You don't have any serious interest in conserving anything, except what you have. Do you really believe it is better to let the rich own as many homes, as many private palaces, monuments to their own bad taste, than to share in the building of a better, a great, country?"

The face of Angela Murray had gone three shades of red, her stare so intense it might, if fixed on dry paper, have started a fire.

"This country is only great when it allows private enterprise to flourish. Without that, there is no freedom. What you're trying to do - everyone gets a free education, gets one if they join up. And then, on top of it, we're going to forget our obligations here on earth and start this endless exploration of the universe! It's all about what government is going to do! Government, that's all you talk about, what government is going to do. We all know what that means. More taxes, more regulation. You're going to make it impossible for business to succeed."

"You don't want government involved; you don't want anyone telling you how to run your business. Is that correct?" asked Julian, sharply.

"No, I don't want government involved at all; government doesn't know what it is doing."

"You don't want government involved in your business, but not the other way round?"

"What do you mean - 'not the other way round'?"

"You don't want anyone in government telling you what to do, but you have no hesitation telling people in government what they should do."

"That's different; that's to keep government out of things it should not be involved in."

"Has anyone in government ever threatened you?" he asked, his voice calm, precise, and ominous. Angela Murray blinked twice in rapid succession as she tried to calculate how far he might go. "Anyone ever threatened to use the powers of government to destroy your business, your career? Because that is exactly what you have been doing."

She stalled, playing for time, afraid whatever she said might be a tripwire that would lead to disclosure of the private conversations with which, through Ismael Cooper by way of Conrad Wilson, she had already been threatened. She looked at the president as if she had no idea what he was talking about.

"It's what you have been doing, isn't it? It is what you're doing now. What else would you call it, the millions, the tens of millions, you and your friends have been spending threatening members of the House and Senate if they refuse to do what you want, if they refuse to oppose what I'm trying to do. How many of those sitting here in the room would still be undecided if you - or your various agents - had not let them know they might be facing an opponent, a well-funded opponent, in their primaries next year if they vote the wrong way? What is that, Ms. Murray, if it isn't threatening them with the destruction of their career?"

"Are you saying that we don't have the right to express our opinion on an issue we think vital to the country?" cried Chambers, eager to divert the president's attention from what was becoming a potentially dangerous confrontation with Angela. "Are you suggesting we don't have the right to support whatever candidates we wish?" he asked, careful to speak in a polite, completely civil, manner.

Julian's gaze remained fastened on Angela Murray.

"You can support anyone you like, Mr. Chambers," he replied, cool and detached. "But you can't threaten someone with a promise to do this against a public official unless he votes the way you want."

"But that's done all the time!" laughed a congressman.

Acknowledging with a nod that this was true, Julian bent forward on his elbows, pressing his left hand against the side of his head.

"If someone offered you money for your vote, Congressman Baker, you wouldn't take it, would you? It's bribery, and you would go to jail. If giving someone money is a crime, it isn't clear to me why a threat to take away something of value should not be a crime as well. We'll give you money if you vote our way, we'll give it to someone else if you don't. What is that but politics as extortion?"

"I might agree with you in principle," replied the third term congressman, a Republican from Tennessee who knew he was vulnerable to a challenge from the right. "But the possibility - the threat, if you want to call it that - is always there; it's implicit in every request that you vote in favor, or against, a bill."

"Which is a very good reason to take private money out of politics, but that is another issue," said Julian, turning away from the congressman to look again at Angela Murray, sitting stiff and outraged at the other end of the table. He leaned back and, dropping his head to the side seemed to study her, slowly calculating what he was going to say.

"You have threatened these men and women; threatened them with the end of their careers. I would like you to stop; I would like you to announce, here, now, that everyone is free to vote according to their own best judgment and that nothing will be done to try to influence the next election. I'm willing to have this decided on the merits, and so should you. Don't hesitate. It is really quite simple. Should Congress represent the people who elected them, or should they allow you to buy them?"

Everyone was watching, tense and expectant, wondering how Angela Murray would respond. No one liked her very much, but they feared her and what she and the money she represented could do. No one leaped to her defense, but neither did anyone take the president's side. They waited, silent witnesses to a battle of wits, their only serious interest the effect it might have on themselves.

"You don't think these undecided members of Congress should decide on the merits a bill of this importance? You think they should instead be subject to your threats of reprisal?" Before she could reply, he turned to Rachel Good, sitting just a few feet away. "I think we'll all be interested to read what you write tomorrow, whether Congress or a few - what did Teddy Roosevelt call them? - 'malefactors of great wealth' - are in charge of this nation's future."

Julian said this with such buoyancy, such astonishing eagerness and energy, that it was almost as if he knew in advance everything that was going to happen. It seemed in that moment to Rachel Good, and not just to her, that he could not be beaten and that everyone knew it. The story, the one she was going to write, had already been written. She wondered how many of the undecided senators and congressmen knew that their decision had already been made, and how many would have to wait until tomorrow to realize that their choice was now between being seen as acting for the public good or voting the way they had been told. Angela Murray was too angry, too frustrated, to think even that far ahead, or to think at all.

"A question of the merits!" she exclaimed, throwing up her hands, impatient of all the stupidity she had been forced to endure. "If it weren't for you and your rhetorical gifts, making promises that will do nothing but harm sound like the greatest things that could ever happen; if it weren't for this reckless self-indulgence in make-believe grandeur; if it weren't....On the merits? If it were on the merits, you would withdraw the bill!"

"I asked you here to help clarify the issue," replied Julian, ignoring her outburst. "I understand that you, and a great many others in the business community, think it is too expensive; you understand that I don't. The difference between us on that point is clear. What other reasons - if any - can you give these undecided members of the House and Senate to vote against the bill?"

"Mr. President," interjected the Senate Minority Leader, Mary Ellen Overland of California who was leading the opposition in the Senate. "As you may imagine, I haven't the same objections as Ms. Murray, or any of the other conservative Republicans who think lower taxes - at least on the rich - is the only answer to every problem we have. We're opposed to the bill because we think college should be free for everyone. Requiring military service as a condition for the kind of education everyone needs now to have any chance at a decent job, a decent life....This will only add yet another burden on the poor."

The tension began to dissipate. Senator Overland was a colleague, and one of the more likable ones, not just willing to listen to an opposing point of view but known, on occasion, to change her mind as a result of what she had heard. She had the additional advantage that, a woman in her early fifties, the men in the Senate, most of whom were in their sixties or seventies, found her rather more fascinating than their wives.

"I certainly have no objection to anything that would make college more affordable," said Julian. Overland was sitting half way down the left side of the table. "There was a time in California when a student could go from kindergarten to a Ph.d. at Berkeley free. No one had to pay for an education. Nothing was more important than a well-educated citizenry. We should get back to that. The bill I've put forward is a different matter. It is only indirectly concerned with the cost of higher education. I tried to explain this. It isn't enough to adopt policies - tax policies, spending policies - that attempt to improve the condition of the poor; it isn't enough to reduce the existing disparity of wealth. Why do we have this disparity, why do the rich keep getting richer, and everyone else has to work harder and harder not to fall back? There is only one reason: somehow we have convinced ourselves that private wealth - how much money someone has - is the only real measure of success. We thank ours soldiers, we thank our police, our firefighters - we thank our teachers - for 'their service,' and, because we would never think of doing anything like that ourselves, never think of them again, unless to complain about the cost. What has gone missing is a sense of responsibility, the belief that our first thought should be not for ourselves, but for those around us, for our country. This bill - think it through. Four years of college, not just tuition - which is what I think you are proposing - but board and room. You may, if you wish, think of it as a reward, the payoff, for four years of military service. You could also think of it the other way around: four years of college as an incentive, as a reason, to join. It is an interesting question, which some of you may wish to consider: which is the most important objective, four years of college to learn what they think they need to know, or four years of service in which they will learn what those who would guard this country should be taught?"

There were other questions, some of them quite specific. Julian did his best to answer them all. The meeting had been scheduled for an hour and a half; three hours after it started it was still going on. Others might get tired or hungry, they might have things scheduled, people waiting for them, but no one makes excuses when you are the guest of the president, and Julian Drake, whatever else anyone thought of him, seemed to live for this, an endless argument over what should be done. Members of Congress who were only undecided because they had not yet been offered something tangible for their districts, sank low in their chairs, wondering if they could bring things to a close by announcing that they had heard enough and were now willing to throw their support behind the president. The rest of them seemed actually to become more energized, more interested and alert the more they listened and, listening, were swept along by the debate.

"I used to read a lot of British history. The House of Commons met at night and on an important issue, someone like Disraeli or Gladstone might speak for three or four hours; speak, by the way, without so much as a note to remind them what they wanted to say; speak for three or four hours and never lose their audience. But then, they did not have our advantages; they did not have television or any of the other electronic devices by which we have made ourselves incapable of attention for anything that lasts more than a few seconds. They would debate - trade speeches - sometimes all night long; stay there until break of day. We should do that here," he added, as if he thought that now would be a good time to start.

"That might be a good idea," said Angela Murray, who had been sitting in agitated silence for the last half hour. "Perhaps we would be better off following the British. With a parliamentary system only someone who led his party could become prime minister. Isn't that correct, Mr. President? You couldn't do it with just one speech; you would have to work your way up, become the leader of your party before you ever became leader of the nation. We might then become a real conservative party, and a real conservative - someone like a Margaret Thatcher or a Winston Churchill - could get elected."

To her astonishment, Julian seemed to agree.

"I didn't used to think so," he began, weighing his words with unusual care. "But now, with the way money and celebrity have come to dominate everything, I wonder if that might not be a solution. As you say, it requires years of involvement in the work of government, and, in addition, the ability to speak, not just a few incoherent sentences, but speak in whole paragraphs on a subject on which you are completely versed. It doesn't allow, the way our system does, any room for those who have spent their lives in business or certain of the other professions. Thatcher, Churchill? - I'm not sure I would put them in the same category; I'm not sure I would put anyone in the same category with the greatest statesman, and the greatest historian, of the twentieth century."

Thatcher, Churchill - any famous name from recent history - that was all she, and others like her, knew: the names, and what those names had come to symbolize for those whose knowledge was limited to what they had heard. It was hard not to laugh. Churchill had been a conservative and so was she, and what could that mean except that Churchill was everything she could have wanted in a politician.

"You would like someone like Churchill to lead the country?" asked Julian, with what seemed innocent curiosity.

"Churchill was a great man," she replied, defiantly. "He was -"

"The leader of the effort to bring what we call Social Security to Britain; the leader of the effort to create a national health service so that every citizen gets the medical care they need. Churchill understood, what you seem unwilling to concede, that government has an obligation to make sure no one gets left out or left behind. There is something more. By the end of the Second World War, which, without Churchill, would probably have been lost, he believed the upper classes had forfeited the right to lead the country the way they had in the past. The Battle of Britain, the air battle in which the RAF beat back the German air force, the battle that meant Britain would be safe from invasion, was not won by pilots who had gone to Oxford or Cambridge. It was not won by pilots from wealthy, titled families. The pilots who won the Battle of Britain came from the British middle class. Churchill understood where the people who had thought first about their country had come from and that these were the people who should now begin to lead. That, it seems to me, is what a conservative should do: make sure that those who give the most to their country are in the best position eventually to lead their country."

Julian looked around the room, his gaze resting for a brief moment on each member of Congress, encouraging them to take seriously what he had just said.

"The question before you, ladies and gentlemen, is not so much how you are going to vote as why. Vote what you think is right and, if you do that, whether you vote in favor or against the bill, you will always have my respect. I wish you well in your deliberations."

He started for the door at the side, but then stopped to whisper something in Ismael's ear. The meeting was over. Ismael stood at the main entrance, as he had nearly four hours earlier, and shook hands with everyone as they left. He did not shake hands with Angela Murray.

"The president wants to see you."

"When?" she asked, irritably. "This week is really -"

Ismael did not let her finish. "Now," he said, abruptly. "Follow me."

She walked beside him down a long corridor to the Oval Office. Isamel did not speak a word. He opened the door for her and immediately shut it behind her. She was alone with Julian Drake.

"Come in, come in," he said, motioning to her from behind his desk.

He was sitting with his legs crossed, leaning back in the leather chair, glancing casually through some document. He did not look up, and when she came nearer, gestured toward the straight back chair in front.

"Sit down. I just wanted to…." He finished what he was doing and for the first time turned to her, a faint smile on his lips and something deadly serious in his eyes. "You might want to look at this."

He said this in a way that seemed to imply a question, though what that question might be she had no idea. When he handed it to her and she saw what it was, she almost laughed.

"I've seen this," she remarked with studied indifference as she put it back on his desk. "Your Mr. Cooper gave it to Conrad Wilson and told him to use it to threaten me - and Rufus Chambers and everyone else who is standing in your way."

"Yes, I know what Ismael did; he told me after he did it."

"I doubt he would have done it if he did not think you would approve."

"Ismael did what I would have done under the circumstances. He did what I expected he would do, knowing what he thought he knew."

"What he thought he knew?"

"And you did what I thought you would, knowing what you thought you knew."

"What I thought I -"

Raising an eyebrow, Julian seemed to taunt her with her own ignorance. There was something she did not know; something, he seemed to suggest with that look of his, that changed everything.

"You thought - Ismael thought - that your telephone had been tapped and that you had been recorded talking with Rufus Chambers about my assassination. You thought -"

"No one was serious! It was just talk, that's all it was," she insisted, indignant that anyone could think otherwise. "It was stupid. I admit that. I was angry, upset; I didn't like - I don't like - what you're trying to do. And so I said some things that I'm sure I shouldn't have said, but -"

"But you didn't just say things, did you?" he asked with a piercing stare. "You did more than that." He pointed toward the FBI report that lay just beyond her reach. "Read it again."

"Read it…? All right, but I don't…." she said, as she turned to the first page.

"No, not the first few pages - that's what you read before, what Ismael read before, the reason he went to New York, the reason he did what he did. That was all I let him see. He doesn't know about the rest. No one does. And if you do what I ask, no one ever will."

She glanced through the first few pages, the ones she had seen before, and then, suddenly, she froze.

"It's all there," said Julian, in a calm, strangely soothing voice. "The payment that was made, the name of the hired assassin, the time, the date, the place where it is supposed to happen, everything, every last detail."

Her mouth was so dry that when she tried to speak her voice cracked.

"What is it you want me to do? You want me to tell everyone I've changed my mind, that after our meeting I'm now convinced that you're right after all, that the bill should pass. I can do that; I can make it sound like its true."

Julian seemed almost sympathetic, and in a way he was.

"No, I don't want you to do that. I meant what I said in there: I want everyone to vote the way they think they should. No, I don't want your support. I was something else, something you'll never understand, something no one would ever understand. Let me explain."

An hour later, when Angela Murray finally left the White House, her hair had turned white.

CHAPTER TWENTY-SIX

It was late, or was it early? Time lost all meaning when Julian wanted to talk. It was two-thirty in the morning, everyone else in Washington was asleep. Ismael had gone to bed a little after eleven, knowing there was always the chance that long before daybreak there would be something Julian would suddenly want to discuss. He was used to it; more than that, he looked forward to it. Five minutes after the telephone next to his bed rang, he was dressed and on his way to the Oval Office. Julian, wearing a coat and tie, looked completely rested.

"I got a couple of hours," he explained. "This is the best time to be awake: when everyone else is asleep. No one can bother you. It's quiet; you can think - you can study."

Ismael took the chair on the side of the desk, a quarter turn from Julian.

"It's been an interesting few weeks, don't you think?"

"Interesting? I wonder if that is what F.D.R. said after his first hundred days. It isn't the word most people are using. They're a little more emphatic: 'revolutionary,' 'catastrophic', 'visionary', 'foolish', 'the work of genius,' 'the work of idiots.' But, yes, you could say it has been an interesting few weeks."

"And now Louis is in the hospital, dying. He did what he said he would - what I said he would - stayed alive to finish his work. He got the votes we needed in the Senate. Without that…."

"That isn't what he thinks. I was with him at Bethesda yesterday. He's convinced it's all because of what you did in that meeting with the undecideds. No, that isn't exactly right," said Ismael, correcting himself. There was a shrewd gleam of recollection in his eyes. "He said it was all because of Rachel Good."

"I know that. If she hadn't…."

"Louis said if you hadn't invited her nothing would have changed, everyone would still have been afraid of what would happen to them in their next election. But once Rachel reported the threats that were made, the threats that were repeated, then the question became one of political courage."

"And courage in politics can be a very great political advantage," said Julian, with a wry grin, "as long as it isn't kept hidden from the public."

"Every undecided senator and three quarters of the congressmen voted in favor, and so did four senators and more than a dozen members of the House who had gone on record in opposition."

"A cynic might say that the lesson in all this is that if you want to buy a senator or a congressman make sure you do it in private," remarked Julian with a frown. "The better lesson is that the same ambition that makes them vulnerable to those who can threaten their political careers, makes them understand the importance of their own reputations. That was the reason I wanted Angela Murray there, the reason I said I didn't think I could win without her."

Ismael sat back, crossed his left arm over his chest, and with his right hand began to stroke his chin. He studied Julian with more than curious interest, with something that almost seemed a challenge.

"You want to know what happened in that private meeting I had with her." For a brief moment he held Ismael's gaze in his own, and then looked past him. "Nothing, really. I told her I knew what she had done, that I had read the FBI report; I told her that what happened next was up to her."

Ismael did not entirely believe him. He was certain there was more to it, that more than what Julian had just described had taken place. Julian was holding something back, but Ismael knew better than to ask.

"You've heard what happened?" Julian looked at him with a blank expression. "She resigned her position, quit without notice, and seems to have pretty much disappeared. No one knows where she is or what she is doing. But you…?"

Julian ignored the question. There were other things on his mind.

"It worked, the bill passed. It's done. Everything is done."

"Everything? I don't understand."

"There were two things that needed to be done, two pillars that needed to be built. Everyone now has the right - which will soon enough be seen as almost an obligation - to serve four years in the military, four years learning the lessons of discipline and honor and shared sacrifice, the importance of looking out for one another. There aren't any differences of wealth, there aren't any inherited privileges, in the military. No one worries about whether someone else is having a good time. They aren't going to be entertained. This isn't some kind of mindless game and they aren't going to be idle spectators. Four years of training, four years learning what makes both an individual and a nation great.

"That is one pillar, the other is what we have just done: making the space program the highest national priority we have, getting Congress to approve as much money as can be spent. These people who criticize it, who say that it is the stuff of Hollywood, the movies, science fiction, they're more right than they know. What has caught the American imagination more than the possibility of exploring the universe? Remember when I told you it was all a question of what you look up to, what a country looks up to? We have always looked up to the stars. That's the reason those movies have always been so popular. They appeal to the natural curiosity about our own existence, why we're here, what it means to be a human being, why we inhabit this one particular planet in what seems an endless universe. Look around you. What is missing from American life? - A common sense of purpose, a dedication to something of lasting importance, something that together we can all help achieve, something that will let us leave our mark."

Ismael did not entirely disagree. There had been too many late night conversations in which he had heard Julian, as he had just now done again, talk about the importance of those two accomplishments. But those were not the only things Julian wanted to achieve. The list was endless, there did not seem anything he did not want to change. When he reminded him of that, Julian tapped his hand on a thick, thousand page volume that sat on top of a stack of things he had been reading.

"Plutarch. Everyone, at least everyone who wants to be reasonably well-educated, should read this and learn what great men there used to be. Read how Lycurgus, when he gave the Spartans their laws, made them agree that they could not be changed without his consent; read how he then left Sparta and did not come back for ten years. They had ten years to get used to their new way of life; ten years so that what was at the beginning an innovation, a change from how they had lived before, could become a habit, a tradition. When the ten years ended, no one wanted change; they understood that if Sparta was to endure no one could even think to question what the laws required. Which isn't to say that they did not understand that conditions, circumstances, sometimes change and the laws then have to change as well. That was the reason they allowed anyone to propose a change in the laws if he thought one was needed. If everyone agreed, he was honored as having benefitted the city; if his proposal did not pass, he was killed," explained Julian with a look of such eager malice that Ismael started to laugh.

"Shall I call the Speaker in the morning and tell him you think they should add that to the House's rules of procedure?"

"That would be unkind. He would spend all day trying to figure out if you were serious, and he's so dull-witted he might decide you were."

Julian's eyes were darting all around; his mouth, even when he was not speaking, could not stop moving, as if he were in mad pursuit of so many different thoughts that as soon as the words to express one of them came into his mind, they flew away, chased off by another, more insistent thought.

"That is the problem, don't you see? We did what we said we would, we did what scarcely anyone thought we could - but only because we moved as quickly as we did. Louis understood. When you're first elected, when you first become president - if you have won it in a way that leaves no doubt you have the country with you - the hopes of everyone are with you, everyone wants you to succeed. It doesn't last; it can't. Once you have done something, especially if it is as fundamental as this, a reaction sets in. Once you've done something, there is something to criticize, something with which to find fault. The question isn't what you can do in the first hundred days; the question is how you can protect what has been accomplished; protect it long enough that it becomes part of the very fabric of American life."

"For ten years, like Lycurgus?"

Julian stared out the window at the darkened sky. A strange, enigmatic smile moved slowly across his mouth.

"Or like Empedocles," he said in a low, almost inaudible voice. He turned to Ismael with a sparkle in his eye. "Do you know the story? Empedocles, if he is remembered at all, is remembered as a footnote in the brief history of pre-Socratic philosophers. He lived in Sicily, in Agrigento with the ten Greek temples arranged like step stones to the sea. He was a physician who, it was said, once brought a dead woman back to life, but he was also, like Pericles in Athens, the dominant, the controlling force in that city's democracy. Other less able, more ambitious, men drove him out of power. He left Agrigento and, according to the legend, threw himself into the volcano, Mt. Etna. One of his golden sandals was found just inside the crater. He left a message telling the citizens of Agrigento that he had gone to take his place among the gods. Lycurgus left for ten years so that the Spartans would not change the laws he had given them. Empedocles left forever, left this earth to join the gods, so that the city would not be quite so willing to make the kind of changes those who had replaced him had in mind, to say nothing of his desire to make them take seriously just who he had been."

Julian looked at Ismael in a way that told him there was more to the story, something that gave it a whole new meaning.

"A single golden slipper! The only proof that Empedocles did what he said he was going to do. And just how do you suppose that single slipper was not destroyed, consumed by the molten lava into which Empedocles had leaped? Or did he die at all? Was it instead, as some later thought, all a grand deception, that Empedocles had left that single golden slipper in exactly the place where it would be found, and then continued on his way, across the Strait of Messina and eventually to Greece where he lived out the rest of his life, undetected in his honorable deception?"

"Are you thinking of doing something like that: jumping into a volcano?"

"Or making everyone think I did," laughed Julian. "And what kind of note would I leave? - Tell everyone that, like Empedocles, I have gone to join the gods? Don't you think enough people already think I'm a little strange? No, suicide doesn't really work," he said, rolling his eyes. He became serious. "The question is how to give permanence to what we've done. We need time, a few years, four or five, so that millions of people have done four years service, time for the idea to take hold that life is a great adventure, that we don't have to involve ourselves in other people's quarrels, that we can lead better by example, by what we set out to do, exploring everything the eye can see."

Twisting around, Julian bent forward, his left hand on the arm of the chair, his right elbow on the desk. He began to draw circles in the air as he talked.

"People talk about American exceptionalism, that the laws of history don't apply to us. There are two problems. There are no laws of history; history does not have a purpose. But there are laws of human conduct, there is a difference between good and evil, and a nation that forgets that difference is almost always doomed to pay a price for its ignorance. What is exceptional about America is how often the best presidents have been lucky, not just in their lives - the way that, sometimes from the most unlikely beginning, they became president - but lucky in their deaths. Adams and Jefferson both died the same day, the fiftieth anniversary of the signing of the Declaration of Independence. Astonishing, when you think about it; singularly fitting that it should happen that way, political rivals who became great friends. It is the story of America. Then consider Lincoln. If he hadn't died when he did, if he had not been murdered by John Wilkes Booth, the country might have been saved a lot of what happened in the years of Reconstruction, but we would have lost the sense of tragedy that will always surround Lincoln's greatness, the belief that Lincoln embodied what was best in us and always would. Always would - that is the point. Without Lincoln, without Lincoln's death, we would be a different people. Whatever depth we still have we owe to him. And then, if Kennedy had lived - well, who knows what might have happened. But with his death he became someone everyone looked up to, a memory people wanted to honor by following where they thought he wanted to lead."

Julian tapped again the book he had been reading.

"The parallel lives, one ancient Roman matched against one ancient Greek, the comparison always in favor of the Greek, but written in a way that Plutarch's Roman audience would not be offended, because written in a way they would not notice it. Whatever the differences among them, there is not one man among them, whether Greek or Roman, who ever spoke about a long life as something desirable by itself. What they wanted to last was what they built, what they created. That is the real reason, one of the reasons, why its important we talk about the exploration of space as a great adventure. It is the last, best chance to treat this obsession with comfortable longevity with the contempt it deserves. What difference does it make if anyone lives to be a hundred, what difference does it make if someone dies at forty or fifty? The only serious question is what kind of life they've led. Mozart died at - what? - thirty-five. Ask people whether they would like their children to lead long, happy lives or die at thirty-five but have done something as remarkable as what Mozart did. You might be surprised at the answers you get. Nothing important is measured by time. You do your work, whatever that work may be; do it as well as you know how, and if you get sick, get better so you can work again. But if you can't, if you cannot be put back in condition to go on with your proper work, it is - or was for the ancients - only sensible that you die. Some people still understand that. What did Louis tell you when we did not have the votes we needed in the Senate? - That he would get them, and wouldn't die before he did."

Remembering what Louis had done, Julian's mouth curled down at the corners. His eyes tightened in the dismal recognition of what he could not change and what he had to do.

"I haven't been to see him; I'll do it this morning."

Louis Matson's room at the hospital was clean, private, and full of monitors and machines measuring with soulless precision the condition of a dying man. The little light left in Matson's eyes took what seemed the last bit of strength he had.

"They told me you were coming," he said, his labored breath louder than his almost soundless speech. "I told them not to let you come. There's nothing you can do. I didn't want you to see me - to remember me - like this."

Julian sat next to him and took him by his fragile, feeble hand.

"It's the best you've ever looked."

He said this with the lying insincerity that, for those who have passed their lives in politics, gets closer to truth's deeper meaning than spoken honesty ever could; a cynic's bridge, if you will, between the world's false sentimentality and what a decent respect for another man's courage and intelligence requires. What might have startled, and even shocked, someone who happened to walk past, witness to a scene he did not understand, made Louis Matson come back to life.

"They were always telling me how much good a little rest would do me."

They were alone in the room. The door was shut. No one could hear what they said.

"Rachel told me she would have married me, if I had ever asked her. I never suspected, never thought she had any interest in me - like that. And I'm not sure she ever really did. She meant it when she told me. That's what she believes now, what she would have done then. We do that, don't we? - Think back about what we might have done, then convince ourselves that it is what we really wanted at the time. But it was decent of her to tell me that. I would have done it, and then I might have been happy and contented, instead of a frustrated politician, always hoping for something better, and always seeing things get worse. Until now. For all my faults, all my failures, I helped get you the presidency." He grasped tighter Julian's hand. "And the strangest thing of all is that I knew it would happen - I could feel it - the first time I heard you speak. Even the night you had to quit the Senate race, I think I knew that somehow, someday, it would happen, that there would be another chance."

"What's important, is that you got the bill through the Senate. No one else could have done it. We have a chance now. We can become a serious country again," said Julian, with a look of the utmost confidence. "A place where everyone competes for honor instead of money, where the future is not what we want for ourselves, but what we want others to look back on with astonishment and pride. You did that; more than anyone else, you made it possible."

"Listen to me," said Matson, his voice a low, hoarse whisper. "I tried to tell you, years ago, in politics, politics in the best sense, everything has its uses.

My death. Take advantage of it. Remind everyone that my name is on the bill, that it was my signature accomplishment - There is a statement, something I wrote, in my desk in my office. I left instructions to release it on my death."

He stopped speaking and tried to regain his breath. His eyes, which had become dull and lusterless, suddenly glittered with something remembered from the long forgotten past.

"Churchill planned his own funeral. He wanted to be sure it was larger than the one given the century before for the Duke of Wellington, because, you see, Wellington's funeral had been larger than the one given, the century before that, for Churchill's ancestor, the Duke of Marlborough. Churchill wanted that honor to come back to his own family."

Very gently, Julian freed his hand from Matson's grasp and stood up.

"What would you like us to do?"

"Invite all my friends," he replied, with a faint, dry grin on his tired, desiccated mouth. "I have three of them: Rachel, Ismael, and you." He reached for Julian's hand. "This is important. Have you talked to the governor? I don't trust the son-of-a-bitch. He promised to appoint Ismael when I resigned from the Senate this summer. But I'm not resigning, I'm dying - he may think that gives him a way out. Don't give him the chance. The day I die, announce that Ismael Cooper is going to take my place, that it was my wish and that the governor has agreed. Now, go. I can't tell you how proud - how grateful - I am."

Three days later, Louis Matson died in his sleep. Rachel Good was with him at the end, more certain than ever that she would have married him if he had only asked. She tried to write a fitting obituary for her paper, but after two failed attempts at a first paragraph, knew she could not do it and asked that someone else write it instead. It was, she discovered, too difficult to separate what she knew and what she felt; too difficult, really, to even be quite sure she knew the difference. Everything was all jumbled up: the memory of what she had covered in her long years as a Washington reporter, the memory of her changing sense of things, what Louis Matson had been like, not as a congressman or senator, but as a human being: what she had liked about him, what had drawn her close to him, made her believe - made her know - that he was almost the only man she could always trust to tell her what he really thought. Maybe, she decided, it was better that they had never married. She might not have known him as well if they had.

The funeral was not what Louis Matson had asked for. They were there, the only three people he considered his friends, but so was half of Washington, crowded into the National Cathedral, listening to Julian Drake tell the story of how, without bothering to ask his consent, Louis Matson had made him president.

"He had a great respect for the power of language, a regard for the way everything, almost everything, depends on the way we speak to one another. He understood, as few others have, that without the ability to explain clearly what we have to do and why we have to do it, nothing of importance ever gets done. He understood that without clear, persuasive speech, we are nothing but those idiots of Shakespeare's marvelous description, telling tales that only fools believe. He understood the tragic irony in those famous words from Lincoln's Gettysburg Address that, 'the world will little note nor long remember what we say here.' The world will remember nothing, and not remembering, never learn, without words that once we hear them we can never forget. Louis Matson was not a great speaker. He was something better than that. He was a great listener, which made him a great judge of what was important and what was not. Louis Matson was my friend, but, more than that, he was one of the best friends this country has ever had."

When the service was over and, under a sunny sky, the crowd had dispersed, when everyone else had gone back to their busy lives, the only three people Louis Matson had wanted at his funeral, the only three friends he had, stood at the gravesite at Arlington National Cemetery. Each in turn tossed a handful of earth onto the lowered casket and then, with this, their last, goodbye, Ismael Cooper and Rachel Good turned and walked away. Julian stayed behind, wanting, as he explained, to spend a few more, private, moments.

Rachel held onto Ismael's arm and, as she would remember later, felt a sudden breeze on her face, the air sweet and clear, and thought it a kind of solace, a reminder of something permanent amidst the passing lives of friends and strangers, the gift of existence that death, instead of defeating, only makes more vivid. She took a long, deep breath - she remembered that -

and then a few more steps, and then, just as Ismael turned to say something, she heard it. They both heard it. They turned, the two of them, to look back and - she remembered - there was that brief moment, an instant, in which their eyes met and they knew, knew before they had turned to see, knew with all the certainty of a death foretold, that the shot they had heard had been an assassin's bullet and that the president, Julian Drake, was dead.

CHAPTER TWENTY-SEVEN

It would have been difficult to know whether Hobart Williams was more bewildered or more exasperated by Rachel Good's refusal to accept the fact that no one was going to solve the mystery of Julian Drake's death.

"A year - more than a year - that's how long its been, and you still think there is a story there? We know who killed him, we know who fired the shot. Do you think he was just some fall guy, that someone else did it? Is that what makes you keep insisting…?"

He knew what she was after; they had had this same conversation almost every week since the assassination: one more lead, one more rumor, she wanted to follow up, the chance - maybe the last chance - to get to the truth; and always the same bitter sarcasm in her voice, the same bristling anger in her eyes, the wrenching contempt for what everyone else was willing, too willing, to believe.

"The 'lone gunman' all over again, another Lee Harvey Oswald, only without the convenience of a Jack Ruby to kill him on national television. He's dead all right - in a car wreck, the car explodes, the driver burned beyond recognition. But the gun, the sniper's rifle, found, conveniently enough, in the trunk! Accidental death, could have happened to anyone," she remarked, shaking her head in derision. "Careful enough when it came to killing a president, careful - precise - enough to fire the shot from hundreds of yards away, but couldn't keep his car on the road, the dry road, on a clear night; just drove off the goddamn bridge. Maybe he was drunk," she said, as she threw back her head and fixed him with a caustic stare; "maybe he just forgot he was driving around with the murder weapon in the trunk. Maybe…maybe he commited suicide. But it isn't really important how he died; it isn't even that important if it really was an accident and he wasn't murdered to shut him up. What is important is who hired him. I know, I know!" she cried, waving her hand with impatience, "there is no evidence he didn't act alone. He was former army, former CIA, former - former a lot of things. Couldn't hold a job, history of domestic violence, no friends, no relatives - perfect candidate for the kind of half-witted maniac that makes everyone think nothing else was going on, that no one else was involved."

Wilson turned toward the window and the glass canyons of New York shining bright in the midday sun. His reporter's instinct told him she was right, that there had to have been more to it than what had become the official version of events, that there had to have been some kind of conspiracy, that no assassin had done this on his own. His editor's judgement told him that Rachel Good had been too close to the story; that she was, in a way, part of the story herself, not just as a witness to what had happened, but involved, personally involved. Julian Drake, Ismael Cooper, Louis Matson had, all of them, told her things they had told no one else. This was not a story she wanted to cover, it was an obsession.

"More than a year, Rachel; more than a year since it happened. How long do you think you can - how long do you think you should - pursue this? Every law enforcement agency, every intelligence agency - no one has ever found anything. What do you think you can -?"

"Angela Murray."

Williams leaned forward on his desk. If he had not known her for years, if he had not known what she had been through, how deeply affected she had been by the death of Louis Matson, how traumatized she had been by the death, the violent death, of Julian Drake when she was just a few short yards away, he would have thrown up his hands in frustration and perhaps even anger. He looked at her instead with the resigned sympathy of an old friend who knows there is nothing he can do to help.

"Not again, Rachel; please," he said quietly. "You can't keep doing this. We have been through this before. There are a dozen stories - good, solid stories - waiting for you to write them, including stories about the influence Ismael Cooper has already managed to acquire in the Senate. Write about that; we can't keep -"

"I know where she is."

"You know…? What difference does it make? It's old news. Ismael Cooper testified that there was an FBI report, that she and Rufus Chambers talked about the possibility; but that was all - the possibility. They checked on Chambers. Nothing to link him to the assassination; nothing to link him to anything. And Angela Murray - who knows what she might have been capable of doing, but after that breakdown, that collapse of hers…."

"If there really was a breakdown, if there really was a collapse, or, even if there was, if she had already started things in motion before it happened."

"There was no connection, nothing - nothing to link her to anything."

"No one ever talked to her."

As gently as he could, he reminded her that she had forgotten what should have been obvious.

"No one talked to her because she was locked up in a private sanitarium, damn near catatonic, from what the doctors said."

Rachel got up from her chair and looked at Hobart with something close to the same sympathy with which he had looked at her.

"She isn't in a sanitarium anymore, and she sure as hell didn't seem catatonic when she called me an hour ago and said she wanted to see me!"

Angela had been asked to come the following day at six, late afternoon on a mid-summer day. The air was thick and stifling as she drove along the Potomac shore. Less than three miles from Mt. Vernon, where George Washington had presided over what was almost a country of his own, Angela Murray had attempted to build on a bluff overlooking the river something like what, nearly a century earlier, William Randolph Hearst had tried to do on the other side of the country, high above the Pacific: a castle filled with priceless works of art from all the capitals of Europe, collected, catalogued, kept not for her enjoyment, but as a measure of her worth. Whatever the intention, it failed to achieve the same effect. Hearst's castle had a massive, unworldly quality, a movie set, a provisional attempt at an image of permanence. There was nothing especially theatrical, or even particularly interesting, about the light gray, three story stone structure with a green slate roof that loomed in the distance as Rachel drove through the open iron gates and down the long, tree-lined drive. It may have been designed by a famous French architect, it may have been based on the plan of an 18th century chateau somewhere in the Dordogne, but, even in America, another hundred years would have to pass before someone who had never seen the original would think it anything but a poor imitation. That had never been the point, of course. The issue was not authenticity; the issue was the sheer expense of it, the notoriety, the statement that something this colossal made. The impression of wealth, unlimited wealth, was the only thing that mattered.

A butler answered the door and showed Rachel through an enormous living room, across a hard polished gray marble floor, out through the French doors to the terrace where a wrinkled, white-haired old woman sat waiting in a wheel chair. Angela Murray pointed a long, bony finger to a yellow cushioned chair next to the table just in front of her.

For one of the few times in Rachel's life, she was at a loss for words. She had never seen such a change: Angela Murray had gone from a vibrant, sharp-eyed woman, a woman arrogant, self-willed, eager to let you know that however intelligent you thought you were, you could never match wits with her, to a mere shadow of what she had been, a broken wreck whose next, labored breath, might well be her last. Her hands, the fingers of which had once moved with such quick, meticulous precision, were like gnarled claws, the nails pressed hard against the palms, as if they had been turned to feeble fists by beating against the walls. Her face, which had been thin and taut, had become cadaverous. She looked at Rachel as if she were not quite sure who she was. Then, suddenly, she started to laugh, her eyes filled with more than recognition, hatred. There was no mistake. It was hatred, pure and simple, but hatred, as Rachel grasped immediately, that was not for her, or rather, not for her alone: it was hatred for the world and everyone in it, especially herself.

"I was surprised to get your invitation," said Rachel, in as pleasant a voice as she could summon. "You didn't say why you wanted to see me, only that...."

Angela Murray rang a bell tied to her chair, and a moment later, and not more than that, a maid appeared.

"Where are my manners? What would you like? Anything at all: coffee, tea, wine, whiskey, coca-cola, gin, scotch...?" she asked in a voice that, strangely, had not lost any of its clarity or force. The sound of it, the sound of her own words, seemed, like the notes of a long-forgotten song, the echo of another time, the lost memory of someone else: a friend, an enemy, someone she knew when life still had a meaning, to enliven her. She glanced at the maid, a young, dark-haired woman who stood in rigid silence. "I'll have a gin and tonic."

Rachel asked for coffee. Black.

"People used to come here, dozens, hundreds. There was a party once, more than a thousand. They all came. You know what they say, how they describe it, in the society page of the papers, papers like yours - 'everyone in Washington.' Only it was not just everyone in Washington, it was also everyone in New York. It may have been the greatest assemblage of money and power ever gathered together in one place. There were three former presidents - and even more important people," she added with a cruel smirk, "the kind that make and break governments, the kind that used to keep the country doing what it is supposed to do."

Rachel gave her a look that did not pretend either to sympathy or understanding.

"You mean the kind that controlled - tried to control - everything before Julian Drake. Is that what you are trying to say?"

Raising an eyebrow, Angela Murray fixed her with a tight, knowing smile.

"I'm going to tell you a story, the biggest story of your life, maybe the biggest story of all time, certainly the biggest story you're ever going to hear. I'm going to tell you everything: how, and why, the president was killed. And you're going to get it without conditions. It isn't going to be off the record, it isn't going to be deep background, it isn't going to be not for attribution. I'm going to tell you I arranged to have Julian Drake assassinated and you will never print a word!"

"How you -?" cried Rachel, halfway out of her chair

"Sit down, sit down," insisted Angela Murray, flapping her hand in the air.

"You're going to tell me how you…? You're going to confess, on the record, and -"

"Yes, all of that, tell you everything. Confess? Yes, exactly. Confession, that's what I am going to do: make my confession and, when I do, your only thought is going to be how you can make sure no one else ever hears, much less reads, what I am going to tell you!"

"And why would I do…?

There was something evil in the way Angela Murray looked at her, as if the secret she was about to share would have the same effect on whoever heard it as what she had done - arranged the assassination of the president - had had on her. Rachel went cold inside.

"I've read what you have written, all the stories about the death of the president, the investigations, the rumors, the speculation. Everything you wrote - at least most of it - was true, and all of it, without exception, was false. There was no conspiracy to murder the president. I made all the arrangements myself. Rufus Chambers!" She laughed, shook her head, and laughed some more. "You know, men who make money, most of them, have no idea how they did it. They think that because it happened they must be smarter than anyone else. Rufus was a fool. He never made an important decision in his life; the only risk he ever took was with what belonged to someone else. Men are too weak, but - never mind. I should have said most men, because Julian Drake….You want to know - well, all right - he had to be got rid of, there was no other way. I knew that, I knew the hold he had on the country; I knew he would make it impossible for people like me, people who know what it means to be a success. So, yes, I made the arrangements. I did not know he was already planning what I was going to do. I didn't -"

"He? - Who do you mean, 'planning what I was going to do?'"

Angela Murray drew back and studied Rachel as if she were trying to anticipate the reaction to what she was going to tell her next.

"It is the reason you'll never use this," she said, slowly, emphasizing each word; "the reason why my 'confession' is something you'll take to your grave, the reason why it will be buried with me. I made the arrangements for the assassination, but he found out, and then…he made me go ahead. Julian Drake ordered me to have him killed!"

It was the way she said it, the deathlike certainty with which she uttered what, in any other circumstance, would have seemed the lunacy of a thoroughly demented mind, that convinced Rachel Good she was telling the truth. She was shocked in a way she had never been shocked before. She had to be sure.

"Are you saying, are you trying to tell me…? Do you really expect me…? The president, Julian Drake, 'ordered' you to have him killed?"

"That is exactly what I am telling you. You were there, that day he had that little debate of his with the undecided members of Congress. You remember. He had you there so you could write all about it. Right after that, when it ended, Ismael Cooper told me the president wanted to see me." A rueful smile, a smile that seemed to acknowledge the brilliance with which Julian Drake had played his hand, slipped across her mouth. "I hated him, I hated everything he stood for, hated him for everything he wanted to do; hated him, if I really want to tell the truth, if I really want to make a completely honest confession, because I envied him, envied the ease with which he seemed to do everything; hated him, to get right down to the core of it, because of his astonishing indifference. There was nothing I could have done, nothing I could have said, that would have had the slightest effect. A lot of people hated me; a lot of them had good reason. But not Julian Drake. It wasn't even that he looked down on me - he didn't look at all. That is what I learned that day, that day he told me that he knew all about what I had done and that I now had no choice: I was going to have to go through with it."

Suddenly, she remembered that she had not explained what had happened before, that in her furious attempt to explain herself, she had left out part of the story.

"He wanted to see me. When I walked in - I thought Cooper was coming with me, but he left me alone in the Oval Office - he was reading something. He motioned for me to take a chair in front of his desk. Then, a moment later, he handed me the report, the FBI report, the one you wrote so much about later on. You got that from Cooper; the same one Cooper had given to Conrad Wilson to show to me, the one they tried to blackmail us with so we would stop our opposition. He shows it to me, slides it across his desk. I almost laughed. I reminded him that I had seen it before. That is when he sprang the trap," she said, still dazzled, and a little puzzled, by how she let herself be outmaneuvered. "He told me to keep reading, that I had only seen part of it, the same part - he told me this! - that he had let Cooper see, the only part Cooper knew existed. They had everything, everything I had done: the money, the wire transfers, all the names, all the countries, through which the arrangements had been made."

Rachel had sufficiently recovered to begin to question what seemed at least a potential inconsistency.

"If he wanted you to do what you were planning - if he wanted to be killed, though God knows why he ever would have wanted that - why bother telling you that he knew? That would have seemed the surest way to make you change your mind. The report...."

The eyes of Angela Murray turned inward, her head shook with what seemed regret, regret not so much for what she had done as for her failure to have known from the beginning, as it were, that she had never had a chance, that she had been used in a way that, even now, no one else could ever possibly grasp.

"That report was the guarantee that I would. He gave me a choice: I could go through with it - his assassination - or I could stop it; but if I stopped it, that report, everything in it, would be used to prosecute me for conspiracy to murder the president."

"Are you serious? Are you...?"

"If I went through with it, the report would be destroyed. I would be safe. But first, I had to resign my position, leave all that behind, and disappear, have a breakdown, pretend I had, do whatever I had to do to make everyone think I was no longer someone who had to be taken seriously. An interesting choice, don't you think? Save the president from assassination and spend my life in prison and go down in history as the most evil woman who ever lived, or conspire with the president himself to commit a crime that would make him, more than a president, a legend."

"A legend? Is that what he told you, that he was going to do this - have you do this - to become a legend?"

"He didn't tell me anything. But what other reason could he have had? It's what has happened, isn't it? I asked him, I asked him why, why he was doing this, why...."

"And? What reason did he give you?"

"He didn't give me an answer. He wouldn't say anything about it at all."

Rachel had only one more question.

"The place, where he was murdered, the grave site at Arlington. You couldn't have known when Louis Matson would die, you couldn't have known the president would be at the grave site."

"That was the one thing I had to change, the one thing he insisted on. He said he wanted to make sure no one would be close enough to get hurt."

Angela Murray was right: It was a story Rachel Good could never - would never - use. The world would think Julian Drake a mad man. And even if she had not cared about that, there was nothing to prove anything of what she had been told, nothing but what Angela Murray had said, and Angela Murray, having made her confession, had made it clear she was not about to confess to anyone else. There was only one person Rachel could talk to, only one person who would believe that it was even possible, and, more to the point, only one person who might be able to explain why it had happened, why Julian Drake, who had everything to live for, had decided to die.

Ismael Cooper was waiting for her at the same Georgetown restaurant where she had once sat waiting for Louis Matson. As she made her way through the crowded tables full of political gossip and other bright minded noise, she wondered what Louis would have thought, what his reaction would have been to have Julian had done. For an instant, she heard his voice echoing in her mind, insisting that "Julian had a reason; Julian always had a reason," the voice that had never known the meaning of a doubt, the voice that never second-guessed, never showed a moment's hesitation, the voice that never pretended to a false sympathy, the voice that with a single word stopped any attempt to sympathize with him. If Julian had himself killed, Julian had a reason, and that reason, whatever it was, would almost certainly put things in a new perspective, something so far from the normal run of things as to make you wonder how someone like Julian Drake had ever been possible at all.

"When I got your call....You sounded....What is it? You look like -"

Ismael leaned across the table and grasped her wrist. "You said you talked to Angela Murray. You found where she- ?"

"I need a drink," she insisted, before he could say another word. She signaled for the waiter, and then, after she ordered, looked around to make sure no one was close enough to hear. Her eyes were shining, wild with what seemed to Ismael something close to desperation.

"What did she tell you? What did she tell you about Julian? Did she tell you that she did it, that she was behind the whole thing? Did she tell you that -?"

"Yes, she told me. She did it, just like you always thought. But there is a catch, something you never suspected, something no one ever suspected. Something no one can ever know."

"No one can ever…? Don't tell me you agreed not to use what she told you, that you're not going to expose what really happened, how she -"

"Julian made her do it."

"Julian!" exclaimed Ismael. He looked at Rachel as if she had lost her mind, but then, suddenly, he saw it in her eyes, the painful certainty that it was true. He sat back and stared down at his hands, pondering this new reality, and, as he did so, a smile started to edge its way across his mouth. Julian's death had not been the result of some tawdry, mindless conspiracy, an act of political terrorism, but had been his own free choice, done at his own direction. Julian had died exactly as Julian had wished. There was more solace in that knowledge than he would have thought.

"Tell me what she told you," he said, calmly, and so much in control of himself that Rachel began to feel almost calm herself.

He listened to it all, never stopping her to ask a question or to make some observation of his own; he listened, measuring everything Angela Murray had said against everything he knew about Julian and what, to the degree to which he had come to understand it, Julian had wanted to achieve.

"He said something to me once," he remarked, when Rachel finally finished. "We were sitting alone, upstairs at the Hay-Adams, the night of the election, waiting for it to be over, waiting for what he knew was going to happen, and he was talking about what those who had become president must have felt when it was all over, when all they had to look back on was what they might have been able to do if things had been different - if they had lived in a time of war or some other great conflict, if they had not been blocked by Congress, if they had only known at the beginning what they knew at the end - how much more than could have accomplished, how much better they could have been. And then he said that those who died in office, but especially those like Lincoln and Kennedy who were killed in office, were the ones who were remembered and most respected. Just a few days before he died, he told me that everything had been done, everything that it was important to do, and the real issue was how to make sure it would not be changed. And he talked about how someone's death can help preserve not just their memory but help make permanent their achievement."

"You think Angela Murray is right, that Julian wanted to become a 'legend?'"

"No, not Julian. What he did had nothing to do with vanity, some desire for posthumous fame. There would have been something deeper, more important, than that. And I can think of one person who might know, one person, the only person, Julian would have told."

Three days later, Ismael was walking, alone and unnoticed, part of the anonymous crowd, on the cobbled streets of Paris, on his way to see Marcel Dubose, a man he had never met, but whom, in one brief telephone call to arrange his visit, he knew already was as serious as anyone, other than perhaps Julian Drake, he had ever encountered.

"Senator Cooper, you are exactly what I expected," said Marcel Dubose, as he invited him inside the small book filled apartment with the view of Notre Dame across the clustered rooftops in between. He bent his small, round head to the side and nodded twice in confirmation. "Exactly the way Julian described you - a thoughtful, intelligent face. Please, sit down," he said, as he took the chair at his desk and reached inside a drawer. He pulled out a thick bundle of envelopes, each of them opened with the surgical precision of someone who never wasted time, and then, the letter read, put back inside so carefully that to a cursory glance it would have seemed never to have been opened at all.

"These are all from Julian, written while he was president, some of them quite long, a record of everything he tried to do. More than that, really: the connection between how, in his mind, they all together formed a plan, a new foundation for what America was in the beginning supposed to be all about. Did I say, more than that? - Much more than that: the connection to everything he had read, everything he had studied."

"He wrote all these to you because…?"

"Two reasons, really. First, writing helped him think. Writing concentrates the mind, forces an order on our thoughts, and, with someone like Julian, brings to the surface what he might otherwise not have known he knew, if you don't mind my putting it like that. The second reason was to leave behind a record - a history, if you will - of what happened: what he intended to achieve and what he managed to accomplish. Not just a record, a chronology of events, but the reason why he did things, and the reason why he did them the way he did. Julian was his own historian. Which did not mean that he did not want someone else to write their own account, someone who had been in position to know what happened and the broader context in which it all took place. It did not mean," he added, with a significant glance, "that he did not want you to write this history."

Marcel Dubose looked around the room, remembering the last time he had seen Julian, that winter night, when to his immense pleasure and surprise, he had climbed the stairs and they had talked for hours.

"When Julian first told me he was going to write me, write regularly - this was after the election, at Christmas, when he came to Paris and was meeting with all the important people - he said that I was to keep everything, and that if something happened to him, I should then decide whether there was anyone who might benefit from reading them. If I decided there was not, I should burn them. As you can see, I did not burn them. I have been saving them for you. Later, after he started writing, he asked me to keep them until you came. In the last letter he wrote, the morning of the day he died, he said he was sure that, eventually, you would."

Ismael remembered, and remembering, felt a fool.

"Yes, of course. He said you were probably the only person who would ever understand what he was going to do. I didn't know what he was talking about, what it was he was going to do. I never assumed it had anything to do with...."

"With the reason he arranged his own assassination?"

Ismael started. "You knew, knew that he was going to do that?" There was a trace of anger in his voice, an accusation he was only half-conscious of having made. Marcel Dubose was not offended.

"The letter in which he informed me of this was the same letter in which he directed me to save his correspondence for you. It was dated the day of his death. But, so there is no misunderstanding between us, even had he written me early enough to have done something - though I don't exactly know what that would have been - warned you, perhaps, and let you decide whether anything should be done to stop it - I would not have done anything except respect his decision. This was not some irrational act, some thoughtless, meaningless surrender to blind impulse. He knew exactly what he was doing."

He pulled from the bundle of letters the envelope on top.

"Here, after he describes what he has set in motion, how he has taken advantage of the criminal desires of this woman, Angela Murray. 'The term of one's existence is no measure of anything. Everything that comes into being goes out of being; what difference whether that comes sooner or later; the question, the only question, is how a life has been lived. What I wanted to do, what I thought important to have done, has been put into place. The only way to make it all a permanent part of how the country thinks about things is to make sure that no one will even think about changing things back to the way they were. What better time to die, what better way to die, than by your own death make permanent things you think better for your country."

Marcel Dubose folded the letter, put it back in the envelope, and then, reaching into another drawer, pulled out a book of matches and lit the letter on fire.

"This is the only letter he asked me to burn, after I read it to you." He paused, watching the letter turn to ash as it drifted down to the empty wastebasket below. "He was right, wasn't he? The effect his death has had. Everything he did, all his speeches, all his legislation, the example of how he spoke and how he governed. Death has made permanent everything he did, everything he was. Or, rather," he added with perhaps the most astonishingly kind eyes Ismael Cooper had ever seen, "what everyone thought he was. Because, as you and I both understand, he was, and will always be, too far beyond the common measure to be known at all."

THE END

ABOUT THE AUTHOR

D.W. Buffa studied under Leo Strauss, Joseph Cropsey and Hans J. Morgenthau at the University of Chicago where he earned both an M.A. and Ph.D in Political Science. He received his law degree from Wayne State University in Detroit. He served as Special Assistant to United States Senator Philip A. Hart, and was a criminal defense attorney for nearly ten years. He is the author of 15 novels and four works of non-fiction.

The *New York Times* called *The Defense* 'an accomplished first novel' which 'leaves you wanting to go back to the beginning and read it over again.' *The Judgment* was nominated for the Edgar Award for best novel of the year.

D.W. Buffa lives in Northern California. You can visit his Official Website at dwbuffa.net.